TASH *hearts* TOLSTOY

ALSO BY KATHRYN ORMSBEE

Lucky Few
The Water and the Wild
The Doorway and the Deep

TASH *hearts* TOLSTOY

♡

Kathryn Ormsbee

SIMON & SCHUSTER BFYR

NEW YORK   LONDON   TORONTO   SYDNEY   NEW DELHI

SIMON & SCHUSTER BFYR

An imprint of Simon & Schuster Children's Publishing Division

1230 Avenue of the Americas, New York, New York 10020

Text copyright © 2017 by Kathryn Ormsbee

Jacket photograph copyright © 2017 by Getty Images

SIMON & SCHUSTER BFYR is a trademark of Simon & Schuster, Inc.

For information about special discounts for bulk purchases, please contact Simon & Schuster Special Sales at 1-866-506-1949 or business@simonandschuster.com.

The Simon & Schuster Speakers Bureau can bring authors to your live event. For more information or to book an event, contact the Simon & Schuster Speakers Bureau at 1-866-248-3049 or visit our website at www.simonspeakers.com.

Book design by Lucy Ruth Cummins

The text for this book was set in Adobe Garamond Pro.

Manufactured in the United States of America

First Edition

2 4 6 8 10 9 7 5 3 1

Library of Congress Cataloging-in-Publication Data

Names: Ormsbee, Katie, author.

Title: Tash hearts Tolstoy / Kathryn Ormsbee.

Description: First Edition. | New York : Simon & Schuster, [2017] |

Summary: Fame and success come at a cost for Natasha "Tash" Zelenka when she creates the web series "Unhappy Families," a modern adaptation of Anna Karenina— written by Tash's eternal love Leo Tolstoy.

Identifiers: LCCN 2016032661 |

ISBN 9781481489331 (hardcover) | ISBN 9781481489355 (eBook)

Subjects: | CYAC: Internet television—Production and direction—Fiction. | Fame—Fiction.

Classification: LCC PZ7.1.O744 Tas 2017 (print) | LCC PZ7.1.O744 (eBook) |

DDC [Fic]—dc23

LC record available at https://lccn.loc.gov/2016032661

To Virginia Sebastian,

who puts the "great" in great-aunt

If it is true that there are as many minds as there are heads, then there are as many kinds of love as there are hearts.

—LEO TOLSTOY, *Anna Karenina*

TASH *hearts* TOLSTOY

You've just watched another unfortunate episode of *Unhappy Families*, a web series brought to you by Leo Tolstoy and Seedling Productions.

CAST		CREW	
Anna	Serena Bishop	*Producers*	Jack Harlow and Tash Zelenka
Alex	Jay Prasad		
		Director	Tash Zelenka
Dolly	Klaudie Zelenka		
		Editor	Jack Harlow
Kitty	Eva Honeycutt		
		Writers	Jack Harlow and Tash Zelenka
Levin	George Connor		
Stiva	Brooks Long	*Graphics*	Paul Harlow
Vronsky	Tony Davis	*Music*	Tony Davis

Tune in for new episodes every Tuesday and Thursday at 11 a.m. eastern!

Isn't it funny how something can be a joke for so long until one day it isn't?

You laugh at an awful new pop song until the fateful day you end up playing it twenty times on repeat, totally un-ironically. You laugh at the idea of deep-fried okra until the fateful afternoon your family stops at some boondocks diner and, as a joke, you order deep-fried okra, and it is suddenly your new favorite snack. You laugh at clowns until the fateful night you stay up past your bedtime to watch the movie *It* and are forever scarred.

Even in ancient times, I'm sure the Roman aristos probably hung around the local bath complex like, "Ha, Gaius, wouldn't it be hilarious if one day all those barbarians came roaring into town?" "El oh el, Titus Flavius, that imagination of yours."

For a long time, my two best friends and I joked that one day we would be famous. It was a stupid little refrain that popped up when we daydreamed: "One day, when I'm famous, I will own all of Nova Scotia." "One day, when I'm famous, I will buy Kate Hudson's dress from *How to Lose a Guy in 10 Days*." "One day, when I'm famous, I will own a DeLorean and travel everywhere at exactly eighty-eight miles per hour." We would speculate, and we would laugh at the grandiosity and absurdity of it all. It was a joke.

Until it wasn't.

One

Here is the first thing you should know about me: I, Tash Zelenka, am in love with Count Lev Nikolayevich Tolstoy. That is his official name, but since he and I are so close, I get to call him Leo.

I met Leo in a bookstore when I was fourteen years old. It was the beginning of the school year, and I had ambitious goals for myself. Freshman English was too easy for me. After two weeks, I was already bored senseless. So I googled a list of famous novels, and I made a short list of the books I would read that year. The first on the list was *Anna Karenina* by Leo Tolstoy. You might say it was Anna Arkadyevna Karenina who introduced us.

It was love at first line. In case you're curious, here is what that line was: "All happy families are alike; each unhappy family is unhappy in its own way."

Isn't that *perfect*? Leo knows just what to say to sweep a girl off her feet. That night, I stayed up until 3 a.m. reading the first twenty chapters of *Anna Karenina*. I was infatuated, and have been ever since.

Leo and I have a bit of the Romeo and Juliet thing going on. Talk about some majorly crossed stars. For one thing, my father doesn't approve of Leo because he is so very Russian. Dad would rather I be infatuated with a nice Czech author like Václav Havel or Milan Kundera, who are perfectly decent boys and all, but have you tried reading *The Unbearable Lightness of Being*? More like *The Unbearable Pretension of Pretentiousness*, am I right?

Another obstacle: Leo is dead. Very dead. He's been pushing daisies for 107 years.

The course of true love never did run smooth.

Here is the second thing you should know about me: I'm a film-maker. Or at least, a filmmaker-in-training. And no, I'm not trying to make the next *Citizen Kane* yet, but I do run a YouTube channel with my best friend, Jacklyn Harlow, and right now we're in the midst of filming a web series. And not just any web series—a modern adaptation of *Anna Karenina*. See? We've come full circle, and in case it wasn't clear before, now you know: My man Tolstoy is a major part of my life.

"Can we run that again? Starting with Eva's line, 'I know what it says.'"

It's late Friday afternoon, and we're at my house, shooting a pivotal scene in the series. I'm situated behind the DSLR camera, while Jack is monitoring sound levels. Jack's older brother and my other best friend, Paul, stands off camera, holding a boom mic over the heads of the talent—George and Eva.

Today's shoot isn't complicated, exactly, and it only requires two of our seven-person cast. Still, it's absolutely vital we get everything right, because this scene reveals a huge plot point that's been dozens of episodes in the making.

And it is a kissing scene.

Filming a kissing scene is not as awkward as you think it is. It's *ten times* more awkward. For one thing, you are asking two people who are not in love to make out as though they were. For another, you are sitting on the other end of a camera, recording it all like a demented voyeur. Which is particularly funny in my case, because I don't even find that kind of thing appealing. And for *another* thing, you're asking these two people to kiss *multiple times*. Like, *Oh sorry, you didn't move your lips in exactly the right way*, or *Oops, there's a bit of saliva just there, we'll have to do another take.*

In this particular case, we're on our fourth try. I'm uncomfortable, but I'm trying to be professional. That's my artistic creed: professional under all circumstances. But this would all be a lot easier if George and Eva weren't in the middle of a fight.

"Hang on," says George, after I give my direction. "I need a minute."

"Oh my God," says Eva. She plops her head in her hands as George launches into a breathing exercise, followed by some elocution practice.

He's looping "bah, boh, buh, beh" through puckered lips, when Eva cuts him off, yelling, "We're not even talking, we're *making out!*" Which causes Paul to snicker so hard that the boom lowers into the frame, quivering from his laughter.

I've begun to despair. At this rate, we are never going to capture the golden shot—that take where everything comes together and the actors' performance seems like the most natural happening in the world. Usually George and Eva get along really well. This tiff of theirs came about all because George insulted Eva an hour earlier by saying her breath smelled and she'd have to suck on some mints before he would film with her. And while this was admittedly a dick move on George's part, I wish Eva would let it go, because though she might be a good actress under normal circumstances, she cannot pull off a besotted gaze right now, when there is murder in her eyes.

"Do we need to take five?" Jack asks, tugging off her headphones.

I nod. "Yeah. Okay, take five, both of you. Walk around or something. Get it out of your system."

Eva doesn't need to be told twice. She hops up and leaves the room in a flurry. A moment later, I hear the sound of the tap turning on in the kitchen. George remains where he is and continues his elocution practice as though nothing has happened.

I turn to Jack with a "kill me now" expression. She shrugs. Jack can be infuriatingly chill sometimes. I know she's got to be frustrated too.

Our series, *Unhappy Families*, isn't doing too well. I don't mean monetarily, because we don't make a cent from our YouTube site. I mean our fan base isn't what we hoped it'd be when we first started this project last December. Our goal was to hit one thousand subscribers, which was definitely a reach, but reasonable. It's nearing the end of

May, and we're at a measly four hundred, not even half our target.

It's not that Jack and I expected to become an overnight Internet sensation à la Bieber, but we did think we'd get, I don't know, a little more attention. As things stand, we've got some faithful viewers who leave comments on our biweekly videos, but that's about it. No fan network. No clamoring calls for the next episode. No thousand subscribers. Jack and I haven't said as much out loud, but I think we're both pinning our remaining hopes on this episode between George and Eva. Because if anything is going to give our web series a shot in the arm, it's a kissing scene. As Jack once put it, "Masses love the kissy face." Which I don't get, but hey, I will play by the rules.

George is running through a tongue twister ("red leather, yellow leather") when I lean forward and tap his knee.

"Hey."

He gives me a look, like he's affronted I would dare interrupt his solemn thespian ritual, but he stops and lifts his brows, expectant.

"Um, do you think you could apologize to Eva?"

George looks even more affronted. "Why?"

"Because you were kind of harsh earlier, and she's mad at you, and none of these kisses are believable."

"I'm not sorry, though."

I push out a sigh, trying to remain calm. Sometimes directing is like babysitting preschoolers—it requires a lot of patience, a sturdy set of lungs, and the ability to coax egomaniacs into doing what you want.

"Right, I know you're not," I say. "And I completely understand. But could you do me a huge favor and *act* like you're sorry? We're not going to get a good shot unless you two make nice, and I'm asking you to talk to Eva because you're always such a class act on set."

I can feel Jack watching me—probably both impressed and disgusted by my shameless flattery. It's no secret George considers himself the best actor in our cast, and while I'd usually deem his behavior worthy of the title "prima donna," I can change that to "class act" for the sake of a good take.

George takes the bait. Just an additional *"Please?"* from me, and he gives a wordless nod, then leaves for the kitchen like a soldier marching up to the front lines.

Once he's gone, Jack gives me a dramatic slow clap.

Paul says, "Masterfully handled."

"Just doing my job," I say. "Paul, you don't have to keep holding the boom."

"Really? Oh, thank God." Paul lowers the boom pole to the floor, carefully leaning it against the living room couch, where George and Eva have recently been not convincingly kissing.

"Yeah, you'd better save your strength for tomorrow," says Jack.

Tomorrow, Paul is graduating from our school, Calhoun High, along with my older sister, Klaudie. I'm trying not to think about that. It's impossible to imagine Paul *not being* at Calhoun. At least he's staying in town for college.

Kathryn Ormsbee

There's a soft "ahem" at my back. I turn to find George and Eva in the doorway. He looks a little annoyed, but pleased. She looks a little annoyed, but placated. That's an improvement, at least. I can work with a little annoyance.

"Okay," I say. "Ready to try this again?"

George and Eva get back in place, sitting on the edge of the couch in front of a game of Scrabble. Paul picks up the boom and assumes position. Jack snaps her headphones on and gets the clapper board ready, positioning it in front of the lens.

This time, it's going to be better. This time, we're going to get our golden shot. I can already tell. The energy between George and Eva has changed. The anger's faded from Eva's eyes. Our actors are finally ready. Now it's just a matter of rolling the camera.

"From the top of the scene," I say. I hit the record button and nod at Jack, who drops the clapstick and then pulls the clapper board out of frame.

"And . . . action!"

Two

I am going to die of heatstroke before I see my sister obtain a diploma.

The sun is blazing down on the bleachers of Calhoun High's football stadium, where I sit wedged between my dad and Jack. Paul has just walked, and we are now crossing the wide alphabetic wasteland that remains between *H* and *Z*. It's eighty-five degrees, and the humidity is so high you could pull out a straw and suck in the surrounding air like a beverage. I thought I'd been smart this morning when I chose to wear my lime-green linen romper. I was thinking the linen would keep me cool. I didn't consider that I would work up enough butt sweat to create two embarrassing crescent marks on the seat of the romper. I haven't looked in a mirror, but I can feel the damage. When it comes to perspiration and periods, a girl just *knows*.

So here I am, terribly toasty and probably dehydrated and wondering how I can exit this stadium without ever standing up again, when Jack leans in close and says, "Check your phone."

They've only made it to the *M*s onstage, so I figure I'm not going to miss any fireworks by sneaking a peek.

"It's eleven thirty," I tell Jack.

"No, no, check *the site*." Jack shoves her own phone in my face.

I squint. "I can't see, the sun's too bright."

Jack drops the phone in my lap. "Look at it."

I cup my hands over the screen in a way that renders it still dark and reflective but readable. The setup of our YouTube home page is the same as always. There is the salmon-colored banner with the words "Seedling Productions" scrawled in spindly script, the logo of a watermelon atop a sunburst, and two running playlists: one for my personal vlog, and one for the web series. Nothing out of the ordinary.

Jack isn't smiling, so I'm expecting the worst.

"What?" I bug my eyes in an attempt to see past my apparent blind spot. "What's wrong, did someone hack it? I don't see—"

"The subscriptions. Look at the subscriptions."

I usually check subscriptions once a week, on Sundays, when I upload a new Monday morning vlog. This past Sunday, we were at 409. I remember the exact number because it launched me into vigorously humming the Beach Boys around the house all day long, until Klaudie shouted from down the hall to shut up and holy crap was she glad to be moving out in August.

On average, my personal vlog gets about a hundred hits a week, and *Unhappy Families* gets a bit more. It's a small but loyal following. I guess that's all you can really expect when you are a seventeen-year-old amateur vlogger with a full school load. It's all I expect, anyway, when I look at the red subscription box.

43,287.

There are more than *forty thousand* subscribers to Seedling Productions.

"Dude," I whisper.

My dad thwacks my knee with his bunched-up program. He gives me a mock-stern look and nods toward the stage. I throw back a mock-repentant look but don't put away Jack's phone. I stare some more. I refresh the page, certain it has to be a fluke. Instead, I get *43,293*.

Jack's eyes are dilated and her electric-purple hair looks more electrified than usual. Color has exploded in her cheeks, and while some of it might be sunburn—damn whoever invented outdoor graduations—I think most of it is due to sheer bewilderment.

"Dude," I repeat. "That can't be right, can it?"

"Something's happened," says Jack. "Some big shot must've mentioned us. That's the only explanation."

I'm still staring at the screen when a hand swoops in from my left. I look up to find my mom reaching across Dad's lap with an *actual* stern expression. She pinches her fingers tight around the phone and raises a brow that says, *Natasha Zelenka, is it too much to ask that you devote one hour of your time to this momentous rite of passage?*

I shake my head. Appeased, she releases the phone. That's the thing about Mom: stern, but so easily satisfied, the sternness is rendered completely ineffective. I return the phone to Jack and train my eyes toward the stage like a model daughter, which is the joke of the day, really, because everyone knows that role is already filled by Klaudie.

Klaudie is prettier, taller, and smarter than I am. No one has ever had to tell me this. It is amputation-without-anesthetic-painfully obvious. She's going to Vanderbilt in the fall, and after that she plans to get her doctorate in chemical engineering. After *that*, she will engineer chemicals and get married and have seven children and maybe become president on the side.

I honestly don't begrudge Klaudie's perfect future, because it means far less pressure on Future Me to get married and produce offspring. My theory is this: So long as the older sibling does all the right things, the younger sibling can go wild. Take William and Harry, for instance. I am Prince Harry. Only I'm the descendant of Czech political dissidents and Kiwi fishmongers, not inbred British monarchs. Also, I am not the hotter sibling, as has already been established.

Klaudie can have the perfection and procreation. I am more than happy to cheer from the bleachers, figuratively and, in today's case, literally. But dude, over *forty thousand subscriptions*. And I haven't even checked the views yet.

As the *P*s trot across the stage, my mind is far from a high school football stadium in central Kentucky and lost in the wilds of the Internet-sphere. Jack is right: Someone—someone *big*—must have thrown a mention out there. Who? And whatever they said, was it . . . *nice?*

My tongue high-dives into my stomach. I was thrilled to see those magical five digits in the subscription box, but now I'm beginning to wonder if this is a bad thing. What if we've been slammed? But no, people wouldn't subscribe to a channel with a bad rap. Would they? Who even knows these kinds of things—PR experts? Is there a video tutorial out there for what to do when you go viral?

Viral. I've always thought that's an ugly way of putting it. As though the population of the Internet is one perpetually ill body, ravaged by disease after disease. Isn't there a pleasanter substitute? For example, "going supernova." Way more epic, and probably the better analogy: a colossal burst, followed by a gradual fade from memory.

And now, it seems, Seedling Productions is going supernova. Bursting forth in a crazy display of light and color at this very moment, when I am supposed to be pondering a commencement speech and tearing up as my sister moves a tassel from right to left. Why couldn't this have happened in mid-January, when everything was dead and cold and time moved at half its regular pace and I had nothing better to do than binge-watch all ten seasons of *Friends* on Netflix? Why is it happening now, as another Important Life Event is going on?

Out the corner of my eye, I see Jack's knees bouncing, her fingers flicking across the phone screen.

One hour, I tell myself. *You can wait one hour.*

My body disagrees. My stomach feels like it's overproducing acid, and my mind is whirring with possibilities. Hashtags, fan art, raving blog posts—all devoted to Seedling Productions. Maybe even . . . a Golden Tuba.

Whoa there, Tash, I tell myself. *Calm down.*

They've made it to the *T*s. Klaudie's row—the very last—is filing toward the stage. I can make out Klaudie from here; her hunter-green graduation cap is bejeweled with the words *Music City Bound*.

Maybe once Klaudie hears the news, she'll decide to stay in Lexington and keep filming with us. Maybe she'll reread all the articles I once sent her about how people who take gap years between high school and college are much more well-rounded and fulfilled individuals.

"It would be great if I were going to drama or film school," Klaudie replied at the time, "but no engineering program is going to be impressed that I spent a year fiddling around with a camera."

This comment led to a giant fight back in March, and even now I am smarting from wounds that haven't scabbed over properly. I don't mind that Klaudie is perfect or that she has a plan, but there's no need for her to be so damn condescending about it. It is a toss-up, really, as to whether Klaudie will be genuinely happy about going viral or will say, with tight lips and bored eyes, "That's nice, Tash, I know how much your little project means to you."

Ever since Klaudie received her acceptance letter from Vanderbilt, she's been wearing a lot of those tight lips and bored eyes, droning out her constant refrain that August can't come soon enough.

"Klaudie Marie Zelenka."

My row, mostly relatives and friends, strains forward, at attention, as Klaudie takes the stage. She crosses the platform in measured steps, posture excellent, and she wears a big-but-not-goofy smile as she shakes Principal Hewitt's hand and he hands over the diploma. A few high-pitched cheers ring out from the graduate section—probably Klaudie's friends Ally and Jenna. Then Klaudie is gone, and the very last of the seniors, Charlie Zhang, steps forth for his own fleeting moment of glory. And that's that.

It's all so . . . anticlimactic.

I guess this is how things will be a year from now, for me and Jack and all the rest of us rising seniors. How depressing. Though who knows? What with Seedling Productions' forty-three thousand subscribers (and counting!), I might not even need to graduate a year from now. I might have already made a life fortune and be sitting pretty in a Californian mansion.

This time, I don't tell my imagination to calm down. Because the thing I've joked about for so long is no longer a joke. It's *real*.

As you might expect, my bedroom is decked out with a lot of Tolstoy-related items. I have one giant poster of him hung over my dresser. I also have a half dozen or so quotes of his written on colored card stock and taped to the walls. Every few months, I look for new quotes, write them up, and change them out.

Kathryn Ormsbee

Here is one of the quotes currently hanging in my bedroom: "The two most powerful warriors are patience and time."

So true. Like how, after the graduation ceremony is over, time moves so. So. SO slowly, just to spite my patience. I want nothing more than to lock myself in my bedroom, throw open my laptop, and figure out the why and who and how of the subscriber explosion. But just because Graduation the Event is over doesn't mean Graduation the Day is over. After the photographs and hugs outside the stadium—during which I keep my hands fanned over my backside in a ducklike attempt to cover the butt sweat stains—there is an after-party on the agenda, at the Harlows' place.

I like to think I would still be die-hard, lifelong friends with Paul and Jack Harlow had they not lived on my street. That all the bike races and water gun fights and backyard camping trips would've happened even if the Harlows lived on the opposite side of town. What I have with the Harlows is an ironclad friendship that has floated through doldrum summers and weathered overlong winters. It is an almighty mess of belly laughs and broken ankles and outdoor voices and first cusses. Friendship like this has to be destined. My bond with Paul and Jack transcends the convenience of location, the sheer luck of our parents' real estate decisions. You can't convince me otherwise.

Of course, location comes in handy on a day like this, when Paul and Klaudie have a joint graduation party. The Harlows are providing the backyard, because they are the ones with the inground pool and the better grill. We Zelenkas are providing food because my dad is basically the MasterChef of Lexington, Kentucky. It is a perfectly symbiotic relationship that requires only a fifteen-second drive from 12 to 24 Edgehill Drive. We've done a lot of birthdays this way. Paul and I share a birth week in August and have insisted on co-planning a joint party for years. I'm pretty sure I can beat anyone for the number of childhood pool parties in their past. Anyone but Paul, of course.

It's the first joint party at the Harlows' that hasn't directly involved me, and I was kind of surprised Klaudie agreed to go along with it. She's never been part of the trio. She never wanted to be. She's only fifteen months older than me, but since toddlerhood she's felt the need to act like she is the mother figure. When I made friends with Paul and Jack, Klaudie wrote off the whole set of us as childish little trolls. She was never *mean* to us, exactly, but she sure kept herself untouchable.

So, considering this history, the news that Klaudie planned on celebrating graduation with Paul was brow raising. Though I guess it isn't so much that Klaudie and Paul are celebrating together as the Harlows and Zelenkas are celebrating together, and *that* is very natural.

At the moment, this Zelenka is on the lookout for her Harlows. I need to find Paul to properly congratulate him on surviving more than a decade of public education. And I need to find Jack to process exactly what's going on with Seedling Productions. I checked the site again on the drive here, and the subscriptions have passed forty-five thousand. For some reason, my eyes have started watering. I'm not sure my body

Kathryn Ormsbee

is capable of handling whatever new emotion I'm experiencing.

Since my arrival at the party, I've been running a gauntlet of family friends and relatives who think it's necessary to congratulate me for my sister's graduation, as though I had any hand in it. I've just escaped another well-wishing neighbor's clutches when I spot Jay Prasad up ahead, standing by himself at the edge of the pool. Or more like wobbling at the edge of the pool. Jay always gets wobbly when he's uncomfortable.

"Jay!" I cry, throwing my arms around him.

Jay wobbles backward, taking me with him. We both do some crazy wobbling together, then regain our balance.

Jay is Paul's friend, and of course mine, and of course not Klaudie's. He is short and slight and an invaluable member of the Seedling Productions team.

"I don't know any of these people," Jay says, adjusting his askew glasses.

I glance around, assessing the crowd. "Yeah. You were really sweet to come. Paul will be so glad you're here."

I grab his hand and lead him along the pool's edge. Paul is sitting on the diving board in a muscle tee and his graduation cap. He appears to be engaged in some kind of dare from a set of guys at the diving board ladder.

"Paul!" I shout. "Look who's here!"

"JAY!" Paul bellows. He scoots halfway across the diving board, then gets to his feet and shoos the guys from the ladder. He gives me the impression of a king processing down a staircase and waving aside his attendants.

He and Jay exchange backslaps before Paul turns to me and chucks me on the cheek.

"Where've you been hiding?" he asks.

"I was going to congratulate you earlier, but relatives kept getting in the way."

Paul peers closer at me. He points at my eyes, which are still watery.

"Have you been crying, Tash? Are you mourning my loss? No more cool points for knowing me."

"I never got them from you, loser," I say. "If anyone is responsible for lending me cred, it's Tony."

Tony is a rising senior at Calhoun and also in the web series. He has a three-inch Mohawk and is undoubtedly the coolest person I know. He is also Jack's ex.

"TONY!" Paul is an individual who takes advantage of every chance to bellow people's names. "Is he here?"

Jay gets wobbly again. Some people wear their hearts on their sleeves. Jay wears his as a giant patch embroidered on his chest, like a tacky Christmas sweater.

I say, "He's probably making his rounds at all his many friends' parties."

"I dunno which friends' parties are more important than mine." Paul pouts. But it isn't a real pout. I've never seen Paul be petty about anything.

"*There* you are," says a sharp voice at my back. Jack. I side-shuffle to allow her into our forming circle.

"I've figured it out," she says.

"Figured out what?" says Jay.

Paul folds his arms and pushes his eyebrows up so high they disappear behind his toppling mess of long dark hair.

Jack's voice is deep and low as she says, "Seedling's going viral."

Which is met with a pair of "*What?*"s from the guys.

"Well," she says, "not exactly *viral*. Ellen DeGeneres isn't going to come calling anytime soon. But there's been this crazy spike in views and subscriptions. I think we might hit fifty thousand subscribers today."

An echo of even more incredulous "*What?*"s.

"This is the best part," Jack continues, and I marvel at how she can deliver all this news without the hint of a smile. "Guess who's responsible? *Taylor Mears.*"

"WHAT?" This time, I join Jay in a baffled screech.

Paul is wearing a guilty expression that I've become very familiar with over the past couple years. Paul isn't into this stuff—web series, acting, drama in general. There are some conversations he just can't engage in. There are too many names and terms and backstories that have built up during months of filming. Taylor Mears is one of those.

"She's this really famous Internet personality," I explain, so Paul doesn't have to ask. "She basically invented the web series. Like, years and years ago, when not everyone who had a camera was making one."

"*Wuthering Bites*, man." Jay is awestruck by Paul's ignorance. "You've never heard of *Wuthering Bites*? These girls never forced you to watch an episode?"

"I've heard of it," Paul says, pinking at the ears. "I just didn't know . . . the name. Taylor Spears?"

"Mears," corrects Jack. "She helped write and produce, *and* she starred as Cathy. She's a goddess. And she has this vlog, and she mentioned us on it. She said we were one of the most well-acted amateur series she's seen."

"She *said* that?" I near-scream.

I grab both Jack's hands and squeeze them in excitement, then shake them in excitement, then raise them in excitement. The effort is entirely on my part. Jack is not the kind of friend I can squeal with about anything. She is cold, bordering on the freezing point, and she has this perpetually grim expression. But even though Jack would never debase herself by jumping and squealing, she's just as excited as I am. I can see it in the slight quirk of her purple-lipsticked mouth.

"You have to show it to me," I tell her. *"Now."*

"Oh, don't worry, I've got it pulled up."

Jack whips out her ever-handy phone and brings up the YouTube page, where Taylor Mears's face is paused in a cheery grin. She punches the volume up to the highest tick, then presses play.

Kathryn Ormsbee

The title of the video is "New and Notable!" It begins with Taylor explaining that she's been browsing through dozens of little-known web series produced by amateur filmmakers working with small budgets. She then says she wants to share what she considers three "undiscovered gems" that aren't getting enough attention. *Unhappy Families* is first on the list.

"You guys," Taylor says with huge, earnest eyes. "*You guys*. Don't walk, *run* to this series. They are already forty episodes in, so carve out time to binge. I don't know how the hell these girls have managed to make a giant Russian novel so darn accessible, but believe me, they have. They've taken a super smart approach by whittling down the cast of *Anna Karenina* to seven main characters: Anna, Alex, Vronsky, Dolly, Stiva, Levin, and Kitty. And oh my God, I *love* what they're doing with the Levin/Kitty storyline. Both actors are crazy talented and adorable, and you will feel *all the feels*. So, whether you want a fun alternative to SparkNote-ing this book for your world lit class *or* you just want to stay up late watching well-crafted drama, check out *Unhappy Families*."

Jay's response is, understandably, "Holy shit."

My response is silence. Silence so long that Jack asks, "Are your organs shutting down? If you're still with us, blink twice."

But I'm not with them. I am dazed and quiet for the rest of the party. I can't even properly taste the cake. People's words sound staticky in my ears.

"You look so spaced," Paul tells me after a while.

"I can't believe . . . ," I begin, but don't finish.

Paul taps my cheek and says, "Go home, Tash. No one's going to care. You're useless to all of us now."

Harsh words, but I know Paul doesn't mean them that way. His eyes are soft with affection.

"Paul's right," says Jack. "Go recoup."

My best friends know me well. I need to be home, curled up in bed, finding out everything I can about the site's stats and any buzz on social media. I need comfy pajama shorts and a gigantic cup of Twining's Earl Grey and the new St. Vincent album on full blast. Everything between me and that ideal setup is white noise, a pointless parade of movement.

"Thanks," I tell them. Then, to Paul, "Enjoy your big day."

He responds with a two-fingered salute.

As I'm running back home, I have a thought, and immediately after I wonder if it is unforgivably selfish. The thought is this: *Yes, it's Paul and Klaudie's big day, but it might be* my *big day too.*

Three

I hit the repeat button. Again. It's my ninth time watching Taylor Mears's vlog.

When I got home, my first order of business was to switch on the electric kettle. Then I tore off my sweaty romper and threw on pajama shorts and an oversize T-shirt. I poured the boiling water into the biggest mug I owned, dunked a bag of Earl Grey, and sprinted upstairs to my bedroom. I pressed play on St. Vincent and turned the volume all the way up. Then I realized I couldn't listen to music *and* Taylor Mears at the same time, so I nixed the St. Vincent and proceeded to watch "New and Notable!" eight more times.

Finally, after this ninth time, I tell myself I need to focus on something else or I will permanently break my brain. So I do what I've been half-craving, half-dreading since arriving home: I visit Seedling Productions' home page. There are 48,063 subscribers. I click on the first episode of *Unhappy Families*, entitled "Stiva Jones Is a Mofo Cheater." There are more than 80,000 views. *Eighty thousand views.* Sure, that number is a mere drip of water to someone like, say, Beyoncé, but for a humble web series, it's huge. I click through the rest of the playlist. The view count decreases sharply at the second and third episodes, which is to be expected, but by and large stabilizes for the remainder of the playlist, hovering around 34,000.

Thirty-four thousand people have watched *Unhappy Families* through its most recent episode. Okay, maybe not *quite* 34,000. The first 500 or so views on all those videos were the result of me and Jack punching the refresh button for a half hour straight. But *thousands of people* have watched our web series. Our writing, our direction, our sometimes shoddy camera work. Thousands of people I've never met. Thousands of people not related to me. People all over the country. Maybe all over the world.

I am giggling uncontrollably. I grab the hem of my T-shirt and lift it to my chin in childish glee. Is this what people mean when they say "drunk with fame"? Or is it "drunk with power"? Whatever, I feel positively tipsy.

Still squeeing, I check on the other playlists—my personal vlog, *Teatime with Tash*, and Jack and Tony's music collaboration channel, *The Echo Boomers*. Their music used to be the most popular of our projects, but they haven't uploaded any new content since their breakup in February, after which Jack quietly took the playlist off the main page. The vlog and *The Echo Boomers* don't have anywhere near the numbers *Unhappy Families* does, but there's still a significant increase in views.

And there are comments. More than the usual half-dozen comments we always get from our small band of devoted fans. There are *fifty-two comments* on my first vlog, which is just me sipping some English Breakfast and rambling incoherently about the Winona Ryder version of *Little Women*.

omg, she is the cutest!!!!!

Someone thinks I am the cutest. THE cutest. (!!!!!)

I spy a St. Vincent poster. Good taste. <3

Finally, someone who shares my devotion to St. Vincent. (Jack says she is pretentious. Paul says her lyrics are too cryptic.)

Then I notice the Like/Dislike counter. Four hundred thirty-two people have liked the video. Nine people have given it a thumbs-down.

Nine thumbs-downs?

There's a tiny pop of panic in my stomach. Not just one random hater, but *nine*? What don't they like? Is my voice annoying? Are they not fans of *Little Women*? Why would they go to the effort of disliking my vlog? This episode is just a silly ramble, really. Who wastes their time disliking silly, rambling videos?

Maybe I'm overthinking this.

I decide to return my attention to comments. So. Many. Comments.

I start with the first episode of *Unhappy Families* and begin sorting through them chronologically:

Kitty/Levin IS a thing, right? Uuuuuuugh, now I'm going to have to read the book.

Omg, that look Dolly gives Stiva at 3:11. I know I'm supposed to be sad for her, but hahahaha

want Anna's shirt. WANT. Where can I buy?

Stiva's such a douche but I love him. Guess that's the point.

who cares about Vronsky, give me Kevin, more Kevin.

Hit after hit after hit. I can't get enough. Is comment reading a classifiable addiction? Is taking them all in like this, one after the other, at a breakneck pace, some reprehensible act of narcissism?

Though it's not like these comments are about *me*. They are about the actors, and about a book by my dead Russian boyfriend. A book that Jack and I have adapted—quite cleverly, according to these commenters and Taylor Freakin' Mears herself. An adaptation we directed. A project that is entirely our doing.

My phone rings. It's Jack.

"Are you seeing what I'm seeing?" I ask.

"I am if you're looking at Tumblr."

"I'm still on the main site. Have you read the comments?"

"Not yet, but have you checked our hashtag on Tumblr? People are already making GIFs. Legit GIFs. And there are all these new followers and messages. People want to know how long the series is supposed to last and if we're going to post any bonus content and if there's going to be a second season and if we're going to do a Kickstarter. Someone actually *asked* if we're going to do a Kickstarter."

"Oh my God."

"And we've got tons of mentions and retweets on Twitter. I haven't checked the Seedling e-mail yet, but I'm sure it's jammed with questions. Are we supposed to hire someone when it gets this big? I'm kind of panicking."

"It's not *that* big yet."

"Uh, fifty thousand subscribers is pretty big. For people like us, anyway."

"Are we sure this isn't a shared hallucinatory experience?"

"Paul is being a total ass over here. He was like, 'Wait, who's Kevin?' and I had to give him a crash course on shipping. He didn't even know what shipping was, Tash. Can you believe that? How has he hung out with us this long and not picked up the art of naming ships?"

"That's our Paul."

"Effing clueless," Jack agrees.

"Though you have to admit, Kevin is a pretty crappy ship name."

"Still better than Litty. Something about Litty sounds . . . dirty."

"Eh. Yeah. So, how do we want to handle this?" I ask. "We should come up with a game plan. Taylor posted that video last night, so we need to respond soon."

"I'll come over to your place tomorrow and we'll figure something out. I want to run next week's edits by you before I upload, anyway."

"But we should at least e-mail the cast about it tonight. In case any of them haven't seen the news."

"Oh yeah, good idea. My God, can you picture George's reaction?" Jack's voice descends into one of her deep, malevolent cackles. "That effing prick is going to think he's the next Laurence Olivier."

I tell Jack I'll take care of the e-mail. When I hang up, there's a text waiting for me. It's from my dad.

Hey there Sneaky Pete, dinner at 7 should you decide to emerge from your cave.

I check the time. Just after six o'clock. Maybe I will be calmer and more sated by seven. At present, I don't feel like coming out of my cave for the next forty-eight hours.

I open my personal e-mail and hit compose. How to phrase this? *Congrats, cast, you've become stars!*?

That's when I notice the new mail sitting in my inbox. My eyes hook immediately on the one from Thomnado007@gmail.com. My chest spasms, then explodes, then collects its scattered pieces and reassembles itself. *Thom.*

I click open the e-mail.

Kathryn Ormsbee

Tash—

Okay, I know I haven't responded to your last e-mail yet, but holy shit, I just saw, and I had to say CONGRATULATIONS. SO INSANE. Crazy proud of you.

Btw, I've been thinking . . . And you can totally say no. But would you want to exchange phone numbers? It might be nice to text in real time. But if that's weird, I get it.

Anyway, huge congrats on the mention. If anyone deserves it, it's you.

Thom

My chest has just sorted itself out when it explodes a second time. A grin takes over my face, holding my cheeks hostage. *Crazy* proud. That really means something coming from Thom Causer, a semi-famous vlogger in his own right. And he wants to exchange numbers. Thom Causer is *asking for my number*.

Though Thom is my age, he's been making videos longer than I have. He first got popular when he was fourteen and he and his friend Wes Bridges made a series of prank videos at their school. Then he moved on to the more serious business of *Beaker Speaker*, a series of weekly ten-minute episodes in which Thom discusses the science in famous movies. He started the vlog about a year ago, the same time I began *Teatime with Tash*—a series of weekly ten-minute episodes in which I drink a new type of tea while discussing a classic book adaptation.

Thom's vlog is much more popular than mine, since he already has a built-in audience from his prankster days. But one day, a couple months back, someone tagged both me and Thom in a tweet about fun movie-related vlogs. I was gratified to be mentioned in the same line. I definitely wasn't expecting Thom to message me saying he liked my videos and asking how long I'd been interested in filmmaking. We exchanged e-mails, and we've been writing back and forth regularly for the past six weeks. It's just blasé stuff, like our favorite fandoms and movies, but my chest still goes into self-destruct mode every time Thom's name pops up in my inbox.

I haven't told anybody about Thom. Not properly, anyway. I mentioned his first message to Jack, back when it happened, which earned a half-interested shrug and nothing more. I haven't told her about the correspondence that's followed—long, chunky paragraphs glimmering with wit and filled with parenthetical asides and even, on occasion, footnotes. E-mails that have recently begun walking the unstable tightrope between friendly and flirty.

I'm not sure why I never talk about him. It's not like I'm ashamed. It's not like I'm doing anything deviant. Maybe I feel weird because I've never actually met Thom in person, never even heard his voice. Well, okay, that isn't technically true. I hear his voice every week when he posts a new episode of *Beaker Speaker*. But I've never heard his voice directed specifically at *me*. I've never even heard him say my name.

But now he wants to exchange phone numbers, and I can't help but feel this is something big. Something significant. A Step in a very definite Direction. Texting seems so much more intimate than e-mailing. More immediate and personal. If Thom and I have been teetering on a tightrope, is this the shove that pushes us from friends over into . . . something else?

Again, maybe I'm overthinking this.

It takes me an embarrassingly long time to write a reply. I keep second-guessing my words, even my punctuation. I don't want Thom to think I'm even remotely weirded out by his request for a phone number, but I also don't want to come off as too desperate. Eventually, I settle on a cheerful little thank-you for his congrats and the assurance that I'd love—no, scratch that, *really like*—to text. Then I give him my digits. Then I click send. Then I bury my face in a pillow and groan, all wheezy and pathetic.

I need a distraction. Luckily, I have one. I click out of my e-mail—I'll compose that cast letter later—and log into Seedling Productions' Twitter account. I scroll through the notifications, favoriting mentions that only require favorites (*Oh my god, just binged all of @Unhappy_Families, and you NEED this in your life.*) and leaving the ones that demand answers (*@Unhappy_Families, PLEASE tell me you guys are going to adapt Dostoyevsky next?*) for later, when Jack and I have decided how we're going to handle this almighty event.

It feels like I've only been weeding through notifications for a few minutes when Dad shouts from downstairs that dinner is ready. I blink at my laptop screen. I'm definitely hungry; I was too hyped up at the graduation party to eat a proper meal and only managed a forkful of cake. But my very soul is hungry for more, more, *more* comments and questions and general adoration.

Which means I might have a problem.

Which means I should probably join my parents for dinner.

I look at the wall facing my bed, where my 36-by-48-inch poster of Leo Tolstoy hangs. It's a grainy black-and-white photograph of him at the age of twenty. Leo sits with his elbow propped lazily on the curved armrest of a fancy chair. He's wearing a heavy, lapelled coat and thick scarf. He's staring straight at the camera. Or, I should say, *scowling* at the camera. As though to say, "Why must I pose for this picture, I am so busy being a troubled and intelligent youth."

I prop my chin in my hands and ask Leo, "Do I have a problem?"

Leo scowls at me from under his dark brows.

"I should eat dinner with my parents like I'm one of the living, huh?"

Leo scowls.

Gotta love that man.

"Yeah, I thought so."

In a feat of admirable self-control, I close my laptop and hop off the bed. I head downstairs, and I don't even bring my phone with me.

It's probably a healthy break, but an hour later I'm back in my room. I stay up until four o'clock in the morning, scrolling through videos, notifications, and hashtag collections. It's around one o'clock that I begin to devise a plan. I fall asleep with one hand still on the trackpad.

Four

Jack and Paul come over the next morning, right after breakfast. Jack is here to plan. Paul is here because, according to him, watching me and Jack plan is more interesting than staying home alone on a Sunday morning.

Jack and I sit on my bed, and Paul lies sprawled on the floor, his arms and legs flung so far apart he looks like he's stretched on the rack, awaiting torture. Leo is there too, of course, scowling out from his poster.

"Is that comfortable?" I ask Paul.

"I'm meditating," he replies.

"That's not—"

Paul holds a finger to his lips and says, "You've got your ways, I've got mine."

I don't argue. I meditate, though I'm not exactly a committed Buddhist like Mom. I'm not proud of this, but I kind of half-ass it when it comes to religion. I blame this on having an Eastern Orthodox Christian for a dad and a Zen Buddhist for a mom. I like to excuse myself by saying I'm confused, which I honestly was as a kid. You'd be confused too if your dad ate steak and your mom didn't and your living room contained pictures of patron saints as well as a toddler-size statue of the Buddha and if you spent the week of Christmas going to candle-light church services *and* meditation nights at the Zen Center.

So yeah, I was a confused kid, but now that I'm seventeen, the only real explanation for my half-assery is that I'm lazy. I keep telling myself I should get my crap together, because if there is one thing all religions agree on, it's that half-assing is reprehensible. There's no way I'll reach enlightenment this way, and there's this Bible verse I heard a long time ago at an Easter service that's freaked me out ever since: "But since you are like lukewarm water, neither hot nor cold, I will spit you out of my mouth!"

So. My point: I suck in the religion department and therefore have no right to tell Paul how he should meditate.

"I've already written up something," I tell Jack, turning my laptop screen for her to see. "I worked out everything last night."

Jack glances over the Word document, lifts a brow. "You sleep at all last night?"

"Five hours."

"Mmm-hmm." Jack taps her nail on the screen and reads.

Jack: Reply to Twitter and YouTube questions.
Tash: Reply to Tumblr and e-mail.

Kathryn Ormsbee

Jack: Post on all platforms, thanking fans for engagement.

Tash: Send thank you e-mail to Taylor Mears.

Jack snorts. "Really? You think Taylor Mears cares?"

"She cared enough to mention us on her vlog."

"Well, yeah, but that's what she does for a living: finds new content and mentions it. She doesn't expect a gold-leafed thank-you note every time. She's probably already forgotten about us. Anyway, it seems kind of . . ."

My face darkens. "What?"

"Like we're kissing her ass."

"You don't even have to write it. It's my job."

"But it's a pointless job. You should ax it."

"No."

"Uuurgh, fine, whatever."

From the floor, Paul says, "Thank-you notes are sweet."

"See? Paul thinks thank-you notes are sweet."

Jack says, "Paul eats grape jelly on pizza, which makes all his opinions invalid."

We return to the list, where I've typed, *Joint Effort: Finish script, solidify filming dates this summer, brainstorm new project to keep up momentum.*

Jack laughs, which, coming from Jack, isn't a particularly happy sound. It's on the sinister side, like she's laughing at the pain of her enemies. She pulls her purple hair into a sloppy bun atop her head, still laughing.

"'To keep up momentum,'" she quotes through the laughter. "Jesus, Tash. This isn't a business venture."

"That's *exactly* what it is," I say, irritated. "Film is an art, but it's also a business. We could get money from this. Not just from a Kickstarter, but if we, like, monetized ads. And we have to keep people interested. If we don't, it'll be worse than never getting discovered. We'll be a flop."

Jack leans against the wall, eyes dim and unperturbed. She yawns. "You stress out way too much. We literally just got famous overnight. We're allowed to take our time figuring it out."

"But I've already figured it out," I say, raising my voice. I hate when Jack gets like this—apathetic and unreachable. "I stayed up until four figuring it out."

"Well, I didn't ask you to do that. I thought we were going to plan *together*."

Jack and I did technically agree to do that, so all I can say is, "You're being really negative."

Jack quirks her pierced brow. "Um. Have you met me?"

"I *mean* you can't shoot down my ideas unless you have alternatives."

"Okay. My alternative to writing Taylor Mears is *not writing her*. My alternative to going all type A on this is *chilling the hell out*."

This is not how I envisioned our meeting going. I expected Jack to

Kathryn Ormsbee

be grateful I'd already written up a game plan and to agree that it was smart and fair. I expected Jack to be supportive. So really, *have* I met her? There's no way Jack—the *real* Jack—would ever behave that way. No matter how many times we get into one of these spats—me pulling toward organization and Jack pulling toward chaos—I can never fully wrap my mind around how Jack can be so infuriatingly . . . *chill*.

I don't want to fight on a Sunday morning, so I retract my claws and press on.

"We've written out tentative filming dates for the end of summer," I say, scrolling to the second page of the Word doc, "but I think we should go ahead and set those times in stone. We want to make sure we have solid commitments from the whole cast. With a bigger audience, we can't afford to miss an upload."

Jack has closed her eyes, and her head is tilted against the wall. "We can afford to miss whatever we want to miss. People take hiatuses, mid-season breaks. Sometimes there are technical difficulties. It's going to be fine."

My claws are coming back out, and I can't control them this time. I'm a werewolf under the light of a full moon.

"Okay, you always say 'It's going to be fine,' but you know who *makes* it fine? Me. It's fine because there's always a plan. Because I think through the logistics. I know you suck at leading, but don't bash me when I'm the one doing all the work."

Jack opens her eyes. She straightens up. "You're doing all the work.

Wow, all that footage must just edit itself then. And I guess next week you'll be saying *you're* the one who wrote the best novel of all time, huh? Tolstoy who?"

"That's not what I meant. Come on."

"Whatever." Jack crawls off the bed. "I'll leave you here to do all the work, shall I?"

She slams the door behind her.

Paul says, "Hmm."

I get down from the bed, a pillow in hand. I nudge Paul in the side.

"Move over," I say. "I'm meditating too."

Paul flops onto his stomach, creating a whole body's worth of space. I drop the pillow and settle the edge of my butt on it, then cross my legs and compose myself.

"Do I need to leave the room?" Paul asks.

I shake my head, turning my palms upward, touching thumbs to index fingers.

"Okay," says Paul. "I'll just be quiet."

So Paul is quiet, and I begin a loving-kindness meditation toward Jack, because at the moment I want nothing more than to punch her, hard, in the face. I follow the usual routine, which my mom first taught me when I was ten. First, I steady my breathing—in through the nose, out through the mouth. Then I focus on the cutest animal I know: a cocker spaniel puppy. I feel affection and unconditional tenderness toward the puppy. Then I concentrate on those emotions, and I transfer

Kathryn Ormsbee

them slowly, steadily toward Jack. I wish Jack nothing but good. I wish her peace.

Over five minutes later, I'm still pissed, but it's lessened from a boil to a simmer.

"Were you picturing Jack as a puppy again?" Paul whispers.

I made the mistake once of telling Jack and Paul how I do my loving-kindness meditations, and Paul responded like it was the most hilarious thing he'd ever heard. He still thinks it's way funnier than it is.

"They say you should never go into business with your friends," I say.

"That's stupid. Lots of friends have gone into business together. Lewis and Clark. The Wright brothers. Uh. Siegfried and Roy."

"You're stretching it."

"Well, maybe. But you two aren't even in an actual business. You make art. Art is all about collaboration."

"She drives me crazy."

"You drive her crazy. That's why it works."

I sink onto my back. I turn to Paul, whose face is half mushed into the carpet.

"*We* don't drive each other crazy," I say.

"What are you talking about, Zelenka? I hate your ever-loving guts."

"Ha."

Silence settles on us, along with the dust motes I can make out in the light streaming from my open window. I inch my left hand across the carpet and take Paul's hand captive. Our fingers slip into familiar slots and bend together. We've held hands like this since we were kids, before it was weird. And it isn't weird, even now. I mean, it would be with any other guy. Anyone but Paul.

I ask, "When do you register for classes?"

"Couple weeks."

"Do you know what you're going to take?"

"Yeah, it's all a bunch of basics first semester. They want to make sure I can spell and add, which is . . . up for debate."

"Hey, stop." I knock my ankle into his.

When it comes to school, Paul is constantly talking himself down. So okay, yes, he was held back twice, in first and fifth grades. No, he doesn't have a stellar GPA or scholarship-worthy scores on his admissions exams. But Paul applied to BCTC, Lexington's community college, like it was his only option. He wouldn't even consider the possibility that he could cut it at UK, let alone go somewhere out of state.

Paul won't leave Lexington because of his dad. Mr. Harlow scared everyone four years ago when the doctors discovered the beginnings of prostate cancer during his annual physical. The doctors said they were lucky to have spotted it early, and they immediately put Mr. Harlow through the appropriate procedures and treatments.

Everything after that happened the way I'd seen it happen in movies: Mr. Harlow began to look sickly and wilting, and he didn't leave the house for long periods of time. All the Harlow family's friends rallied around them with prayer chains and favors and casseroles. Mrs. Harlow shared several sobbing phone calls with my mother. My dad fixed a ton of meals. And then, one day, the doctors came back with the joyous news that Mr. Harlow was in remission.

What the movies didn't prepare me for was the effect all this cancer stuff would have on Jack and Paul. It was toughest with Jack. She's always been sullen, and sometimes it was hard for me to tell when she was actually sad. I would be sitting on the bed with her for minutes before I noticed the tears streaming fast down her face. That was the year Jack first dyed her hair—a shocking half-and-half of pink and orange. I was surprised Jack went that route. It was so . . . predictable. But Jack didn't seem to care that she was fitting into everyone's expectations. Jack's never really cared what anyone thinks, to the point that whenever she suspects someone like a teacher actually has a good opinion of her, she'll sabotage herself by cussing in class or purposefully failing a test. I've seen the pattern again and again, since elementary school, but it got especially bad when Mr. Harlow was sick.

With Paul, it was more obvious—the fear and uncertainty. He isn't the kind of guy who's afraid to cry or hug in public. So I had a better idea of how bad it was for him.

I saw the months of Mr. Harlow's hormone therapy rip Paul from the inside out—his faltering smiles and space-out moments the telltale signs of internal bleeding beneath. I hugged Paul a lot that year. I found that even when I was trying to comfort him, he hugged back in a way that made me feel like the comforted one.

Even after the good news, Paul wasn't all smiles with the rest of us. He told me later, when Jack wasn't around, that he had a bad feeling.

"It's going to come back," he said.

I was so shocked I could only robotically blurt, "The doctors say his chances are really good."

"I know, but I can't shake the feeling it's going to happen again, right when it shouldn't. On his birthday, or Jack's wedding day, or over Christmas break. It always happens when it shouldn't."

And while I had difficulty picturing Jack ever agreeing to a traditional wedding, I couldn't argue with the rest of it. Mr. Harlow received his diagnosis right when he shouldn't have, the week after he'd been given a demanding promotion at work and three days before Thanksgiving. But then, is there ever a time when horrible things like that *should* happen? What's an opportune time for bad news?

"I never thought I'd leave Lexington," Paul told me. "I've never felt restless to get out like I guess you're supposed to when you're in high school. Now I know I won't leave. I can't."

I didn't agree with his reasoning, but I didn't feel I had the right to say so.

I do, however, have the right to tell Paul to stop beating up on himself. I stare at him when he doesn't reply to my reprimand. Again I hit his ankle with mine, this time harder.

"Your teachers are going to fall in love with you," I tell him, squeezing my palm against his. "You are the perfect student. Always attentive. Always asking questions."

"Stupid ones. What are you even saying? It doesn't matter that I suck at homework and tests so long as I dazzle my professors?"

"No. But a lot of grading is subjective. Sometimes teachers nudge your grade up because they like you."

"And you know this because . . . ?"

"Because *I know things*." I use a dramatic whisper that's supposed to be mysterious but comes out as just plain disturbing.

"You can be so fucking scary sometimes," says Paul. "Scarier than Jack."

"When you grow up and become a freelance graphic artist," I say, because this really is Paul's plan, "I am going to buy a lot of burner phones, and I am going to prank you every week. With impossible commissions. Or a scary whisper or two."

"I look forward to that."

I flop up into a sit, feeling more rag doll than seventeen-year-old collection of flesh and bone.

"I should find Jack," I say.

Paul nods his nose into the carpet. "Right. Let's find Jack."

He pops to his feet and offers me the same hand I was holding, hoisting me up with such gusto that I fly forward a few steps to the door.

It doesn't take long to locate Jack. She's sitting at the kitchen island eating the first of two open-faced peanut butter and honey sandwiches. Paul has a severe peanut allergy, and the Harlows choose not to keep any peanut products in their house, which means Jack is constantly snacking on peanut butter when she visits.

"My kryptonite," says Paul, noting the sandwiches and hanging back by the fridge.

I screech out the stool next to Jack and sit down. I take the second of her sandwiches, bite off a piece, chew, swallow.

I say, "I'm sorry. I know you do a ton of stuff."

"I know you know," sniffs Jack. Then, "Did you picture me as a fluffy puppy?"

I wipe peanut butter off my lower lip. "So fluffy."

"Look," she says. "I'm cool with how you divvied things up. I'll do my half, and if you want to write some sycophantic letter to Taylor Mears, be my guest. I just . . ." Jack taps the edge of her plate, rotates it forty-five degrees. "I'm not letting this take over my life. Art does that: takes over people's lives. Maybe you're cool with it, but history shows some of the best artists were total assholes to the people around them. Like Tolstoy. And I'm not going to turn into that. I'm not going to abandon my family to go out into the fields of rural Russia and live like a peasant."

"That's good to hear, because I worry about that every night: Will Jack run off to Siberia?"

I ignore the slight to my man Leo, because that is not the point of this conversation.

Jack gives me a disgruntled look. I return it. We've made nice.

Kathryn Ormsbee

"There's one more thing," I say. "We should talk everything through with the cast. Next Sunday's an all-cast day, so that works out."

Jack snorts. "Ten bucks says George has already written his Golden Tuba acceptance speech."

Paul says, "I think I'm getting hives."

Five

That night, it's just me and my parents at the dinner table. Klaudie is hanging out with Ally and Jenna and intends to stay out all night as part of her weekend-long graduation celebration. I know this is tough for my dad. He doesn't play favorites, exactly, but he and Klaudie have this special bond. It's funny because by rights, he should like me more. I am generally loud and demonstrative, like him, while Klaudie is more reserved, like Mom. I wonder if he likes Klaudie so much because she's different from him personality-wise but the same as him interest-wise. Klaudie likes cooking; I can't tell you with 100 percent certainty what a spatula's official use is. Klaudie likes talking college basketball stats for hours; I will scream my heart out during March Madness same as the next Lexingtonian, but it's pointless to memorize stuff like free throw percentages when the players are just going to go pro the next year. Klaudie is into engineering like Dad's dad was; I'm okay at math but prefer drama and fiction and no right answers.

It would probably bother me more, this special paternal bond I'm not part of, if I weren't certain that I'm my mother's favorite. Not in an epic, Steinbeck-novel way—just a slight, unspoken preference. Maybe a lot of it—the leniency on rules that were way stricter for Klaudie, the extra smiles and winks—is normal for any youngest sibling. Maybe it's because I meditate regularly, while Klaudie publicly announced her sophomore year that she was just atheist now, and not a Buddhist. Maybe.

Anyway, even if I hadn't picked up a Major Sad Vibe off Dad, I would've known his mood based on the meal. He's cooked goulash, and he only cooks goulash—the ultimate comfort food—when he is mopey. The air in the dining room is drenched with a rich, meaty scent as Dad sets thick, freshly sliced dumplings on each of our stew-filled plates.

Technically, the meaty smell is only coming from Dad's plate, since Mom and I don't eat meat. This is normal in our house: Dad's the cook, and he always fixes a meat-based dinner for him and Klaudie and a vegetarian version for me and Mom. Most of the time this works just fine, but when it comes to goulash it's kind of depressing, because pretty much the whole point of Czech goulash is the beef.

The recipe is Nana Zelenka's, and as such it demands to be eaten in the place where my grandmother's spirit is most present—here, in the dining room, surrounded by the rows of floral-trimmed china and crystal pitchers accumulated over the fifty years since my grandparents' move from Prague to Lexington.

Gramps and Nana Zelenka died in a car accident when I was nine.

Car crashes are an awful way to go, no matter what, but it's especially unfair that's how my grandparents went out, because up until that point their life had been so magnificent, and driving off a country road late at night is such a trite end.

Gramps and Nana lived in Prague back during the Cold War. They were in their twenties in early 1968. In case you don't know Czech history that well, that's when the local Communist government implemented a lot of reforms granting more rights to Czech citizens, who went wild with their new freedom and did a lot of super artistic and daring stuff like distribute uncensored newspapers and experiment with rock 'n' roll. Nana Zelenka would say, "It was a terrifying time. Terrifying and splendid." She said this so much that Klaudie and I made up a whole new word—"splendifying"—and you'd be surprised how much it comes in handy.

Anyway, in July of 1968, my grandfather received an offer to serve as a visiting professor of chemical engineering at the University of Kentucky. So he and Nana Zelenka moved to the States, and three weeks later the Soviets were like, "WHAT'S ALL THE RUCKUS IN PRAGUE, WE'RE COMING IN WITH TANKS. WE ARE THE BORG, RESISTANCE IS FUTILE, YOU WILL BE ASSIMILATED." My grandmother didn't say that; that's half me, half *Star Trek: The Next Generation*. Nana had a more eloquent way of putting it, which was, "Then those Soviet bastards came in and did what Soviets did best: Shat all over everything."

Kathryn Ormsbee

Whichever way you look at it, this was bad news for the Czech population, and my grandparents considered themselves lucky to have gotten their visas and shipped across the Atlantic when they did. Gramps's visiting professor stint turned full-time, and that's how two young Czechs came to live in the middle of Kentucky. And that's why we, their progeny, are eating goulash in a shabby midcentury modern house in a suburb west of Appalachia. Life is weird like that.

I take a dumpling and soak it in my goulash. I watch as the sauce permeates the soft bread, staining it brown.

"You're very quiet, Tasha," says Mom.

Klaudie and I joke that our mom is constantly trying to get people to talk. It's a joke because she's a speech pathologist, but it really is true. Mom has this calming, subversive way of siphoning words out of people. I suspect it has something to do with her Kiwi accent, which she hasn't given up even twenty years after leaving New Zealand. I say "given up," not "lost," because Mom is an accent expert. She could pass herself off as a Scottish Highlander if she wanted; she could definitely pass as a Midwesterner. But she chooses not to.

"I'm thinking about Gramps and Nana," I reply truthfully, before considering this might not be the best thing to say when Dad is already feeling gloomy. I cast a glance his way and am pained by the glassy, distant look in his eyes. Then he catches me looking, shakes himself, and grins.

"Well!" he says, slamming a hand on the table. "And wouldn't they be proud of you two. Sister heading off to Vandy, and you a budding Woody Allen."

I make a face. "Dad, I've told you, I hate him. If you're gonna go there, make it Orson Welles. Or Elia Kazan."

Dad forks a hearty helping of beef into his mouth. Talking around it, he says, "Aren't *we* ambitious?"

He shoots me a cheery wink, and I shoot back a "har har har" eye roll.

"Actually," I say, before realizing I have no idea how to phrase my news.

It's too late to backtrack, though. My parents are watching me with interested expressions.

"Actually?" Mom coaxes.

"Um," I say. "Well, the web series got a big boost yesterday. Someone famous mentioned us, and our views are shooting through the roof."

"Tasha, that's *wonderful*," Mom says warmly.

"Excellent news," says Dad. "Is this the one about tea?"

I remind myself that my parents are thirty years older than me and cannot be expected to keep this stuff straight. I say, "The one about tea is my vlog. The web series is the modernization of *Anna Karenina*."

"Ambitious," Dad repeats, grinning. "That's my girl."

I am genuinely pleased by Dad's pride, and also proud that I've distracted him from his darker thoughts. But as it turns out, the distraction is only momentary, because the next thing he says is, "Hard to

Kathryn Ormsbee

believe this is how dinners are always going to be. You'd better get used to being an only child. We're going to lavish all our attention on you, so you should forget about dating, because it will only end in tears."

"Thanks, Dad," I say drily.

I decide not to add that this isn't how dinners will *always* be. It's how they'll be for a year. Then I'll be gone to college too. Vanderbilt is at the top of my list. Actually, it's the only school I want to apply to, period. I love Nashville, and Vandy has an excellent film track. But Ms. Deter, my guidance counselor, keeps stressing again and again that with my grades, Vanderbilt is a reach school and that choosing film as an undergraduate degree isn't a wise decision.

"Don't specialize early," she advised back in March. "You want a university where there are plenty of options. That way, if you decide film isn't for you, you'll have a wide array of other majors to choose from. And if film really is what you want to do, you can head to L.A. or New York for an internship or graduate degree with a more versatile B.A. in hand."

Not only does Ms. Deter think I shouldn't specialize in film, she thinks I should forget about Vandy altogether and go to the University of Kentucky instead.

"You can still get a solid foundation in communications, art, or maybe English," she said in a valiant attempt to, I don't know, counsel and guide me? "Also, you'll pay basically nothing for tuition, since you're in-state and a Governor's School for the Arts attendee. Just think about it, Tash."

I've thought about it. What I think is, *If I don't get out of Lexing.*
now, I'm going to be stuck here for the rest of my life. I'll make excuses fo
why things didn't work out and become some drunk has-been straight out
of a Bruce Springsteen song.

I know very well I'm not Klaudie. I'm not smart enough to earn an
academic scholarship at a private university like Vanderbilt. I'll be lucky,
very lucky, just to be admitted. And yes, it will cost me a ton of money, but
isn't that the case for everybody these days? Isn't everyone in their twenties
laden with bone-breaking college debt? And it's *Vanderbilt*. It is stonework
and lattices and ivory towers. UK is sorority row and ugly, experimental
buildings from the seventies. It's wind tunnels and insane traffic during
football season. And it's so . . . familiar. I've grown up riding through its
streets and taking piano lessons at the School of Art and attending plays at
the Singletary Center. I need something new. Something non-Kentuckian.
A place where half the graduating class of Calhoun won't end up.

And it's not like I am being entirely irresponsible. I have a plan. I've
already looked into loans and departmental scholarships, and I am working part-time at Old Navy this summer. And okay, yes, I know that my
entire summer wages from Old Navy won't even cover one semester's
worth of books, but I am *doing something*. I am working toward my
dream. This is what working toward your dream looks like. Isn't it?

"Your father and I were thinking of watching a movie," Mom says,
slicing her fork through a dumpling. "Want to join? We could run
down to Kroger, see what's at the Redbox."

Kathryn Ormsbee

I chew my food slowly. Lately, Mom and Dad have wanted to hang out a lot more than usual. Graduation is an emotional upheaval for parents, and no doubt mine want to smush me between them on a couch in an attempt to dull the pain of their other daughter's imminent departure. It wouldn't be an appealing proposition even if I didn't have a laptop to get back to and stare at for the remainder of the evening.

Cautiously, I say, "I'm actually pretty tired."

Dad looks a little crestfallen when he says, "Maybe another night sometime soon, hmm? All four of us. We'll let you girls choose the movie."

Which really means they'll let Klaudie choose, since Klaudie and I have diametrically opposed tastes in movies and Klaudie gets the trump card all summer long, because it is her "last summer."

"Yeah, that'd be nice," I say. "Tonight, I'll let you two have a nice romantic evening."

Mom laughs—an airy, glittery sound. "Me, your father, Tom Cruise, and a bottle of chardonnay. Very romantic."

"We live the high life," says Dad, reaching across the table for Mom's hand.

"Get a room," I say pleasantly, taking my plate and glass into the kitchen.

I wash up, then blow a final kiss to my parents before heading upstairs to check on Seedling Productions' most recent stats and notifications. I feel only a little guilty for giving them a rain check.

Six

It's Sunday, the last day of May, and I'm sweating again. I always think I've turned up the AC enough for a cast meeting, and I'm always wrong. It's kind of terrifying how quickly the body heat of nine people can turn my bedroom into a sauna. And that's *before* we switch on any of the set lights.

Everyone is here except Eva, who's texted me that she's running ten minutes late.

I'm sitting straight-backed on my bed next to Jack, my reading glasses on and a thick yellow binder in my lap. Jay Prasad sits on Jack's other side and is shaking the bed with laughter at a joke Serena Bishop's just told. Serena is on my desk, legs crisscrossed, still doing a killer impression of some character from a raunchy adult cartoon. Serena can whip out celebrity impressions with a flourish that would put the whole *SNL* ensemble to shame. She's super talented. Obviously. That's why we cast her as Anna Karenina.

I met Serena during the first week of Governor's School for the Arts.

I'd been friends with Jay since orientation, when Jay asked if he could sit next to me because I was wearing a Pokémon shirt and, according to him, "anyone who's a Charmander fan must be legit." Jay and I were in separate tracks—Jay was Drama, I was New Media—which meant we didn't share any classes, but we met up during meals and free time. Serena was in the Drama track with Jay, and once Jay made friends with Serena, Serena made friends with me.

That's how it was at GSA: instant friendship by proxy. I think it worked that way because everyone who attended GSA was by and large from the same social stratum. We were the weird, slightly hip, artsy kids. The ones who put in the extra practice hours after school. The ones whose weekends were tied up with rehearsals and tech and concerts. The only real distinction that remained was between kids who went to public schools and kids who went to arts schools. Here's what I'll say about that: Not everyone from arts schools is a pompous asshole, but all the pompous assholes are from arts schools. A square, rectangle kind of thing.

Serena goes to SCAPA, Lexington's arts school, and is tall and gorgeous, in an elegant, already-grown-up way. She intimidated the hell out of me until a few days after I met her, when I was sitting with a handful of the drama kids in the dining hall and Serena stood on a chair and chugged a two-liter of Fanta on a dare. By the end, the soda was running down her chin and neck—orange rivulets cutting across her dark skin. I looked on in awe as I realized Serena Bishop was crazy and fun and not the least bit egotistical.

TASH *hearts* TOLSTOY

For the next two weeks, Jay, Serena, and I were inseparable. We exchanged tearful good-byes the last day. Serena's and Jay's were particularly spectacular. (Actors. Typical.) But we took comfort in the fact that we lived within thirty miles of each other—Serena and me in Lexington, and Jay right outside the city in more rural Nicholasville. We promised to keep in touch, and the promise turned out to be much harder to break when Jack and I held auditions for *Unhappy Families* last December.

Serena and Jay were shoo-ins for the roles of Anna and Alex, but Jack was weird about the casting decision for a couple days. She kept saying things like "Yeah, but they might not be the best fit" and "We shouldn't make a *final* decision yet. Anna and Alex are *the roles*, and there are more video auditions rolling in."

I finally called her out on it.

"This is because I met them at GSA, isn't it?"

Jack didn't answer, which meant "yes."

Jack didn't get into GSA, but not because she wasn't qualified. She actually sent in an application for the Visual Art track, complete with portfolio and teacher recommendations and personal statement. It was the personal statement that disqualified Jack. It read:

Dear High and Mighty Pricks,

You know you're basically the sorority of the arts world, right? There you sit, smug with your MFAs and your training at Juilliard or whatever the

Kathryn Ormsbee

hell, choosing us for your summer program like this is a popularity contest.

I know plenty of talented artists who've applied to your program and been turned away. You know why? Because the arts are subjective, and in the end it comes down to what the judges like and don't like. But you act like getting into your shitty camp is a badge of honor. Like your graduates passed some magical test and all the rejects failed.

It doesn't work that way.

You think Van Gogh or Clapton or Tarantino would attend your program? No. They'd be too busy actually making art, trying and failing on their own without some Artificial Authority telling them they were good enough.

Here's my portfolio. I think it's fabulous, and that's all the approval I need.

Fuck you very much,

Jacklyn P. Harlow

I spent several days desperately begging Jack to reconsider sending in that application. Each time, Jack calmly responded, "I'm not going to change my ideology, so why would I change the letter?"

Here's the thing: I totally understand where Jack is coming from. I know plenty of really talented students at Calhoun who were turned down by GSA. And yeah, I know it's a kind of beauty pageant, and that's not fair. But if I had a chance to learn about filmmaking and screenwriting from qualified professionals, to meet artists my age from across the state, to earn scholarship money for college, why wouldn't I take it? Sometimes you have to play by the world's unfair rules. Unless, of course, you are Jack Harlow. Then you play by your own rules, no matter how many opportunities you have to deny yourself for the sake of "ideology."

I don't like Jack when she gets like that. Honestly, it scares me, because when Jack takes a stand that unflinching, it means someone has to be right and someone has to be wrong. And while I like to think Jack was just being way too persnickety about GSA, there's this suspicion in the darker part of my mind that maybe *I'm* the one who's wrong. Maybe I am weak in spirit, a total sellout, the kind of human that ancient Greek philosophers warned against associating with. Maybe Jack is the stronger person.

Jack didn't give me a hard time for applying to GSA. She said nothing snarky when I was accepted. She sent me letters and packages during my three weeks on Transylvania University's campus. There was no lofty pontification, no judgmental looks, no eye rolls. When I came home with a digital copy of my group's short film, Jack watched it with adequate enthusiasm. She even said that Serena was talented. But when it came right down to it, as we sat on my bed in a mess of résumés and headshots and scrapped lists of cast combinations, Jack wouldn't give her wholehearted approval to Jay and Serena, and I knew why: They were GSA kids. They were snotty sellouts, and by extension so was I. And that hurt.

Kathryn Ormsbee

"You're not better because you didn't go," I told her.

"That's not what this is about," she replied.

"It isn't?"

"Look," Jack finally said. "I'm worried you three will form some kind of inner group, okay? Because you have the three weeks in common. And you'll be talking about that and making inside jokes I won't understand."

Jack's vulnerability was so unexpected, I couldn't fault her.

"We won't be like that," I said. "Promise. We're all busy artists with our own projects to worry about. We won't be talking about the past. We'll be talking about the future."

That convinced Jack. Maybe not entirely, but enough for her to agree on the final cast list, with Serena's and Jay's names at the top. And just like I promised, the three of us really didn't bring up GSA. Not often enough for Jack to throw a fit, anyway.

We found Eva, George, Tony, and Brooks through a cold-reading audition we held in the Calhoun auditorium, thanks to some help from Mr. Vargas, our drama teacher. Eva Honeycutt was only a sophomore, but I knew her from some school plays I'd stage-managed. Eva was assigned the usual roles of Flower Girl #3 and Chorus Member that all underclassmen have to endure before seniority grants them stardom. But I'd done enough improv exercises with Eva to know she had the chops to pull off a leading role. Plus, she has the perfect face to play Kitty—delicate bone structure and rosy cheeks and a celestial nose. Eva does modeling for local businesses, and it shows. She knows how to turn her chin and lower her lashes to achieve optimum cuteness. She has a thin, airy voice to match. None of the other auditionees came close to capturing the sweet naivety of Kitty Shcherbatsky as well as she did.

George Connor is one of those notorious arts school pompous asses I was talking about earlier, but dammit if he isn't a pro. He's one of Serena's friends from SCAPA, and he's already flown out to London twice to tour the Royal Academy. He's all business all the time, and he's constantly asking me if he can "tweak a line or two" of his dialogue, which really means a lot of improvisation on his part. Trouble is, I can never get all that angry with him because his improvisation is *good*. Even, I'll admit, better than the script. When the camera rolls, George turns into good-natured, overearnest Levin. His chemistry with Eva is on point. Everyone can see that. So everyone tends to turn a blind eye when George is an ass, and we only laugh at him when he's not in the room.

Brooks Long is a sophomore theatre major at the University of Kentucky. Jack and I were a little shocked when he showed up for auditions. Sure, we'd put up flyers around campus, but we never actually thought a college student would walk into a high school auditorium and take our project seriously. I know how young Jack and I look, and how—to steal a word from Dad's books—*ambitious* our project sounds. Comically ambitious, really, if you sit down and ask me and Jack how many classic novels we've adapted before (none), or how many web series

Kathryn Ormsbee

we've directed (none), or how much experience we have with a DSLR camera (very little).

Lucky for us, Brooks gave us the benefit of the doubt. Extra luckily, he's perfect for the role of Stiva. He plays him as weathered but convivial, full of faults yet lovable. Off camera, Brooks is professional. He doesn't ever stick around for our after-parties, but he isn't standoffish. He's just . . . older. He's on the other side of that as-yet-uncrossable chasm between the last semester of high school and first semester of college.

At the moment, Brooks is leaning against the doorframe of my closet, chatting with Klaudie. He's asking her about Vanderbilt, of course, because that's what college students talk about: college. As I look over the red markings in today's shooting script—shorthand directions about character placement, camera angle, lighting choices—I catch an occasional sound bite from their conversation. Brooks is asking Klaudie why she won't consider minoring in theatre, because she's very good at it. Klaudie's saying she wants to focus all her energies on engineering, because she is so perfect and simply has too many talents to choose from.

Well. That's basically what Klaudie is saying.

Sometimes, I regret suggesting Klaudie play Dolly. A year ago, Klaudie wasn't such a pill. A year ago, when Jack and I told her our big idea, she was genuinely excited and told us we should stop second-guessing ourselves and just make the web series before someone else beat us to it. So I told her she was how I pictured Dolly, the nurturing and heartbroken partner of cheating husband Stiva (updated to cheating *boyfriend* Stiva in *Unhappy Families*). Klaudie said it'd be fun at least to audition, and from there on out, everything clicked. Klaudie has a good rapport with Brooks, and her memory's a steel trap, so I can always count on her to recite her lines verbatim. That's how Klaudie joined the cast.

And then there's Tony Davis, our Vronsky, whose interest in *Unhappy Families* is about as natural as a professional golfer's interest in nuclear physics. It just doesn't compute. Tony's social calendar is already booked. He attends parties. He plays in a band—a band that sounds like nails being sent through a food processor, but *still*, a *band*. Before the web series, he never once came near school plays or drama club. I didn't even know he could act. But then Tony showed up on audition day, in all his Mohawked, leather-jacketed glory. Tony *was* Count Alexei Kirillovich Vronsky. Typecasting in its purest form.

Thus we formed our merry little company: seven actors, two filmmakers, nine companions. Exactly like the Fellowship of the Ring. Okay, not exactly. Only in my mind, where I've assigned myself the role of Gimli, because come on, who is better than Gimli?

"Don't you think we should get started? Someone can fill Eva in."

I look up from the script to find George standing over me, arms crossed.

"She'll be here any minute," I say, capping my highlighter.

"Yeah, but it's not fair that we're all here on time like professionals and she's holding us up."

Kathryn Ormsbee

This is normal behavior from George—all this talk of profession-alism and how everyone aside from him doesn't know what that is. Usually, I'm cool with it. Like I said, it's a small price to pay for good acting. But today, my fuse is shorter than usual. My mind is half script, half social media mentions. Last night, I *dreamed* of weeding through notifications.

"George," I say, pressing the heels of my hands to my forehead. "Just . . ."

"Fine. We'll get started."

I shoot Jack a surprised glance. Jack is never one to give in to George. But judging from the look on her face, she has no fuse whatsoever this morning.

"Okay, everyone." Jack doesn't shout. She only shouts when she's angry, not when she's happy or excited and certainly not to get any-one's attention. Her get-attention voice sounds like a bored recitation of phone book entries. No one hears her.

I don't have a problem with shouting.

"Guys!" I stand and wave my arms. "Hey, we're gonna go ahead and get started."

George seats himself in my desk chair with a smug smile on his oh-so-punchable face.

The room quiets, aside from a grizzled sound emitting from Tony's earbuds. He looks up from his place on the floor and yanks out the earbuds with a quick "Sorry." Before the music cuts out, I recognize the song and realize Tony has been listening to *himself.* His own band. Jesus. If egos were helium-filled balloons, this bedroom would detach from the house and float straight to the moon.

Everyone has turned their attention to me. I clear my throat and tug on the sweat-lined collar of my T-shirt. I really wish I'd dashed into the hall and punched down the temperature before starting this prepared speech of mine. But it's too late for that; I've activated public speaking mode.

"Okay," I say. "So by now, I'm assuming you've all read my e-mail and seen the explosion online. As of this morning, we're at almost sixty-five thousand subscribers, which is pretty wild. This is what we've been working toward—more exposure, more fan engagement. It also looks like we'll be able to fund more projects. And, of course, if we create a Kickstarter, we'll budget a certain amount to pay you retroactively for your work as actors. We want each of you to get a cut, because we know what it's like to be poor, broke artists, and Jack and I both think it's important to pay artists for their time whenever possible."

"Amen," Brooks says, shooting me a wink.

"Right," I say. "So we're going to continue filming as usual. Jack and I have printed out a final schedule of our remaining shoot dates this summer, so make sure you grab one before you leave and double-check it with your calendar. We've tried to work around everyone's vacations, but that means a few weekends spent filming. Sorry."

I glance down briefly at the bullet points I penciled out this morning.

Kathryn Ormsbee

"The main thing to keep in mind is that Jack and I will take care of all interactions on social media. We don't want you to have to worry about that, and it'll be more controllable if we answer everyone's questions from the Seedling Productions account. So if anyone tags you individually or asks you to engage, send it our way."

There's a click at the bedroom door. Eva slips in, sending a repentant smile around the room.

"Sorryyyyyy," she stage-whispers, making a show of tiptoeing in and then performing a cute little leap over Tony.

"Let me get this straight," says Tony. "Are you telling us we can't interact with our groupies?" He's grinning the same way he does when he makes a smart-ass remark in social studies.

"We'd just rather you didn't," I say. "It's not that we don't trust you guys or anything, but believe me, it gets exhausting, fielding stuff like that. And we all know how things can get weird fast on social media. One misinterpreted comment or a slip about something that's coming up in the series, and we'll have to do major damage control."

"Makes sense," says Serena. "I'm glad you brought that up, actually. I've gotten a couple mentions on Twitter—just nice things. But I don't want to be answering questions."

"Right," I say. "This way, you won't have to. Speaking of questions, any of you have them?"

Serena raises her hand and says, "This isn't a serious question, exactly, but have you all seen the GIF sets floating around? It's *awesome*. George and Eva, everyone is obsessed with you. Or should I say, '*Kevin*'?"

The smugness in George's smile has spread to his eyes. He leans the desk chair onto its back two legs and shrugs as though to say, *Can I help that I'm fabulous?*

Eva releases a pleased giggle and says, "No one's a bigger Kevin fangirl than me."

"It's perfect timing, too," says Jay. "Right before the Scrabble scene? People are going to go crazy over that."

Jay is referring to one of our upcoming episodes, which we shot last week. It's our adaptation of the scene when a previously scorned Levin returns to a changed Kitty and proposes marriage a second time—this time with happier results. It's *the kissing scene*. And like I hoped, after all the effort, it turned out perfectly.

In *Unhappy Families*, Levin isn't a farmer but a college freshman studying agriculture. Kitty isn't a socialite waiting around for a proposal of marriage but Levin's childhood friend and a professional ballerina. And of course Levin doesn't ask Kitty for her hand in marriage, just out on a date. In the book, the reconciliation happens by way of a word game, using chalk and a card table. It was my idea to update this to a poorly played game of Scrabble. Jack has already shown me the edited footage, and it is undeniably adorable. Like Jay said, this is perfect timing. Nothing pleases a crowd quite like a beloved ship setting sail.

That's when I say something I haven't written down. "You guys. I'm really, *really* excited."

Kathryn Ormsbee

I'm met with grins and thumbs-ups. There is energy crackling in this room. I can practically see it—lightning bolts of neon pinks and greens and blues. There's a feeling that *something is happening*. Something big and uncertain and out of control. It is splendid and terrifying—*splendifying*. I guess that's how filming has always been. The thrilling unknown of auditions. The utter largeness of watching dialogue Jack and I wrote coming out of actors' mouths, then turning into a coherent playlist of videos. Nothing else compares.

"We just can't go the route of all rock groups," Tony says from the floor. "We can't let fame turn us on each other or make us fall into a cycle of substance abuse. And no selling each other out to the tabloids."

Everyone snickers at the remark. Everyone but George, who says, "Are we going to get to filming now?"

"Yep," I say. "For this first shot we need Levin, Kitty, Dolly, and Stiva. We'll be in the living room. The rest of you, feel free to look over lines up here or grab some snacks in the kitchen. We'll take a break at twelve thirty for pizza."

I turn to Jack. "Ready to set up lights?"

Not that I need to ask. Jack is always ready to film.

In the living room, Jack works in knit-browed silence to adjust a reflector on our actors. We fall into our usual prep sequence: check white balance, check sound levels, check frame for any weirdness. Then Jack brings the clapboard into focus, and *snap*, the scene comes to life.

I am officially the director of *Unhappy Families*, since Jack and I decided it would be less confusing if we designated one person the actors should approach with questions about interpretation or movement. It also means Jack can edit the footage with some amount of objectivity, since she wasn't the one behind the camera during filming. Today, I have very little direction to give. There are no forgotten lines, no awkward cadences, no gaffes. Our actors are hitting every single line right on the first take.

An hour in, Jack asks for a quick break to check over sound recordings. I head for the kitchen, where we've set up a snack station, to fix a plate of carrot sticks. I walk in on Tony and Jay in the middle of a shouting match.

Jay is brandishing a plastic fork at Tony's eye while yelling, "I hope you know it's your fault if she dies! Don't you ever forget that: It's your fucking fault."

"She's not going to die," says Tony, who's blanched to the shade of parchment paper. "She's not going to die."

I'm frozen in the doorway, entranced. Tony and Jay stand in front of the fridge, less than a foot from each other, their bodies tensed and prone. Tony's shoulders are rolled toward Jay in a downward slant. The guys are just rehearsing, but I can't shake the feeling there's something about this that isn't artificial.

"Don't kill each other before the actual take," I say, walking up to the counter.

Kathryn Ormsbee

Both of them start. Jay lowers his fork and backs a step away. Tony laughs. He has a magnificent laugh—hoarse and cascading and always a little self-deprecating.

"Can't make any promises," he says. He reaches past me to dip his index finger straight into the dish of ranch dressing on the vegetable tray.

"Jesus Christ, Tony," I yelp, smacking his hand away. "That's disgusting."

I know I'm reacting exactly the way Tony wants me to, but seriously, there are certain hygienic rules you don't break. How does Tony get away with this behavior at all his fancy parties? Is everyone there too drunk to notice?

As I scoop up a handful of carrots, Tony says, "I licked all those."

I give Tony a "you're better than that" look and bite one of the carrots clean in half.

I say, "You guys are up in ten. Where's Serena?"

"In your bedroom," Jay answers. "She said we were distracting her, so she went upstairs."

That's not hard to believe. If the shouting wasn't distracting enough, the tension between Tony and Jay definitely would be. Part of me wants to shove the two of them together, screaming, "Kiss already!" But the larger part hasn't forgotten that Tony and Jack were an item a few short months ago.

Even now that Jack and Tony are broken up, I suspect Jay might never say a thing. Not because Tony doesn't swing that way—he took a guy as his date to prom—but because Tony dated Jack, and Tony, Jack, and Jay are all involved in the web series. I believe this is called "discord in the ranks," and it kind of makes me feel like I live in season nine of a primetime drama, when the writers have run out of decent plotlines and begin pairing off all the main characters with each other.

I head upstairs to my bedroom. The door is cracked, and I knock lightly before pushing it open and finding Serena bent over her script, eyes closed and fingers pressed to her temples in concentration.

"Hey," I say softly. "You're up in ten."

Serena glances up, looking a little dazed. Then she grins. "Thanks."

I'm closing the door when Serena calls, "Tash?"

"Yeah?"

"Okay, I'm about to be kind of cheesy, so ignore this if you want, but, um . . . I'm really glad I met you last summer."

"Me too."

Serena bunches her shoulders toward her ears, grin still on her face. "I just have this feeling we're doing something that's once-in-a-lifetime, you know?"

I nod.

Yes. I absolutely know.

Kathryn Ormsbee

Seven

We film until eleven o'clock at night. It's an hour past what we originally scheduled, but no one has Sunday night plans that begin at ten, and there's a dogged excitement hanging around the house. My parents obligingly retired to their bedroom with Chinese takeout boxes, so we've had free range of the place. Today was a rare all-cast day, when we shoot scenes with either every or nearly every character in the series. Thanks to today's shoot, we have four important episodes' worth of footage.

In the coming weeks, we'll resume our regular schedule, which usually only calls for Levin and Kitty or Anna and Vronsky, the four primary roles. Jack and I film roughly two weeks in advance, which means Jack is now uploading episodes this week that we filmed mid-May. It's a packed schedule that must take into account actors' vacations and school plays and other commitments, but I've planned it all out on an Excel sheet in what Jack calls "a display of unadulterated dorkdom." According to this schedule, now finalized to its very end, filming will wrap up the first weekend of August.

I wake up at one in the morning with an acidic monster in my stomach. I fix myself a bowl of leftover coconut rice I find in the fridge and watch some Netflix, hoping the bright light will tire my eyes. It doesn't. I can't shut off my brain for another hour, and when I wake up Monday morning I am slightly nauseated, head aching, my skin tight and itchy.

Of course, this *would* be my first morning at work. With great effort, I drag myself out of bed, stare at myself in the bathroom mirror, and decide my hair isn't *that* greasy and therefore can go into a bun and therefore I can sleep a little longer. I fling myself back into bed for ten minutes. Eleven. Twelve. Then I come to the grim conclusion that if I plan on shelling out money for a private college education, work is a thing that needs to happen.

This is my third summer working at the Old Navy in the mall. It's boring, but the employee discount is nice, and I like most of my coworkers.

"Hey, Ethan," I say, walking in and casting a wave at Ethan Short, a UK student who's been working here since last August. He's generally pretty quiet, but we get along.

I head to the back room to store my knapsack in a cubby. I check my phone one last time before I must enter a seven-hour blackout of absolutely no contact with the outside world. There's a text from Thom. No, *two* texts from Thom.

The remains of the Pop-Tart I ate for breakfast sprout wings and take flight in my large intestine.

Kathryn Ormsbee

Even though Thom and I exchanged our numbers over a week ago, neither of us has texted. I guess we've both been playing it cool, attempting to prove that we aren't annoying texters who need to talk about every blasé thing ever. But it really began to bother me over the weekend. Had Thom changed his mind? Maybe we weren't taking this thing to the next level—whatever level that was. Maybe we'd just made things irreparably awkward. Maybe we were going to go on sending e-mails like this phone number thing never happened.

But no. In two simple texts, Thom has set my anxious mind at ease.

Testing, testing, one two three.

(It's Thom. In case you haven't added me yet.)

In case I haven't added him yet. Ha. Not that Thom needs to know I added his contact info the moment I got his number. I stare at his messages, trying to formulate a response.

I text, *HEY! Tash, reading you loud and clear.*

I frown, nix the exclamation mark. An exclamation after all caps is too enthusiastic. Then I start reconsidering the second sentence. It's too obvious. Duh, of course it's me and I can read him loud and clear. So maybe I should keep it brief. Just the "hey." In all caps. No exclamation point. I try tapping the text box to make my edits, but I accidentally end up hitting the send button.

Damn.

I hope there are a lot of shirts to fold today. I need all the mindless distraction I can get.

. . .

When I arrive back home, Klaudie is in the den watching *Dancing with the Stars* on DVD. She pauses the show and cranes her neck toward the kitchen.

"Hey," she says.

"What's up?" I ask, bringing in a bag of wasabi-flavored snap peas. I sink into the couch beside her and tilt the open bag in her direction.

Klaudie shakes her head. She's wearing this funny expression, like she's on the verge of a sneeze.

"Why do you look like that?" I ask.

"Like what?"

Klaudie sounds annoyed, which annoys me into saying, "Like you're constipated."

Klaudie's look turns from funny to full-on ugly. "I want to talk to you."

"Okay." I chomp into a snap pea. "So talk."

"Oh my God, Tash, can you not eat for a second. That crunching is disgusting."

I narrow my eyes. I place the remaining half of the snap pea in my mouth and chomp as disgustingly as possible. I'm not exactly proud of myself, but these are the rules of sisterhood. Once Sister One says something obnoxious, Sister Two must launch back a *more* obnoxious rejoinder, and so on and so forth until both parties feel pretty shitty about themselves and remain so until the next day, when they pretend the tiff didn't happen.

Kathryn Ormsbee

But because I don't want this to turn into a full-blown argument, I roll up the bag of snap peas and set it aside. Crossing my arms, I say, "Happy?"

"You're so immature," Klaudie replies.

"Is that what you wanted to tell me?"

"No. Um. Well, there's not really a good way to say it."

"Just *say* it. What?"

So Klaudie says it, all in a rush: "I can't be in *Unhappy Families*."

I stare at her. My face is blank. Actually, I'm not sure I can feel my face anymore. From the floor, the bag of snap peas begins to unroll itself—a loud, crinkling sound.

"What?" I ask.

"I've been wanting to tell you for a while now. Way before Taylor Mears. I've been thinking it through, and . . . I don't have time for all the filming dates. I'm volunteering with the engineering camp at UK, and that takes up a lot of time, and if I'm doing filming too . . . I want enough time to just hang with my friends. It's my last summer in Lexington. I think I need to spend more time enjoying it."

I shake my head slowly. "But you enjoy filming."

Klaudie blows out a long breath. "That's not what I'm saying. Yeah, I enjoy it. But there's other stuff I enjoy . . . more."

"Oh. Right. Like Ally and Jenna."

"*Yes*, like Ally and Jenna. They're my best friends, and we're all about to go in different directions, and I want to have a summer where I'm not stressed or overbooked, and I'm *sorry*, I know this project means a lot to you, but I don't have that big a role, anyway, so—"

"Exactly," I snap in. "You don't have a big role. It's not *that* many filming dates. Only, like, nine total. That's basically nothing."

"It's *three whole weekends*. That's, like, a *third* of my summer. And it's been hard for me to decide this, but I need to quit now. I need to do what's best for me."

I can't look at her. I cannot look at my sister right now. Instead, I stare at the television. The screen is frozen on a blond actress in a shimmery pink dress cha-cha-cha-ing with a man wearing a matching pink bow tie. I angrily realize there are tears in my eyes.

"So all that's more important to you," I say. "Your stupid engineering camp and freakin' Ally and Jenna. Not me."

"This is about the show, not you, Tash." Klaudie's voice is surprisingly gentle. "I know you think I'm a total bitch right now, but I really am sorry. I've looked over all the scenes I have left to film. It won't be *that* hard to cut me out."

I whip back toward Klaudie. "You have *no idea*, do you? How much work goes into scheduling. How much work we put into the script. It's not that easy. We can't just cut you out. Plenty of stuff still hinges on Dolly. Lots of lines. Character development. And what about Brooks? Did you think about him? Most of his scenes are with you. What are we supposed to do about those scenes now, throw them out? So that means Brooks gets, like, half the screen time he's supposed to."

Kathryn Ormsbee

"You don't have to shout at me." Klaudie hugs her knees to her chest, and I am so pissed at her for acting like she's the wounded one. "I told you, I'm *sorry*. I just can't be in a web series right now."

"No, you *won't*. You're so freaking selfish, you know that? You don't even have a good reason for quitting."

"I have a—"

"Oh right, sorry. You have a great reason. You want to 'enjoy the summer.'" I throw up disdainful air quotes. "Like filming with us is total hell."

"Well, sometimes it is."

"Excuse me?"

Klaudie's distant eyes turn sharp. "I said, 'Sometimes it is.' Sometimes you make it hell. You get so high-strung and start focusing on the 'aesthetic' and all the technical details and getting a shot *just right*, and you forget that some of us are your friends. You forget I'm your *sister*."

"Is this about when I corrected your lines on Sunday? Because I correct everybody."

"No, it's not that. It's . . ." Klaudie shakes her head, lets out a frustrated groan. "I've already told you. I'm obviously never going to give you a good enough reason, so you're going to have to accept it, okay? I'm quitting."

I shake my head. I shake and shake and shake my head. "You are. So. Unbelievable."

But Klaudie is right about one thing: She won't ever give me a good enough reason for this betrayal. I can't stand to be in the same room with her for another second. I grab my snap peas and storm out.

"If she wants to go, there's nothing we can do about it."

Jack sounds calm, teetering toward bored, on the phone. I try not to be annoyed. Jack always sounds bored, even when she's talking about her crushes and favorite bands.

"She made a commitment," I say. "She made a *promise*."

"Yeah, and she broke it. That's life. Happens all the time. We'll have to figure out a way to write her out of the script and still give Brooks some decent lines."

I glare at the twinkle lights wound around my bed frame, until my vision grows wet and blurred.

"I'm so pissed," I say.

"Well, you're allowed to be. But it's Klaudie. She isn't going to change her mind, so we need to deal."

"You don't think . . . ," I begin, but don't finish.

"What?"

"That it'll have a bad effect on everyone else? Like, once she leaves, do you think they might peace out too?"

"Hell no. Were you watching them yesterday? They're as pumped as we are. This is great exposure, something solid they can put on their résumés. Klaudie's not an actor, so she doesn't get that. But no one else is going to leave, I guarantee it. They'd be idiots."

Kathryn Ormsbee

I recall what Serena said to me yesterday: *We're doing something that's once-in-a-lifetime.*

"Yeah," I say. "I guess."

"So, how're things in your corner of the Internet?"

Jack is referring to my list of duties. It's been more than a week now since Taylor Mears's vlog posted, and while our subscriptions and view counts are ever growing, they've slowed to a far less alarming rate. Same with the social media situation. Mentions and fan content crop up daily, but it's more manageable now. I spend about an hour each day getting caught up on my end of things.

"It's fine," I say. "A lot of nice comments. I retweeted some stuff tonight."

I don't mention the five-paragraph e-mail I sent Taylor Mears, thanking her for the shout-out. In retrospect, it *might* have been too much. I think I overused the word "amazing."

"I seriously wish we could afford a personal assistant," Jack says. "I went into this line of work because it meant I wouldn't have to interact with people. This is interacting. With people. Not a fan."

I smile against the phone. Jack often feels the need to remind me she is a misanthrope.

"While we're near the subject of quitting," I say, "I have something to tell you."

"Tash. If you bail on me now, I will effing—"

"Shut up and listen, okay? I've decided to put my vlog on hiatus for a bit. I don't think I can do the web series *and* all this social media stuff *and* my summer job *and* the vlog. Something's got to go."

"Huh. Yeah, makes sense. You can always pick it back up when things settle down."

"That's what I was thinking," I say, though I feel a pang beneath my ribs. I was hoping Jack might try to dissuade me at least a little. Say something like "Oh, but everyone loves *Teatime with Tash*!"

But then, putting the vlog on hiatus is the only solution, and it's not like I would change my mind even if Jack did fight it.

"Okay," she says. "I've got to get back to Sally's face."

Which sounds weird but is the norm coming from Jack. A few years ago, she started making these Tim Burton–inspired clay figurines and selling them online. She's gotten really good at it and ships out about a dozen a week. Now that she's no longer singing with Tony on their *Echo Boomers* channel, she's been especially devoted to her Etsy shop.

As is the norm for *me* upon hearing Jack mention her business, I launch into a magnificently flat rendition of "Sally's Song" from *The Nightmare Before Christmas*:

"I sense there's something in the wiiiiind—"

"God, Tash."

"—that feels like tragedy's at haaaaand—"

"I'm gonna hang up now."

And she does.

Kathryn Ormsbee

. . .

I don't want a repeat of my last restless night, so I go downstairs to brew a cup of chamomile tea—a special loose-leaf Grandmum Young sent from Auckland last Christmas. The television is on in the den, a rarity after ten o'clock. After switching on the electric kettle, I peek inside. The lights are off, and a black-and-white Bette Davis movie is playing at low volume. In the shifting flashes of light, I see my mom curled into the corner of the couch. She isn't watching the television, but some space of wall to the left of it. She's crying.

My throat goes dry. I'm used to these tears one day out of the year—January 14, the day my mother left New Zealand for the States. But finding her like this on such a run-of-the-mill night is unexpected and . . . kind of embarrassing.

The kettle water begins to boil. Mom looks up at the sound and sees me in the doorway. I smile weakly and try to think of something to say.

"Tasha," she says, wiping a hand beneath her eyes and tipping up a smile. "I didn't see you."

"I was making tea."

"Mmm. Mmm-hmm."

"Would you like some?" I offer, the first sensible thing to come out of my mouth.

A long moment passes, during which Mom recovers steady speech, then says, "That would be lovely, yes."

I nod and slip back into the kitchen as the kettle clicks off. I measure the tea into two strainers, then fill the mugs with piping hot water and return to the den. I hand one mug to Mom and snuggle beside her on the couch.

There's nothing I can say, so I just keep close, and we sip our tea as Bette Davis fills each frame with wide-eyed assuredness. It's only many minutes later, when I've drained my chamomile to its dregs, that Mom says, softly, "I miss them."

I know this isn't a simple stating of fact, but a confession. Even now, after twenty years, Mom feels the pain as badly as she did the day she left her home in another hemisphere. I know Mom's angry at herself for feeling this way. She thinks it's some kind of failing on her part. But I don't think she feels like this because she doesn't meditate enough or because she is too attached to the physical world. My mother is also a daughter. She is human, and she feels deeply, and some deep wounds don't ever heal.

Mom was—*is*—very close to her parents. She's their only child, and they were as close-knit as a family can get. Then, when she was at college, she won a scholarship to study abroad for a semester. She was writing her linguistics thesis on dialects of the southern United States, and it was the perfect opportunity. So she left, and then she met my dad, and suddenly she was staying and staying and *staying* abroad. To study. To earn her doctorate. To marry Jan Zelenka. To start a family. The way she tells it, it's not like she regrets coming here. She loves my

Kathryn Ormsbee

dad and our life in Lexington. But she loved her life in Auckland, too. And she didn't know when she left that she wouldn't be going back for a full eight years. It was hard on her parents, and it was hard on her, and even though she Skypes with Grandmum and PopPop every week, it isn't the same.

I get that. It'd be hard for me if I left all this—Mom and Dad and Jack and Paul and all my favorite places—behind. It *will* be hard, when I go to Vanderbilt.

Mom rests her head on mine. We're less mother and daughter now, and more one nameless entity. Mom confided in me once, nearly a year ago, that she knows she won't reach enlightenment in this life. It wasn't a possibility after she left Auckland, because parting from her family was a pain she could never remove herself from, never rise above. I disagree. I think that *because* Mom has suffered in this life she *deserves* a better existence in the next one. I know this perspective isn't strictly in keeping with what I've heard at our local Zen center, but I refuse to believe my mom gets a spiritual setback just because she moved a few thousand miles from her childhood home.

I remain still. My fingers are warm from the mug of tea. I feel a drip of hot liquid trickle down through my hair and touch my scalp. My mom's tears are utterly silent.

I say, "I love you, Mom."

On-screen, Bette Davis descends a staircase, dressed in diamonds and a stunning satin dress.

More hot tears water my hair. I fall asleep like that, and wake only much later, curled on the couch, just as Mom is covering my legs with a quilt. I pretend I'm sleeping, and soon I really am.

In the morning, I climb upstairs and lock myself in my bedroom. I open my laptop and click the Final Draft document labeled "UF 15.2." Calmly and efficiently, I cut every single one of Klaudie's lines.

Eight

The next day, I'm back at the mall. I while away the hours checking out the occasional flip-flop customer and bouncing a light-up volleyball between my register and Ethan's. The soundtrack is a nice mix of pop remixes and cheery oldies like "Walking on Sunshine" and "Ain't No Mountain High Enough." Overall, it's a boring morning, but I leave in good spirits and stop by the food court to buy a blue raspberry ICEE. Then I settle on one of the benches outside Macy's to read through a series of texts Thom sent during my shift.

As it turns out, my "reading you loud and clear" text did not bring about eternal shame and mortification. Thom just replied with an innocuous "AWESOME," and somehow we ended up on the topic of food and beverages. At the moment, Thom is espousing the merits of bubble tea, and he's flabbergasted I've never tried it before.

It's shocking, Tash. Totally shocking.

You're only half a person until you've burst a tapioca bubble in your mouth.

I didn't think Kentucky was THAT backwards.

That last text makes me indignant. I know Thom is joking around (or flirting?), but I take offense whenever anyone makes a slight about where I live. Like I reside deep in the woods and wear a coonskin cap and talk like one of those crazy hunters on *Duck Dynasty*. Yes, Thom is from L.A., and yes that makes him somewhat cool, but it's not like we live in the year 1805, when hip new developments took decades to reach the landlocked states. We live in the brave new twenty-first century, where the trends in Lexington are now only a season behind the big cities and everyone is learning to talk in the standardized Midwestern accent all the newscasters use.

I text back, *Bubble tea has been out for ages, and I KNOW WHAT IT IS. I just never ask for it when I go to coffee shops.*

Then I add, *I go for the frappes.*

Just in case Thom wants to buy me one when we meet up one day. Not that I've pictured that scenario at all. Not that I've imagined Thom taking me to Starbucks, where we'll get lost in conversation for five whole hours. Or how he will slurp the last bit of his iced coffee, but in a cute way. Or how, when we finally leave the store because they're closing, he will casually drape his arm around my shoulders and whisper, "I'm so glad you're here."

Kathryn Ormsbee

Like I would imagine that. Ha.

My heart peps up when I see that Thom is texting back.

Uuuuugh, he replies. *Seriously? Frappes? They are like the Appletinis of the coffee world.*

I text, *What do you have then? I bet you're a purist. I bet you only order triple espresso shots.*

Thom texts, *It's an acquired taste. Don't worry, you'll grow into it.*

I frown, both at the text and the brain freeze I've brought on with an extra long slurp of ICEE.

Maybe Thom is just flirting, but if this is flirting, I'm not a fan. I don't feel like defending my beverage choices, and I don't like Thom treating me like I'm naive. It's not attractive; it's something an annoying older brother would do.

Though not an older brother like Paul. He and Jack fight, but I've never once heard him tease her. I think this has to do with the fact that Paul was bullied a lot in elementary school. In the end, it got so bad that Mr. and Mrs. Harlow held Paul back in the fifth grade, because of the bullying *and* his trouble in classes.

Paul.

I want to talk to him about Klaudie. I called Jack expecting sympathy, which was stupid of me. Jack doesn't do sympathy, but Paul does. Paul does it very well. I decide I'll go over to the Harlows' later today, after I film the vlog announcing my hiatus. Jack will be working her shift at Petco then, so I can have Paul all to myself for a few hours. It's been a while since we've hung out, just the two of us.

I also decide not to reply to Thom's text. At least, not right away.

"Hey, everybody! So, I know this video is late, and I apologize profusely. As most of you probably know, our web series *Unhappy Families* got a big signal boost last week, and things have been hectic over here. But the good kind of hectic! Because Jack and I want to provide you guys with only the best content, I've decided to put *Teatime with Tash* on hiatus so I can focus more energy on *Unhappy Families*. I'm going to miss sharing tea and talk of dashing young gents with you all, but I hope to be back with brand-new episodes this fall, after we've wrapped up filming for . . ."

I grimace. I feel like I'm saying "Unhappy Families" too often over such a short period of time. I reach behind the camera and jab the record button, putting an effective end to this take. Maybe I can say "wrapped up filming *the web series*." That sounds cleaner.

This video is necessary. I can't abandon my vlog without a reason why, or else our subscribers will think Jack and I aren't devoted to our projects. But deep down, I wonder if anyone will care. All anybody seems interested in nowadays is *Unhappy Families* and the Kitty + Levin OTP. I expect things to go crazy tomorrow, when Jack uploads the Scrabble episode. My hiatus announcement will probably be lost in the hullabaloo.

Kathryn Ormsbee

It's not like I'm jealous of my own web series. I just really enjoy filming *Teatime with Tash*. It's simple and kind of superficial, yeah, but that's what makes it fun. I don't have to shoot a scene fifteen times to get the actors' tones and the lighting and the camera angle perfect. All I have to do is sit down in my desk chair, framed by a backdrop of powder blue bunting and a stack of my favorite books, and *talk*. Drink a new flavor of loose-leaf. Gush about JJ Feild as Mr. Tilney in the underrated ITV adaptation of *Northanger Abbey*. It's the easiest thing in the world. It's just me being *me*, talking about something I love.

Unhappy Families requires a lot more time and effort and planning. I'm not afraid of planning; I love it, and I'm a pro. I just like, on occasion, to do something effort*less*.

I remind myself that there are at least a few people out there who like my vlog. They were leaving encouraging comments way before that Taylor Mears video. At least a few viewers will miss me. A few viewers will be happy when I resume the vlog. And I *will* resume the vlog. Just after this fame explosion dies down.

I lean back to check my reflection in the closet mirror. I sweep away an errant smudge of eyeliner, then tuck a stray shoot of hair back into my messy brunette bun. I take a few deep breaths, then vibrate my lips together the way I've seen Serena and Jay warm up before speaking their lines.

Settled back into position, I press the record button once more.

"Hey, everybody! So, I know this video is late . . ."

When I've wrapped up filming, I text Paul, *Can I come over?*

Paul texts back immediately, *Thought you'd never ask.*

Grinning, I slip on a pair of ballet flats and head out, going through the kitchen so I can snag a box of bite-size white chocolate macadamia nut cookies. Paul will probably need sustenance. Jack is always complaining that Mr. Harlow and Paul would starve if she didn't force them to eat dinner on nights when Mrs. Harlow is away on business—and that's about half the nights every month. They both get so wrapped up in whatever they're doing they forget to eat, which I can maybe understand for Mr. Harlow, but aren't teenage guys like Paul capable of inhaling extra large pizzas without thinking twice? Paul claims he did all his growing when he was seventeen, which might be true. The way I remember it, I started sophomore year several inches taller than Paul and ended it a full foot shorter. Jack and I used to joke that there were fissures in Paul's skin from having to accommodate such a sudden stretch.

When I reach the Harlows', I go around back. The house is a split-level, and I get in using the basement's sliding door. From the patio, through the glass, I see Paul smushed into a beanbag, playing a video game. I stop a few feet from the door and, for a moment, just watch.

I will never tell Paul this, because there's no way to say it without sounding creepy, but I love his face when he's playing video games. It's all tensed muscle and set jaw. The brightness, the sheer earnestness in his eyes is unsettling. Like that, Paul looks ageless—like he could just as well be battling in the Trojan War, or on the fields of Gettysburg. It's a

Kathryn Ormsbee

face that makes me weirdly proud of him, that makes me want to shout, "This is my friend, who is fully human and so alive, and he deserves an epic poem or at least a mural."

It's a face that frightens me a little too. Maybe for the same reason: because Paul is so alive.

I slide open the door and am hit with the sounds of trumpets and clanging metal. Paul looks to me, pauses the game, and tosses the controller aside.

"Thank God you're here," he says. "I'm sucking so bad right now. I'm about to bleed out."

"This shall restore you, soldier," I say, shaking the box of cookies.

I edge my butt onto the beanbag and rip open the box, then the aluminum bag inside. Paul promptly extracts a handful of cookies and shoves them into his mouth, chewing noisily. I roll my eyes. In just a minute, he has gone from demigod to uncouth slob. So strange and changeable. So, so alive.

Paul grabs the remote wedged under his thigh and turns off the television.

"You can keep playing," I say, slipping an arm behind his back as he throws one over my shoulder.

"I was mostly dead, anyway."

"No, you're just being polite."

Paul inhales another handful of cookies. "Polite?" he says, when his mouth is at its fullest. He grins at his magnificent rebuttal.

"I mean, playing host. You never keep the TV on when I'm here."

"Well, it's rude," says Paul.

"Which makes you polite."

Paul tries to look annoyed, which does strange things to his cheeks. "Hey, stop throwing that word around. I have a reputation to protect."

"Hmph," I reply.

"I need to redeem myself." Paul gets up, dusting off the fine layer of cookie crumbs that has collected on his T-shirt. "C'mon, we're gonna play some Ping-Pong."

"How is that redeeming yourself?" I ask, following him from the entertainment room to the game room. (The Harlow basement has such exciting room names. We Zelenkas don't even have a basement, just an eensy cellar we use during tornado warnings.)

"Because I am going to whoop your ass," says Paul, "and hosts generally let their guests win games."

"That's a stupid rule. And you are *not* going to whoop my ass."

He is, actually. Paul is way better than I am at anything requiring hand-eye coordination. Still, I like playing Ping-Pong with him, because I'm good enough to make the game interesting, not humiliating.

The Harlows' Ping-Pong table is University of Kentucky blue. The paddles are two-toned—blue and white. The balls are white with tiny blue UK logos. The walls of the game room are covered in old posters boasting about national championships and broken records. (Example:

Kathryn Ormsbee

UK2K! for the first NCAA basketball team to reach two thousand wins. Yeah. UK fans are that obnoxious.)

"Ready?" Paul asks, picking up a paddle and tossing one to me. I catch it by the handle, and Paul grins, clearly impressed. I grin, clearly proud.

I say, "Let's get this thing started."

Paul starts off with an inhumanly rapid serve that flies off my side of the table before I can even think to make a lunge for it. I'm not too worried, though. He is undoubtedly going to beat me, but I'll sneak in a few points by the end; Paul always gets lazy after a few rounds. In the minutes that follow, the room fills with cheers of victory, screeches of defeat, commiserative laughter, and, under all of it, the unsteady *pit-pat* of the Ping-Pong ball. After five rounds, Paul remains the undefeated champion.

I lose my last point by raising my paddle over my head and crying, "You're rude and a terrible host, okay?"

Paul takes a bow. Then, maybe because I'm woozy with adrenaline, I climb atop the table and lie out diagonally. Deeming this a good plan, Paul does the same on his end of the table. I glance over and snicker at how awkward a sight it is—Paul's legs hanging a good two feet off the edge. He wriggles around, trying to get more comfortable, and eventually settles on pulling up his knees.

It's quiet for a while. I turn toward Paul again, squinting through the netting in an attempt to get a better look at his face.

"You okay?"

Paul laughs.

I prop myself up on an elbow. "Paul?"

"I'm *fine*. God, Tash, you freak out every time I'm quiet for more than fifteen seconds."

"That's not true."

Silence.

More silence.

"Okay, fine," I admit.

"So let's talk about you," says Paul. "Tash Zelenka, how are you handling fame?"

I wince. "It's very surreal and kind of annoying."

"Oh yeah? I thought you were loving it."

"No, I am. It's awesome. All the comments and, oh my God, someone posted this fan art of Kevin yesterday that was, like, breathtaking."

"Who's Kevin?"

"Too late," I say. "Jack already told me you tried that on her. You *did* know what a ship name was before that, didn't you? Please. It's important for me to hear that you knew this."

"Yeah, yeah, I knew. I'd have to be really dense not to catch that after hanging around you guys so long. Denser than usual, anyway."

I chuck the Ping-Pong ball I'm holding at Paul's face.

"Ow! What was that for?"

"You're doing it again," I say.

Kathryn Ormsbee

"What?"

"Cutting yourself down. Stop it."

"What are you, my guidance counselor?"

"You're smart, Paul. You're really smart."

Paul doesn't respond to that. Instead, he says, "Jack told me about Klaudie quitting. Sorry. That sucks."

I don't like him changing topics, but this particular topic is something I really want to talk about.

"She totally blindsided me," I say. "Getting all this attention has been stressful enough, and now I have to figure out how to rewrite the rest of the script."

"Guess there's not a guidebook for how to handle fame and its complications, huh?"

"Nope."

As an afterthought, I say, "Maybe Thom would have some good advice. . . ."

Paul is quiet for a moment. Then he asks, "Who's Thom?"

"I've mentioned him before."

"I don't think so."

"Oh. It must've been to Jack."

"Sooo, who's Thom?"

"Well, first off, to give you a better visualization, it's Thom with an 'h.'"

Paul horks out a laugh. "That's horrible. What a pretentious-ass name."

"No, it's not," I say crossly. "It's short for Thomas, so it's more . . . accurate. He's a vlogger, like me. That's how we met. We've been friends for a while now."

"Internet friends?"

"Yes, Paul. *Internet friends.* Real friends who happen to use the Internet. It's not that weird."

"Have you met him in person?"

"No."

"Do you talk on the phone?"

"No." I quickly add, "But we text and e-mail, and I know he's not some elaborate hoax or serial killer because I watch his vlogs every week. He's totally normal."

"Is he hot?"

Silence. I'm at a loss for words.

"Shit," says Paul. "I didn't mean—"

"No, it's fine. He's nice to look at."

"Really?"

The table creaks. Paul's curious face edges into view.

I look him in the eye. "I can find people attractive without wanting to see them naked, you know."

Paul nods slowly. "Sorry. I didn't know. I mean, after what you . . . Sorry. I just assumed."

A memory blooms and hangs over us—a conversation from several months back that feels just as fresh and awkward as though it took place an hour ago. But I don't want to remember it, and I don't want to talk about it now.

So I say, "You don't have to say 'sorry.'"

"Um. So. Sorry, but do you *like* him?"

I'm pretty sure there is boiling sludge, not blood, beneath my cheeks. "Um. I guess. But not . . . I mean, not like . . ."

"Right, right. Okay."

"Anyway." I wince at how tense I sound.

"Hmm. *Thom.*" Paul tests out the name with an audible smile, wheezing the *h*.

I wish I had another Ping-Pong ball to throw at him. "Your name isn't any better."

"I never said it was."

I feel a sudden pressure and release on my head. Paul is tapping me with his Ping-Pong paddle.

"What?" I ask.

"I'm challenging you to another game," he says. "You were close to winning that last one."

"Only because you were soft on me."

"That is insulting. I was giving it my all."

I rise to a sit, shaking my head. "You just want an ego boost."

"Maybe."

"So pathetic," I say, swinging my legs off the table.

An almighty cracking sound rings through the room. I lose my balance, suddenly and inexplicably off-kilter. I'm sliding downward, along the table, but at an angle I don't understand. I hear Paul shout just before I crash into him, and a sharp pain slices across my leg.

It takes a few stunned moments to piece together what's happened. When I do, I burst into tear-filled laughter.

"Holy crap," I say. "We broke Ping-Pong."

Kathryn Ormsbee

Nine

Paul and I stand surveying the wreckage. Paul's theory is that we placed too much weight on the middle of the table, which explains why the middle legs buckled and sent the two pieces of table smashing into each other in a spectacular splinter of blue wood.

"It wasn't made well," he says. "Or maybe the screws in the legs weren't tightened all the way."

"Or maybe two full-grown people weren't supposed to sit on it?" I hypothesize.

Paul looks dubious. When I offer to help pay for the damage, he waves me off.

"I am a man," he says, "and therefore if it was a matter of weight, mine was to blame."

I give him an unamused look but don't protest. I'm not in the mood to talk comparisons between my weight and Paul's. I am well aware that I'm thirty pounds over what an issue of *Cosmopolitan* deems beautiful.

Only when we leave the entertainment room do I notice blood on my foot. There's a long, thin cut along my leg that takes three regular-size Band-Aids to cover.

"My parents will never let me play with you again," I say very seriously. And while I'm on the topic of parents, I add, "We should tell your dad."

Paul nods but says, "He's not here. He's at some meeting for work."

"Well, you shouldn't have to tell him on your own."

"Tash, I'm nineteen. I've got the balls to tell him."

"Okay," I say, unconvinced. "But if you need me to come back over, I will. Or if you want to blame it entirely on me, that's fine too."

"You could stay over if you want. Jack will be back soon."

"I told my parents I'd eat dinner with them. Though I do feel kind of shitty about breaking your stuff and running away."

Paul shrugs. "I'm a bad host, you're a bad guest. We're even now."

For dinner, Dad makes a giant spinach salad filled with goat cheese, sliced plums, caramelized onions, and roasted almonds. He's baked and sliced a chicken breast for his own salad, but I'm confused by the second piece of chicken I see sitting on aluminum foil in the kitchen.

"Is Klaudie not here?"

"She texted she was staying out with Jenna," says Mom.

Right, I think. *Out enjoying her summer.*

Klaudie and I haven't spoken since our fight. The past couple days have been nothing but frigid glances and a shoulder brush in the stair-

Kathryn Ormsbee

well. Our very own cold war is officially under way, and I'm certainly not going to be the first to warm back up. Klaudie is in the wrong here. I've had to spend hours on the script, both with and without Jack's help, fixing the structural havoc Klaudie wreaked.

Dolly isn't as important a character as Anna Karenina, or even Kitty, but Jack and I wrote an airtight script, where every single episode hinges on the next, where no dialogue is superfluous. Cutting Klaudie's lines was easy enough—therapeutic even—but it's been much harder to reconstruct the story after the demolition. I'm most worried about how we're going to work Stiva, Brooks's character, back into the plot. Almost all of his scenes are with Dolly, and I don't want to take away Brooks's screen time, especially now, right when we're getting popular.

I know I shouldn't be this angry with Klaudie. If I went to one of the teen meditation classes at the Zen Center and talked to Deirdre, my group leader, she would tell me my anger is only hurting me and that Klaudie has her own path to follow. But I haven't been to the center in a few months now. I've been wrapped up with filming and college entrance exams, and though I tell myself I'll start going back once things settle down, it doesn't look like things are going to settle down anytime soon—especially now that I'm "mildly famous," as Jack likes to put it. I do my ten-minute breathing meditations most nights, but sometimes I curl up with my laptop and get so immersed in all the new tags and mentions that I lose track of time and end up too sleepy to get up and brush my teeth before bed, let alone practice mindfulness.

. . .

I have trouble focusing the next morning at work. The Scrabble episode posts in the middle of my shift, and I'm itching to see the fans' reactions. When Jack tweeted from the *Unhappy Families* account two days ago, hinting at what was to come, our followers promptly created the hashtag #KevinThursday, which produced equal amounts of exhilaration and panic within me. I kind of wish Jack hadn't hinted, because now everyone has high hopes for today's episode, and what if it disappoints? *I* think it's great, of course. But I have not one iota of objectivity, no way of knowing if the episode is good because I know how much work we put into it or because *the episode is actually good*.

I've already decided I'm not going to check my phone during my ten-minute break. Whether the reaction is good or bad, I wouldn't be able to unpack it all in just ten minutes, and I'd be even more of a mess on the floor than I am at the moment. I've already screwed up two checkouts—first by double scanning a bathing suit, then by misentering a birthday coupon code. Stupid mistakes. Maybe it would've been better to call in sick today.

"You okay?" Ethan asks me when I zone out and totally miss the volleyball he's tossed my way.

Apologetically, I say, "I'm not where I want to be."

Ethan laughs and says, "You and me both."

. . .

Kathryn Ormsbee

My man Leo once said, "Nothing is so necessary for a young man as the company of intelligent women." Which might be sexist. Or not at all. Or a little. It's hard to tell sometimes with guys who lived more than one hundred years ago, when sexism was just the Thing to Do. Anyway, I like to modify his words to the following: "Nothing is so necessary for a *person* as the company of intelligent *people*." Because really, if we didn't occasionally hang out with smart people—especially people smarter than us—we'd probably end up turning back into single-celled organisms floating around in swamps.

Jack is smarter than me. Meaner and weirder, too, maybe, but definitely smarter. It's been helpful to hang around her the past couple weeks, during this fame explosion of ours, because she knows how to keep it in perspective. Her most recent favorite saying is "Yes, this is nice, but everyone will probably hate us tomorrow." That's why I need to be with Jack now, on #KevinThursday—to get some perspective on all the fan feedback.

When I walk up to the Harlows' house, Mr. Harlow is watering the front garden. For a moment, I consider if it would be unacceptable behavior for me to throw myself into the hedges and army-crawl to the backyard, hidden from view. Don't get me wrong—most days I like talking to Mr. Harlow. He's funny in the same twitchy-mouthed, deadpan way as Jack. He's also much easier to approach than Mrs. Harlow, who is usually in the Northeast on business or, if not, typing away in her home office.

But today, the memory of the broken Ping-Pong table is fresh in my mind. Paul must have told him about it by now, and I'm not sure I want Mr. Harlow unleashing his devastating wit on *that* incident.

"Hey there, Tash."

I look up, startled, to find Mr. Harlow shading the sun from his eyes with one hand, holding a watering can in the other. I can tell the can is full because of the little sprays of water that shoot out every time he moves. Too late now to duck and crawl, I suppose.

I approach the garden. "Hey, Mr. Harlow. The dahlias look nice."

I'm saying this purely for the sake of conversation. I don't know what the hell constitutes a nice dahlia; I'm just proud of myself for knowing what a dahlia *is*. Mr. Harlow began to garden after he went into remission. His oncologist recommended it as a stress-relieving activity.

Mr. Harlow snorts. "You didn't come here to talk flowers." He nods toward the house, causing more water to splash out of the can. "Jack's inside."

"Um, thanks."

Is that it? Not even a hint at the Ping-Pong table incident? Maybe Paul *hasn't* mentioned it yet, which makes me even more uncomfortable, because it means I have to anticipate a joke about it the *next* time I see Mr. Harlow.

"I really wasn't kidding about the flowers," I call, throwing open the storm door. "You've got the nicest yard on Edgehill."

Mr. Harlow keeps a straight face and waves me off. I head inside,

Kathryn Ormsbee

toward Jack's bedroom. She doesn't look up when I come into the room, just pats the space of bed beside her. She's frowning in concentration at her laptop screen.

"Seen anything yet?" She clicks something on-screen, then unleashes a furious burst of typing.

"No," I say, my impatience ringing in the word.

I pull my laptop from my backpack, not bothering to hook up the power cord. Nothing is working as fast as it should. My username and password are taking too long to process, the Harlows' Wi-Fi is taking too long to kick in, my Internet browser isn't popping up new tabs quickly enough.

But finally, *finally*, all of #KevinThursday is at my fingertips.

"I'm working through Twitter," Jack says. "People retweeted the *shit* out of this thing. We've got a couple hundred more followers."

"So, what's the reaction?" I ask. "Good or bad?"

"Overwhelmingly positive. The video comments are mainly fan-girling. In terms of Rotten Tomatoes, I'd say this episode's certified fresh. Stop doing that to your face or you won't be able to fit the Jell-O spoon in your mouth when you're eighty."

But I can't stop grinning, even after minutes of scrolling through a deluge of screenshots and GIFs and exclamatory reblogs. Nearly an hour passes before I tear my eyes from the screen, look around the room, and ask, "Where's Paul?"

"Playing basketball with some guys," Jack says, before launching into another burst of typing. "He'll be back in a couple hours." She slows her typing to a dramatic *punch . . . punch . . . punch* as she cocks her head toward me. "I heard about Ping-Pong."

So Paul told *someone.*

"Ha" is my reply. The welcoming white glow of my computer screen is rapidly sucking me back in.

"If I didn't know any better, I'd think it was the result of wild monkey sex."

That's enough to permanently shock me out of my Internet daze.

"*Excuse* me?"

"But I do know better, of course,"

"Yeah." I scowl at Jack. "You do. Gross, Jack. Why would you even say that?"

"Oh my *God*, it was a joke. It's funny because it's totally inconceivable."

"It's not . . . It isn't . . ." I let out something between a growl and groan. "What's that supposed to mean? Why would you say something like that?"

"Like what?" Only Jack isn't being flippant anymore. She's shut the lid of her laptop and is looking at me with an atypically earnest gaze. "What did I say wrong?"

"Paul's a guy, and . . . and I'm a girl. I still *like* guys."

Jack is very quiet. "You like Paul?"

"*No.* That's not what I said. I mean you don't have to talk like I'm some sort of . . . robot."

Kathryn Ormsbee

"God, Tash. That's not what I meant at all."

I press my hands to my face. "Yeah, I know. But that's what makes it worse. Like—like you *automatically* look at me like I can't feel stuff for anyone."

"I don't think that," Jack says, with ten times the feeling she usually allots to her words. "I'm sorry. I don't think that at all. It's just . . . you weren't exactly clear when you told us . . ." She breaks off. In a mumble she says, "I didn't know you felt that way."

I lower my hands, if for no other reason than to show Jack I'm not angry. I don't blame her for being confused. Sometimes *I* still feel confused when I attempt to describe it, to put it into words that don't sound crass or sensational. I'm not happy with how I explained it last September, when Jack and Paul and I were sitting around their pool, wrapped in towels, with sodas in hand. I'd just broken up with Justin Rahn, my first boyfriend. Jack was saying how there were plenty of other not-stupid guys out there and how they'd come out of the woodwork now that they knew I was in the dating ring, and I blurted out, "I don't want to."

"Don't want to what?" she asked. *"Date?"*

I grew quiet. With Jack's and Paul's eyes on me, I said, "I guess I've never really wanted to do . . . stuff. That dating people. Want to do."

To their credit, Jack and Paul said nothing.

"Like, I've *never* wanted to," I rushed on. "At all. And when Justin asked me out, I thought it was a good idea, because maybe I just needed to, you know, *do it.*"

Jack made a strangled sort of sound, and I hurriedly added, "Not *do* it. Just be around a guy. Like that."

I felt hot all over. Hot from the sun and hot from the inside. I concentrated on my pruny toes and said, "This is really awkward, I shouldn't have brought it up."

Jack got up from her deck chair and joined me on mine. She swung an arm around my shoulder.

"You know it's cool, right?" she said. "Whatever you like. Whatever you don't like. It's cool."

I melted into Jack's shoulder, suddenly tired to the point of sleep. When I opened my eyes, I saw Paul looking at me the way he always did—affectionately.

"Ditto what Jack said," he said. "It's cool."

And we haven't brought it up since.

I mean, I'm sure Jack and Paul have brought it up when it's just the two of them (a thought that makes me cringe with embarrassment), but they never bring it up around *me*. Which doesn't mean nothing's changed. I've noticed things. Little things. Jack has stopped pointing out guys' backsides in the cafeteria. Paul has stopped cracking quite so many dirty jokes. I guess they feel as awkward about it as I do, and I guess they've been waiting for me to broach the subject again. And I tell myself I will, when the timing is right and I feel more confident about however the hell I see myself these days.

In the spring of my sophomore year, I decided I had to make a choice:

Kathryn Ormsbee

Either I liked guys *all the way*, or I wasn't allowed to like them, period. So when Justin Rahn invited me to his junior prom, I saw it as a sign. I liked Justin. He was funny, he wasn't bad to look at, and he always complimented me on every date we went on that summer. I didn't even mind that much when we kissed. That is, until the kisses began to lean further and further into something else altogether. Something involving loosening limbs and quickening fingers and shallower breaths. And I couldn't, just *couldn't*. I wasn't afraid, I just didn't *want* it.

The week before school started back up, I told Justin I needed to focus on school. Junior year is supposed to be the most stressful, after all. It wasn't a messy breakup. Justin was hurt, but he said I should do what was best for me—which only made me feel guiltier than ever. I considered for a moment, just a moment, telling Justin the truth. But how was he supposed to understand the truth when I was still figuring it out for myself? I couldn't help the way my body felt. But I couldn't help the way my heart felt, either.

That fall, when I wasn't working with Jack on Seedling Productions planning, I was bundled up in bed, scrolling through forums with purple color schemes, browsing through topics, clicking on every single one that contained the words "heteromantic" and "likes guys." Still, no matter how many posts and replies I read, no matter how much more knowledgeable I became about terms like "ace" and "graysexual" and "allosexual," no matter how supportive everyone on those forums seemed, I could never convince myself it was *okay*. That the way I felt was normal, that it was lasting. That it was really part of who I was. Because how could I like guys—want one to ask me out, to put his arm around me, to tell me he liked me, *loved* me even—and not want to have sex with them? What if everyone on those forums was just . . . confused, like me?

Over winter vacation, I formed this horrible habit of staying up late every night and laying out all the facts in a Word document on my laptop. How, to me, guys could be as beautiful as works of art. How I wanted one to kiss me on the forehead, but nothing more. How I'd never *gotten* sex—not when Jack started talking about it in middle school and not when I watched *Titanic* at my friend Maggie's thirteenth birthday party and the girls fanned themselves and said how "hot" the car scene was. When it was my least favorite scene. When I sank my face into my knees and waited until it was over before I looked again. I definitely didn't get sex when, during my sex ed class at Calhoun, Ms. Vance told us, "Sex is a normal part of life. We're all sexual beings." And all I could think was, *Not me, why not me.*

Every night, just before I drifted to sleep, I clicked out of the document without saving changes and without feeling any wiser.

That's how it was after September. That's how it was for nearly nine months. Nine months. Like some bizarre gestation period of sexual identity that led to . . . what? It's a girl! Sort of? Because how could I be *a girl*, when apparently all other girls were *sexual beings*?

Toward the end of spring semester, I started to spend a lot more

Kathryn Ormsbee

time on the forums. This time I wasn't just creeping on other people's posts. I signed up with the username videofuriosa and began joining in discussions, even starting my own threads. I made friends with several users over personal messaging, exchanged e-mails with a couple of them. Then, in April, I came out. It seemed fitting there, in the place I'd spent so much time sorting myself out, accepting this part of who I was. There, I could call myself heteromantic ace, and everyone would understand and think of me as totally normal.

But as cathartic as that experience was, I can't shake the guilt that I've come out to these people, who I don't even know in real life, but I haven't come out to Jack and Paul. Not really, not in a way that isn't botched like it was back in September. It doesn't bother me that my family doesn't know. Why do they need to? If I ever date again, I'll date guys, like they're expecting. Anyway, what kind of family dinner conversation would that be? *Hey, Mom and Dad, that thing you did to produce me? Not a fan of it myself. In fact, I find it mildly unsettling.*

But with Jack and Paul, it's different. We've talked to each other about crushes and dates ever since they were actual things in our lives. More than that, Jack and Paul *know me*. In ways my parents and Klaudie never will. It's wrong to hold out on them. It's bad for them and bad for me. I've wanted to bring it up for weeks now, wanted to tell them both at the same time, in the right way. Instead, over the course of two days, it has spilled out of me all messy and haphazard. On a Ping-Pong table. On Jack's bed.

So now, while Jack is apologizing and looking genuinely mortified—both big rarities—I can do nothing but say, "It's okay. I haven't been exactly clear about everything."

She still looks fidgety. "Do you . . . uh, do you want to talk about it?"

"Um. Did Paul say anything else about last night? Other than us breaking the Ping-Pong table?"

Jack looks like she's about to answer one way. Then she seems to change her mind and says, "He said that you like a guy."

A blush is sheeting my face. "Right. Okay, so. Crap. I really wanted to tell you and Paul the right way. Like, together. In a . . . non-awkward way?"

"Probably not possible. Just say it, Tash. I told you before, I'm cool with whatever."

I nod. I haul in a long breath and then say, "I like guys, but I don't like sex. So that makes me, um . . . It's called romantic asexual? Not that I really like labels. And I know it sounds like an oxymoron, but . . ."

"No. It doesn't. I know what it is."

I blink. "Um. Yeah."

Jack nods.

"How . . . You do?"

Jack gives me an incredulous look. "Please. Don't you think I did a shitload of research after you told us that stuff in the fall?"

I suddenly feel magnificently stupid. Of course Jack has looked into it. *Of course*, but I haven't once considered that possibility before now.

Kathryn Ormsbee

I have talked through dozens of possible explanations for Paul and Jack, all ways of defending myself. Like I need a defense. Like Jack isn't already on my side.

Jack is on my side.

The relief is sudden and all-consuming. I begin to cry.

"Oh God," says Jack. "Do you need a hug, or do you want me to pretend you're not leaking?"

I blubber out a laugh. "I'll be fine, just give me a sec."

Jack nods and flips her laptop back open. She pretends to be tending to her social media duties, but I see her sneaking an occasional glance as I sop up my tears and return to stasis.

"Do you want a tissue?" she offers.

"No, I'm good. I'm fine now. Sorry."

"Hey, don't apologize." Jack continues to click around, frowning at her screen before edging her gaze back to me. "So. So, Thom? With an 'h'?"

"I *know* I told you about him."

"Yeah, Thom Causer. The dude with the sci-fi blog."

"Sci-fi *and* actual science."

Jack gives me a look. "Okaaay. So, what? You like him? Like, you *like* him?"

I scratch my forehead, just to give my hand something to do. "I mean, we've been talking a lot, over e-mail and text."

"But is it, like, something more?"

I'm blushing again. "I don't know."

"Okay. And does he know about . . . ?"

"No. Only you and Paul know about that."

Jack is quiet for a long moment. "Really? You haven't said anything to Klaudie?"

"Why would I say something to Klaudie?"

"I just . . . didn't know we were the only ones."

"Well, you are," I say. "And I don't feel like I have to make that big a deal of it, or—or 'come out' in some big way or anything. I don't want to."

"No, I get that. I've never had the urge to stand in a public square and say, 'I wanna do the dirty with menfolk.'"

"Exactly."

"Hmm."

And that's that. We've said what we need to say. There's no pressure to prettily tie it up. I return to my laptop screen, and Jack to hers, and we descend into a comfortable clicking silence. That is, until Jack makes a squeaking sound and says, "Tash. Tash, I need your help."

She turns her laptop toward me, her expression unreadable.

"What?" I say, frowning at an e-mail Jack has pulled up.

"Am I hallucinating," she says, "or did we just get nominated for a Golden Tuba?"

Kathryn Ormsbee

the moment I've only made videos that are a copy of Leo's own work or largely unedited footage of me throwing back tea and rambling about how much I love the 1995 BBC version of *Pride and Prejudice*. See? Not so impressive.

But this might be the turning point, because *Unhappy Families* has just been nominated for a Golden Tuba, and that is the most impressive thing that has ever happened to me.

The Golden Tubas have been around for three years, and during those years they've reached a status in my mind on par with the Oscars and Emmys. Three years back, *Wuthering Bites*—Taylor Mears's wildly popular modernization and parody of gothic romances—uploaded its last ever episode, and the People of the Internet decided that something had to be done about all the great small-budget, independent web series being produced—most of which had been directly inspired by *Wuthering Bites*. Sure, there were the Streamy and Webby awards, but they were for bigger names and super sleek productions. Some people of the Internet wanted a more low-key option. So these people decided to create a two-day convention and award ceremony—a celebration of amateur vlogs, web series, and other creative video ventures. Both the event and the awards are called the Golden Tubas. Apparently the name is an inside joke, or maybe it's a palatable substitute for Golden YouTubes, which just doesn't sound right. Whatever the case, the event was a smashing success its first year. The award ceremony was

Kathryn Ormsbee

Ten

Count Lev Nikolayevich Tolstoy lived one extremely impressive life. He was born into a wealthy, well-known family and was a member of the Russian nobility. He was your typical spoiled rich boy until he joined the army and traveled around Europe and got a taste of the real world. Then he began to rethink his whole life, and he began to write. He wrote *War and Peace* and *Anna Karenina*, which are basically the two best and most famous novels of all time. He was pals with Victor Hugo. He grew an out-of-control beard. And in his later years, he was a pacifist Christian anarchist (which, yeah, is just as crazy as it sounds) and a big advocate of nonviolent resistance. He died of pneumonia in a railway station. Thousands of peasants flocked to see his funeral procession.

My life is not as impressive. I was born to a suburban, middle-class family. I do okay in school. I suck at any sport. I want to spend my life making important documentaries that change people's minds, but at held in a decked-out ballroom at an Embassy Suites in Orlando. Naturally, the bulk of the awards went to Taylor Mears's production team, Latte Love League, and the cast of *Wuthering Bites*.

I stalked social media with giddy envy that weekend. People who'd only been screen names and credits in the description box of a video suddenly had faces—happy faces. Everyone looked like they were having the time of their lives. The absolute worst and best part was the pictures of the *Wuthering Bites* cast hanging out at the Wizarding World of Harry Potter. Best, because is there any better combination of awesome things than Taylor Mears, Joe Samson, and Kate Palomo clanking frosted butterbeer mugs? Worst, because I wasn't there clinking mugs with them.

But now I have a vivid picture in my head: me, Taylor Mears, and Thom Causer standing in front of Hogwarts Castle, forming peace signs with our right hands, holding bottles of pumpkin juice in our left. I already have the perfect Instagram filter in mind. Because why not? At this point, why freakin' not? Anything is possible.

That's what I'm thinking as Jack reads aloud the e-mail that arrived in Seedling Productions' inbox late this afternoon. She's not hallucinating. Or else, we're sharing a hallucination when we take a look at the Golden Tubas website. Sure enough, there's a list of nominees that includes *Unhappy Families* in the category "Best New Series."

What I'm having a hard time getting over is the fact that the e-mail we've received has been personalized. Not a generic "Congratulations!

You've been nominated along with ten other so-and-sos." It's a letter from someone on *the* Golden Tuba nomination committee, who's written to say:

We're so glad we were alerted to your charming web series just last week. Your nomination came in a little past the cutoff date, but we've decided to make an allowance since you would no longer be eligible for "Best New Series" next year. We hope to see you in Orlando in August!

"I wonder who nominated us," I say. "Doesn't it have to be some higher-up?"

"Probably Taylor Mears," says Jack, "as she is obsessed with us."

According to the e-mail, the entire cast and crew are invited to attend the event the second weekend in August. We've been offered free passes and a complimentary dinner Friday night, but we have to pay for our transportation and accommodation.

Upon reading this information, Jack slumps and says, "Okay, yeah, let me magically shell out the money for a flight to Florida during vacation season."

"It's not impossible," I say. "What about your Etsy profits? And Petco?"

"Yeah, that money's for daily life, not two-day trips. There's no way I can afford something like that. I don't think most of the cast could."

I deflate. I know money's tight in the Harlow household. It has been ever since Mr. Harlow's medical treatments. And I really want Jack to come with me. Because of course I am going to find a way to go.

"Maybe," I say slowly, "we could do our Kickstarter now?"

"No," says Jack. Sharp, immediate. "That's sleazy, asking fans to pay for us to go to some award ceremony when we might not even win."

Jack's right, of course. She and I have already decided we don't want to do a Kickstarter campaign until we've wrapped up *Unhappy Families*. We want to give our fans a finished product before asking them to fund a new one. It's a matter of principle.

"Jack . . . ," I begin.

She shakes her head. "You have to go. One of us needs to be there. Just let me live vicariously through you, and I won't complain."

It's a weighty commission Jack's giving me, but I nod soberly. I will find a way to go to Orlando. This is my *dream*. I have a little over two thousand dollars saved up from my last two summers' worth of work. Granted, it's supposed to be money for college, but at the moment higher education is looking a whole lot less important than a Golden Tuba.

In the morning, Jack walks with me back to my house. She's been pretty quiet ever since last night's news.

When we come to a stop in my driveway, I ask, "You okay?"

Jack nods. Pauses. Shakes her head. In a cloudy voice, she says, "Dad hasn't been feeling well."

This isn't even close to what I was expecting. *"What?"*

"He didn't start complaining until a couple days ago, which means it's probably been going on for a few weeks. He says he's getting really bad headaches."

"Do you think it's . . ." I don't finish. I refuse to say the "C" word more than is absolutely necessary. Saying it out loud makes me feel like I'm lending it power, like I'm complicit in its existence.

"I don't know," says Jack. "He says migraines run in the family and that he used to get them when he was younger. Maybe that's all it is. But he won't go to the doctor to get it checked out. Mom's mad at him, but he keeps saying he'll just wait until his next oncology checkup, which isn't for weeks."

"That's crazy."

"Yeah, that's what we keep telling him. But he's Dad. There's only so much we can do to change his mind."

"Jack. I'm really sorry. Why didn't you tell me earlier?"

"I guess . . . because I don't want it to be real? And Paul would be so pissed if he knew I was telling you. He said not to."

"Why?" My chest twitches in discomfort.

"I dunno. He probably doesn't want you worrying, because we don't know what's up yet. Headaches can mean anything—that you've had a long day, or you're dehydrated, or you have a brain tumor and are about to die. There's no way of knowing."

"Until he gets checked out."

Kathryn Ormsbee

"Yeah."

In the silence, an unspoken request passes from me to Jack. In response, Jack fixes me with a heavy-lidded glare.

"Fine," she grouses.

I pull Jack into a loose but solid hug. Then before she can shove me away, screaming, I let go.

"Just let me know what happens, okay?" I say. "No matter what Paul tells you."

Again, my chest twinges.

Jack says, "Do you ever wonder what horrible things I must've done to earn such bad karma?"

"What?"

"I mean, for Dad to get sick the first time, and now this. I must've done some awful shit when I was kid. Maybe something I don't even remember. Maybe I killed a family of squirrels and then suppressed it."

"It doesn't work that way," I say softly. "You could be getting bad karma now for something you did lifetimes ago."

"Or maybe it's not karma, and shit just happens."

"*Dukkha* happens," I say, smiling.

I'm not sure how we've come to this place, making Buddhist jokes about the horrifying possibility that Mr. Harlow's cancer might be back. But I have a feeling the only alternative to joking about it is crying.

"I don't know," says Jack. "You'd think some cosmic authority would put a limit on how many hard knocks people get in a lifetime."

I think of my mom's tears, illuminated by the flashing light of a television.

"Yeah. That would be nice."

"So," Jack says, "when are you going to tell everyone about Klaudie dropping out?"

"Um. Well, Brooks knows, and he's the one it affects the most."

Jack gives me a hard look. "I should send an e-mail."

"No," I say. "I'll do it."

"I don't think you will. I'm going to send them an e-mail."

"Jack . . ."

"Everyone deserves to know. Anyway, we also have to tell them about the nomination. It'll be killing two birds or whatever."

Defeated, I say, "Fine. Just *please* be nice about it."

Jack looks affronted. "What's that supposed to mean."

"You know you can come off as . . . snippy in your writing."

"I think you mean 'bitchy.'"

"Jack."

She raises her hands. "Okay, okay. I'll be nice. I'm sure they'll be too excited about the nomination to even care about Klaudie."

I nod. The nomination is a huge deal. A *Golden Tuba*. Things just keep getting better for *Unhappy Families*. Now if only that could be the case for *our* families.

· · ·

I texted Thom about the Golden Tuba immediately after Jack showed me the e-mail. Now, at last, I get a reply.

That's AMAZING, Tash!! Congrats. Don't know if you've seen the full list yet, but Beaker Speaker got nominated for Best Vlog. Which means I'll be there. So you know what THAT means.

I blink at the screen.

I know what that means.

Wait. *Do* I know what that means?

It means Thom and I will finally meet in person, right?

It means I will finally hear his voice saying words directed at me.

It means we could go on a . . . date?

Is that what it would be? A date?

My thumbs hover over the keypad, but no coherent reply is forming.

What I want to text is, *I know what that means, but I don't know what it MEANS.*

Like now, in this moment, what if I replied to him with *Yes! Can I call and talk about it?*

I could do it. I could text those eight words, two punctuation marks. I could change everything.

What I text instead is, *YES. We should hang out.*

We've been texting for a while now, and neither of us has mentioned the possibility. I know why I haven't: I am terrified. What if Thom doesn't want to take it there? What if he does, but when we do finally talk it's stilted and a complete disaster? I'm not sure of Thom's reasons for skirting the issue, but I like to hope they're more noble than my own.

Part of me wants to call him up right now. I could dial at any time, and he could pick up, and we could talk, actually *talk* to each other. I stare at our conversation for a couple minutes, willing that blessed bubbled ellipsis to pop up. Thom sent his text only fifteen minutes back, so there's a good chance this will turn into an actual conversation. But another minute passes, and there is no sign of life on Thom's end.

I groan and throw the phone into a wadded-up fleece blanket at the foot of my bed. I reflect, not for the first time this week, that the twenty-first century is a screwed-up place to be. How is this even a normal human interaction? Back in the old days people waited weeks, even months, to receive letters, and that had to suck. But on a regular day, when they were out and about having normal chats, no one had to wait in crippling suspense to see if their conversation partner would deign to answer them. If said partner remained unresponsive for a full three minutes, the only possible explanation would be that they'd had a stroke, not that they'd heard the question and didn't want to answer for another few hours.

But Thom hasn't heard the question. Probably not. He's a busy guy, and he hasn't had the chance to check his messages yet. He wouldn't keep me in suspense on purpose. Right?

My phone chimes, and I bolt up, making a convulsive grab for it.

Kathryn Ormsbee

As I read Thom's text, I'm hit with sweet relief. He's written back *OF COURSE*, and he tells me to let him know when I buy my tickets and the exact dates I'll be in Orlando.

I've yet to bring up the Golden Tubas with my parents. I'm pretty sure they won't give their wholehearted approval to their daughter blowing her college savings and flying out of state, alone, for a weekend. But I'm seventeen, and the money is mine to spend, and this is a big deal. Also, my parents don't have a history of keeping me under lock and key. I have a reasonable curfew, and I've gone on plenty of overnight school trips and vacations with the Harlows. I just have to phrase this right, at an opportune time. Meanwhile, I've already found the cheapest flight to Orlando. Because I am so freakin' professional.

Eleven

Kisses bring viewers out of the woodwork. That's pure and simple fandom fact, and #KevinThursday is a prime example. A kiss is the culmination of everything unspoken—all the hints and hopes and uncertainties in a budding romance. Until that moment, it's heat and simmer, heat and simmer. It's a look, a word, a gesture. But the kiss is the boiling point. It's what everyone waits on and cheers for.

I get that, but personally? I prefer what happens before the kiss: the accidental brush of a shoulder, the spark of a stolen glance, the seemingly throwaway comment that is steeped in history and means so much more. That's what I love best, and it's what I best direct.

Like today, as I film George, Eva, and Brooks. The scene is post-kiss, but Kitty and Levin aren't all over each other because their friend Stiva is in the room. He's rambling along happily, as Stiva is wont to do, and Kitty and Levin are trying to figure out how to tell him they're an item. And as Stiva gushes about his new favorite restaurant and how choice the onion rings there are, Kitty and Levin are sneaking looks at each other, smiles tipping up both their mouths. Out of Stiva's sight line, their fingers inch closer and their hands entwine. Kitty bites her lip, looking sharply to the distance, as though she's liable to burst into a gut laugh at Stiva's chirpy obliviousness.

It's our fifth take, and the second after I asked Eva to try the lip biting. It's perfect and adorable, even if Jack is rolling her eyes off camera. When I call "Cut," it's clear the others are happy with the performance too.

Eva giggles the moment Jack lowers the boom. *"Brooksss,"* she whines. "You can't keep changing it up like that, I almost lost it."

They're both cracking up, because Brooks has been slightly altering his delivery with each take, and it's been getting progressively funnier. Even George is in good spirits for—well, for *George*. He's actually smiling, for God's sake, and he hasn't once asked to tweak a line or complained about how anyone else is "carrying themselves."

Jack was right about the nomination: It completely overshadowed the news of Klaudie leaving. Brooks is perfectly chill about changing later scenes and losing a few lines. "It's show business," he said, as blithe and amiable as Stiva himself.

"So what's up?" he asks now. "Want another one?"

"Nope. That was the money shot."

"AW YEAH." Brooks raises both hands. Eva and George—yes, *even George*—oblige him with high fives.

"The fans are going to love this," I say.

It's true. Even if our viewership won't love it as much as the locking-lips installment, they'll still eat this episode up. And for me, today's shot is a fluff scene at its finest. It's all wrapped up in the safety and warmth of two people who have passed a point of recognition, of openness. I'm not talking about the kiss, either. I'm talking about what came before it. There's a moment in the Scrabble episode—right when the light kicks into Levin's eyes, and he realizes Kitty understands him. That they're on the same page. You can see it so well in George's excellent performance; it's the sheer joy of simply *knowing* another human being. It's here, too, in this episode—that comfiness of being understood, evident in every little look and move. And it might be schmaltzy to say, but I'm proud I've had a hand in crafting it.

George leaves immediately, off to the next bullet point on his agenda, but Brooks and Eva stick around. They hang with me and Jack on my back porch, and together we eat through an entire box's worth of Fudgsicles.

"I know it's not the Academy Awards," Eva says, imprinting bite marks along her Fudgsicle stick, "but it feels *real* now, you know? An awards show. Do you think I can put that on my résumé?"

"God knows I am," says Brooks. "Though I kind of wish they had a classier name than Golden Tubas."

"Yeah, well, Oscar isn't such a classy name, if you think about it," says Jack.

Both Brooks and Eva consider this. Brooks shrugs. Eva's blond hair

Kathryn Ormsbee

blows up in a sudden wind, and strands stick to her fudge-coated mouth. It's a stupid, almost ordinary thing, but something about her reaction—an overdramatic gasp and lurch in her deck chair—sends us into cackles.

"Blergh," says Eva, picking away at her soft, highlighted hair, and still managing to make the process look cute. Put me in that situation, and I'd have you fleeing for the hills. That's why Eva is the talent, not me.

Eventually, Jack and the others head out, but I stay on the deck, feet propped against the wooden railing. I've found a pleasant surprise waiting on my phone: Thom has texted.

How's it going? Filming today, right?

My stomach does a few of its usual backflips, but I'm grinning as I write: *You know that feeling when you GET it? Everything comes together the way it's supposed to? That's what today was.*

To my delight, I see activity on Thom's end. I've caught him in time for a proper conversation.

Oh man. That's the best feeling in the world. Like when I nail a vlog in one go? Minimal editing, good face day? Perfect.

Haha, when do you NOT have a good face day?

Oops. I guess that was flirty. But it's also true. Is it *really* flirting if you're stating a fact?

Thom's response is immediate: *Well, not as good as YOURS.*

Oh my God. The muscles in my hand decide to stop functioning, and my phone goes clattering to the deck.

What is even happening.

I scramble to pick the phone back up. There's a new message from Thom.

. . . Did I scare you off?

My thumbs tap like the wind: *Ha! No. That's sweet.*

I'm pretty sure my face is the color of Sriracha, but I'm okay with that. Since this is such terrifying fun, I decide to keep it going:

Seriously, Thom, you should start your own beauty vlog. People want to know how you do it.

Beauty sleep, that's my secret. A full eight hours every night.

Well! The sleep gods certainly favor you.

Flirting. Yep. Definitely flirting. I've crossed the line, and I don't even care. I feel like I could run a marathon and projectile vomit at the same time.

I'm really excited for you, Thom writes. Deflecting. I get it. It's what I do when someone compliments me too much. *The nomination and the good shoots and your face. You've got it all, Tash.*

My smile is a mile wide, though Thom isn't exactly right. I don't have it all *yet*. I haven't attended the Golden Tubas. I haven't met him in person.

But I'm well on my way.

All four Zelenkas are at the dinner table—a phenomenon that's become increasingly rare over the past few weeks. I hardly ever see Klaudie in

Kathryn Ormsbee

the house. She's started her volunteer work with Connect!—an engineering day camp hosted by the University of Kentucky during which middle schoolers build robots and miniature bridges. At night, she's out with Ally and Jenna and their whole lot of friends. Most evenings, she doesn't get in until really late. I'll hear her plod up the stairs at one or two o'clock in the morning, when I'm still sitting up in bed, clicking through Tumblr posts.

When I do see Klaudie, she looks—different. Kind of haggard. Like tonight, her eyes are pink and watery on the edges. She looks tired. Which is weird, considering the whole point of quitting *Unhappy Families* was to "enjoy her summer," and you'd think that would involve plenty of naps. I'm pretty positive she and her friends drink, and I don't want to think of what else. I guess it's normal, even for perfect, smart people like Klaudie, to kind of go off the rails. It *is* her last summer before college, and that seems to cover a multitude of sins. Or at least, that's how Mom and Dad have been acting. They don't wait up for Klaudie, and I haven't heard them scold her for breaking what used to be curfew during the school year. Even now, at dinner, they don't comment on how quiet she is, or the pinkness of her eyes, or how she's sullenly skewering food on her fork like she's been forced at gunpoint to eat with us.

Dinner is a zucchini casserole. Most casserole nights, Dad makes an obligatory remark about how he never considered any meatless casserole to be a true casserole until he met Mom, who forever changed his mind *and* heart. When we were younger, Klaudie and I would coo at that last line. These days, we act like we're going to throw up.

I don't know how my parents manage it. On paper, they look so different that a mere acquaintanceship, let alone two decades of marriage, seems impossible. Mom is a self-professed communist nomad from New Zealand who's been vegetarian since her fifth birthday, practices daily mediation and yoga, is soft-spoken and tenderhearted, and specialized in a career where she could help people. Dad is the son of two Czech immigrants, a meat-devouring extrovert who loves parties and exotic stouts and cigars, with a fervor for capitalism that rivals John D. Rockefeller's. When the two of them met on a backpacking trip in the Blue Ridge Mountains, they had every reason in the world to hate each other. But they didn't. It worked. It worked so well that they fought through endless visa paperwork to put rings on each other's fingers and say "I do." It's worked for almost twenty years. Which isn't to say Mom and Dad never fight, but their arguments only last a day, max.

I guess it has something to do with compromise. Dad cooks vegetarian meals and is responsible for any meat in his own dish; Mom never judges him for eating said meat. Mom raised me and Klaudie the way she was raised in Auckland, following the teachings of the Buddha; Dad takes us to Christ Church Cathedral for Easter and Christmas services. Mom converted our attic into a yoga studio; Dad can smoke his cigars and drink his stouts in the home office and *only* the home office. It works because of compromise. And, I guess, you know, because they love each other.

Kathryn Ormsbee

Tonight, as we sit eating our dinner, I expect Dad to make the casserole comment any minute. But time passes, and the table remains quiet.

In the end, I break the silence.

"I've got some exciting news," I say.

I haven't noticed how intently my parents have been eyeing their plates until now, when they both look up.

"Does this have to do with your newfound fame?" asks Dad.

"I'm not *actually famous*," I say. "I think I might have explained it to you wrong."

"Hey, I'm glad you're doing something that makes you happy," Dad says, waving a zucchini-staked fork to emphasize his point. "When you do what you love, you're bound to be successful."

"Jan," says Mom, her voice gently chiding. "I don't think that's necessarily true."

Dad hikes his shoulders up in a way that says, *Maybeee not?*

"So," I say, "our show got nominated for an award. Like, I guess you could say they're the Academy Awards of low-budget web series."

"What?" cries Dad. A bit of almond flies out of his mouth and goes skittering across the table. "That's fantastic!"

Out the corner of my eye, I see Klaudie stabbing at her casserole. With more relish than necessary, I say, "Yeah, everyone is really excited about it. The awards ceremony is going to be at this convention in August, and they've invited us to attend."

"All expenses paid?"

I really wish Dad hadn't asked that. It makes what I'm about to say sound even more grandiose than it did when I practiced it in my mind earlier tonight.

"No," I say slowly. "We get free passes to the convention, but we have to pay for our own transportation and accommodation."

I see it: the dreaded unreadable glance exchanged between my parents.

Dad says, "Uh-huh."

Not promising.

"I was thinking—and please, *please* hear me out, okay?—that I could buy my tickets and room with some of the college money I've saved up."

"You mean *all* the college money you've saved up?"

I didn't expect my parents to be jumping up and down with excitement, but I consider this a particularly mean-spirited question for my dad to ask.

"I know how much flights cost," I say. "And hotel rooms. I know it's expensive. But this trip means a whole lot to me. This is what I want to do with my life. I've thought it through, and it's not irresponsible, if that's what you're thinking. It's an invaluable experience, and it'll be great for my résumé, and anyway, someone has to be there in case we win."

"Is Jacklyn not going?" asks Mom.

"No, she can't afford it. But she thinks I should go."

"By yourself," says Dad. "On a plane. Staying in a hotel, on your own."

"You're making it sound so dramatic," I say. "Like I'm some stupid kid who doesn't know what stranger danger is. I'll be safe, I promise. I'm seventeen. I can handle it."

Dad looks like he's preparing to say something very adult and disapproving. I brace myself for impact, but it never comes. Mom must've silently signaled him when I wasn't looking, because he stays quiet, and she speaks instead.

"It's clear you've put a lot of thought into it. Your father and I know how responsible you are, and how much this project means to you. And I understand it's your money, but, Tasha, darling . . ."

Oh no. I am not ready for a "But, Tasha, darling . . ." They only ever end in misery. "But, Tasha, darling, don't you think you should share the cake?" "But, Tasha, darling, couldn't you clean off Klaudie's dish too?" "But, Tasha, darling, don't you already have shoes in that color?"

Some days, Tasha Darling wants to forget that she is supposed to be a kind and responsible entity.

"But, Tasha, darling," says Mom, "I want you to consider what a big expense that is. I know college tuition looks like a bunch of zeros right now, but they do add up."

"I *know*."

"I'm only saying, I don't want you to regret spending all that money on one weekend. You worked hard for it."

"I *know*," I say, irritation soaking my voice. "I was there. Doing the working. And the only thing I'd regret is *not* going to the convention. It's"—not for the first time, I recall Serena's words—"a once-in-a-lifetime thing."

Mom nods, but there's a hesitancy, almost *sadness* in her eyes that I don't get. It amazes me sometimes that Mom and I can be so similar in some ways, but other times I can't read her at all. I wonder if she ever feels the same way about me.

"We'll take some time to think about it," Dad says, in a tone that means this conversation is over.

Then my parents get conspicuously quiet again. Mom lifts her head suddenly, catching me off guard. She smiles. I know that smile. I don't like it. It's the same smile Mom used to tell me and Klaudie that Ralph, our family dog, had passed away, and again, all the times she told me I couldn't spend the night at the Harlows' because of a family obligation.

"What?" I ask, every inch of my body on alert. "What's going on?"

My parents seem . . . *anxious*. Like for once they are the ones breaking curfew, or getting a C on their biology test.

Dad says, "We have something to tell you girls. We'd appreciate if you heard us out from start to finish."

Now it's Klaudie's and my turn to exchange a glance.

What the hell is going on? asks my glance, and Klaudie's watery one replies, *Your guess is as good as mine.*

"All right," says Mom. "There's no easy way to put this, so I'm going

140   *Kathryn Ormsbee*

to say it as clearly as I can. Girls, I'm expecting. Your father and I have consulted the doctor, and she says there's every chance of a healthy pregnancy. If all goes well, you're going to have a little brother or sister for Christmas."

I set down my fork. I stare at Mom. Of all the hundreds of thousands of possible things to come out of my mother's mouth, this is the one I would have never, ever expected.

"Girls, I've decided to spend a month climbing the mountains of Nepal." Acceptable. "Girls, I'm going to dye my hair red." Okay. "Girls, I'm going on a strict sugar-free diet." Sad, but fine. But not this. Not "Girls, I'm expecting." My mom is *done* being pregnant. Door closed. Moved on. She is an almost empty nester. She is a responsible adult. Women her age don't have unexpected pregnancies. That job is left to girls *my* age.

Unless this wasn't unexpected. Unless it was planned. Unless . . .

"Wait," I say. "Christmas. December? So you've known about this for *three months?*"

"Not the entire three months," says Mom, conciliatory. Her large dark eyes look larger than usual.

So it *was* unexpected, I deduce. The thought brings on a rapid surge of repulsion, because I am now contemplating my parents' sex life, and there has to be some fundamental law of the universe against that.

"I don't understand." Klaudie is pale. Her words come out abruptly, like sneezes. "What are we supposed to say?"

"Girls." Dad is solemn. "We know this is an adjustment. It has been for us, too. But your mother would appreciate your support right now."

"I don't get it," says Klaudie. "You've already had kids."

"I know it's a lot to process," says Mom. "But it's what I want, and it's what your father wants too. I think it might be best if we all take some time alone so you two can process it on your own."

I start giggling. I don't mean to. I don't *want* to giggle. I am experiencing an emotion far removed from amusement or happiness. Only, it seems, that emotion doesn't know how to get out of my body the right way.

"I'm sorry," I gasp out, covering my mouth. "It's not funny, I just . . . can't . . ."

Klaudie is looking at me like I'm crazy. Dad looks like he's angry but doesn't know what to do. Only Mom is looking at me with calm, understanding eyes. But I don't want calm understanding from my mother. Not now. I'm still laughing in chest-squeezing bursts when I get to my feet and run from the room.

Tonight, my insomnia returns, full force. At four o'clock in the morning, I kick off my bedsheets and creep down to the kitchen, grab a sleeve of Pop-Tarts, and head to the Harlows'. As I hoped, they've left the basement's sliding door unlocked. I go inside, spread out on the couch in the entertainment room, eat half a Pop-Tart, and fall asleep with the wrapper in hand.

Kathryn Ormsbee

I wake to the sound of Jack saying, "*I'm* not going to effing wake her up."

Groggily, I lift my head to find Jack and Paul standing at the foot of the couch, assessing me as though I am a stray raccoon that has chewed its way into the house.

"You should lock your doors," I mumble. "Or get a security system. If I were a criminal, you would be so robbed by now."

"What're you doing here?" Jack asks.

"Avoiding my parents," I say. Then, "Ow," because Jack is mercilessly shoving me over so that she has a square of couch cushion.

"Anyway," Jack says, turning to Paul. "As I was saying, if you didn't want to go, you didn't have to buy a ticket."

"I didn't say I don't want to go. I just said they're not my style."

I deduce that the conversation my unexpected break-in interrupted is about an upcoming trip to Nashville. Several months back, Tony suggested the whole *Unhappy Families* team take a day trip to Nashville, just for fun. His favorite band, Chvrches, has a show scheduled there in July, so several of us—including Paul—bought tickets.

Jack tells Paul, "Your style is wimpy guitar dudes who sing falsetto by default."

Paul doesn't reply, either because he's too tired or he's being the better person—I can't tell.

When the silence gets too suffocating, I blurt out, "My mom's pregnant."

Paul teeters, then tips off the beanbag, onto the floor.

Jack coughs out, *"What?"*

"She sprang it on me and Klaudie last night." I feel a torrent of words at the back of my throat, ready to break free, and I'm worried that if I continue talking I might not ever stop. "She's, like, already in her second trimester and only now decided to tell us. And I . . . I can't even wrap my head around it. It's too weird. I keep waiting for her to tell us it's some elaborate practical joke, and at this point I don't know if I'd be angrier at her for pulling a joke that cruel or for just *being pregnant.*"

"Holy shit," says Paul.

"Was it on purpose?" asks Jack.

"I'm trying not to think about that, but no. I'm pretty sure it was an accident."

"Why would they want another kid?" says Jack. "They just got done raising you and Klaudie. And your mom's, like, in her forties, right? Aren't late pregnancies extra dangerous?"

"I don't know, I guess."

I catch Paul shooting Jack a reproachful look. He catches me catching him and says, "I'm sorry. That sucks."

"There's something about it that's so royally effed up," I say. "I don't even know where they plan on getting the money. It's not like we're rolling in the dough."

I frown. Where *do* they plan on getting the money? What details would my parents have told me last night if I'd stuck around long enough to find out?

Kathryn Ormsbee

My phone rings. As I grab it, an irrational thought flits through my mind: *Maybe it's Thom.*

It isn't Thom. It's Mom's cell.

I mute the ringer.

"I should go," I say. "Sorry I invaded."

"Boo," Paul says. "You sleep on our couch and then run away? Worse than Cinderella."

Jack grabs the foil packet containing a Pop-Tart and a half.

"I'm keeping this," she says. "As lodging tax."

I nod distractedly and get to my feet, combing my fingers through my tangled mess of hair.

"See you later," I say.

"Mmm-hmm." There is already Wild Berry filling coating Jack's teeth. "Give our regards to your very fertile mom."

I don't go straight home. I have a headache, which I guess has something to do with my unconventional sleeping situation this morning. I head right, not left, down Edgehill, away from my house and toward the neighborhood park.

As far as parks go, Holly Park is a shabby specimen. The jungle gym's tan paint has peeled so severely that it's more bare metal and rust than anything else. The slide is old school—wide and metal, made back in a day when park planners must've deemed thigh burning good for toughening a kid's moral fiber. Just past a row of picnic tables, there's a small pool, skimmed over with algae. I've only recently realized how dismal the place is. When I was a kid, I thought of Holly Park as this magical destination. I was always begging Dad to pack lunches for me, Paul, and Jack to tote off to the park in my Radio Flyer wagon.

Even now that I recognize the park for the little cesspool it is, I can't shake that childhood affection. I still come out here to swing and to walk the park's perimeter—a gravel path lined by trees. I walk the path today in short, even steps. At the moment, the park is empty, and I intend to take advantage of that for thinking purposes.

I'm so mad at my parents. For springing the news of Mom's pregnancy on us, and more than that, for keeping it a secret. I'm mostly angry because of a horrible, unshakable jealousy that's kicked up in my heart.

Maybe "jealousy" isn't the right word. I'm not *jealous* of this unborn kid, exactly. I'm . . . disoriented. Enough is changing—Klaudie's moving off to college and I'm about to head out myself. My parents are the constant, and home is the solid thing. But not anymore. Everything is going to change. I won't be the youngest. My parents won't care as much about my future now that they're worrying about this new arrival's present. Holidays will involve pacifiers and shrieks and toys underfoot. I don't want that. I don't want any of it. But it's happening, whether I want it or not. So somehow, I've got to figure out how to deal.

I'm so dead lost in this angsting on the walk home, I don't notice the bounce of a basketball, the shouts of teenage guys in a driveway, or

Kathryn Ormsbee

Paul's approach. Not until his arms are around me and I am cloaked in sweat.

"Aaack, urrrk," I say, but I don't push out of the embrace, because I'm happy to get some shelter from the sun and from my unpleasant thoughts.

"Hey," says Paul close to my ear, so his basketball companions can't hear. "You okay?"

I nod against his chest. A drop of sweat falls from his brow and smacks my nose. I rub it away on his T-shirt.

"'Cause I can quit the game. Break another Ping-Pong table talking about your feelings."

This time I do shove Paul away, laughing. "I'm *fine*."

Which isn't true, but this is one problem I don't think Paul can help talk me through.

"Dude, enough!" shouts one of the guys in the driveway. "Say good-bye to your girlfriend."

Paul and I exchange a look like, *Ugh, these fools know nothing.* Then he blows me a kiss and I blow one back, just as someone throws the ball, hard, into his gut, and the guys bust into loud, hacking laughter.

Those fools know nothing.

Though . . . I walk the rest of the way home with a tight, bubbly feeling close to my throat—how it feels when I drink too much soda lying down. I kind of like someone mistaking me for Paul's girlfriend. Which is really messed up, I know. Sure, he's not attached to anyone since his breakup with Stephanie Crewe, but I know how he likes to be attached, and it is *not* the way I do.

But that doesn't mean I can help that feeling of carbonated indigestion.

C'mon, Tash. Those fools know nothing.

I tug out my cell phone to plunge myself into a realm of thought-numbing social media. There's a text waiting for me. From Thom. It's about the most recent episode of *Storms of Taffdor*, a new premium cable channel show that's fast becoming all the rage in my nerdier circles online. The text reads:

THE FEELS HAVE SLAYED ME.

And just like that, I'm in a better mood. I grin, stop in my tracks, and text back.

Twelve

Here's another nugget of wisdom from that genius among men, L. Tolstoy: "True life is lived when tiny changes occur." It sounds generic, I know—like a quote you'd find embroidered on a pillow at a Cracker Barrel. But it's more profound if you switch things around and make it negative: "You're not really living if nothing changes." So, like, you shouldn't be afraid of change, because change is one of those reminders you're alive, and something is *happening* in your life.

Sometimes I feel like I do my least amount of living during the summer. The weeks turn into a stale progression of habit—a circuitous movement from my bedroom to Jack's bedroom to the Harlows' basement to Old Navy and back to my bedroom, where it all began.

I wonder if this is how everyone is destined to live: hopping from familiar space to familiar space, until all the familiar spaces turn into one big blurry memory of nothing in particular. I read somewhere that the average American spends six months of their life stopped at red lights. I wonder how many years most people spend in their bedrooms. How much of life happens within those four walls? I probably think about this more than is strictly healthy—usually while in my bedroom.

June gets older and hotter until it passes on a sweltering summer torch to July. I spend three mornings a week at Old Navy, two mornings on filming, and the remaining two thinking thoughts, big and small, in my room.

On the whole, filming is going smoothly. Like Jack, most of the cast shrugs off the idea of actually attending the Golden Tubas because of cost or timing. In the end, George is the only one besides me who plans on going. But the fact that just two of us will be heading to Orlando doesn't dampen anyone's excitement; the nomination is a big deal, confirmation we're doing something *right*.

Things are less at ease in the Zelenka household. The day after Mom and Dad dropped the Christmas Baby Surprise on us, they agreed to let me go to the convention. Which was no doubt their way of trying to win me back into their good graces, but hey, if accepting the offer makes me shameless, I guess I'm shameless.

I'm on speaking terms with my parents, but I'm not really back to full civility. That disorientation I felt in the park? It's still there, occasionally clouding glimpses of the future: graduating from Calhoun while some tiny Zelenka shrieks in the bleachers, or Skyping my parents from college only to find my mom's exhausted from the baby and has already gone to bed. I know it's only speculation—I'm not a freakin' seer. And

Kathryn Ormsbee

I know I can't stop those inexorable nine months from culminating in a kid brother or sister. This is happening. It doesn't make sense to glare at my parents during movie night. But *still*. Why the hell are they shoving another sibling into the family equation? I don't think I'm mad, but I am resentful. I can't help it. Maybe it's something only time is going to fix.

Anyway, *my* reaction is angelic compared to Klaudie's. She's already been spending most of her time outside the house, but now I'm lucky to see her once a week. She bails on all her date nights with Dad, when they usually watch baseball in the den. And on the few nights she joins us at dinner, she's curt and monosyllabic. She eats her food as quickly as possible and leaves the moment she's through.

"Someone's ready for college," Dad says one night after a particularly chilly interaction.

Which is a stupid thing to say, because Klaudie has been telling us how ready she is for college for a year now, and anyway, we all know that isn't the real reason for the ice-out.

The Friday after Independence Day, I'm at Old Navy monitoring the floor and fitting rooms when I see Jay Prasad browsing a row of button-up plaid shirts. With devious intent, I creep up behind him and jab his spine. Jay jumps and swings around.

"Tash," he laughs. "Shit. I thought you were going to accuse me of shoplifting."

I eye the green-and-white button-up Jay is already wearing.

"Actually, you could probably wear one of those out of the store and no one would notice."

"I don't think you're supposed to say stuff like that as an employee."

"I've worked here three summers. I can do whatever I want."

Jay just laughs again and asks, "You off your shift anytime soon?"

I check my watch, which isn't necessary. I already know the time. On slow days like this, I check my watch every couple minutes, as though the mere act will speed along the second hand. An unenlightened exercise in futility, my mom would call it.

"I've got a couple hours left, but my manager won't get too pissed if I talk to you. We've been pretty dead." I gesture to the empty floor. "Walking on Sunshine" is playing in the background for the umpteenth time.

"Looking for anything in particular?" I ask, remembering to be semi-employee-like. "Looks like you've got a good handle on the plaid."

"Plaid is eternal," Jay says. "It's like blue jeans. Everything and everyone looks good in plaid."

I don't agree, but I smile in the "yes, you should totally buy all of it" way I perfected at job training.

"I didn't know you worked here," Jay adds. "How did I not know that? I feel like that's something I should know."

I shrug. "I guess these days we're only talking about the web series."

"Yeah. Speaking of which, did I tell you I got a few e-mails from some web series directors? Nothing huge, just requests for a headshot and résumé. None of them are close to us, of course. One's in Ontario, and the other's outside L.A. They both said they'd accept a video audition if I'm willing to relocate, and I'm like, 'Do I look like a professional actor with endless funds?' I'm not sure they get that most of us are still in high school. But the attention's nice."

"For sure," I say, still digesting the fact that an actual web series in L.A. asked for our very own Jay's headshot.

But Jay's moved on and asks, "Is it really just going to be you and George in Orlando?"

"Yes." I try to keep a straight face that does not betray my distaste. Distaste is not professional.

"Uh-huh. You gonna cut back on costs? *Share a room?*"

"Jay."

"What?" he says, all innocent. "I'm just saying, there's a fine line between hate and love. Opposites attract, and all that. He's a very pretty boy, and now, bonus, he's famous."

"I *made* him famous," I say, feeling lofty.

I am desperate for a way out of this conversation.

Sometimes, I feel like I could tell Jay the truth and he would not act like it's weird. He knows what it's like to not fit into the World at Large's Hopes and Expectations for You. But more often than not, I'm worried that telling Jay will be the equivalent of stomping on his foot. To throw out my lack of sexuality when Jay is getting harangued every day for the expression of his own? It seems so insensitive. It's not like people are telling me I can't get married or that I'm going to hell.

I've been part of Calhoun's gay-straight alliance since freshman year. When I joined, I identified myself as an ally. During one of our meetings this past year, Tara Rhodes said, "Allies are important. They're the 'A' in all our acronyms, after all!" And I wanted to stand up right then. I wanted to shout, "I'm real and here and just as confused as a lot of you!" But I stayed quiet, because I didn't want to *come out* right there, in a basement classroom that smelled like whiteboard cleaner. Still, Tara's comment bothered me for months after that. It made me feel like no one saw my "kind of people." That we didn't exactly *count*. And if I didn't count in an effing GSA meeting, then where the hell was I supposed to go?

"Tash?" Jay's smile has disappeared during my long silence. "Sorry, didn't mean to make you feel weird."

"No, it's fine. I was just thinking, it *would* be a lot cheaper if I could share a room with someone. Just . . . not George. You know, Tony was thinking of going for a while, but I think he decided he wanted a new synth more."

"He loves his music."

Jay is making a careful study of a scarf rack just behind my shoulder.

"Jaaay," I drawl uncertainly. "Um, I know it's not any of my business, but—"

Jay's face crumples. "I don't want to talk . . . about . . . um, about that."

I nod quickly. "Okay."

"It's just . . . you're Jack's friend, and he's Jack's ex, so it'd be weird for us to talk about it, right?"

It really would be. I don't know why I said anything. Only I *do* know: It's because every time Jay and Tony film together, Jay looks like a big-eyed puppy waiting for Tony to pet his head and say "Good boy." Because even on-screen, when Alex and Vronsky are duking it out, you can see a smidgen of wistfulness in Tony's eyes. Or maybe only I see it. Whatever the case, it's painful.

"I mean, I really like him," Jay says, despite the established weirdness. "I think that's obvious to everyone but him. But I don't want to fuck things up with the filming. Because I love Jack, she's great. And it's already kind of topsy-turvy with all the online attention and then Klaudie leaving and George . . . you know, George being George."

Oh. I am so well acquainted with all these stressors.

"Okay, okay," says Jay, without any encouragement. "I'm also afraid Jack will kill me. She seems like the type who could murder someone and cover it up perfectly."

"She is," I say, without thinking.

Jay's face is so crumpled now, it's almost beyond recognition.

"Um," I say. "You're right. This is too weird."

Jay shoves a plaid shirt back on its rack. "Were she and Tony really serious?"

I recall all the long phone calls with Jack during the Tony months, which were filled alternatively with sobbing and swooning. I recall all the playlists Tony shared with Jack, which she subsequently shared with me. I think of the love songs Tony wrote for Jack and the breakup songs Jack wrote about him. I think of the late night back in December when Jack came over and crawled into my bed and confided that she and Tony had slept together for the first time. Two months later, they were broken up.

"Well. You saw them when they were together," I say.

"That was different, though. You guys are always professional when we film."

This pleases me to hear. Professionalism is always the goal. Even after their breakup, Jack and Tony managed to make it through the following months largely ignoring each other rather than fighting in front of the rest of the cast.

"Then yeah," I say. "I'd say they were serious. As serious as life or death."

"You mean 'safe.'"

"Hmm?"

"I think the saying is '*Safe* as life or death.'"

"Same difference."

"Not really."

"Jay, can I interest you in one of our scarves? You seem super into them."

"What? Oh, no, sorry." Jay shakes his head, wipes a hand across his face. "Sorry, like I said, we probably shouldn't talk about it."

Kathryn Ormsbee

I poke Jay's cheek. "So, stop talking."

A too-long-absent smile returns to Jay's face. "We should hang out more often. Outside filming. I miss when we'd just hang out."

"Me too. Everything's been all business for a while."

"You should make that part of the business plan: mandatory hang-out sessions."

"Mmm, that sounds like *lots* of fun."

Jay ignores my sarcasm and, with the charisma of a presidential candidate, says, "If the fun isn't happening, make the fun happen."

"I hope someone attributes that quote to you one day on a big marble slab."

Jay holds up his only remaining plaid button-up. "I'm ready to check out."

I assume my employee face and nod congenially. "*Excellent* choice. Right this way, sir."

"Grandmum, can you hear us?"

The image on the computer screen is pixilated, and Grandmum Young's voice emits from the speakers in gurgled bursts. Sometimes it's hard to catch certain words Grandmum says because of her Kiwi accent, but this kind of lapse in communication is due solely to technical difficulties.

My family has been Skyping with Grandmum and PopPop Young for about an hour when the picture freezes. Tonight, it's just me and my parents sitting around the living room computer. Klaudie skipped out before dinner without telling anyone, and I for one am supremely pissed about it. Klaudie knew we were Skyping with the grandparents. She knew, and she totally stood them up.

In my opinion, all things are sacred where grandparents are concerned, because they are old and you never know if this present interaction with them will be your last. I didn't know the kiss I planted on Nana Zelenka's cheek in the parking lot of an Olive Garden would be the last kiss. Everything seemed so ordinary that night. Nana Zelenka hugged me around the waist and told me to be a good girl, and then she and Gramps were killed instantaneously in a car crash on their drive home.

This very night, Klaudie could be missing out on the last possible conversation with Grandmum and PopPop Young. I mean, I'm not wild about my parents' baby news, but I'm not taking it out on my *grand*parents.

I try to shed the anger—not because Klaudie doesn't deserve it, but because I don't want all the bad emotion to show on my face. Of course, at this point, my grandparents are lucky if they can even make out a featureless blob through the bad connection.

"Mum?!" Mom yells at the screen. "Mum, if you can hear us, we're going to hang up and try you again."

When Mom hits the end-call button, Dad turns to her with clasped hands and begs, "Can we say our Internet went out?"

This is yet another one of those points where my parents differ greatly.

Kathryn Ormsbee

Mom loves lengthy conversations. She asks about the little things, like my grandparents' daily schedule and what they ate for breakfast. She asks how they're feeling, and how they feel about those feelings, and how those feeling about those feelings make them feel. My dad's a talker too, but he prefers loud, hot-blooded conversations. Topics like sports and politics. When it comes to Skype dates with Mom's parents, Mom calls the shots, so our conversations tend to be mild and rambling, with no highlights and no clear ending point. Grandmum and PopPop know about the baby, of course, so that provided them with twenty minutes of somewhat interesting discussion—and silent moodiness on my part, because how could my grandparents be talking about a *new grandchild* like it wasn't the most screwed-up news in the world? But things digressed after that, and by the time our connection went bad Grandmum was complaining about a bunion on her left heel.

I endure these mind-numbing conversations because, again, grandparents are sacred. But also for Mom's sake, because she's said lots of times how guilty she feels that Klaudie and I don't know our grandparents as well as we could. These Skype talks and our two-week visits every five years are all we have to go on. And I know how much this bothers Mom. It's enough to make her weep silently in the den late at night.

Mom dials Skype again.

"You can always tell them good night and leave," she says to Dad. "I'm sure they won't mind."

"I'm sure they won't," Dad says, peevish. "Your mother will be too busy talking bunions to notice."

The Skype call is still ringing.

"Maybe *their* Internet went down," I say.

Dad nods enthusiastically. "Internet down Down Under!"

Mom sighs and says, "Jan, just go upstairs. I'll tell them good-bye from you."

Dad looks like a child trying to process the announcement that school has been canceled for the day.

"Go on," Mom says, swatting his elbow. "You've done your good deed for the month."

Dad sprints toward the staircase, headed for the master bedroom and a few hours of ESPN.

"Men," I sigh. "They have so little fortitude."

Mom gives me a look that says, *That's* not *true, but at the moment it is.* Then the call finally picks up and my grandparents come back into view, much clearer than before.

"Grandmum, can you hear us?" I ask again.

Grandmum Young smiles into the camera. "Yes, sorry, dear. John thought we ought to restart the program. Technology can be a blessing and a curse, can't it?"

I nod wholeheartedly.

. . .

Kathryn Ormsbee

It's past midnight when Klaudie gets in. I'm still up, texting Thom about the most recent episode of *Storms of Taffdor*, during which blood was spilled and tears shed.

I've just sent a text that reads, *I could watch those opening titles on a loop for an entire day,* when I hear the soft thud of footsteps on the stairs. Quickly, I punch in *Sorry, gotta go,* fling off my comforter, and race to the door. I catch Klaudie in the hallway, as she's passing. As if compelled by the instinct of a wild animal, I grab Klaudie's elbow and dig my nails in, hard.

Klaudie shrieks, then tacks on a low cuss and shakes me off.

"What the *hell*? What is your problem?"

"What is *your* problem?" I hurl back. "Bailing on our call with Grandmum and PopPop? That's *rude*."

There's a smell hanging in the hall—vaguely familiar, but out of context. It's tied to my memories of walks downtown and Calhoun High's parking lot. It's smoke. Klaudie smells like cigarettes.

"I already had plans with Ally and Jenna," she says.

"So, you should've canceled your plans. Grandmum and PopPop are family. You're probably not even going to be talking to Ally and Jenna in three years."

Klaudie's face fills to the brim with disdain. It's a hideous expression—something that belongs to a cartoon. It's an expression you wouldn't use on your worst enemy, just your sibling.

"You don't know anything about my life," Klaudie hisses.

"Look, I'm pissed too, but there are some lines you don't cross. And you don't have to be *that* shitty to Mom and Dad when they're paying your freakin' college tuition."

"An *eighth* of my tuition," snips Klaudie. "And I worked my ass off to get a scholarship."

"Yeah, well, they won't be paying for *me* to go to Vanderbilt."

"Oh come on, Tash, you won't even get into Vandy. Get your head out of the damn clouds."

Now I am wearing my own variety of hideously angry face. I am shaking. I feel perfectly capable of scratching Klaudie's eyes out.

"You know what this is actually about, don't you?" Klaudie says, and I smell another familiar-but-unusual scent on her breath. "You know what Mom is telling us? That we're not up to par. We didn't turn out the way she wanted. So she wants a do-over."

"You don't know that," I whisper, even though she's voicing something I've suspected more than once.

"It's dangerous and financially irresponsible, and if you want to go along with it like nothing is wrong, just for the sake of harmony or whatever Buddhist bullshit you still believe in—"

"I'm not *'going along with it'*!"

"Yeah, but you will. Because you'll do anything to stay in Mom's good graces. You're such a suck-up."

"Seriously? You're the one who brings home straight As and gets into

Kathryn Ormsbee

Gramps's engineering program and watches ESPN with Dad and earns National Merit whatever. And *I'm* the suck-up? Don't even—"

"Yeah, fine. Lie to yourself about that, too. Just like you're lying to yourself about getting into a good college."

We aren't being quiet. What began as an exchange of grizzled whispers has now escalated to shouts. When I notice Mom in the doorway of the master bedroom, I have no idea how long she's been standing there. Klaudie catches my change in expression, turns around, stiffens.

"Girls," Mom says in her usual crystalline voice. "It's past bedtime."

As though she's heard nothing. As though the only thing amiss here is that we're up past midnight.

Then Mom turns back around and closes the door.

Klaudie begins to say something, but I don't wait around to hear what.

I slam my bedroom door and sink into a sit against it, processing everything that's just been said. Klaudie has no idea what she's talking about. She's the suck-up. She always has been. Every summer before now she spent earning volunteer hours at the Hope Center and working on extracurricular science projects with the Calhoun physics club. She spent them studying test prep for the SAT. She spent them babysitting and endearing herself to the neighbors. She spent them hanging out with our family. She's racked up so many Perfect Points, she's exceeded the limit and passed on to sainthood.

At least, that's been the case every summer until now. I don't know what the hell she's into with Ally and Jenna, but Klaudie's an adult. If she wants to shake things up, then fine, I guess she deserves it. She *doesn't* deserve to be a bitch about it.

Her words about Vanderbilt won't leave my head, and neither will the look on Mom's face when she caught us shouting irretrievable words.

Once I'm in bed, the thought hits me: For so long, I've always thought of Klaudie as the better daughter. The queen apparent in our sibling lineup. But these days, I'm not so sure. I think her reign might be ending. Not that I'm vying for the crown; Klaudie just seems dead set on losing hers.

Thirteen

"Wait, so we're mad at Klaudie again?"

Jack, Paul, and I are sitting under the metal slide in Holly Park, prepping ourselves for our annual Burn and Earn contest. We've been doing this since fourth grade. The rules are simple: We choose a hot day midsummer and challenge each other to sit, bare-legged, on the metal slide for as long as possible. Whoever holds out the longest reaps a cash reward from the losers. Back in elementary school, the amount was a dollar per contestant. Now, it's twenty dollars and a year's worth of honor, glory, and bragging rights.

Jack is slathering moisturizing lotion on the backs of her legs, which she claims to be the secret behind her success for the past two years. (I haven't won since middle school.)

"We're not mad," I say. "We're . . . frustrated."

"Really? Because we sound mad."

"Why are we using the royal 'we'?"

"We don't know."

I grunt and say, "She's treating me like I'm a traitor for being okay with the baby. Like, what other choice do I have?"

"I already told you my great plan," says Jack, "and you shot it down."

"You mean your plan to make a deal with the devil so that my baby sibling turns out to be the Antichrist and my parents realize the error of their ways?"

"You make it sound so sinister."

I haven't mentioned what Klaudie said about Vanderbilt. That topic is still too tender to touch.

Paul is lying on his back, his long legs sticking out from under the slide. He collects a fistful of gravel, raises it over his head, and says, "How much would you pay me to eat this?"

Jack asks, "How are we related?"

"Maybe we're not. Maybe *I'm* the Antichrist." He waves the gravel-filled hand over his head, shrieking, "Look, Damien! It's all for you, Damien!"

"I'd dare you if it was normal gravel," I say. "But I'm pretty sure that stuff is more contaminated than Chernobyl. It probably hasn't been raked or changed out since, like, the Vietnam War. Do you know how many dogs have probably pooped on it?"

"Or little kids have peed on it?" Jack adds, an instant fan of this game.

"Or cigarettes butts have landed on it?"

"Or birds have mated on it?"

Kathryn Ormsbee

"Okay, okay, you've made your point, sheesh." Then, at turbo speed, he tugs open the collar of Jack's T-shirt and dumps the whole fistful of gravel down her back.

Jack does not scream. She does not whine out Paul's name and bat him off. She locks a cold, murderous glare on him and says, "I will kill you. I will murder you in your sleep tonight, Paul Marcus Harlow."

There's a sudden snap of sadness inside me. Even when Jack is threatening fratricide, I can see it there—how much she and Paul genuinely like each other. How well they get along, like best friends. It makes me sad, and kind of jealous too. By rights, it should be like that with me and Klaudie. She and I are even closer in age, and we're the same gender. We *should* be the best of friends. We should know each other's secrets and share each other's clothes and be confidantes. But we're not. We never were. We're just too different, I guess. Klaudie is student council, I'm the arts crowd. Klaudie is equations, I'm fiction. Klaudie is National Merit, I'm . . . Golden Tuba.

I know it's not something I can change, but times like this, I do wish we got along better. That I could hug and threaten and joke with her as easily as Jack does Paul. For a few months, when Klaudie filmed with us, I thought maybe we were getting closer. That the filming gave us common ground. We spent more time together then and were happy about it. Except *not*, since Klaudie now thinks filming is too time-consuming and highly unpleasant.

So much for sisterly bonding.

Jack doesn't get the chance to elaborate on her threats to Paul, because a flock of small children descends upon us. There are five of them, and judging by the green icing stains on the face of one of the kids, they're part of a birthday celebration. A girl who can't be any older than six stops right in front of our hideaway and shoves her hands on her hips.

"You guys are too *ooold* to be here," she says, pointing accusatorially. "Only kids are supposed to be on the playground. Those are the rules."

"We're still in school," Paul says congenially, "so I think we qualify as kids."

"Nuh-*uh*." The girl stamps her foot. She's wearing light-up sneakers, and an impressive display of blue and green zaps across her toe.

The boy standing next to her, who seems much less concerned about the apparent breach of park rules, says, "You wanna play with us? It's tag, and I'm it, but I'll give you a five-second head start."

A big blue button is pinned to his Transformers T-shirt. It reads, *Birthday Boy.*

Jack says, "Oh, Paul here *loves* tag. I'm sure he wants to play."

She nudges Paul's knee with a malicious smile.

Paul isn't even fazed. He ducks out from the slide and gets to his feet, wiping gravel off his backside.

"Five seconds, huh?" he says.

The boy gives Paul a good looking over.

"Mmm," he says, before smacking Paul's leg and screaming, "YOU'RE IT!"

Kathryn Ormsbee

Paul produces the roar of an angered bear. The kids all shriek in exhilarated terror and scatter. Paul glances back at us and sticks his tongue out at Jack.

"Ha," he says. "Now I'm in with the popular crowd."

He sets off running at a slow, exaggerated pace, and reaches out to tag kids in a series of carefully calculated near misses.

I shake my head at Jack.

"What?" she says. "He's having the time of his life."

"I bet that boy's parents want to know why some random teenage dude is chasing their children."

Jack makes a sputtery snorting sound. "Need I remind you, he stole all my babysitting clients? Parents love him."

"Why do you sound bitter? You hate babysitting," I remind her.

This is indisputable fact. Jack does not have the temperament for child care. She refuses to smile at kids or kneel down to their level or ask them what their favorite school subject is. According to Jack, kids are mini grown-ups who act constantly drunk, and if they refuse to be rational in her presence, they are not worthy of her attention, much less cloying accommodation. She phased out the babysitting thing three years ago so she could devote herself exclusively to her Petco job and Etsy shop.

"I'm not bitter," she says. "I'm just saying he's the guy all mothers love."

For a minute, we watch in smiling silence as Paul and the birthday kids whip around the playground. Paul fits right in, whooping and dodging in and out of the swings with overexaggerated propeller arms.

"Those kids are lucky," says Jack. "It can't have been a good birthday if the parents thought *this* was a nice place to host it."

I shift my gaze to Jack. There's a question I want to ask her, something that's been gurgling around in the back parts of my brain for weeks now. It's not a question I can just ask outright. It requires buildup—a seven-layer dip of increasingly probing inquiries.

"So, are you still planning on going to the Chvrches concert?"

Layer number one.

Jack gives me a look like I'm being unforgivably stupid.

"Uh, *yeah*. I spent good money on that ticket."

"Okay, cool. I just . . . you know, I don't want you to feel awkward. If you didn't want to go, that's all right. I could even stay here with you."

A sloppy layer number two.

"What the hell, Tash? I'm going. Just because Tony and I aren't together anymore . . . Is that what this is about? Because it was his idea? Or that we covered a Chvrches song for the channel, or something?"

"Well. Yeah, I guess."

This dip isn't ever going to make it to the party table.

"You're making something out of nothing. I'm fine, okay? We're fine now."

"You never talk to him." I quickly cut off Jack's protest with "*Hardly* ever. If it's something that's not directly related to filming, you don't.

You won't even sit next to him. I've seen you leave the room when he walks in. So don't tell me you're totally fine."

Jack shrugs violently. "What do you want me to say? Would I rather not interact with him almost every week? Sure. Are things still weird between us? Yeah. But I don't really have a choice. He's part of the cast, and we're *professionals*."

"Bleh. What does that word even mean?"

"Hell if I know." Frowning at the ground, Jack adds, "You know what gets me? Sitcoms. Like, okay, everyone knows they're not an actual representation of life. They're what sad, tired working people come home to and watch so they don't feel like complete shit. But you'd think they could at least be honest about how breakups work. Healthy breakups, anyway. I get it, they have limited resources, and they have to keep the same cast members. But inevitably all those cast members start dating each other, and when they break up, nobody leaves. The ex stays in the picture, in perpetuity. They just stay part of the same friend group, no matter what. It's so dysfunctional. And that's not how it's supposed to work. You break up, you go your separate ways. Nine times out of ten, it's not healthy to stay friends with your ex. Because things will always, *always* be weird."

"You made that statistic up," I say.

"If national television corporations are allowed to make up bullshit love stories, then I am allowed to fudge a few statistics."

"Are you saying *Unhappy Families* is a like a bad sitcom?"

"I'm saying I'm fine, but wrapping up filming has its silver lining."

"Okay."

"So stop being sensitive."

"Okay." But because the topic has already been broached and doesn't seem likely ever to be broached again, I hastily ask, "Do you want me to take the music videos down?"

"Why would you do that?"

"If they make you uncomfortable. I mean, you guys were really . . . affectionate."

The combination of Tony's poppy synthesizer and Jack's throaty vocals was a big draw to viewers, but by far the most endearing quality of their videos was that Tony and Jack were open about being boyfriend and girl-friend and even kissed on-screen at the end of a love song Tony wrote for Jack. If I were Jack, I'd want those videos taken down immediately.

"It's still good music," Jack says. "Our relationship status doesn't affect the quality of sound. Think about it: Plenty of band members have dated and broken up. Jack and Meg White, Gwen Stefani and Tony Kanal. They don't just pull all the records and videos they made when they were dating. When you're a musician, sometimes you don't get that kind of catharsis."

I nod slowly, not sure of a good response. Jack has entered a land where musicians live and I am only an ignorant visitor.

In an attempt to leave Music Philosophizing Land, I ask, "How's your dad?"

Kathryn Ormsbee

"From what he's telling us, fine."

Mr. Harlow stopped complaining about his headaches a couple weeks back. Despite his family's pestering, he didn't get them checked out. They obviously weren't happy about that, but Mr. Harlow is scheduled for his next oncology checkup at the start of next month, and if there's anything to be concerned about, surely the doctors will catch it then.

"INCOMING."

I make room just in time for Paul to come skidding under the slide and hunch with his hands over his head.

"Hey!" shouts Birthday Boy, galloping over to us. "Hey, no fair!"

"It's totally fair." Paul's still covering his head, as though he fears the six-year-old might do damage to him. "I tagged you, so now things stand the way they did before I got involved. You're It. I'm out."

"Nooo," says a pigtailed girl. "You're fun!"

"I've gotta have fun with these two losers now," Paul says, waving at me and Jack. "Sorry. We already had a scheduled playdate."

A whole swarm of glum-faced kids has congregated around us.

"My God," Jack says under her breath. "It's like *Village of the Damned.*"

"Pleeeease," says Birthday Boy, who is now in all-out pout mode. "Play with us five more minutes?"

"Sorry, kiddos. I'm old and tuckered out."

Just as a couple kids begin whining, Jack pokes her head out from under the slide and, in a dead, monotone voice, says, "I'm a witch, and if you don't leave him alone, I'll put a curse on you."

"You're not a witch!" yells Pigtail Girl. "They don't exist, my mommy told me!"

"Your mommy is a liar. *Ow*, stop it, Tash." Jack wiggles her fingers sinisterly toward the girl. "You don't want to test my powers, do you?"

Pigtail Girl looks dubious, but Birthday Boy has backed away, uneasy. With no warning, he jets off again, shrieking, "I'm It!" And Paul is forgotten.

"You're horrible," I tell Jack. "You don't tell a kid their mother is a liar."

"All parents are liars," says Jack. At which Paul frowns and chucks another handful of gravel at her.

"Burn and Earn," he says. "The sun is at its peak position. Let's do this."

We do it. Jack wins the contest for the third year in a row. Eighteen seconds of uninterrupted contact between skin and burning metal.

"Triple Crown winner!" she bellows, before inspecting the hot red backs of her thighs.

The next day, I'm hanging out in Jack's bedroom as she edits footage and I scroll through comments on our newest upload, entitled "Anna's Turned the Corner." Tomorrow is an early morning filming day, and we'll be shooting in the Harlows' dining room, so I've decided to spend the night. We're sitting in a comfy silence, punctuated by clicks, when I notice Jack frowning at her screen.

"What's wrong?" I ask, immediately worried that it's something to do with the footage—that there aren't any usable shots from a certain angle, or there's some glaring continuity error we didn't catch.

"Um, nothing," she says, but her frown deepens.

I scoot closer to take a look at her laptop. "Are you sure?"

Jack throws her hands over the screen, shielding it from view. "Yeah." She sounds weirdly nervous. "It's fine."

"Then why are you covering the screen?" I try to peel back her fingers, without success.

"Okay," says Jack. "Okay, you've got to promise not to freak out."

"Just show me."

So Jack drops her hands. The screen is pulled up to a Tumblr post. A lengthy Tumblr post.

Jack says, "The haters have finally come out to play."

There's a certain brutality about repeating things to yourself, even if those things are good. After you stop purposefully reciting the words, they continue in an automatic loop, wearing down a groove in your brain. I've experienced this before with Taylor Mears's video and with some texts from Thom. Certain words hop aboard the Endless Loop Train and go around the track again and again and again, draining the fuel of my very consciousness.

And that's when it's *good* words. With bad words, it's much, much worse.

I read through the Tumblr post once, twice, three times. Then I react, talking faster and more ferociously with every passing moment. I am in full-on rant mode when Paul comes in the room, basketball in hand. His hair is gathered back in a ponytail and his face is flushed. He smells of sweat and sun.

Jack interrupts my tirade to say, "Don't you dare touch my furniture like that. Floor only."

Obligingly, Paul tosses aside the basketball and dives to the floor. He asks, "What're we mad about?"

"Some horrible person with nothing better to do wrote a critique of *Unhappy Families*. Like, okay, I'd like to see *you* try to produce a show with no money and a ton of logistics to worry about, and I bet he doesn't know we're only in high school, because what kind of creep . . . Jack, *what?*"

Jack looks like she's making a concerted effort not to laugh.

She says, "I like it when you get all vindictive. Suits you."

This makes me angrier, because it reminds me that I am not acting anywhere close to enlightened. I really need some space with this. Space to think and calm down.

"What did this person say, exactly?" Paul asks. "And what makes you think it's a he?"

I shrug. "Why not?"

"Hey," says Jack, jabbing my knee. "That's not fair. Girls and boys can be equally horrible." She leans over the edge of the bed and props her laptop on Paul's chest. "Read it for yourself. It's the one by silverspunnnx23."

Which Paul apparently takes to mean "Read it aloud for us," because he clears his throat and revisits the phrases that are already tearing wounds into my brain:

Okay, I seem to be in the minority here, but why the f*** is everyone suddenly OBSESSED with Unhappy Families? *So it got a plug from Taylor Mears, but everyone knows Taylor's vlogs have turned into throwaway content these days, now that she's busy working on her new project. Personally, I've found the whole series so far to be dull and hackneyed. And so no one can accuse me of being in a bad mood, I've listed the problems I found when watching. Let's take a look, shall we?*

1. ACTING—I guess the acting is decent overall, but the script sounds so forced most of the time. They're obviously trying way too hard to make references to the text, but it just doesn't work.

2. THE STORY—Am I the only one thinking this? There's a reason no one's made Anna Karenina *into a modern web series: BECAUSE IT DOESN'T WORK. It's WAY too ambitious. Tolstoy wasn't writing some cute love story. He was writing a social and political commentary, and that's totally lost here. I'm not saying it's a web series' job to be as epic and insightful as a Tolstoy novel. Most of them are derivative pieces of fluff, anyway. But it's one thing to update some already awful gothic novel. It's another* to attempt to update Russian lit. I bet at this point, the writers are already realizing they bit off way more than they can chew.

3. KEVIN—God, don't get me started here. I can't for the life of me understand what anyone finds attractive about this ship. It's not that great in the book to begin with, but in this series it's a total joke. Levin is an awkward, sniveling pansy rich boy who likes plants. Also, the actor playing him is way too pretty for the role. Kitty is bland and has NO definable personality traits other than being a dancer. Even so, she deserves better than Levin. I don't get why anyone is cheering for these two to get together. WHY.

Conclusion: WTF. Seriously, that's all I can think when I see people junking up my feed with their fangirling over this mediocre-at-best show. I can only hope this is a phase and everyone will move past the #KevinThursday madness soon.

Paul shuts the laptop and stretches both arms over his head to return it to Jack.

"Ouch," he remarks. Then, noticing a pile of Jack's newly molded clay figurines, he picks up a Corpse Bride and Jack Skellington and makes them dance across his stomach in a languid waltz.

"I would sincerely like to see that person write and direct and produce a web series," I say. "What, does he live off tears and negativity? Does he have nothing better to do than burn people who are actually trying to—to make art?"

Kathryn Ormsbee

"Okay, Tash, don't make it so lofty." Jack throws the laptop screen back open. "We're doing *Unhappy Families* because it's fun, not because we got commissioned to spruce up the Sistine Chapel. And the reviewer could be a she. Probably is."

"Whoever they are, they suck. And did you see all those reblogs? Who would reblog something that mean? What, are there hundreds of people out there who hate our show?"

I think back to those nine dislikes on my vlog. I tear up.

"Hey," says Paul, lifting the Corpse Bride to my eye level in a consoling approach. "It's not worth crying over."

"Don't tell me what's worth crying over!" I shout, knocking the figurine from his hand. "Like you've ever done something like this, Paul!"

The silence that follows is awful. Paul's gaze is back on the ceiling, but I can see hurt in his face.

Jack's staring at me. "Jesus, Tash. When did you get to be such an asshole? That's my job."

"I—I'm sorry," I say, miserable. I slide off Jack's bed to sit beside Paul. I nudge him in the shoulder, which is still damp with cooled sweat. "I'm sorry, that was way out of line."

Paul closes his eyes and says, "It's fine."

"Bad reviews are inevitable," says Jack. "We just can't let George see this."

"For so many reasons," I agree, shaking off my remaining disquiet.

TASH *hearts* TOLSTOY

"So. Enough of that." Jack turns the screen for me to see. "Look at this GIF set instead. Isn't that the best?"

Someone has captured three moments from the Scrabble episode: a close-up of the letter tiles, of Levin and Kitty brushing hands, and of Levin and Kitty's kiss.

I smile and nod, but I can't help thinking, *NO definable personality.*

Is that true? Jack and I worked so hard to make Kitty's character sweet-tempered but believable. Is it not enough? Or is it just Eva's performance? Or *what?* What are we doing wrong?

Even late into the night, after Paul has dragged himself off to his room and Jack and I have settled into bed, my mind won't shut off. The words keep whirling around in my mind: *so forced, derivative pieces of fluff, total joke.*

After an hour of trying to fall asleep, I take my phone out from under my pillow and text Thom.

We got a really bad review today. Any tips for how to shake it off?

I don't anticipate getting a reply until sometime tomorrow, so I'm surprised to see typing on Thom's end.

He writes, *That's the worst. I'm so sorry. I've gotten my fair share. Just try to stay away from them, and DON'T read obsessively. Otherwise, you'll remember them for-ev-er.*

I grimace and text, *Too late for that.*

It's going to be okay, Thom texts back. *Remember, there will always be people who don't like your content. It's their right to criticize. It's your right to keep making art.*

I smile. At least Thom thinks I'm making art.

Thanks, I text. *Seriously, that makes me feel better.*

Anytime. Sweet dreams.

I stare at the screen for a full minute.

Sweet dreams. Is that a normal thing for friends to text each other? Are Thom and I friends, or what? It's not like either of us is making protestations of love, but lately Thom has been responding much more quickly and holding out longer in our conversations. Two nights this week, I stayed up past three o'clock in the morning chatting with him about the new material he has planned for his vlog and—my new favorite topic—the Golden Tubas.

Do you ever feel totally intimidated by the Golden Tubas? I texted him a couple days ago. *I know it's not like they're the Academy Awards, but sometimes it feels like that.*

Thom texted back, *Don't let it get to you. I was all hyped up when I first got nominated last year, but I would've enjoyed it a lot better if I wasn't so nervous.*

He added, *Also, if I'd known I wouldn't win, I wouldn't have gone. Lol.*

Why not? I asked. *It's still a great opportunity to meet people.*

I know enough people, Thom replied.

Which, I suppose, is true. Thom is much more established in this world than I am. Last year, *Beaker Speaker* was nominated for three

Tubas—Best Vlog, Nerd of Honor, and Best Personality. He may not have won any of them, but getting the nominations was a big deal. At least I will only have to be a nervous wreck for one round of awards.

I just hope I don't cry, I wrote.

And Thom replied, *I'll bring lots of tissues, don't worry.*

So, no romantic overtures, but still, there's something there. Not romantic yet, maybe, but a tenuous promise. I have a feeling both Thom and I know things will change at the convention. Our meeting will either be a confirmation of what we've been hoping for or a sad realization that reality doesn't match expectations. The thought of that meeting sends shock waves through my body—tangled sensations of fear and anticipation.

I wonder how Thom pictures our first meeting. If things take a good turn, will he expect us to make out? Will he expect . . . more? If he doesn't, there's absolutely no reason to tell him yet. Anyway, how are you supposed to tell a boy you like that you don't want to have sex with him, possibly ever? There are no tips for that in *Cosmopolitan*, no informational paragraph in my health textbook. It isn't something I can ask Jack's or Paul's advice about.

Even if I start a thread on the forums, no one there can tell me exactly how to phrase the text or the spoken words. *So, Thom, I like you a lot, but absolutely no part of me wants to hook up with any part of you.* How do I word that without making it sound like a rejection? Without

Kathryn Ormsbee

sounding like I'm just a prude? I mean, what teenage guy wants to hear that? What person wants to hear that, period?

In any case, there's no reason to tell him now. I have until the Golden Tuba Awards, when that tenuous promise of ours is bound to either come true or break into a hundred tiny pieces.

Fourteen

I wake to a harsh flood of morning light and Jack pouring forth a steady stream of cusses.

"What's wrong with you?" I mumble, glaring resentfully at the windows from which Jack has just ripped away the curtains.

"Get *up*," she says.

I check the clock.

It's 8:52. Eight minutes before we're supposed to start filming.

I forgot to set my alarm last night. And, it seems, Jack did too.

"We've got George and Serena down there already," Jack says, yanking her sleep-mussed hair into a ponytail. "Shit. George isn't ever going to let us live this down. *Come on*, Tash, get your ass out of there."

This can't be happening. This *never* happens. Jack and I are so good about following our schedule, keeping things professional. And now *this*—this is the height of unprofessionalism. I throw off the covers and hurry over to my duffel. I pull out my shirt and jean shorts and am just putting on my bra when the door flies open behind me. I glance over my shoulder and let out a yelp.

"Whoa!" Paul shields his eyes and slams the door shut. A second later, he creaks it back open and says, "Sorry, Tash. Um, I wanted to see if you guys still need my help today. Also, there are people here."

"We are aware," Jack says in a cold voice that warns of impending violence.

"Well, let me know if I can help with something in the meantime."

"Oh *sure*," says Jack. "Why don't you serve our guests some tea and crumpets?"

"Fuck off, Jack." The door slams again, more forcefully than before.

"Don't push him over the edge," I say, zipping up my shorts. "He's all the help we've got."

"He's fine," says Jack. "When it comes to Paul, there's no edge too steep."

Jack and I planned on getting up at seven this morning and setting up the dining room for the day's shoot. The scene is supposed to take place at night, which means we have to BlackWrap all the windows and figure out lighting. There are also lots of props we need in order to transform a corner of the Harlows' so-so dining room into something that resembles a fancy university library.

But Jack and I didn't get up at seven, which means there is at least half an hour of hurried setup to get through before we can even think of rolling the camera.

George isn't happy. Even Serena looks upset. She's sitting in an armchair with folded arms, studying her script, and she only looks up to say, "I have to leave by three. Ben and I have a date."

"We won't run over," I assure her. "It's just now nine."

"Nine is when we *start*," says George, his face twisted in a way that makes him look like he's in labor with a baby elephant. "Nine is when you shout 'Action.' I can't believe this. Eva's not even here."

As though on cue, the doorbell rings. I run to get it. Eva is huffing and puffing and crying that she slept through her alarm but she is never going to be late again.

"You don't have to apologize today," I tell her.

When I return to the dining room, George and Jack are in an all-out fight.

"We're not going to start that late if you help out," Jack is saying. "We've got to cover these windows, move in the bookshelves, and set up the lights. Then we're good to go."

"But that's *not my job*," George says, with a special dramatic emphasis I have only ever heard used by actors. "My job is to study my lines and give a good performance. You do your job, I'll do mine."

"Oh my God, George," says Serena, who now looks more resigned than pissed and is cutting off a long sheet of BlackWrap. "You're not in SAG-AFTRA yet."

"I'm not the one who overslept."

"Well, this is the first time they ever have, so give them a break."

Kathryn Ormsbee

George will not be moved. While Jack, Serena, Eva, Paul, and I set up the room as quickly as possible, he remains at the dining room table, reading through his script and, on occasion, sniffing loudly.

Things don't get better, even once we're ready to film. In her rush to leave home, Eva forgot to bring the lipstick she was wearing in the scene we shot last weekend, which means we have a continuity error on our hands.

"I guess the audience can assume she sneaked off to change her lip color between dinner and drinks," says George. "Girls do that, right?"

"Shut up, George," says Jack, who reached her George threshold an hour ago.

After which point, George purposefully botches his lines. He goes so far as to cut off some of Serena's, and there is only so much she can sustain before, in the middle of a take, she slaps George on the shoulder and yells, "I can't work with this prick!"

"Well, that's not going in the gag reel," Jack mutters.

I stop the camera, and Paul lowers the boom mic, and I tell Eva, George, and Serena to call it a day, because there is no way we're going to get usable footage like this.

"We'll reschedule later," I say, talking over George's protest. "I don't think any of us are in a position to calmly discuss this right now."

George says, "This is so unprofess—"

"Just. Leave."

So the talent leaves, and I throw myself on the living room couch with a muffled wail.

"I can't believe we just wasted a whole day of filming," Jack says.

Derivative piece of fluff, I think.

"That was—" Paul begins.

"A train wreck?" I supply.

"I was gonna say 'high drama.' Have you ever thought about turning the filming process into a reality show? Because I would totally watch that."

This only puts me in a fouler mood, because it reminds me that Paul doesn't watch *Unhappy Families* "on principle." The way he explained it once, he doesn't want us asking for his opinion on the show, because if he hates it, we'll be forever angry at him, and if he likes it, he'll be constantly pestering us to see footage of what's coming next. I think this is flawed logic, but it doesn't bother me that much. Except at times like this.

"You," Jack snaps at her brother. "Go to kitchen. Bring back ice cream."

Paul blows her a kiss with his middle finger. But he leaves the room, and a moment later I hear the telltale unsticking sound of the freezer door.

"We get back in our pajamas," says Jack. "Then we hole up and watch movies, and we are *not* going to think about what just happened for the next five hours at least."

I don't have a problem with this plan. An hour later, the three of us are lounging in the living room among used ice cream bowls, watching *The Dark Crystal.*

Kathryn Ormsbee

"I think I kind of look like Jen," Paul says.

"You're just saying that because you have long hair," says Jack. "Doesn't work that way."

"It does a little, though," says Paul. "There are so few long-haired men in the world."

"Oh, so now you're a man, are you?"

I laugh. "Yeah, Paul, I'm not sure you're in man territory yet. You're still solidly a guy."

Paul looks wounded. "Well, Jen isn't a man either. He's a puppet."

"You can't call looks alike just because you have similar hair," says Jack. "Next thing we know, you're gonna be comparing yourself to Jared Effing Leto."

Paul shrugs. His expression says, *If the shoe fits.*

I thwack him on the head. "Ass," I say, and as I do, I get that tight, bubbly feeling in my throat—the carbonation indigestion, though I haven't had a single soda today.

We watch movies late into the night. Eventually, Mr. Harlow pops his head in the room and asks, "Am I getting my house back anytime soon?"

"We'll clear out," says Jack, switching off the television and gathering up some of the wreckage in the room. Our collection of ice cream–skimmed bowls has since been joined by potato chip bags and string cheese wrappers.

Mr. Harlow gives the three of us an approving nod as we clear the trash and ourselves out of the room. He looks tired—kind of worn down around the eyes. Which makes me nervous, but I've had to train myself to not think every tired look of Mr. Harlow's is a sign his cancer is back. If he'd found out anything about those headaches, Jack and Paul would've told me. He's probably just eager to have the television to himself. Even before we set foot in the hallway, I hear a baseball game blaring from the room.

"Is he mad at us?" I whisper to Jack.

"What? *No.*" She smirks. "You know Dad, he's such a pushover. If we'd told him we wanted to watch movies all night long, he would've let us. He'd rather die than witness a confrontation."

"Good thing he wasn't around earlier, then."

"I've got some stuff to do," Paul says. "See you tomorrow, I guess."

His voice is tight, almost angry. I frown at his back as he hurries down the hallway and closes the door of his room.

"What was that?" I whisper.

Jack shrugs, but there's a troubled look on her face as we head back to her room.

Kathryn Ormsbee

Fifteen

"We need a new plan."

I've finished my shift at Old Navy, where Jack surprised me by jumping out of a fitting room and demanded I share a late lunch with her in the food court. We're sitting at a two-seater table next to the mall carousel. I'm eating a veggie pizza. Jack has bought a Philly cheesesteak and a giant Cinnabon roll and is alternating her bites between the two. She's just stuffed a gooey forkful of cinnamon roll in her mouth when she asks, "What kind of new plan?"

"For how we deal with social media," I say. "It's getting draining. And kind of depressing."

As it turns out, silverspunnnx23 was not an isolated incident. Ever since that post, I've noticed more dislikes on our videos, more negative e-mails and comments (*Ummmm, where'd the plot go?*; *Does Kitty do her own makeup, because it shows*). It's hard to tell if the negative stuff has always been there, just less visible, or if silverspunnnx23's post has opened the proverbial floodgates; it's racked up a *lot* of likes and reblogs.

"I'm telling you," says Jack, "we should hire a personal assistant."

"Yes, with our huge-ass budget. Come on, we need an actual, executable solution."

"Uh, okay, eighties businesswoman." Jack reaches across the table and pats my shoulders frantically. "Oh God, I can already feel the shoulder pads coming in."

"There is nothing weird about approaching life with a plan."

"Nothing fun about it, either," mutters Jack, turning her attention to the cheesesteak. Once her mouth is full, she starts up again. "I don't see what we can change. We can't exactly filter out hate. So unless we're not going to respond to *anything* online, I say we keep up what we're doing."

"Maybe we *shouldn't* respond," I say.

Jack swallows loudly. "Are you kidding? You want us to, what, totally disappear online?"

"No." The plan formulates even as I'm talking. "We'll still upload videos. But maybe we should take a week away from weeding through notifications."

"But when we pick it up again, we'll have a huge backlog to work through. How does that help?"

"I don't *know*," I say, frustrated. "I just don't think how we're doing it now is . . . sustainable. It would help to step back for a week and get some perspective."

"I mean, fine, whatever. I don't mind getting a few hours of my life back."

Kathryn Ormsbee

"Kevin is still strong at least," I say, dunking one of my pizza crusts into a cup of marinara. "*Most* people were happy with #KevinThursday. And did you see how someone started a Tumblr fansite?"

"Dude, that's been up for ages."

"Well, I'm just *saying*." I wad up a grease-soaked napkin and toss it at Jack's nose. Jack ducks, and the napkin hits the head of someone sitting behind her. The someone turns around. It's a middle-aged mother eating McDonald's with her two children. She looks extremely unamused.

"Sorry," I say. "Sorry, that was for my friend."

The woman gives me an unflinching glare. It's faces like this that have me convinced people really did watch gladiators and public executions for fun.

Jack is still bent over, snickering hard.

I kick her under the table. "Shut up. Eat faster."

Jack straightens. She takes a bite of her cinnamon roll. With glee in her eyes, she chews slowly.

When I get home, I look over a flash drive's worth of edited footage that Jack gave me at lunch. As expected, everything looks good. Jack's cuts are perfectly timed, her corrective coloring decent. And I never get tired of watching our five-second intro. Tony composed the theme: a flirty little melody on synthesizer; and Paul did the graphics: an aerial shot of neon train tracks that end in the series title.

When Paul first presented the design, I asked if it might be too morbid, considering Tolstoy's Anna meets her tragic end on the train tracks. (We've planned a less tragic end for our Anna: She just leaves town.) Jack replied that nothing in this life is too morbid, because nothing is more morbid than life itself. I didn't want to offend Paul, who'd done the graphics as a favor to us, so I dropped it. Now, months later, I wouldn't change a thing. Which might be because I've come to realize the genius of our title sequence, but more likely is because I've grown accustomed to it.

Whatever the case, I'm happy with the titles. Unlike a certain Tumblr user named silverspunnnx23 who is all WTF about our entire production. The tone of that post is still so lodged in my brain, I can imagine with vitriolic eloquence how the critique would go:

4. OPENING TITLES — What kind of cheap excrement is this? Low budget? How about NO budget. Congratulations on producing a five-second song more annoying than a car dealership jingle. News flash: Punching out a few notes on a synthesizer does not make you a musician. The graphics? If I wanted to see those shades of neon, I'd take some LSD, thanks very much. And train tracks? Talk about poor taste.

"Ugh, toxic," I tell myself, head on my desk. "This is so toxic, stop it."

I decide to distract myself by checking the Seedling Productions e-mail account. This isn't *technically* social media. Still, before I open

Kathryn Ormsbee

the web browser, I set a twenty-minute timer on my phone. Boundaries.

As always, the inbox is filled with equal parts junk and fan mail. There are lots of e-mails from viewers asking impossible questions, like how is the series going to end, and how do we plan on approaching such-and-such plot point in the book. Several people want to know where they can listen to more of Jack and Tony's music, even though a cursory glance at the videos' description boxes would provide them a link to Tony's Bandcamp site. A few just want to say how much they love the show. At this point, I feel like I've seen every possible type of letter. Turns out I'm wrong. My eyes catch on an e-mail sent this afternoon with the subject line *"YOUR SHOW SUCKS."* The body of the e-mail is only a little more verbose: *I think your show really sucks, would you stop making videos already.*

The whole experience is so sudden—just a click and a couple seconds to process—that I find myself reeling away from my desk like a drunk woman. I pace the room a few times. I look at my poster of Leo. He scowls down on me. I scowl back. Then I return to my laptop and delete the e-mail. I tell myself that whatever person gets their kicks from sending nasty letters deserves my pity, not wrath. That's that.

I wish I could rid myself of silverspunnnx23's criticisms as easily. The trouble is, silverspunnnx23 didn't write an uninspired, juvenile e-mail. She (I've begun to think of her as a *she* now) wrote a coherent criticism using good grammar. Worst of all, she's pressed on parts of me that are already bruised and sore from self-doubt. I've wondered at times, when reviewing the script, if certain lines are too stilted, too forced. Jack and I discussed doing a modern adaptation for months and months, and we were both leery of how massive *Anna Karenina* was. It *is* an ambitious project, sure, but we liked our approach of simplifying and updating the story. We weren't setting out to make a masterpiece. It's not like anyone on YouTube is clicking around in search of the next Francis Ford Coppola. But no matter how many times I tell myself silverspunnnx23 is out of touch, out of line, just doesn't *get* it—her biting words keep playing over and over again.

In a last-ditch attempt at distraction, I return to my e-mail. This time around, scrolling through my inbox feels like walking through a field now known to be hiding land mines. I sift through a few more inquiries about Tony's music before I come to the subject line "*INTERVIEW REQUEST.*" This is another variety of e-mail I've yet to encounter. Leaning closer with interest, I click open the letter.

Dear Jacklyn and Natasha,

My name is Heather Lyles, and I'm co-founder of the lifestyle blog Horn-Rimmed Glasses Girl. *Every month, we like to spotlight girls who are doing new and innovative things on the Internet. If you're interested, my co-blogger Carolyn and I would love to interview you for our August slot. Feel free to browse around our blog and check out past interviews (links below). Just let us know in the coming weeks if you'd like to take part.*

Kathryn Ormsbee

Sincerely,

Heather Lyles

Creator & Blogger, Horn-Rimmed Glasses Girl

I went looking for a distraction, and here it is. An *interview* request. Like Jack and I are celebrities. Like we have something worthwhile to say in a Q&A. Best of all, I've actually heard of the *Horn-Rimmed Glasses Girl* blog before. Which means this is not just a distraction but a somewhat big deal. Five minutes later, I've composed a reply thanking Heather for the opportunity and informing her that absolutely, we'd love to interview.

My twenty-minute timer goes off a few seconds after I press send. Perfect timing. I've ended things on a good note. I close my laptop and retreat to my bed with my phone in hand. Thom texted me during work this morning. I read his words quickly at break, but now I take my time, studying every letter as though it's a hieroglyphic.

Hey, read the Tumblr post. That girl is an idiot, don't let it bother you for a second. She was basically criticizing all web series, not to mention TOLSTOY HIMSELF. Not worth your time.

Thom's got a point: Silverspunnx23 did seem critical not just of *Unhappy Families* but of everything in general. She's probably one of those people who goes out on a sunny summer day and says, "Ew, there's a cloud in the sky, my life is ruined." And she *did* slight my man Leo, which is not only offensive but laughable, because he is the best novelist in the history of novelists. These are all good reasons to let it go. Maybe now I'll finally be able to.

I text, *Thanks. You always know what to say.*

A moment later, Thom writes back. He's been texting a lot more promptly over the past few days, and I don't know if that's because his schedule is less hectic or if it's something else. Something having to do with me.

I always know what to TEXT. You ever think how weird it is that we've literally never said anything to each other?

I sit up straight in bed. I want to text back that yes, I've been thinking that for weeks now. But that would come off as way too desperate.

Very weird, I write. *But that'll change soon.*

Is Thom going to bring it up? Is he going to suggest we call each other? Skype, even? Maybe he isn't going to text back at all. Maybe he's going to be spontaneous and call me on the spot.

But no. No call. He texts back, *Are you sure you're okay?*

And I can't be mad at him for that.

I'll be okay, I write. *Just a lot of things I wasn't expecting, all happening at once.*

Thom can't know this, but I'm not just talking about the web series anymore. I'm talking about the health of my best friends' dad and my mom's out-of-the-blue pregnancy and the ever-widening rift between me and Klaudie and the sinking feeling that my dream school is a *pipe dream* school.

I fall asleep before Thom's reply arrives. In the morning, I read the message waiting for me: *Buckle up, it only gets crazier.*

Sixteen

Later that morning, I walk to Holly Park. We've been getting some unseasonably cool weather the past few days, and, given all the recent weirdness and negativity, I decide now is as good a time as any to meditate.

I walk along the shaded path, ten steps in one direction, ten in the other, keeping my eyes lowered and my breaths steady, and trying to block out the occasional interference of sound bites like *junking up my newsfeed* and *script sounds so forced*.

When I hear a car honk, I don't register the sound as pertaining to me. It's as much a part of the outside world's white noise as the birds and wind and distant traffic. But when I change the direction of my ten-step walk and chance a look up, I see a familiar blue Camry parked on the side of the road. The window is rolled down, and my mom is in the driver's seat.

She leans out and calls, "I'm sorry, darling! I didn't realize you were meditating."

I'm always taken aback when I hear Mom shout. Most days, she's so soft-spoken that I start thinking she's incapable of speaking at any level over the "2" tick on the volume knob. But here she is shouting—not angrily, but with perfect articulation; from yards away, I hear every word.

I hesitate for a second longer, then set toward the car in a jog. I stop at the open passenger window and wipe at my forehead, which has picked up a fine coating of sweat.

"It's fine," I say. "I was just finishing up. I hadn't done a walking meditation in a while, and . . ."

"Now seemed like a good time," Mom finishes. Her smile is so incisive I have to look away, or else I'll get cut.

"Would you like a ride home?" she asks.

I smirk. "My mom taught me never to get in strangers' cars."

Mom laughs at that, in a water-glass-melody way. She unlocks the door, and I get inside. Once we've pulled away from the curb, she says, "Full disclosure: I still have some errands to run."

I gasp at this betrayal and unclick my seat belt.

Laughing again, Mom says, "Before you throw yourself to the pavement, hear me out: Graeter's is on the way."

"You should've led with that," I say.

I have a time-honored affection for the ice cream shop Graeter's same as for Holly Park, only unlike the park, Graeter's is wholly worthy of such affection. I know my mom is shamelessly buttering me up with the offer to take me there, but I'm not ashamed to accept this kind of buttering.

We drive in silence for a few minutes, following a familiar route toward downtown. We merge onto New Circle, the circular highway that connects the city's main roads like spokes on a wheel. Once we're settled at a steady pace in the right lane, Mom turns to me.

"You know, your father and I spent weeks trying to figure out the best way to tell you girls about the baby, and even then we messed up."

"Yeah," I say. "I'm sorry I laughed that night."

"Sometimes our bodies react strangely to big news."

I nod. I remember when I was in seventh grade and Mr. Harlow was diagnosed with cancer, Jack didn't cry for the longest time. It wasn't until months later, when the two of us were watching *Monsters, Inc.*, that she burst into hiccuping tears and couldn't stop for a half hour.

"Mom?"

"Yes?"

"How are you going to afford it? I mean, isn't raising a kid expensive? And I know you told me you'd match my college scholarship, but . . . like, is that going to change?"

Mom makes this occasional humming sound as I talk, so I know she's listening, but she doesn't speak until she's taken her exit and turned onto a less trafficked road.

"Some things are going to change," she says. "Dad and I are going to live on a much tighter budget from here on out. But we made you and

Kathryn Ormsbee

your sister that promise several years ago, and we won't go back on our word. We'll match whatever scholarship you get."

"Which might be nothing," I mutter. "Not at Vandy, anyway. Klaudie's twice as smart as I am, and she's only getting, what, like five thousand dollars a year?"

"Tasha, darling."

I bristle. I know exactly what Mom's going to say. I open my mouth to protest, but she waves for me to listen.

"I'm only going to say this once: I'm not sure Vanderbilt's the best choice for you. I know you're in love with the campus and Nashville and the idea of going to a private school, but you should count the cost. If you don't receive any kind of scholarship, you're going to have six-figure debt the moment you graduate. Which is one thing if you plan on becoming a neurosurgeon, but another thing entirely if you're going into filmmaking. And I am *not* in any way belittling filmmaking. I'm only saying, a profession in the arts is a financial gamble, and I don't want you starting a life saddled with debt and no way to pay it off.

"You could get just as good an education at UK for a fraction of the cost. You'd earn a much better academic scholarship there, and half your tuition is already paid through GSA. I want you to think about it, that's all. And now I've said my piece."

We pull into a metered parking space in front of a boutique cooking store called Whisk & Dish. Mom puts the car in park but doesn't cut the engine. She's riffling through the console compartment for quarters.

"So," I say, "Klaudie can go to Vanderbilt. That's fine, because she's smarter and going be an engineer. But I can't because I want to make movies?"

Mom clicks shut the compartment, two quarters in hand, and gives me a hard look.

"You know that's not what I mean. I'm going into this store, and I will be out in fifteen minutes, and when I come back, *then* you can say whatever is still bothering you. Fair?"

No, I do not think this is fair, but it's not like I have a choice. I'm used to this; it's how my mom has handled conflict since I was a little girl. With her, conflict is all about taking time to cool off and think things through. I'm convinced Mom invented the whole "take a deep breath and count to ten" method. What pisses me off the most is that it usually works.

Today is no exception. By the time Mom returns to the car with two pink paper bags in tow, I don't feel like arguing anymore. I've tilted back the passenger seat, directed all AC vents toward my face, and punched the radio to an oldies station playing "Tainted Love." I know I can't ignore everything Mom's said about money and my foreseeable future. But for now, I'm going to. I've stored away the advice in an airtight compartment, to be reviewed at a later date when I'm not hot and irritated and craving ice cream.

We go to Graeter's next. I order a double scoop of strawberry chip in a bowl and Mom orders an old-fashioned sundae. We sit at a window booth and talk about the renovated Kroger store opening down the street and the premiere of a new summer television show, *13 Saint Street*. We talk about any and everything that isn't the baby or my college education.

It's then I know I'm still upset with my parents about the baby, but I'm too tired to keep acting that way. When we leave Graeter's, Mom slides an arm around my waist, pulling me into a side hug. I don't return it, but I don't shirk out of it either.

When I get back to the house, there's a notification e-mail in my personal inbox informing me that Thomnado007 has posted a new video. I click the accompanying link, but I'm confused. Thom updates his vlog every Monday; today is Wednesday. The video pops up, its title "Public Service Announcement." I punch up the volume and press play.

Thom sits in his usual habitat: a green leather desk chair surrounded by world maps, dinosaur figurines, and a stack of books with titles like *A Brief History of Time*, *Cosmos*, and *Death by Black Hole*. It's clear from his opening sentence, however, that this is not a normal episode of *Beaker Speaker*. I can't believe it at first. I pause the video, drag the tracker back to the start time, punch the volume up some more, and begin it again.

"Hi, guys, Thom here, with some unscheduled programming. Most days, I'm talking science and sci-fi, but today I've got a more general announcement to make. It's something that's really been weighing on me the past few weeks, and I don't think I can sit by as a member of the vlogging community and not say something.

"I know it's easy to exist on the Internet without a face or real name or any identification that makes you personally responsible for what you say. It can lead to online bullying and a lot of unchecked hate that wouldn't be cool in any other outlet. For example, if you absolutely despise some web series you see online, you might tell a few friends, gripe about it in private, and then move on. But some people out there decide to share the hate online, in a public forum. Now, as a fan of science, I'm all for peer review and open discussion, but I think it goes too far when people share the hell out of a post that's only meant to hurt and offend.

"So this is a little note from me to you awesome people: Next time you're about to post a comment or a blog that's entirely negative, think about who's on the receiving end. Most of us are just like you, playing and experimenting and trying to get better at what we love. We're people, and the majority of us don't get paid for what we do. So let's make a concerted effort to dial back the hate, okay? Let's keep this a positive place. That's it. Stepping down from soapbox. Don't forget to tune in this coming Monday for a scintillating discussion of Christopher Nolan, nuclear explosions, and wormholes."

I pause the video on the last frame, at the point where Thom has just finished saying "holes" and is flashing a warm parting smile at

Kathryn Ormsbee

the camera. His brunette hair is overgrown, a single lock encroaching into the right lens of his thick-framed glasses. He's wearing an Iron Man graphic tee.

I told Paul the truth back on that Ping-Pong table: Thom is nice to look at. His face is drawn in pleasing lines, at good proportions. His arms are kind of lanky, but I hold out hope they're good for cuddling. Still, I'm not sure Thom is what people consider "sexy." I can't figure it out from a cursory glance at the vlog comments, the way I can on videos by more popular girl vloggers. People are always making sexual comments there. Things like "10/10, would bang" and "she's so hot." Or "what a fugly hag, who would tap that?"

I don't get it. How can people judge sex appeal as easily as that? By a simple video, one narrow look at a human, people whittle them down to a single quality: fuckability. I know trolls aren't worth my attention. But there are so many of them. So many that I sometimes wonder if that's how *most* people are wired: to assess procreational potential on first glance. It seems so animalistic, so superficial. But it also seems so . . . essential. Such a basic part of everyone around me. Which leads to the inevitable question: Am I *missing* something essential?

I shove that question into yet another one of those airtight compartments in my mental storage, as I've done dozens of times before. Right now, I want to focus not on Thom's appearance but his actions. Because he's done this for *me*. There's no other explanation. Maybe he didn't mention me or *Unhappy Families* by name, but the timing can't be coincidental. Thom has done this because I've been upset, and he could tell.

I grab my phone. I have to let him know I've seen the video and how much I appreciate it. But as I sit staring at a blinking cursor, nothing comes to me. What's a good way of putting it? I don't want to make it awkward. I don't want it to sound like I've assumed he made his PSA for me, even though he obviously did.

First, I text a simple *Thanks.*

Too fawning. Delete.

I saw your video.

Too stalkerish. Delete.

Good day so far?

Boring and oblivious. Delete.

I shut off the screen and try a new method of concentration: staring at the uneven Windex streaks on my bedroom window. I am so deep in thought and the text tone is so unexpected, I let out a squeaky little yelp. Then I look at the text. It's from Thom.

Posted a video today. Stay strong, Tash. I think you're great.

I tug in my lower lip until I feel like a pug dog. Is it possible for your whole body to grin? The answer is yes.

Seventeen

"Vronsky, you've got moon pie on your teeth."

It's the last full-cast filming day, and despite starting on time and maintaining levels of utmost professionalism, we are running behind schedule. I'm beginning to think maybe it was a bad idea to break for lunch. If the cast were starving, they'd be more motivated to finish their scenes. As things stand, everyone is either in a food coma or high on caffeine or, in the case of Tony Davis, covered in chocolate.

"Whoops," says Tony, vigorously brushing his index finger against his teeth. "Sorry. Got it?"

"No, there's still some there, to your left. No, *your* left."

"Gotcha. Good now?"

Serena, who is posed next to Tony on my living room couch, has been watching this entire scene with unreserved horror.

"Tony, that's disgusting." She turns to me and says, "I am not kissing him after that. He should brush his teeth. And wash his hands."

"You're pissed at me in this scene, anyway," says Tony. "It'll play into that."

Serena glares. "I am an excellent actor. I don't need your poor hygiene to help me along."

"You guys, *come on*," I plead from behind the camera. "We're running late. Pull it together."

"Do I really have to wash my hands?" Tony asks.

Serena throws me an "I mean business" look.

"Yes," I tell Tony. "And check the rest of your mouth while you're at it. I don't want us to discover another chocolate-covered tooth in post."

Tony sighs his displeasure, but he leaves for the hall bathroom.

I feel a tap on my back, and turn to see Eva toeing the carpet.

"Um, Tash?" she half-whispers. "I was wondering, since I'm only in one more scene, could we go ahead and film that next? My sister's got a swim meet at two, and I'd like to make it if I can."

I want to say that no, Jack and I have drawn up a shooting schedule for a reason. No, not everyone in this damn cast can get special treatment. And anyway, if Eva needed to attend that swim meet so badly, she should've put it on her conflict calendar back in the spring. But I bite my tongue. Everyone else here may be falling apart, but I need to hold it together. That's what directors do: Call the shots, and hold it together.

"We'll see," I say. "This was supposed to be a quick take, but maybe I can ask Serena and Tony to stay a little later."

Kathryn Ormsbee

"What?" yelps Serena. "No way, Tash. I've got plans with Ben."

I want to say that it is Serena and Tony's own fault for producing a series of mediocre performances these last five takes. I want to say that a convincing climax of *Unhappy Families* is way more important than a date. I bite my tongue so hard I wonder why my mouth hasn't turned into a reservoir of blood.

Hold it together.

"Fine," I say. "Believe me, we're trying to go as fast as we can."

Jack walks in just then from the kitchen, where the rest of the cast are gorging themselves on pizza and Cokes and moon pies.

She looks around. "Where's Tony?"

"Flossing, I hope," says Serena, who is checking her eye makeup in a compact mirror.

I give Jack a sad-dog face. Jack pats my shoulder.

"You want me to take over?" she whispers, just for me to hear.

I shake my head. What kind of question is that? I've directed this entire series to date. I direct, Jack edits; that's the deal. I'm not about to show weakness now. I am the one who holds it together, even on crappy filming days.

"I've been checking the weather," says Jack, "and there's a high chance of thunderstorms in the next couple hours. So if we want those shots in the backyard, we'd better get hopping."

"Okay."

"But . . . we can do my scene before that?" Eva squeaks.

"Okay." My vocal cords have missed the memo to keep it together and are heaving toward screech territory. "I'm doing the best I can here. Where the *hell* is Tony?"

Days like this, I wish I could fast-forward to the time when I'll have made it in the film industry. I wish I had an entire crew on hand to help out. Someone to dress the set and check on makeup. A director of photography to ensure everything is where it ought to be. Most importantly, a production assistant to yell at people like Tony.

But I am not a renowned director, and I don't have a budget to pay for decent lighting, much less a PA. Jack and I handle all the work, and while we do an admirable job of it, thanks to my careful planning and Jack's unshakable composure and Paul's occasional help on set, sometimes I'd like to lock myself in a closet and cry.

Jack must see this desire written all over my face, because she says, "Hey, no pressure on the outside shots. That's what makeup dates are for."

She's right, we did build a makeup date into every month of the schedule with hectic days like this in mind. But we already have lots of footage to make up, thanks to the day Jack and I slept in, and if I have to add yet another filming day to our schedule, I seriously might break down.

"Take ten," I tell the room, shutting off the camera and dismounting from my adjustable stool.

I head straight to my bedroom and close the door. Mom would tell me this is the perfect time to do a mindfulness meditation. Dad might

Kathryn Ormsbee

tell me to shoot up a quick prayer for patience. But I do neither. I sit on the edge of my bed and stare at my poster of Leo.

"It's just a bad day, right?" I ask. "You must've had bad writing days too, huh? Long nights where you ended up swigging a ton of vodka?"

Leo's reply is a scowl.

"I thought so."

The day improves. When I return to the living room, Serena and Tony are waiting and ready to film. They both look chastised, which means Jack must have given them a talking-to in my absence. At last, their delivery finally convinces me that Anna is jealous of Vronsky, while Vronsky is torn between his affection for Anna and the stifled feeling of being locked into a highly publicized relationship. I fit in Eva's scene afterward, and we manage to wrap up the last of the outdoor scenes just as rain begins to spatter on the camera. It would seem Leo has scowled down benevolently upon us.

Only when the cast and the equipment are safely inside do the heavens open up. Thunder crawls closer and closer, until it sounds like someone is wrapping our house in aluminum foil. We gather in the living room, where all the lamps are switched on and it feels like it's midnight and not five o'clock in the afternoon. Jack is lying on the carpet, eyes closed, face reld. Thunderstorms are her favorite thing.

"It's darkness and unpredictable fireworks," she explained to me once. "What's better than that?"

Tony has commandeered our upright piano and is showing off with a minor progression of seconds against thirds. Brooks and Jay sit on the couch, where Brooks is cracking a joke that involves the word "balls." George has claimed the cushiest armchair and is busily tip-tapping away at his phone on business that's far more important than any of us.

Tony abruptly stops a run of arpeggios, cracks his knuckles, and begins to pound out chords that are tantalizingly familiar. It's a song by the Yeah Yeah Yeahs. More than that—it's one of the songs he and Jack covered for their YouTube channel.

I stare dumbfounded at the back of his Mohawk. Is he trying to hurt Jack? Or is this some attempt at restoring normalcy amid the weird tension that's existed between them since February? Whatever the case, it's not comfortable.

I still don't know all the reasons behind Tony and Jack's breakup, but it was pretty ugly. They were always what you'd call a tempestuous couple. In the six months they were dating, they didn't go a single week without fighting. And I don't mean the cutesy "No, *you* hang up first," "No, *you* take the last M&M" fights either. I mean *fights*. *Altercations. Battles.* In hindsight, their entire relationship was a series of battles, so I guess it'd be more accurate to call it a war rather than a relationship. The Six-Month War of Jack and Tony. Their battles were waged with smirks and jabs and cruel winks and, most commonly, earsplitting screams. They could start with something as simple as Jack not wrapping one of Tony's amp cords right and end up with

Jack bellowing that Tony was the most narcissistic musician to come along since Liam Gallagher.

According to Jack, though, fighting requires a ton of passion, and when she and Tony weren't busy expending their passion on fighting, they were using it for more . . . enjoyable activities. Tony was the first guy Jack had sex with. The only guy, as far as I know. When she told me about it, she didn't go into detail, for which I was quietly grateful, and she only brought up the topic one more time, a few weeks later, when she confided in me that she was worried she and Tony did it too much, and that even though they were always safe, the laws of pregnancy probability were less and less in Jack's favor the more they did it. She looked guilty the whole time she talked about it, and I knew it wasn't because Jack felt guilty about the sex but because she was talking to *me* about it. So I told her she was fine, it didn't bother me much, and that even though I was no expert on sex or statistics, I didn't think that was how the laws of probability worked.

Two months later, she and Tony broke up. The only explanation Jack gave was that they were driving each other crazy, and since that alone was obvious and comprehensive, I let it rest. All the details were left to my imagination. I didn't know if Jack or Tony had been the one to call it off, or if it was mutual. During the frosty, awkward period that followed, I asked no questions, did nothing to rock the boat.

But now, here, out of the blue, Tony seems intent on not just rocking the boat but capsizing it altogether. Though maybe he doesn't realize that. Maybe he's totally oblivious. In matters of affection, Tony does have a track record of being dense.

He's still pounding out the melody, but I swear, it's its own kind of silence. The others have picked up on the weird vibe; even George has pocketed his phone and is glancing apprehensively between Tony and Jack.

Then Jay speaks up. "Want some accompaniment?"

I think he meant it to sound lighthearted, just a teensy bit teasing. It comes out kind of scared.

Tony stops playing. "No, it's not in your range, man. Anyway, only Jack can do a mean Karen O impression."

I shoot Tony a look. Is he trying to hurt Jack *and* Jay? Maybe he's got gigantic blinders when it comes to Jay's crush on him, but what he's said is super rude, crush or no crush. I'd like to inform him that Jay is a crazy talented singer and he had to choose between music and drama when he was accepted into Governor's School for the Arts, because he'd participated in a rare double audition and both departments clawed each other to get at him.

Tony's too quick for me. He swivels toward Brooks and asks, "You're still cool with driving, yeah?"

Brooks's eyebrows bounce sky-high. "To Nashville, you mean?" He's looking at me of all people, as though I can grant him confirmation that it's not wrong for him to have this conversation with Tony after what's just gone down. "Yeah, of course. It's still seven of us, right? 'Cause I can't do more. It's a big SUV, but there's a legal limit, and considering most of you are, like, underage, I think they'd lock me up for decades."

"You talk like you're planning on getting pulled over," says Jay, who has recovered from Tony's lack of decency with infinite grace.

Brooks shrugs. "I speed. It happens."

I'm grateful my parents are not in the room to hear this conversation. They aren't too happy about me heading to Nashville with a carload of other young people, most of them males, for a big, bad alternative concert—especially when I casually mentioned we planned on driving back straight afterward, in the dead of night, to save on hotel fare. I finally managed to set their minds at ease by telling them Brooks was driving, and he was a mature and responsible college student with an extremely safe SUV.

"He's basically Mister Rogers," I told them. "Mister Rogers driving an armored tank down I-65. Nothing bad will happen."

Good thing I didn't mention our Mister Rogers has a need for speed.

I might be more interested in the current conversation if I weren't trying to assess Jack's emotional state. Her eyes have remained shut this whole time, and she is motionless. I have this theory that Jack moves less than most humans. Not in a slothful way. It's just, once she hunkers into a position, she keeps it. No fidgeting. No adjusting. She simply exists in that allotted space. And that makes it so hard to figure out how she's feeling. I can't tell if she's upset or livid or not even bothered at all.

Meantime, I feel more jittery than usual, and it's not until later, after the rain has let up and everyone's left the house, that I realize why. Back in early spring, when we bought tickets for the Chvrches concert and planned our mini road trip to Nashville, I was daydreaming about Vandy. Back then, I thought the trip would be a great second look at the campus. (I've already visited once, with Klaudie my sophomore year.) I thought our trip to Nashville would be a preview of my life to come.

Now I'm wondering where I found all that boundless, stupid optimism. Klaudie's right: I'm not smart enough to cut it at Vanderbilt. My grades are more high Bs than As, and my standardized test scores are only slightly above average. Mom's right too: It's a gamble, paying full price for a private education to earn a degree I might never be able to pay off. UK would be way cheaper, almost free. And that's an opportunity not everyone gets. Just like Klaudie has an opportunity I can't get.

I want to leave Lexington, but maybe that feeling is more about finding my own space to breathe. About leaving my house more than my city. I could live in a dorm with Jack. I could start fresh there. On all fronts, that looks like the best decision. It's the *smart* decision, and I guess making it means I'm a responsible adult. Still, I can't help mourning the dream of life on a picture-perfect campus. I can't help that our upcoming trip to Nashville makes me more glum than excited.

Later, I'm in the living room watching *Mrs. Doubtfire* with Mom and Dad when Klaudie gets in from another night out with Ally and Jenna.

Dad says, "Hey, sweetie, want to join?"

Even though we all know she won't, and she doesn't. She says nothing, and we say nothing back. I watch her stride down the hallway at a cool, measured pace. She doesn't know how lucky she is. She doesn't know the damage she's causing. My anger toward her runs through me like boiling blood, and I don't think that's something even a dozen loving-kindness meditations or chats with Leo can completely purge from my system.

Eighteen

Jack doesn't want to talk about Tony. I know because she slipped out with the rest of the cast the moment the rain let up, and when I gave her a look that asked *You okay?* she replied with a smile. Something's wrong when Jack smiles like that. But if she doesn't want to talk, I'm not going to push. Jack doesn't react well to pushing.

Sunday's filming passes without incident, and in the end we only have to schedule one makeup shot for Monday—a scene between Brooks and George. Both being the consummate professionals they are, they arrive on time, give a perfect performance on the first take, and are out of the Harlows' house by noon. Afterward, Jack tells me she has a load of laundry to take care of but that I should head down to the basement, where Paul's been hiding away, and she'll be down shortly.

When I get to the entertainment room, I hear the sound of a Ping-Pong ball tapping between solid surfaces, which is odd, because last I heard the Harlows still hadn't gotten the table repaired. I creep down the hallway to the game room and peer inside. The splintered Ping-

Pong table has been folded and moved to one side of the room. At the opposite side, Paul is playing what can best be described as Ping-Pong racquetball. He drops the ball to the linoleum floor and hits it on its way up, causing the ball to bounce off the wall and back to his paddle. I watch in silence from the doorway as he makes it to eleven hits in a row. On the twelfth, the ball ricochets off the wall with such force that Paul misses, and it heads straight for me.

It takes me a jolting, pained moment to realize what's just happened. I stare at the blue and white ball at my feet, then raise a hand to my right eye.

"Ow," I say. It's an afterthought more than a reaction.

"Holy shit! Tash, you freakin' scared me."

Paul jogs across the room to where I stand, still stunned.

"You okay?" he asks, peering at my eye.

"It's just a Ping-Pong ball," I say, dismissive.

I snatch the ball off the floor and lob it at him. He takes it on the chest with a relieved smile.

"Is this what you've been doing all morning?" I ask.

"Eh. I watched the last half of *Alien vs. Predator*. Played some *Bloodborne*. Ate a box of Cheez-Its."

"Busy man."

"You know it. Are you guys through? I didn't hear any screaming up there, so that's a good sign, right?"

I grimace. "Definitely better than last time."

"Cool." Paul sits down in the middle of the room and looks to me, expectant.

I join him and say, "Is there a reason we're choosing tile over the cushy couch in the other room?"

"I like sitting here. Lots of space and no windows—it's a good place for thinking."

It does seem like a good place for thinking. Or a good place to drive yourself crazy.

"I'm taking astronomy this semester at BCTC," Paul says, leaning back on his elbows, then sinking into an all-out flop. I swear, Paul's default position is horizontal.

I remain sitting and tap my hands on Paul's shins as though they are a drum set.

"Astronomy's cool," I say. "Is that for a science credit?"

"Yeah, it seemed like the easiest option. No way I'm taking chemistry or biology again."

"You'll have to pass along all your wisdom," I say. "Tell me how great the odds are we'll get wiped off the face of the universe by meteors in the coming decades."

Paul nods dutifully. "It sucks I can't take any design classes yet. I talked to admissions again, and they say I can transfer to UK my sophomore year, no problem, if my grades are good. So I guess I'll take the easiest classes possible this year and get into the good stuff later."

I release a peppery sigh and ask, "Do you ever wonder when that stops?"

"When what stops?"

"Doing gross crap so you can get to the good stuff later. When do we finally get to the good stuff?"

"Ew, Tash. Don't be all cynical like that. You sound like Jack."

Paul closes his eyes, and in that moment he looks so much like Jack it derails my train of thought. A lot of people assume Jack and Paul are twins or comment on how much they look alike. Personally, I don't see it. Except when Paul's eyes are closed.

When he speaks again, it takes a moment for me to remember what my question was. "I think we've got some of the good stuff now. It gets sprinkled into the rest of your life, same as the gross crap. The whole yin-yang idea. Isn't that Buddhist? You believe that, don't you?"

"More like Chinese philosophy," I say. "But . . . yeah, maybe I believe it."

"You're not experiencing that much gross crap, are you?"

"No. I'm really not." I think about today's filming and how much I wish I could be living in L.A. already with a dozen accolades under my belt. "I didn't phrase it right. I guess I mean I always feel like I'm . . . waiting. Waiting until I get older so people will finally take me seriously and I can do what I want."

"It's kind of messed up, isn't it? We just want to be older, and people our parents' age complain about how they wish they were young again. It's depressing."

"It's *dukkha*," I say, shrugging. "I know I'm not supposed to fight it, but sometimes I really, really want to."

"Then let's do this," says Paul. "You tell me all the reasons it's good for me to be nineteen—"

"Almost twenty," I interrupt.

"And I'll tell you all the reasons it's good for you to be seventeen."

"Almost eighteen."

I can't help it. These are important distinctions to make.

"I'll start," says Paul. "First, you don't have to pay for your own health insurance."

Without missing a beat, I say, "You can lie down on a cold, hard floor and not complain about your arthritic joints aching."

"You have access to millions of songs, all at the mere brush of your fingertips."

I frown. "That's more like a modern-day perk, not an age perk. Eighty-year-olds have millions of songs at their fingertips too."

"Yeah, but how many of them actually know how to access them?"

"I bet there are plenty of technologically savvy eighty-year-olds."

Our little game has quickly tanked, but it's put me in the mood for music. I tug my phone from my jeans pocket and start Chvrches' most recent album. Paul groans.

"Uuugh, it's bad enough I'm going to the concert. Why're you torturing me like this?"

"I am going to convert you, Paul Harlow. You will like them."

"It's not that I *hate* them. They're just not my style."

"Mmm-hmm, your style is mopey British bands. And, like, 'Carry On My Wayward Son.'"

"I like what I like," he says buoyantly. "Anyway, as I said, they're not my style, but I can appreciate the talent. Also, the lead singer—what's her name? I'm a little in love with her."

I give Paul a look like he's an asshole. "How can you be in love with her when you don't even know her name?"

He gives me a look like I'm a hypocrite. "How can *you* be in love with someone you've never spoken to?"

I stop drumming Paul's shins in time with the music. I stop touching him altogether.

"What?" he says. "What's the difference?"

"There's a huge difference. Thom and I have had tons of conversations. Maybe they haven't been conventional, but welcome to the twenty-first century. And I never said I was *in love* with him."

"Okay, fine. But obviously you care a lot, because you're red in the face."

I *am* red in the face, but I can't help it, and I am so pissed at Paul for pointing it out, which makes me go even redder. I scoot back and lie down a good yard from him, my arms crossed tight against my chest.

"Tash, *what*?" Paul props himself up and tries to get a good look at my face, but I keep shifting around, not letting him. "I was just pointing out what I *liked* about the band. They're talented. I have a crush on the lead singer. Those are good things."

"Yeah, okay."

Paul slides to his back, and the only sound is the music—a melody of synths and poppy electronic pattering.

"She's not just a singer," I say. "Did you know she has a degree in journalism? Did you know she can play drums and keyboard, too?"

Paul is quiet awhile before he says, "All the more reason to crush on her."

I know he says this thinking it will make me happier. But it doesn't. His words pick up the fleshy mound of my chest and wring it tight, like a washrag, draining away all the vital fluids. Why am I *sad*? I can't place it. Paul has always been open about girls he likes. He told me and Jack every little detail about his relationship with Stephanie Crewe, up until the day he broke up with her, which, from what I gather, is pretty rare for a high school guy to do.

So I'm used to this. I'm used to Paul talking about girls. And not for the first time, I reflect that Paul has probably never, ever considered me in that way. Because if he did, he wouldn't feel like he could talk about his love life so openly when I'm around. Couldn't tell me the exact same things he tells his sister. And after my poolside confession last year, how could he *ever* think of me that way? What normal guy would crush on me after I said I flat out didn't want sex?

I shouldn't have unreasonable expectations; I know I shouldn't. But this weird sadness of mine grabs hold of my until-now-dormant fear of meeting Thom next month, and basically my emotions are little better than a pot of melted Jell-O.

Kathryn Ormsbee

"What's going on here?"

I tilt my head back to see an upside-down Jack standing in the doorway. She's changed into a pair of long fleece pajama pants and an Edward Scissorhands graphic tee.

I think, *I am leaking out all over this linoleum.*

I say, "I'm forcing Paul to like Chvrches."

"Cool," she says, joining us on the floor.

After a chorus's worth of no talking, I nudge Jack and ask, "Did you watch that video I sent you?"

Her only reply is a snot-filled snort.

"What?" I say. "Don't you think it was sweet of him? He clearly made it for me. For us, I mean."

"Sorry, who are we talking about?" asks Paul.

"T*h*ooom." Jack huffs the *h* and draws out the *o* in precisely the same way Paul has done before. Which either means they have sibling telepathy, or—the far more likely option—Paul and Jack have talked about Thom behind my back. My mood goes from sad to irritable.

"It was super nice of him," I say, glaring over at her.

"It was super *condescending* of him. Like he is some great Authority come down to help us downtrodden novice filmmakers."

"That's not how he meant it."

"You know we have more followers than him now, right?" says Jack. "We don't need him defending our honor. Anyway, what good does he think that video is going to do? He's preaching to the choir. Everyone knows there are trolls on the Internet. Haters will hate, no matter how many PSAs he puts up."

I say nothing. I'm making a careful study of a canvas print on the wall that reads, BIG BLUE NATION.

"What?" says Jack. "Paul, stop looking at me like that. I'm allowed to say whatever s*hit* about T*hom* I want. And I say he's making a power play to convince us he's in a position of benevolent privilege, and it's weird. So sue me. Tash. *Tash.* Don't give me the silent treatment."

I shrug off Jack's tap on my shoulder. "Fine. Everyone hates Thom, I get it."

"I didn't say I hated him. I've never even met the dude. And, may I remind you, neither have you."

"Yeah, well, I'm going to," I bite back. "Soon."

"Uh-huh, okay." Things get quiet again, save for the electronic clatter coming from my phone. Then Jack abruptly gets to her feet and says, "Hang on a sec."

She's gone for a couple minutes. When she returns, she's got two flashlights in one hand and a laser pointer in the other. She flicks off the game room's light switch with her elbow and pushes the door shut with her foot, casting us in complete darkness. Then there's a sudden wash of light, and I shield my eyes.

"Ow! Jack, what're you doing?"

"You get a flashlight," she says, and I feel the weight of a small, solid object on my stomach. "Paul gets a flashlight. I get the laser pointer. If you

Kathryn Ormsbee

insist on assuming the stargazing position while listening to this music, we are gonna make the most of it. We're gonna do an effing light show."

I open my eyes and grab the flashlight. My irritation from earlier is forgotten—which I guess is Jack's master plan.

"Ha!" Paul cries, switching on his flashlight and creating a dizzying circular pattern on the ceiling.

I try a strobe-light effect, pulsing the light on and off with the music's driving rhythm. Jack, meantime, shoves me closer to Paul before lying back down beside me. I try to figure out what shapes she's envisioning as she drags the red laser across the ceiling in precise strokes. A skull, maybe. A pyramid. Her full name.

I start making a *bloop-bloop-bloop* sound, imitating one of the electronic layers. Paul cracks up and adds his own more convoluted and therefore more amusing imitation. It sounds something like *peoooow, scrsh, scrsh, bow!* Jack comes in with a sensual *unst-unst.*

For a minute, it's this chaotic swirl of music and sound and lights. It's all so stupid and absurd and wonderful. Then the songs ends, and we've reached our limit. We explode into laughter. Even Jack is cackling, totally uninhibited. I love it when Jack laughs like that.

The next song starts up, and we keep up our light show, though we all silently agree not to continue the vocal accompaniment. It's a slow song, and I use my flashlight beam to paint long, ephemeral strokes across the ceiling. The room grows warm and sleepy, and when a peppier song follows the slow number, I don't feel the energy to pick up my light show game. Paul yawns loudly. Jack has calmed her laser work to a predictable series of figure eights.

I keep my flashlight on and pointed upward but nuzzle my face into Jack's shoulder. My body has decreed that I shall nap, and nothing will stand in my way. With my eyes closed, I listen as Jack's breathing grows slower, fuller. We're all going into hibernation, it seems, and I get this odd picture in my head of us as sleepy bear cubs snuggled in a den. It's so ludicrous that a laugh trickles out of me. I feel a hot, slight pressure on my arm. The arm nearest Paul. He's resting his knuckles against my elbow, and I like it. I like the warmth and the sensation of safety that comes along with it.

I turn and peek open an eye and find Paul peeking back at me. I creep my hand over to his—the one resting on my elbow, and I fit my fingers into his in the usual way.

"Hi," I say.

"Hey." Then, "You know I think you're the best, right? Way better than the lead singer of Chvrches."

I laugh, but Paul doesn't. He squeezes my hand. I squeeze his back.

"I think you're better than the band Kansas," I whisper. "Like, the *entire* band."

I expect Paul to laugh at that at least, but he doesn't. The muscles around his mouth get tight. He looks the same as when he plays video games—the war-mural, ancient-statue Paul. And I get that feeling in my throat—carbonation indigestion.

230   Kathryn Ormsbee

"Don't frown at me," I say, because his face needs to stop looking that way.

"Am I frowning?"

"Yes. It makes you look bad." Which is a super impressive lie.

Paul's face transforms into an exaggerated, toothy smile. I snort and make a swipe at his nose with my free hand.

"God, Zelenka, what do you want from me?"

The smile is gone, and Paul sounds so genuinely mournful that I inch in closer and tuck my head under his chin and say, "Nothing. You're good like this."

He doesn't answer. He squeezes my hand again, just once. The feeling in my throat subsides, and I feel safe and okay again.

That's what I'm concentrating on when I fall asleep.

Nineteen

My phone wakes me.

It's a ringtone I haven't heard in a while: "Let's Get Together" from the old sixties version of *The Parent Trap*. Klaudie and I programmed the song into each other's phones back when we first got them in middle school. Or at least, I was in middle school. Klaudie was already a freshman at Calhoun, and she was so pissed that we got our phones at the same time—me a whole year earlier than her.

After Klaudie's anger wore off, we decided we needed matching ring-tones, just for each other, so we'd always know when the other was calling. *The Parent Trap* was our favorite movie when we were little, so the choice was a no-brainer.

I answer the call just as Hayley Mills is singing *"We can have a swingin' ti-ime."*

"Klaudie," I heave out groggily. *"What?"*

The game room is, as before, cast in windowless darkness. It could be later afternoon or past midnight—there's no way of knowing. All I'm really certain of is the crick in my back.

"Tash? Thank God. I thought I was going to have to call Mom and Dad. Tash, you have to come get me."

I sit up straight, rubbing at my eyes and kicking my brain into operative mode. Beside me, Jack stirs. Paul is snoring softly; he's always been a heavy sleeper.

"Come *where* and get you?" I say in a bad attempt at a whisper.

"Um. *Um.*" Klaudie's crying, I realize. "It's . . . the Dairy Queen near the mall. The Lansdowne shopping center? By the post office."

"Okay. Okay, I can be there in, like, twenty minutes."

Klaudie sniffs. "Can't you come sooner?"

"No, because I'm at the Harlows', and I have to walk back home to get the car, and that Dairy Queen is fifteen minutes away from our house, anyway. So just calm down, I'm coming as fast as I can."

I now have a very strong suspicion that Klaudie is drunk, in which case telling her to calm down probably won't help, but I don't know what else to say. I've never dealt with a drunk person. I never imagined I would have to deal with a drunk *Klaudie*, of all people.

When I hang up, Jack is quick to speak.

"Was she in an accident? What's wrong?"

"I don't know, she just said she needs me to pick her up."

"Want me to come with?"

Something about Jack's offer, so immediate, like a reflex, draws tears from my eyes. Yes, I do want her to come. I want someone else with me as I deal with this potentially scarring mission. I want someone to sit in the passenger seat and tell me Klaudie is fine and that I'm perfectly justified in being simultaneously worried about and angry with her. But then I think about what Klaudie would want. What would I want if I were Klaudie? Obviously she's in a desperate place if she's calling me and not Ally or Jenna. And would I want one of Klaudie's friends seeing me desperate and crying and probably drunk?

"No," I say. "It should just be me."

"I could at least walk you home. It's pretty late."

I check my phone. It's almost two o'clock in the morning.

"Damn," I say.

Because I realize that not only has Klaudie yet again broken curfew, I technically have too. Sure enough, there's one missed text from Mom on my phone: *Where could Tasha be?*

I type back, *Sorry!! At Harlows, fell asleep early. Will be back in the morning.*

Paul hasn't stirred. Jack looks at him, then me, shaking her head.

"He'd be the first one dead in a zombie attack." She doesn't even try to whisper.

I know she's trying to cheer me up, so I throw back a halfhearted laugh. When I get to my feet, Jack grabs my wrist. It's so dark, I can barely make out the edges of her face, but I feel the concern on her.

Kathryn Ormsbee

"Hey," she says. "It'll be okay."

I nod rapidly. Jack can't see the tears on my face, but I know she can feel them the same way I can her concern.

Paul's still sound asleep when I leave the room.

I run down the sidewalk, slow to a brisk walk, then speed to a run again. I don't have my own car yet, but I borrow Klaudie's sometimes, and I have a spare key. Halfway home, I have the panicked thought that Klaudie drove herself tonight and that her car's abandoned in a ditch somewhere. But then my house comes into view, and I see Klaudie's white Honda Accord parked in front of the house, per usual.

When I open the door, I'm hit with a pungent wave of perfume. I don't know the physics behind it, but Klaudie has mastered the art of making her car smell like a Juicy Couture store. I gag, and then breathe through my mouth as I turn on the engine and crank the AC to full blast. It's a hot, sticky night, and the cold air helps thin out the sugary fumes. The radio turns on, blaring a dubstep remix. The beat has just dropped, and the whole car thrums with the bass line before I can turn down the volume.

I don't cut off the song entirely. I need something to distract me from my anxious thoughts. The streets are deserted, and I hit three green lights in a row. When I gave Klaudie my ETA, I wasn't taking into account the fact that there'd be no traffic. I'm only going a little over the speed limit, but I can already tell I'll make it to her in half the usual time. Good.

I pull into the empty parking lot of the Dairy Queen, and for a moment I freak out, because all the lights are off, and there's no sign of Klaudie. No Klaudie by the door, no Klaudie on the patio. It's only when I get out and round the building that I see her sitting on the curb, just past the drive-thru window.

She turns her head at the sound of my approach, and moonlight illuminates her tearstained face.

"So . . . ," I begin.

"Don't say anything," she says. "Just drive."

We get in the car, but I don't turn the key yet. I'm staring at Klaudie in the fuzzy blue darkness, trying to figure out if she's really drunk, or if she's high, or if she needs medical attention. Her pupils are pretty dilated, but then, it's dark, so I guess mine are too. Her movements don't seem *that* uncoordinated. But maybe Klaudie's not that kind of drunk. Maybe she's the quiet and surprisingly coordinated kind.

"Stop trying to look at my eyes," Klaudie says, covering her face. "I'm not stoned."

I reach over the console and fumble around the floorboard of the backseat until I grab hold of what I'm searching for: a water bottle. It's half-empty and lukewarm, but it's something. I unscrew the cap and hand it over to Klaudie.

"Drink," I command.

I expect her to resist, but she doesn't. She chugs all of it in one go. She releases the bottle from her mouth with a noise that's half hiccup,

Kathryn Ormsbee

half cry. It's an embarrassing noise that makes me turn on the engine in hopes that the radio will make things less awkward.

I pull out of the parking lot and get back on the street, but I don't turn where I should to get us home. Maybe Klaudie notices, or maybe she's too intoxicated to care. Whatever the case, she doesn't say anything, just props her sneakers on the glove compartment and rests her head on the passenger window. We're passing through a nice neighborhood of ranch homes from the fifties. I like driving this route. On this quiet night, driving down these uniform, symmetrical streets, I can almost imagine I live in a world where there's no war or embezzling or ignorant Facebook posts. No online haters, no silverspunnx23. No Internet whatsoever.

"I don't have to tell you anything," Klaudie says.

Which is totally uncalled for, because I'm not trying to extract information from her, even on the sly. I was perfectly content to drive in silence. But now I feel like I have to defend myself, so I say, "I didn't have to pick you up."

Klaudie starts crying again. Loudly. I slow to a stop at a red light, even though we're the only car at the intersection. I wonder, would I really be breaking the law if I ran it? If a tree falls in an empty forest, does anyone hear it? The light changes before I can contemplate these and deeper mysteries of the universe. I drive on. Klaudie keeps crying.

She finally says, "I had a fight with J-Jenna and Ally. I told Jenna she was t-t-too drunk to drive, and she wouldn't listen, and so I made her pull over and drop me off. O-only I didn't think she was going to actually *do* it. I thought she'd pull over and we'd just wait it out. But she didn't, she's such a *bitch*. They b-both are."

I use the ensuing silence to debate whether Klaudie will remember any of this in the morning, and if it's even worth engaging in this conversation. Klaudie reads my mind.

"I'm not *that* drunk," she says, rolling down her window.

"Ugh, Klaudie, stop. It's so humid out there."

She hangs her head out the window. I wonder if she's going to puke, but after a half minute, she pulls herself back in and rolls the window up.

I feel bad about my last comment, so I say, "You did the right thing, at least. Friends don't let friends drive drunk, or whatever."

Klaudie coughs out a hard, brief laugh. "Yeah, that's me. Being good even when I'm bad."

I laugh too, because Klaudie has voiced exactly what I've been thinking: Even when she's trying to go delinquent, it seems she can't help but sabotage herself with responsibility.

We're silent for a second, and then she says, "Stop."

"Stop what?"

"Psychoanalyzing me."

"I'm not saying anything."

"You're thinking."

"God, excuse me for thinking."

"You don't know what's going on with me."

"Okay, *fine*."

"I'm not trying to, like, see what it's like to be bad for once. That's not what this is."

"Okay."

Silence.

"You're still doing it."

I slam on the brakes. We're at another intersection, and our light is green, but I shift the car into park. It doesn't matter. No one's here but us.

"Get over yourself," I say, my voice quick and tight. "I'm allowed to analyze you in my head. God knows it's what we've all been trying to do this whole summer."

"What are you talking about?"

"C'mon, Klaudie. Skipping dinners and treating Mom and Dad like shit—"

"I haven't—"

"Yeah, you *have*. Look, I get it's your last summer. I get you're trying to carpe diem or whatever the hell. But you screwed over all of us in the process."

"Oh my God, see? See, that's *it*. That's why I can't *do* this anymore. Anything out of line with you guys makes me a freakin' *disappointment*."

"I didn't say I was—"

"Forget it. You're missing the point."

"So *tell* me the point."

Klaudie shakes her head. "You don't know what it's like. You get a free pass. You get to mess around with your movies. I'm the oldest, so I have to keep my shit together."

I'm silent for a second, processing. "But . . . you *like* keeping your shit together."

"Okay, yeah, most of the time. But sometimes I can't. Sometimes it's not enough. And Mom and Dad—"

"What? They never say—"

"They don't have to!" Klaudie shouts over me. "They don't have to say it in so many words. It's just the way it *is*."

Klaudie drops her forehead onto her bent knees. Above us, the traffic lights go through another cycle: green, yellow, red. I want to be angry at Klaudie, but I'm not. I guess I'm too stunned.

She turns in her seat and says, "You know what Dad did, when I told him I wanted to study engineering? He *cried*, Tash. He freakin' cried. And he said Gramps would be so proud of me, and I was going to carry on the Zelenka legacy."

"What's . . . wrong with that?"

"It's the *pressure*!" Klaudie shrieks. "Who wants that kind of pressure?"

"He didn't mean—"

"No, of course he didn't. But it's there. It's *there*. And it's going to be there, even when I'm away at Vanderbilt. The Zelenka name is on my

Kathryn Ormsbee

shoulders. That's what will be in the back of my mind every time I take a test or give a presentation. Like, did Gramps and Nana come all the way from behind the Iron Curtain just for me to fuck up a thermodynamics final."

"Klaudie, that's messed up. No one wants you to think like that."

"But—"

"No," I cut in. "No, you know what? Sometimes you don't realize how lucky you are. You're complaining about going to this great, expensive school that I can't even get into."

I don't know what I want Klaudie to do—if I want her to lash out or fight back. She does neither. In a whisper, she says, "I know. I'm sorry. I shouldn't have said that to you."

But I don't need that apology. It's taken me weeks to get a grip on Vanderbilt, but I think I finally have. I shrug, surprised by my composure. "I read this article that followed graduates from public schools and prestigious private universities, and twenty years down the road they end up with the same jobs and salaries. So it doesn't really matter where I go."

"I thought you were trying to make *me* feel better." Klaudie sniffs, and somehow it turns into a little laugh.

For the first time since she got in the car, the silence that falls between us isn't tense. It's just silence. I think about shifting gears and driving on, but I'm scared that will break this quiet, strangely comfortable moment.

"Do you ever . . . ," Klaudie begins. She shakes her head and rubs her wrist beneath her nose. "Do you wonder if Mom and Dad would be different if their families were around?"

"What?"

"Gramps and Nana were all Dad had. And Mom's, like, thousands of miles away from her family. I know at first I was saying Mom was having this kid because she thought we weren't good enough. I knew that was stupid, but . . . it kind of felt like it. But now I've been thinking, maybe this kid is just them trying to expand the family. Give themselves what they don't have enough of, you know?"

"Well," I say, "it was an accident, so I don't think there really *is* a reason."

Klaudie tips her head toward me. "No. Maybe not."

It's in the air. I know: We've reached an open place. A moment where we can peel back our skin and expose all the poorly threaded veins and bad blood beneath. It's a place only Klaudie and I can go, because we're sisters, and we know each other this well.

So at last, I voice my own doubt.

"Do you think they're being stupid to have the baby?"

"I don't know." Klaudie's tracing an unknowable pattern on the window with her pinkie finger. "But I don't blame them."

Somehow, this makes sense to me. Even though Klaudie clearly *does* blame my parents—and I do too—we don't blame them *in that way*. Not in a moral way. Morally, I think we understand. The way we blame

Kathryn Ormsbee

our parents is personal. A daughter-to-mother, daughter-to-father way. We might feel it to different degrees, but the question is the same: Why change everything forever, when everything was just fine?

The intersection blinks through yet another cycle, turning our light green. I shift the car into drive. I'm driving with purpose now, though still not toward home. Klaudie doesn't ask questions. If she doesn't know what I'm doing at first, she does when I pull into the lot of a twenty-four-hour Kroger and say, "Let's buy flowers."

We buy a bouquet of sunflowers and a bouquet labeled "Summer Celebration"—a collection of daisies, orange roses, and button mums. In the self-checkout lane, we both grab a bottled Coke from the display fridge. Then we load back into the car, and I drive us to Evergreen Memorial Gardens. The cemetery is older, on the outskirts of town, backing up to horse farm territory. The gates are shut, but the wrought iron fence is low and relatively easy to climb. I go first, and Klaudie hands the flowers and sodas through the bars before following me. I use my phone flashlight to guide us.

I've never found graveyards scary in the way most people do. I don't believe in ghosts or hauntings, just life after life. But it's more than that, I think. I was young when my grandparents died, and I got so accustomed to visiting their graves that the cemetery was never a spooky unknown to me. It was a routine part of life, the same as my annual checkup at the doctor's or a visit to the hairdresser. And how could I believe that anything evil was buried here, in the company of Gramps and Nana Zelenka?

We visited here a lot after the accident, all together as a family. We brought bouquets for Nana and drank sodas for Gramps, because his favorite thing to do when we visited their house was sit on the porch drinking Coke. And then, around high school, we stopped coming so often, until we only made an annual visit every October. But whenever we came, I felt good. I felt safe, not sad.

A grave is just a grave, and I don't think Gramps and Nana are sentient ghosts who know we're paying them a visit. But the memories I have of them—Nana's goulash and early morning games of rummy and Gramps laughing harder than we did at cartoons on television— those are still alive, and they grow much brighter when I'm at Evergreen Memorial.

I thought I knew the path to the graves better than I do, because we get turned around twice before Klaudie points ahead and says, "No, no. It's this way. It's just there."

She's right. We come to a stop at the large, rounded cut of limestone that reads:

Dominic Jan Zelenka
February 7, 1942–October 2, 2008
Irma Marie Zelenka
September 23, 1945–October 2, 2008
Beloved parents and grandparents
You were loved.

Kathryn Ormsbee

"Hey, you two," I whisper, crouching at the grave. I scoop up a collection of wilted roses, then pull back the plastic from my sunflower bouquet and set it in the old bouquet's place.

Klaudie settles into a cross-legged sit beside me. She tears away the plastic from her own bouquet and rests it beside mine. Then we sit there, and I hear the faint, stuttering sound of Klaudie crying.

I don't feel sad, but I'm thoughtful. I'm thinking of what Klaudie said, about Mom and Dad trying to make more family for themselves. The pregnancy was an accident, but what this kid is? What this kid is going to be? Maybe there's a reason in that. Maybe our family—some of us dead and some of us halfway across the world and some of us readying to leave town—maybe we do need an addition. This baby is going to turn everything upside down, no doubt. But maybe, in a weird way, we will be more stable, too.

Klaudie's mind must be wandering the same wood as mine, because she says, "Nana would love the news. She'd call it *splendifying*."

A gust of damp wind whips through the cemetery, blowing back our hair. I stare, mesmerized, at Klaudie's moon-kissed face. She looks so dark and severe. She looks like a witch. Not the ugly, wart-covered kind. She is sleek and young and beautiful and misunderstood—a witch of Salem. Not that I would ever tell her that; Klaudie wouldn't understand. Still, I can't help but feel that if one tried to cast a spell over this graveyard, it would work.

My eyes grow sore from staring so long at Klaudie. I scoot closer and lean my head on her shoulder. We sit. We drink our Cokes. We stay there through sunrise. Though my eyelids are prickled and sticky from lack of sleep, they lift as far as possible to let in the pink sherbet light of dawn, thrown in sharp relief by a border of gravestones and cypress trees and a solitary mausoleum.

Kathryn Ormsbee

Twenty

It's the morning of our Nashville road trip. We've all gathered around Brooks's Ford Explorer outside my house. We're waiting on Tony. He's twenty minutes late.

"I say we leave without him," says Serena, who's been on the outs with Tony ever since the moon pie incident. "If he can't respect the schedule, we don't need to respect him."

I shake my head. "He's the one who suggested the concert in the first place. I say we give him ten more minutes."

"Has anyone gotten ahold of him? Do we even know if he's awake?" Brooks is sitting sideways in the driver's seat, legs hanging out the open door. He's smoking a cigarette, and I'm really hoping neither of my parents is watching us from the house. The whole smoking thing doesn't really jibe with the Mister Rogers story I fed them.

"I texted him," mutters Jack. "He's coming."

I shoot her a look of mild surprise, but it slides off her, unheeded. I've given up trying to talk with Jack about Tony. That entire situation is a lost cause, suitable only for the likes of St. Jude and high-risk gamblers.

Paul pokes my arm and leans in to whisper, "The hell's going on there?"

I raise my shoulders to my ears, conveying my own woeful lack of information. Then I smirk at his T-shirt. It's black, the words *Pure Heroine* written across the front in silver lettering.

"What," he says. "What're you shaking your head for?"

"How can you like Lorde and not Chvrches?"

Paul nods eagerly, like I've just asked him to define a vocab word he reviewed this morning. "Easy. I only like mainstream."

"Chvrches have gotten pretty mainstream," I argue.

"Nope. Mainstream means your *parents* recognize them."

"Is that according to Webster's?"

Paul's answer gets lost in the roar of a motorbike. Tony's motorbike. He grinds it to a stop just behind the Explorer, and as he takes off his helmet, I swear I hear Jack whisper "fucker" under her breath.

"Hey!" cries Tony, swaggering—and I do mean *swaggering*—toward us with an easy smile and open arms, as though he is the Messiah à la *Godspell*. I'm dead certain he's about to burst into "Day by Day."

I really need to stop hanging around so many theatre kids.

"Where've you been, asshat?" says Brooks. "Burning daylight."

"I'm not that late," Tony replies, all smiles.

Serena looks ready to punch him in the gonads.

"We're all here," I say. "We should load up."

Kathryn Ormsbee

Everyone is more than willing to do just that. Brooks turns himself right-side in the driver's seat, and Serena calls shotgun. Jack, Paul, and I claim the middle row, which leaves the back two seats to Tony and Jay. It wasn't intentional, but as soon as I realize the setup, I watch attentively as they climb into the back. Jay has been quiet ever since he arrived at the house, but I chalked it up to him not being a morning person. His expression now isn't tired so much as . . . uncomfortable. Maybe even a little pissed. He claims the seat nearest the window, plugs in his earbuds, closes his eyes, and drifts into a sonic world that is, for all intents and purposes, five thousand miles away from this SUV. Tony looks uncomfortable too, and I know I'm not making this up in my head, because Paul says, "You okay there, dude? Do you get carsick or something?"

"Huh? Oh. No, no, I'm cool." The discomfort lifts off his face as easily as a paper mask. He's the bohemian Messiah once more.

I don't know why it's so hard to stay mad at Tony. I want to be angry, not because he was late, but because he didn't apologize for being late, like any civilized human being would. But then Tony grins straight at me, a grin that says, *Remember when?* and *Isn't life grand?* Times like this, I can see what Jack saw in him. I can also see why it was always hot and cold between them.

Brooks wasn't kidding: He *speeds.* Once we're on the Bluegrass Parkway, he keeps us at a steady ninety miles per hour.

"You guys are my lookout," he tells us. "When we come to overpasses or those wooded medians, especially. If I get pulled over with twelve other eyes watching my back, then I *deserve* to get a ticket."

Tony's reply is just, "Nash Vegas, baby!"

Jack whips out her unicorn pillow pal and turns toward the window for a nap. I wouldn't be surprised if she sleeps through the whole trip. She gets bad motion sickness, so I don't blame her for checking out. It's actually pretty ideal, because I've been having a good conversation with Thom, and my fingers are itching to get my phone back out. I've already crafted the perfect reply to his last text.

I write, *You have a time machine that you can take to ANY TIME AT ALL, and you choose to meet H. G. Wells?*

Even though I left the conversation dangling this morning, nearly an hour ago, Thom is still around and quick to pick things back up.

He texts, *He's my hero.*

I reply, *You're not supposed to meet your heroes. That's Fangirl 101.*

Okay, Miss High and Mighty, where—I mean WHEN would you go?

I've already thought up an answer to this one, too. It came to me while I was brushing my teeth: *I would go to June 28, 1914, and prevent the assassination of Archduke Franz Ferdinand.*

I'd like to claim I just knew June 28, 1914, off the top of my head, but AP U.S. History was *last* year. I looked it up on Wikipedia, because the full date makes my proposition sound more credible.

Thom: *WHAT. Why??*

Kathryn Ormsbee

Me: *That's what started WWI. It was the straw that broke the camel's back. So if I stop the assassination, I stop WWI. And probably, as a result, WWII.*

Thom: *Nope. Wasted time travel. There would've been another straw. The war still would've gone down.*

Me: *You don't know that.*

Thom: *You don't know that No WWI = No WWII.*

Me: *If Germany hadn't been forced to pay all those reparations, then Hitler probably wouldn't have risen to power.*

It takes me three tries to get autocorrect to supply the right spelling of "reparations."

Thom: *I don't know, it's a dangerous game, messing with history that much.*

Me: *H. G. Wells might have been a complete ass in person. You really want to shatter your illusion?*

Thom: *I'll take my chances.*

I'm in such a feverish headspace that I don't notice Paul leaning in close, and I startle when he speaks.

"Dorking out, much?"

I drop the phone in my lap and glare at him.

Paul gives me a weird look. "Is that how you two flirt?"

"Rude," I say. "It is so rude to read someone else's private text conversation."

"You know what's actually rude? Texting some Internet guy when you're sitting right next to someone who can talk to you *in real life*."

"You weren't saying anything."

"Yeah, because you were texting. I'm bored."

"Only boring people get bored."

"I have never claimed to be an interesting person."

I wave toward the front seats. "Talk to Brooks, or Serena."

Serena raises a hand and says, "Nope. Sorry, Paul. Studying lines."

Last week Serena landed the role of Maria in the Lexington Community Troupe's production of *West Side Story*. The performance isn't until mid-September, but she's already prepping like a fiend. Brooks, meantime, seems intent on pretending he hasn't heard us.

I sigh with much feeling. I don't pocket my phone, but I do flip it screen-down on the seat, cross my arms, and turn to Paul. "Okay. You've got my undivided attention. Now what?"

Paul still has a funny look on his face, like he's trying to identify a flavor for a taste test. But then he smiles and says, "Alphabet game."

"*God*, Paul. *No.*"

"Okay, fine. I Spy."

"You are eight," I say. "You are eight years old, you know that?"

But I'm laughing, so we play I Spy. Tony joins in, and Serena does too after griping that she can't concentrate on her script. We're half an hour in when Jay takes off his headphones and says, "I spy with my little eye something that's green," and we guess for five whole minutes before Tony guesses it's Jay's jacket zipper, and the whole carload goes into an uproar, because Tony is the only person in the vehicle who

Kathryn Ormsbee

could actually see the zipper. Jay is unapologetic and clearly pleased with himself for holding the longest record of stumping the car. Serena calls him a dirty cheater, and Jay roars back, "You're the cheater, Anna Arkadyevna Karenina!"

Serena plays right into it by screeching back, "I was unhappy, Stiva! You stifled me!"

Everyone is convulsing with laughter. Everyone but Jack, who's woken from her nap with all the grace of a grizzly bear. She groans into her unicorn pillow, "If I barf in here, it's your all's fault."

Our laughs are still loud and long when Tony grips my headrest and lunges forward, yelling, "Shit, shit, shit, cop at eleven o'clock!"

It's to Brooks's credit that he doesn't slam on the breaks, given Tony's melodramatic delivery. He decelerates quickly but steadily, just as we fly through the underpass where the cop car is hiding out. We collectively hold our breaths, craning our necks back to watch and wait. We drive farther and farther out. No siren. No sign of pursuit. We settle back in our seats. There's a beat of silence. Then the laughter picks up again.

"I spy with my little eye . . . the effing Batman building."

We're all hunched in to see the Nashville skyline though the windshield. I-65 provides a dramatic introduction to the city; nothing like an entrance to Lexington, which is all horse farms and strip malls. Lexington's tallest building—our cobalt blue 5/3 Bank tower—would develop a severe inferiority complex in a place like this.

It's an obvious choice, but my favorite building in the Nashville lineup is the AT&T building, affectionately known as the Batman building because of the two pointy spires poking out the top like Batman's mask. When Klaudie and I were younger, Dad had both of us convinced those spires shot out every single cell phone signal worldwide. I held fast to that belief for much longer than I care to admit.

Our first stop in the city is Hattie B's, which, according to Brooks, has the best hot chicken in town. Of course, chicken isn't an option for me, so instead I load up on à la carte orders: baked beans, black-eyed pea salad, and pimento mac and cheese. And then, because this *is* a special occasion, I go all out and order banana pudding and a large cup of sweet tea. For everyone else, there's a chart listing five types of chicken cooking styles in increasing level of hotness. Jack and Tony are the only ones to order the hottest level: *Shut the Cluck Up!!!*

Being Jack and Tony, neither of them complain or betray so much as a wince of discomfort as they eat. I do note, however, that they take many long gulps of soda in between bites. When Tony gets up for a refill and asks Jack if she'd like him to get her one too, she actually lets him.

We have several hours to kill before the concert, so we all pitch in a few bucks toward parking and Brooks finds us a place in Midtown that's close to our venue and to Centennial Park.

"Did you want to go on Vandy's campus?" Paul asks me as we unload from the Explorer. "Poke around the media arts department?"

I haven't talked to Paul or Jack about the college thing yet. I've wanted to be sure I'm committing to UK before I tell them, because the only thing worse than leaving the state for college is leaving the state after promising I'll stay in town. But now, the discussion seems like an inevitability. I anticipated this conversation on the ride down, but only as a vague fear that might not come true if I didn't think about it too hard. But here it is, and because I haven't done any hard thinking, I don't have any good answers on the tip of my tongue.

"No, that's okay," I say, shrugging, still hoping Paul and Jack won't read anything into it.

Of course, they do.

"What do you mean, *'That's okay'*?" says Jack. "You've been talking about visiting again ever since we planned this trip."

"Not recently," I mumble.

We've reached a crosswalk, and the seven us begin to break off. Brooks is heading to a nearby café to meet up with a friend. Serena and Jay are going to a boutique Serena follows on Instagram and wants to check out in person. Paul, Jack, and I are, of course, a natural grouping. That leaves Tony the odd man out. At the intersection, he decides to cross the street with Serena and Jay while the rest of us wait for a light in the opposite direction. That's good, at least. I wouldn't want to have this very personal conversation in front of Tony.

It isn't until Brooks has waved us good-bye and headed down his own street that I say, "Vandy's not happening. Even if I got in, which is doubtful, it'd be too expensive."

Jack and Paul are quiet. I know they're exchanging a look behind my back. Apparently, Jack has been appointed the emissary, because she says, "Um, that's new information."

"I've been thinking it through for a while now. I was just figuring out how to tell you."

"How to tell us? We're your best friends, Tash. You don't have to bullshit us. You just *tell* us."

Bristling, I say, "I'm allowed to figure out things on my own before I tell you."

Jack makes a short humming sound I take to mean "fair enough."

We haven't discussed where we're going instead of campus, but we seem to have all silently agreed to head toward Centennial Park. We step onto one of the many paths leading off the main sidewalk and into the shade of trees. There's a distant sound of plashing water—a fountain in the park lake, currently out of sight.

"So . . . does that mean you'd go to UK?" Jack turns and bats her lashes. "With meee?"

It's so sudden. I feel short of breath, and my chest fills with warmth. I don't know if it's Jack's childishness or the beauty of the park or the simple contentment I feel at walking sandwiched between two of my favorite humans on earth, but this feels . . . right. *This.* Because even if UK means staying in Lexington, it means staying with *them.*

"Yeah," I say. "That's what it means."

She's fighting down a smile when she says, "I'm sure you know I'll make a horrible roommate, but I'm still going to guilt you into living with me."

I fling one arm over her shoulder, one over Paul's, and start singing the chorus of "With or Without You," whisper-screaming into her ear my modified lyrics: *"You can't liiive with or withooout me."* It's obnoxious, but I don't care, and neither does Jack or Paul. Paul adds his own imitation of a cymbal crash and drum crescendo. Jack joins me for Bono's climactic wail just as we come to a clearing in the trees and get our first view of the Parthenon.

In this moment, I'm overwhelmed with love for them both to the point of queasiness. Jack and Paul don't care if we make a scene. They would never be embarrassed by me. Why would I leave that for a fancy school and a six-figure college loan?

We shake our heads at the Parthenon, because that's really all you can do when faced with a full-scale replica of an Athenian temple plopped down in the middle of Tennessee. It's such a stunningly odd sight, because it has the potential to be tacky, and maybe some people think it is, but I don't. Here, in this park, it looks eternal. A structure that will remain even after all the nuclear wars and alien invasions and epidemics wipe us out. Maybe the Batman building will fall, but not the Fake Parthenon. Never the Fake Parthenon.

There's already a decent line outside the concert venue when we arrive. I spot Serena, Jay, and Tony a couple dozen people ahead of us and shoot them a wave. Tony motions for us to join them, and I notice a few of the people between us turn sour-faced, already prepping themselves for a line-cutting confrontation. They don't need to. My friends and I may be annoying, but we are not jackasses. I shake my head and ignore Tony's pouty face.

Doors open soon enough, and we meet the others on the floor. It's a big warehouse space with the stage on one end and a full bar on the other. We all wear big Sharpie-drawn *X*s on both our hands, branded underage losers for the remainder of the night. Serena shows us a necklace she bought at the boutique—a silver pocket watch with a teeny bird on the end of the second hand. Tony and Jay stand close beside her, but even closer to each other.

Brooks doesn't find us until the break between the opening act and Chvrches. His face is flushed from alcohol, but he doesn't drink any more while he's with us, and his tipsy grin fades into a far more sober one over the course of the night. When Chvrches takes the stage, we all might as well be drunk. We're a frenzied ball of energy, and I shriek shamelessly as they begin their opening number—my favorite of their songs.

When the band's set is over, the audience cheers them back onstage for an encore. And it's during the encore that I look over and see Jay and Tony kissing. Jay's standing with his back against a metal support, just the teensiest bit wobbly, and Tony is leaning over him, chest-to-chest, drawing out kisses from his mouth in a steady, constant rhythm, like a heartbeat.

Kathryn Ormsbee

At last, our Vronsky and Alex are together, and I ship it even more than Kevin.

It's a good concert, though as we're leaving, Jack whispers to me what I've been thinking: "A little anticlimactic." I haven't been to too many concerts, but so far experience has taught me that a lot of them are this way—just not big enough to live up to all the mental hype.

Brooks doesn't seem tipsy when we leave, but there's an interaction between him and Serena that I don't catch, which results in Serena taking the wheel. We can't have been on the road for more than five minutes when Brooks starts to snore in the passenger seat. The rest of us snicker softly, and Serena just cranks the radio louder.

I fall into a tired but comfortable fog. Everyone's quiet, sleeping or half-sleeping. There's a spooky, bluish glow behind me from one of the guys' phones. After several minutes, it disappears, casting both back rows into darkness.

When I wake, we're still on the interstate, passing a semi in the right lane. I've fallen asleep on Paul's shoulder, where I've deposited a trickle of drool on his T-shirt sleeve. Luckily, he's sleeping and unaware of this disgusting little surprise. Jack is breathing deeply on my other side, and Brooks is out cold in the front. I shift toward the backseat and see that Jay is awake, listening to music and staring out at the passing cars. There's just enough light to make out his hand atop Tony's in the space between their knees. Jay shoots me a grin. I grin back, point at him, then Tony, and give a giddy thumbs-up. He points at me and the back of Paul's head and lifts his shoulders in an inquisitive "what about that?" shrug.

I make a face. Me. And . . . Paul? Is he suggesting what I think he is? What Jay does next leaves no room for doubt. He puckers his lips in a kissy face and winks. All I can do is stare, dumbfounded, and finally shake my head and whisper, "No."

In response, Jay grins bigger at me and shuts his eyes, returning to the world of his headphones. I turn back around in my seat, close my eyes, and tell myself to sleep, but my mind is racing.

Me and Paul. If Jay only knew that Paul sees me as a sister, same as Jack. That even if he didn't, it wouldn't work out because I'm not a fan of sex, and I know, thanks to Paul's candidness about his relationship with Stephanie Crewe and a couple other less serious dates, he most certainly is.

Still, I can't shut my mind off. The bubbly feeling is in my throat, like it was the day Paul hugged me in front of his basketball friends and one of them called me his girlfriend. Those fools knew nothing. I'm no one's girlfriend, and Paul is just . . . Paul.

He shifts beside me, and I have a panicked, irrational thought that all this time Paul has been a telepath, and now he's going to tell me as much in the most humiliating way. But Paul doesn't say anything. He smiles sleepily at me and, still panicked, I whisper-blurt, "I drooled on you."

He follows my finger to the dampened portion of his sleeve. In response, he snorts and tugs me in close to deposit a raspberry atop my head. I wrinkle my nose and punch him in the chest. He smiles against my hair and says, "Even." Then he closes his eyes again, but his arm remains where it is—loose around my shoulder. And it's the most confusing moment, because Paul has *always* been like this, and resting here, tucked in his side, can be as easily familial as it can be something else.

It's nothing, it's something. It can't, it could. It's Paul, but Thom.

Thoughts pester and peck at my brain, keeping me wide awake. My mind is racing when we pull into my driveway and Serena opens her door and a steady *ding-ding-ding* wakes everyone else from their slumber.

Twenty-One

The Golden Tuba Awards are in exactly two weeks. I've drained almost the entirety of my college savings on a round-trip flight to Orlando and a two-night stay at the Embassy Suites, where the conference is being held. My remaining trip budget is tight. I've already planned on making a clean sweep of the continental breakfast and sneaking some waffles and fruit back to my room for a makeshift lunch, but I know I'm going to have to pay for a couple meals at some point.

At least Thom will treat me to an iced coffee. Probably. *Hopefully.*

After a week of what I call our "social media fast," Jack and I get back online with a new plan: We will weed through notifications in an efficient manner, disregarding the hate as best we can and responding only to fellow web series accounts or very pressing questions. It isn't ideal, but we agree it's the only way to stay sane.

Since our cemetery sunrise, Klaudie and I haven't been fighting. We haven't been giving each other mani-pedis, either, but we've reached an understanding. Our *splendifying* morning with Gramps and Nana made me see things differently. I guess I secretly thought it was Klaudie's fault we weren't ever closer. She was the one who was too snooty to hang out with me and Jack and Paul. She was older, so it was up to her to draw me closer. But she didn't, and we spun further out from each other, growing irreconcilably different. I blamed that on her. But I don't think it's her fault anymore. It was personality and birth order and a lot of other factors neither of us can control.

So now we're two grown sisters with a sizable gap between us. I still can't cross the gap, but I can at least see to the other side, to a place surrounded by the pressure to perform. Klaudie was right: That's pressure I've never felt, never even thought about. I may not feel it myself, but at least now I know she does, and that makes it a little better. And while Klaudie hasn't made peace with our parents just yet, she's been much milder in her interactions. There are fewer quips, no more sullen eye rolls, and she's begun to eat most dinners with us again.

The day after my Nashville trip is one of those days when you sleep in so late that you're completely worthless for the rest of the day. Despite getting a solid twelve hours, I'm a wreck when I walk into the dining room that night. But then I see what Dad's fixed, and I perk up. He's made his homemade calzones, each one to our liking: green peppers and onions for Mom, mushrooms for Klaudie, bacon and pepperoni for himself, and four cheeses for me. The only dish I like more than Dad's traditional Czech meals is his calzones. The sight of them, piping hot on the table, is like a shot of adrenaline straight to my heart. I'm

suddenly wide awake. I need all my senses on red alert to fully appreciate this explosion of cheese.

"What's the special occasion?" I ask, taking my seat.

"Family movie night," Dad says. "That's a *very* special occasion."

In a way, I guess it is. The last movie night all four of us were together
was way back in February, when we were snowed in and Mom and
Klaudie had the flu. We snuggled in the den with blankets and cider
and watched all three of the original *Star Wars*. For a while after that,
once the roads were clear but the snow was deep on the lawns, Dad
would leave for work each morning brandishing his windshield scraper
like a lightsaber and yelling, "Just another day on Hoth!"

Tonight, we're watching *The Goonies*, which means before Dad will
press play on the DVD menu, we must do our best truffle shuffle.
Klaudie and I whine and moan, but we secretly love it. We hop onto
the couch and raise our T-shirts above our bellies, wiggling them as best
we can with accompanying growling sounds. Dad nods approvingly and
says, "All right then." We point fingers at him and demand he do it
too. So Dad turns around very solemnly, untucks his button-down shirt,
and wiggles his tubby midsection with the most dramatic and accurate
gurgle-growl yet. I don't think Dad missed his calling—he makes a great
salesperson—but he could've totally made it on the stage, too.

Mom joins Klaudie and me on the couch. I suspect it's a calculated move when she sits between the two of us. I *know* it is when she
oh-so-casually slips her arms around both our waists.

Kathryn Ormsbee

"Mom," I say. "We're not going anywhere."

Mom presses a kiss to my temple. I lean forward to check Klaudie's reaction and am shocked to find she's resting her head against Mom's collarbone. Mom's begun to show—a small bump beneath her emerald-colored blouse. And since she's taken the liberty of wrapping a hand around my side, I press the tips of my fingers to the bump. None of us say anything. We relax into each other's bodies and watch as a giant skull and crossbones fills the TV screen.

Later, once I'm in bed, I text with Thom. I've brought up the Golden Tubas again. I can't help myself. With the end of filming fast approaching, the awards seem like a culmination of everything Jack and I have been working for in the past year. It's like some universe-ordained close to the whole *Unhappy Family* experience. It's reached a beyond-epic proportion in my mind, which I know is dangerous. The ceremony and convention aren't going to live up to my expectations; I keep reminding myself that. I have no chance of winning the Golden Tuba for Best New Series. None whatsoever. Half my mind is wholly convinced of this. The other half is on a wild rampage of boundless optimism. I think about it way more often than is healthy, so it's inevitable that some of it leaks out into my conversations with Thom.

The negativity online didn't get any better after Thom's video. Not that I expected it to. But despite Jack's disapproval, I'm grateful for Thom's PSA, not only because it showed he cares about my feelings but also because it served as a kind of turning point. Our conversations really began to pick up after that. And even though Thom mainly wants to talk about sci-fi or his work or the latest online phenomenon, I like those topics well enough too.

At the moment, I am expressing some cutely worded anxiety, and Thom, as always, is cutting straight through it.

Tash, RELAX. If you don't win, you don't win. At least you'll get a good vacation out of it.

What I want to text him is, *But not a real vacation, because I don't have enough money to go to Harry Potter world.*

Instead, I write, *I know I know I know, you're right.*

There's a pause. No text bubble on his end, and no typing on mine. I'm about to tell him good night, when he begins typing. I wait for his message.

Are you in bed?

Yup, I write back. *All snuggled up, no makeup on. I would scare you so badly.*

It's only a joke, but the moment I hit send, I second-guess myself. Maybe that was too far. Did it sound like I was fishing for a compliment? I hate when people do that—smash themselves to pieces and then hand you the glue stick, screaming *FIX ME.* I make an antsy squeal and shove the phone under my pillow, as though this will somehow prevent Thom's reply from coming through. I only take it back out a minute later and read his reply: *I'm sure you look beautiful. ESPECIALLY all snuggled up in bed.*

Kathryn Ormsbee

I turn to stone.

My bones have transformed into marble, my tendons to granite. My blood has hardened into vein- and artery-shaped stalactites. Because Thom Causer really texted that. He called me beautiful. He basically said he was picturing me in my bed. And I want to think so badly that's all it is. Just an innocent, offhand comment. That he's picturing us snuggling together, and that's it. But that can't be all there is, because he is a guy, and he is seventeen, and the chances he could be like me are about a million to one. It's there, between the bubbles of our rambling, flirty conversations: *sex*. It snakes through our exchanges, stealthy and sure, flicking its forked tongue to coat every word with the hint of its presence. I hate it. And I know I should probably tell Thom at this point. I just can't figure out the when, the *how*. There is no un-awkward way of bringing it up, and once I do, everything will change.

I've done my research on relationships between aces and sexual people. There are a lot of different perspectives out there, but the general consensus is this: It's really hard. It requires openness and compromise. Sometimes the sexual person stays committed emotionally but finds sexual satisfaction elsewhere—either on their own or with other people. Or sometimes the ace is cool with having sex every so often, to make their partner happy. Sometimes it all ends in tears. But any way you slice it, the details sound so clinical and ugly, and is it wrong of me to not want to think about them yet?

I stare at the ceiling, remembering all the nights I've stared at this ceiling before, my imagination in a totally different place—trying, *try-ing* to picture any scenario where I would want sex, where I'd crave it. One weekend, when my parents were away for a mountain getaway in Pigeon Forge, I hauled a stack of movies up to my room. Movies I knew had sex scenes in them. I watched them, I rewatched them, I paused them, I *tried*.

This is the conclusion I came to: My lack of desire isn't due to any lack of effort. I've tried it for myself plenty of times. I don't hate the feeling. It's fine—satisfying, even, to reach that point of release. But it's not what I'm supposed to feel. Not according to the movies and television shows I've seen, not according to the talk at school, or my conversations with Jack. I'm supposed to feel more. I'm supposed to want it like *they* do. Either that, or everyone around me is just faking it. Sometimes I wish they were. It would be disillusioning, but at least I wouldn't be the freak.

At the beginning of last year's English class, my teacher, Mr. Fenton, told the class that the motivation behind every single piece of literature is sex or death, and usually both. Jack dissented very vocally in class, and outside of it she said that Mr. Fenton only thought everything was about sex because he was a guy.

"I guarantee you," she told me, "Jane Austen's main motivating fac-tor wasn't sex. Or death. It was satire and social commentary, because she was a grown-up. Men can be so effing basic. It's hard for them to get around their own damn phallic-shaped monument to manliness. That's why the best male writers are almost always gay or bi. Give me Wilde! Whitman! Capote! Impeach Fenton!"

Mr. Fenton was not impeached, but it became a running joke in the classroom that when pressed for an answer we didn't know, we should say, "Sex."

Maybe Jack and I didn't agree with Mr. Fenton, but I think he got what he wanted, anyway. The thought of sex hung heavy on that room, the same as it did outside, in the school hallways, and farther outside, in the world at large. It's everywhere, like a second skin on everyone I know.

I wonder if it's too much to ask for a pass into an alternate dimension, where it's just not an issue. Because stuck in this particular dimension, I wonder if I'm only ever going to be a disappointment. A not-quite-right human. A girl in need of fixing. If there are a mere two driving forces behind every story out there, does that mean the only driving force left to me is *death*?

I'd like Mr. Fenton to answer that question. I'd like *anyone* to answer it.

I don't reply to Thom's text.

I stare through the dark at the fuzzy outline of my Tolstoy poster.

"Leo," I say. "Will you be the only man in my life?"

It's too dark to see, but I know he's scowling back at me.

Twenty-Two

I have this theory that the second half of summer goes by twice as fast as the first. June begins as a bright, blazing burst. All the energy that's been building through spring semester can finally be released on swimming, barbecues, amusement parks, and best of all—doing nothing. The days are long. Night doesn't arrive until nine. Everything is stretched out and saturated with sunlight. Then Independence Day strikes. The days get shorter, and school lurches nearer, and it feels like every subsequent day is robbed of another hour, until it's August, and the scent of suntan lotion is replaced by that of freshly sharpened pencils.

This summer is no exception. The July weeks whiz by, a fast train of blurred colors. It's a cycle of work and hanging out and, most importantly, filming. We inch closer and closer to our final film date, until suddenly, with no fanfare or ceremony, it's here: the first weekend of August, the last day of filming.

It's a Saturday afternoon, and the only two actors at my house are

Serena and Eva. They sit on my bed, their backs against a wall of dried flowers and pictures of snow-covered Paris that Jack and I carefully arranged the night before. We're on our fifth take, but it's not because I'm frustrated or Serena and Eva aren't hitting their lines. I'm just being a perfectionist about it. It's the last scene of the series; it has to be flawless.

Since Jack and I decided to only reply to pressing questions online, we've definitely saved ourselves a lot of time spent on the Internet. But some days, just for fun, I poke around the hashtags and the fansites out there. The love of Kevin is going strong, and there's even some girl on Etsy selling handmade jewelry engraved with quotes from the series. I guess that might be some kind of copyright infringement, but I don't care, because it's fan art people want to buy, and how cool is that? Not to mention, we're the original thieves who stole our entire story from dear, darling Leo.

There's still criticism out there too, but the last time I sniffed around—a couple days ago—the biggest issue wasn't so much a critique of what we've done as speculation about what we *might* do. So far, our plot has made some significant deviations from the novel. Obviously, we couldn't condense the entire book with all its characters. None of our characters are married, just dating. Anna doesn't get pregnant with Vronsky's kid, just really ill with pneumonia. And, as silverspunnnx23 so sagely pointed out, we don't grapple with Tolstoy's commentary on the political climate in imperial Russia; Levin's relationship with his activist brother, Nikolai, was cut altogether. So now that we're reaching the end of the story, fans want to know whether our Anna will or will not play true to the original plot and throw herself under a train.

Spoiler alert: She doesn't. Jack and I decided this at the very beginning. We wanted a positive twist. We wanted Anna to find comfort, not in her relationship with Vronsky or any other guy, but in a friendship with Kitty. Was it fudging around the original plot? Sure. In the book, Anna and Kitty aren't close. But in our script, they become close, and when life falls apart for Anna, and her past and current boyfriends leave the scene, Kitty's still there to help her process and move on. It's girl power to the tune of the Spice Girls' "Wannabe," and Jack and I wouldn't have it any other way.

That's the way we planned it from day one, but back then, it was just me and Jack huddled on the floor of my bedroom, throwing out ideas and excitedly jotting the ones that stuck in a spiral notebook. All we were thinking about then was the story, the drama, and how it would look on camera. It was pure creative energy, no inhibitions, no fear of what others would think.

Now, it's impossible to look at our script without imagining what our viewers will say. I've read too many of their comments, good and bad, to shut off that way of thinking. I already know what the response will be when our last episode airs. Some will think it's the perfect wrap-up, very feminist, good for us. Some will think it's an oversimplified letdown. Some will say we're idiot teenagers who totally missed the whole point of the novel. I know every variation of the impending criticism. It's scary, but it's a little liberating, too, to be creating something I *know* other people will hate. Because there's no way around it. No matter how Jack and I finish this series, we are bound to make someone mad.

After our tenth and final take, Eva starts crying. It's a quiet, leaking sort of cry. She's obviously embarrassed and keeps touching her knuckles to the edges of her eyes. When Serena sees, she wraps Eva in a giant hug. I join them on the bed, rubbing my hand on Eva's back in soothing circles. I'm crying a little too. So is Serena. Only Jack remains unmoved, watching us not with judgment but definitely like we're an alien species.

"Hey," I finally say. "No more crying until the wrap party, okay? That's what wrap parties are for."

Eva clears the remaining tears from her face and wheezes, "Okay."

"It's crazy," Serena says. "I can't believe it's over."

"Good thing," I say. "Now you can focus on *West Side Story*."

Serena shrugs. "Sure. But there will always be community theatres putting on *West Side Story*. There's only one *Unhappy Families*."

Serena is one of those people who says the thing you didn't know you needed to hear until you hear it.

I'm afraid I'll start crying again, so I just nod quickly and say, "I'm still really glad I met you last summer."

Serena offers me a fist. I bump it, and we pull our hands away, making dramatic spirit fingers.

No matter what happens in the future, we share this: We told a story together, and we wouldn't have been able to do it without each other's help. No one else can share this part of our lives. No one else can fully understand it like the nine of us. This is the breaking of our Fellowship. I, Gimli, shall wield my ax again, but never in this same company.

I think that deserves some tears. And definitely a spirit-finger fist bump.

The wrap party is Sunday night. We're holding it in the Harlows' backyard. Everyone's dressed for the oppressively hot weather—tank tops, flip-flops, and swimwear. We've ordered four boxes of extra large Papa John's pizzas, and the party consists primarily of stuffing ourselves with cheese and then sending our stomachs for a ride by diving too quickly into the pool. Once everyone's worn themselves out, we dry off and head to the entertainment room, where Jack and I have hooked up her computer to play *Unhappy Families* on-screen. The series in its entirety is *long*—over five hours. So we've decided to just play the last hour, which includes this past month's as-yet-unpublished footage. (Jack was up most of last night editing the final shot of Serena and Eva.)

Brooks can't stay for the whole thing—he's a hall director this year and has to attend some mandatory orientation on UK's campus. The rest of us stick it out, including Paul, who's been invited to join the festivities. When the final episode rolls, I look around the room, clandestinely checking everyone's expressions. Serena and Jay are crying. They've got their arms around each other. When the screen cuts to

Kathryn Ormsbee

black, there's a pregnant pause before the room erupts into applause and cheers. Jay leaps up and demands high fives from everyone. Eva blindsides me with a bear hug. She pecks my cheek and says, "It's great, Tash," and she looks ready to do the same to Jack, until Jack says, "I'll take the compliment, not the hug, thanks."

Someone's playing "Another One Bites the Dust" on their phone. Tony, of course. He's doing a sad attempt at the moonwalk while Jay claps in rhythm, looking on with such affection you can almost see little emoji hearts radiating off him.

It makes me happy. And then I feel kind of bad for feeling happy and turn to Jack, who's looking on.

But Jack doesn't look pissed. She doesn't even look like she's trying to be cool with it. She looks *actually* cool with it.

"Everything okay?" I ask.

"It's fine," she says. "I'm serious, it is. Tony talked to me about it. Apparently he thought Jay liked this other guy at SCAPA, and he's been trying to make him jealous."

"Holy crap. They could be their own Tolstoyan storyline."

"Yeah. But, anyway. Tony's a better person when he has someone in his life. And who could deny Jay anything? That guy's an effing angel. He deserves to be happy."

I think this is very big of Jack, though of course I can't tell her so, as she is allergic to affirming words of any kind. I have to be sneakier about it, so I say, "I'm glad things are okay."

Jack says, "Yep."

"You're nowhere close to an angel, but I think you deserve to be happy too."

"Blech, Tash. You used up all your genius on this script. No good words are left in you." Then, "Someone should stop Paul before he breaks his neck."

Paul has joined the Queen dance party—they've moved on to "We Are the Champions"—and is standing on top of the coffee table, belting the chorus into a remote control. When he catches my eye, he motions for me to join him.

I say, "We've broken enough furniture in this basement, don't you think?"

So he jumps off the table, grabs my hand, and twirls me around, all while managing to sing the second verse into the remote. Afterward, we collapse into the beanbag together, and we stay there as the rest of the cast say their good-byes and leave. Everyone says we *have* to stay in touch and they're sure we'll all see each other again soon. George approaches us in an awkward shuffle, as though Paul and I are holding court and he's a peasant come to ask for more grain for the winter.

"I guess I'll see you Friday morning, Tash," he says.

I nod, not bothering to be super enthusiastic. Of course I'm excited about the Golden Tubas, but not so much about being there with George.

"I guess so," I say.

Kathryn Ormsbee

"You nervous?" he asks.

Am I nervous. Ha. I've been wailing about that to Thom for so long, sometimes I forget that the entire-world population does not know how absolutely, completely, incurably nervous I am.

I reply, *"Que será, será."*

Tony, who is leaving through the back patio, pops his head back in and begins singing the Doris Day song, flourishing his hand toward the two of us: "Que será, será! *Whatever will be, will beee! The future's not ours to seee!"*

Jay stands on the other side of the glass, laughing. Beaming.

Unamused, George gives me a look that says, *Can you believe this guy?* And I reply with a look that says, *It's Tony. It's what he does.*

"Anyway," says George. "See you at the airport."

"Mmm-hmm."

I wave as he follows Tony and Jay out of the house. And that's it—that's a wrap to our wrap party.

Jack closes the patio door, shaking her head. "I hope he has a paralyzing fear of flying. Or has to use a barf bag." Then she tilts her head to one side, looking annoyed. "I've got water in my ear. I'm gonna pour in some hydrogen peroxide, take a shower. You sleeping over, Tash?"

"Haven't decided yet," I say, though my current state of laziness, combined with my position—mushed next to Paul in this beanbag—indicates I'll probably stick around. Jack bounds up the stairs, and I close my eyes, listening to her quick footsteps above our heads. I feel exhausted, but in the nice way. My skin is damp and smells of chlorine. My mouth is still coated in a buttery layer of garlic sauce.

Paul shifts slightly beside me and asks, "So, *are* you nervous about the Golden Saxophones?"

I laugh, despite the terribleness of Paul's purposeful mess-up. "You have such dad humor," I tell him.

"Answer the question," he insists.

"Okay, fine. I am extremely nervous. I don't know if I'm more nervous that we'll win or we'll lose. Because if we lose, it will be bad for obvious reasons, but if we win . . . I don't know. It seems the more famous we get, the more people feel like they can post really vicious comments. Like because we've got so many views, we're invincible. I don't want our series to be something people end up resenting. I'd rather it be under-appreciated, I think, than slammed for getting so popular."

"Oh yes. The price of fame."

"Stop making fun of me."

Paul laughs. "I think it's great. Not many people our age can say they've made a five-hour-long adaptation of *Anna Karenina*. So no matter what happens at the Platinum Trumpets, at least you've got that."

"At least I've got that," I repeat distantly, my thoughts taking a familiar bend in the road. "And even if everything else at the convention is a total flop, at least I'll have finally met Thom in person."

"Right. There's that, too." Paul shifts again. It feels like he's trying to move over, put some space between us, but it's wasted effort,

Kathryn Ormsbee

because our weight on the beanbag drags us right back together again.

"It's weird," I say. "We know so much about each other, but it's all these little things, like our favorite fandoms and movies and what we'd do with a time machine. None of the huge things like—"

"Actually talking to each other," Paul supplies.

I smile to myself. "I think that makes it special, though. When we meet in Orlando, it'll be like meeting an old friend. But in another way, it'll be like meeting each other for the first time."

"Oh yeah, total voice virgins. That's really hot."

There's something horrible in Paul's voice. Something contentious and sharp-edged. It's a voice I've only heard him use with Jack and, on occasion, his dad. Never with me. The word "virgin" hangs in the room, flashing like a neon sign. Paul and I are sitting way too close to each other.

I climb out of the beanbag with difficulty, stumbling once before righting myself.

"Tash," Paul says. "I—"

I round on him, heat rushing up my face. "Because 'virgin' is an excellent punch line, isn't it? That's great, Paul."

"Shit, I didn't mean it that way. I'm sorry."

"Why do you get like that? What's wrong with Thom?"

Paul's staring straight at me, but he's unreadable, his brown eyes locked and closed off.

My jaw is trembling. I blurt out, "Are you jealous?"

Paul opens his mouth, but only wide enough to let out a breath, not words. He shakes his head and breaks our gaze to stare at the DVD collection behind me. I move over to block his view.

"*Are* you?"

"Jesus Christ, Tash."

Now I'm the one to shake my head at him, hard and fast and disapproving.

"Because you don't get to be," I say. "Not when you know everything about me. Not when you don't even *want* me. Not when you can't even be a good friend."

A recognizable expression is finally spreading over Paul's face: confusion.

"How have I not been a good friend?" He sits up straight in the beanbag, which makes a loud farting sound. In any situation save this one, we'd laugh about it. Which makes the noise twice as unpleasant.

"You don't tell me things," I say. "You keep things from me."

"Like *what*? Just because I'm not constantly talking—"

"What about your dad?" I take a step forward, pressing the question into him. "Why didn't you tell me about his headaches? That's something a friend tells another friend. But instead you specifically tell Jack not to let me know?"

"You can't call me a bad friend for that. *You* don't tell *me* plenty of things."

"Like wh—"

Kathryn Ormsbee

"How do you really feel about guys?"

I startle, going still and silent.

"I'm just . . . I'm trying to figure it out," he says. "I'm not saying I don't support you or that I don't believe you, I'm just trying to *get* you. Because one minute you're telling me you hate men—"

"I never said—"

"And the next you're telling me that you're falling in love with this vlog dude. Which I didn't think you could do. Because if I'd known, I would've . . . Because I'm *just trying to figure it out.*"

I swallow hard. I should tell Paul it's my fault. I've made things confusing, because *I've* been confused. *I've* been trying to figure it out.

I should, but the words don't come.

When it's clear I don't intend to reply, Paul sinks into the beanbag and stares at the ceiling. His eyes are wet.

"I've had a crush on you since we were kids. I've probably been in love with you since our moms arranged that playdate at Holly Park."

These words are not coming from Paul's mouth. They cannot be. It is surreal, absurd.

I say, "We're best friends, Paul. You and me and Jack. We've always loved each other."

Paul shifts his gaze back to mine. To my relief, he doesn't look like he's on the verge of a cry anymore. But then he speaks, and everything falls back apart.

"Yeah, Tash. I'm jealous. Okay? I'm jealous. Because you have this epic thing going on with a guy you met on the Internet, and you didn't even want to try with me."

I shake my head in disbelief. "*You* didn't want to try with *me*. You're the one who dated Stephanie Crewe."

"I'm the one who *broke up* with Stephanie Crewe."

"Oh my God, don't even tell me that was over *me*. You never saw me that way. You never have. I've always been your little sister, or yeah, your friend. You're just rewriting history now that you definitely can't have me. Because, what? I'm all enigmatic for not wanting to have sex? Or maybe you think you can fix me, if I just give it a try with you?"

Paul's face contorts into disgust. "*What?* No. I never said that. I've never *thought* that."

"Really? Then you're an idiot. Because you're a red-blooded guy, Paul. You want sex. And you can't have it with me. So if you want to be with me, you're an idiot."

"Let me get this straight: I'm either an asshole or I'm an idiot, no in-between. Is that it?"

I'm aware of how unfair I'm being, but it's too late. I'm too committed to stop. "Pretty much."

"Fuck that," Paul says, raising his voice. He propels off the beanbag and comes toward me with disorienting speed, stopping just a foot away. "Fuck that, Tash. You can't tell me how I used to feel or what I want."

"So, you're this totally normal nineteen-year-old guy who doesn't want sex?"

"I didn't say I didn't want—"

"I'm not going to magically change, Paul."

"I never—"

"Just because we've known each other our whole lives, just because you get me more than anyone else—that doesn't mean you'll be the perfect guy who changes my mind. Okay? I know I've been confusing about this, but I know that part for sure."

"If you—"

It could be the adrenaline pumping through my system. It could be adrenaline or anger or just that my self-destructive alter ego has taken over. Whatever the reason, the resulting action stops Paul's words: I yank my T-shirt over my head and throw it to the ground.

I've worn less in front of Paul. Just an hour ago, I was dunking him underwater in my swimsuit. But this is different, because the air is charged, and this isn't my bikini top, it's my bra.

Paul glances down once, briefly.

"What are you doing, Tash?" he whispers.

"You're a liar," I say. "I'm proving it. I'm proving you're a liar."

I unzip my skirt and release the waistband, letting the material fall and pool around my feet. I point a finger at him, drive it into his chest.

"This is what I'm like underneath. Which apparently turns people like you on. And if you want to be my boyfriend, you have to know all the time what you *can't* have, and you might say it's fine at first, but it won't be fine, because you want what's underneath, and it will ruin everything. It will ruin our friendship. It will ruin my friendship with Jack. And I won't let that happen. So yeah, you're either an asshole or an idiot, and I'd rather you be an asshole, because then at least we can stay friends."

That's when I hear movement behind me, on the stairwell. I hear Jack's voice say, "What in the holy fuck is going on here."

And I don't even turn to face her. I stoop to grab my shirt and skirt and I run for the door. Jack shouts my name. I turn the handle and flee, leaving the door wide open behind me.

I hide myself behind Mr. Harlow's well-manicured hedges, where I clumsily re-dress myself. I forgot my flip-flops; they're back in the basement. I run barefoot through the dark, my heels hitting the pavement in uneven thuds as my brain chants, *What were you thinking, why would he say that, why would he say it now?*

When I'm finally locked away in my bedroom, I realize my shirt is on backward and inside out. I don't bother with it. I don't bother with anything but crawling into bed and pulling the covers over my head.

Kathryn Ormsbee

Twenty-Three

I don't contact Paul or Jack. They don't contact me. We exist on the same street, twelve houses apart from each other, and do not exchange words for four days. On Tuesday and Thursday morning, new episodes of *Unhappy Families* go up per usual. It would seem that nothing is amiss.

Except everything is amiss.

The last big fight I got into with Paul and Jack was about whose bike color scheme was cooler. We've never had a blowout over something as big and messy and *adult* as this. Nothing close to Paul telling me he's loved me since the first time we played on the shoddy jungle gym at Holly Park. Nothing remotely involving sexuality or lack thereof. This is uncharted, unfriendly terrain. There's no vegetation here, no signs of life. I know I won't survive if I try to rough it out much longer. Still, I can't bring myself to call, to text, to break into their basement and fall asleep on the couch. I can't, and, it seems, they can't either, and I wonder if this is how friendships end—not with a declaration, but a stalemate, a slow fade.

Not that this is the end of our friendship. I refuse to let that happen. But I can't pick up the phone. Not yet.

I do text Thom. Not about the fight. Of course not about the fight. He doesn't know that Jack and Paul are my best friends, let alone what I would fight about with them. We gab about the usual: Thom's opinion of J. J. Abrams and the most recent episode of *Storms of Taffdor*.

On Thursday night, I bid au revoir to Leo. It's an emotional parting. He puts up a good front, attempting to hide the anguish beneath his scowl, but I know he's heartbroken to see me leave, even if it is only for a few days.

"It's not exactly on a par with starting a dozen schools for newly emancipated serfs," I say, "but this nomination is kind of the biggest thing I've accomplished in my life so far."

Leo scowls.

"Hey, stop judging me, okay? I am not superficial for wanting a tuba-shaped piece of hardware."

Scowl.

"Don't even. You didn't have your shit together when you were my age. You were running around being a privileged aristocrat and blowing your inheritance on gambling and dropping out of school and joining the army."

Scowl, scowl, scowl.

I hoist my shoulders to my ears. "Okay, Leo. But you're gonna miss me when I'm gone."

Kathryn Ormsbee

Then I start packing. I'll be gone only two nights, but I somehow manage to fill my entire suitcase. I keep remembering little things, like my sleep socks and travel perfume and an extra pair of sunglasses.

I'm blaring St. Vincent's *Actor* album, and in the silence between two songs, I hear a knock at my door. I open it and find myself nose-to-nose with Jack. From the look on her face, this isn't her first round of knocking. She's not wearing any makeup, and she's still dressed in her sleep clothes—black flannel pants and a Jack Skellington tee. She pushes past me into the room, sits down on the edge of my bed.

She says, "You've got *so* much effing explaining to do."

There's a blitz of distorted guitar coming from my laptop speakers. I shut the screen, bringing the song to an abrupt end, and sink into my desk chair, facing Jack.

"Where do you want me to start?" I say.

"Well, while I'm tempted to ask why I found you doing a striptease in front of my brother, I think I got enough information from him. The more pressing matter is *this*."

She hands over her phone. The web browser is pulled up to a blog. I recognize the title and logo immediately: It's *Horn-Rimmed Glasses Girl*. The page is her most recent blog post, titled "Unhappy Families, Unsatisfying Production." This must be the Q&A the founder, Heather Lyles, conducted with me in mid-July. I just now remember that I never mentioned it to Jack. For a while, it kept slipping my mind in the usual filming madness. But then I finally decided against telling her at all. Jack doesn't do well when interacting with strangers, and a joint interview with her would have been so much more of a hassle than answering the questions myself. So I answered the questions, and I told myself I'd let Jack know eventually. Now, eventually is here. She's holding the interview in front of me. But when I skim the text, I find no back-and-forth text between bolded names, no trace of a Q&A. It's a post in paragraph form, and it only takes me a few sentences to realize it's a review of the series. A *scathing* review.

"I need to know if you actually gave her those quotes," says Jack. "Because if not, we need to, I dunno, sue for libel or something. And if you did . . ."

I don't have to say anything; Jack gleans an answer from my silence. Her expression remains blank, but she's angry. How could she not be? As I read further, things only get worse. Heather Lyles has lambasted the show, and she's used the quotes I sent her to back up her points. The final paragraph reads:

Young web series "producer" Natasha Zelenka is just seventeen years old and, unfortunately, it shows. The choice of Anna Karenina *as subject matter for a lighthearted series is all the proof you need. Others have criticized the series for oversimplifying Tolstoy's storyline. I'd say it slaughters it. Behind all the Kevin fangirl craze is a meandering plot with none of the drama and passion from the novel. By making the main characters "young adults," Zelenka and Harlow sacrifice critical elements that make the book*

Kathryn Ormsbee

work. Anna dumping her long-term boyfriend Alex for new fling Vronsky isn't anywhere near the heartrending mess of Anna leaving her husband and beloved son to live the life of a social pariah in imperial Russia. And as for the famed end of the novel's heroine? Zelenka says she "can't give away the ending, but our hope is that it's satisfying and does justice to the rest of the story." Not too hard to do justice to a story of so low a caliber, but if you're expecting satisfying, don't hold your breath.

I hand the phone back to Jack and press my lips together, not sure if I'm going to laugh or cry or pass out.

"So," says Jack, "were you never going to tell me you did an exclusive interview with a well-known blog? Without me?"

"I'm sorry, Jack."

"Are you? Because this whole thing looks pretty deliberate on your part."

I don't know how to answer that, and Jack doesn't let me.

"I thought you should know this shit is out there," she says, "especially before you head for Orlando. You left me out, so you get your own quotes used against you. I think that's what you call karma?"

"I'm sorry," I whisper. "I'm *sorry*."

Jack shakes her head. "What the hell is wrong with you, Tash? I get that things are weird here with your family because of the baby and Klaudie leaving. But you don't ever get an excuse to treat Paul like that. Only *I* can treat Paul like that, and only on very special occasions, when he deserves it. So, you want to tell me your side? Did he deserve it?"

"No." My voice is crumbling away into dust. "No, of course he didn't."

"Know what? I've thought about it a lot, and I've figured it out: You take us for granted. Him especially, but me too. I dealt with all your self-indulgence about going to a hyped-up, preppy college. Even when that's not remotely an option for me. Even when you didn't once mention that you'd be leaving me behind. Like living in another city without me was nothing, like it wouldn't affect you. I've put up with your plans and your schedules because I think it's great you care that much about the series. But how much do you care about *me*, Tash? About either of us?"

My chest is shuddering. There are only a few remaining particles of my voice left when I say, "Paul said he's in love with me."

Jack throws her hands up, as though I've made some wildly inappropriate joke. "Well, fucking *duh*, Tash. Of course he's in love with you. What did you expect? You grew up together and, bonus, you're not related. It was kind of inevitable."

She kicks the leg of my desk chair, reflective for a moment before adding, "He was going to ask you to winter formal. Isn't that priceless? He spent a whole damn year whining to me about you after he broke up with Stephanie. 'Oh, Jack, does she like me? It'll screw things up forever,' blah, blah. So he finally comes up with this elaborate plan. He was going to buy fifteen pumpkins and carve a letter into each of them, and he was going to light them all outside your window so they'd say 'DANCE WITH ME, TASH.' And I couldn't stop him, no matter how nauseating the whole thing was. And then, I swear, not a week after he concocts the proposal, you tell us your news."

"Jack. I had no idea."

"Yes, well, you're kind of oblivious to anyone's feelings but your own."

That's harsh, but I take it. I think I deserve way harsher at this point.

"We were . . . confused," Jack says. "The way you told us, I thought you didn't like guys, period. Like, you weren't attracted to anyone. It was something neither of us felt like we could bring up with you. We were both scared we would say something wrong. Which I know was messed up in its own way, but . . . I mean, you've got to understand, it threw Paul for a loop."

"Because he thought I was a normal girl before."

If Jack is allowed to be harsh, I figure I'm allowed some melodramatic self-loathing. But Jack flings me a look that informs me she's not having any of it.

"He was beginning to come to grips with it, and then you got into this . . . *whatever* you have with Internet Thom. All this new information that sounded different from what you told us in September. I'm not saying it's your fault for not liking Paul back. But you have to see things from his perspective. You really twisted him up."

"No, I—I get that now. God. He . . . he was really going to carve fifteen pumpkins?"

Jack nods.

"*Fifteen?* He could've just spelled 'Dance.'"

"Yeah, well he thought you deserved fifteen."

I slump in my chair. There's a puncture wound somewhere in my skin, slowly letting out all the air inside. I deflate faster and faster by the second.

"It's not that I don't like him," I whisper. "I had a crush on him when we were younger too. Like you said, it was inevitable. But then . . . I don't know. It's impossible now. It wouldn't work."

"Because . . . he likes sex?"

"Jack. We are not actually having this conversation."

Jack throws her hands up again, like *What're you gonna do?*

"I know him," I say. "I know the girls he's gone on dates with. The things he's said about them. Stephanie Crewe, all of that. I know what he wants. It won't work."

"Okay, yeah, but maybe that's a little close-minded? I'm not saying it *will* work, but if he wants to try. . . . And anyway, what makes him any different than Thom? Just because you don't know Thom as well, you think, what, he'll be magically perfect for you?"

"N-no."

I can't tell Jack she's put her finger on it. She's called it out exactly. Even though I know it's impossible, that it doesn't work that way, I've been hoping that as long as Thom and I don't talk about sex, it won't become an issue between us. Ever. It's so stupid. It's stupid, and Jack can sniff it out from a mile away.

"Okay." Jack scoots down the bed, closer to me. "Look. I'm not blaming you for feeling the way you do. You know that, right? You can feel or want whatever, whoever. I mean that. I just don't get why half your clothes were off your body the other night."

"I wanted to prove him wrong," I say, even though that makes no sense in the rational light of day. "I don't know, I can't . . ."

"Well, can you not do it again? Can you not *purposefully* twist him up?"

She cuts me off before I can answer. "Look, I can't get mad at you for effing up coming out when I've never had to do it myself. But I can be mad at you for plenty of other stuff. Like going behind my back with this blogger. And treating Paul like shit. Treating us both like shit."

"Jack, I—"

Jack shakes her head viciously as she cuts me short. "No. I'm not done being mad at you. Especially because I don't think you *get* it yet."

Then she leaves me. I watch from the front porch as she heads down Edgehill, past those twelve front lawns that separate us. This time tomorrow, it won't be twelve lawns but eight hundred miles.

Twenty-Four

In the morning, Mom drives me to the airport. I have a seven o'clock flight. There is absolutely no good reason to set an alarm clock for five in the morning when school is not in session, and I am a stumbling, semiconscious mess when I slide into the passenger seat.

Mom smiles sympathetically. "You going to make it?"

"No wonder this flight was cheapest," I groan.

"But it'll be worth it, right?"

I consider this. I nod begrudgingly.

"Call me when you land," Mom says. "And when you check in to your room, all right? I still don't like the idea of you staying in that big hotel by yourself."

"It'll be fine, Mom. I'm not going to be totally alone. George Connor will be there, remember?"

"Yes, that doesn't really put my mind at ease."

"Oh my God, don't worry. George and I don't think of each other that way *at all*."

I haven't told Mom about Thom, though. It doesn't seem necessary, when he's a person I haven't even met in real life. That's my screwy logic, anyway.

The one good thing about that awful review on *Horn-Rimmed Glasses Girl* showing up right before the convention is that I'm way too preoccupied to dwell on it. I didn't even pull it up on my computer last night to reread the goriest pieces and comb through the comments. I know it'll only get me down, and I don't want to be in a bad place for Orlando. I've learned over the past couple months that those kinds of comments stick around in my mind a lot longer than the nice ones. If I don't want them forever filed away, then I shouldn't read them, period.

I try not to think of Paul, either, but that's a harder feat. As I sit curled up by my gate, trying to read an issue of *Entertainment Weekly*, the better part of my mind goes rogue and keeps flashing up images and fragments of sentences. Paul's face when I pulled my shirt over my head. *Fifteen pumpkins. Confused. Twisted inside.* I beat each one down, telling myself that I can't think about those things right now. I should be focusing on Orlando. On what panels and meet and greets I want to attend, on how I'm going to wear my hair for the dinner tonight and what I'll say if *Unhappy Families* wins a Tuba. On Thom.

I open my phone and read the final text he sent last night: *See you SOON.*

Because we're finally going to *see* each other. We're finally going to use our voices to talk. That's a big deal. That's what I need to focus on. My life in Lexington can wait for the next two days.

I look up from my magazine after having read the same sentence five times and deeming myself momentarily illiterate. I crane my neck, looking around for George, and I spot him a few rows over, tapping on his laptop. I try to catch his eye, even wave in his direction, but that only snags the attention of the girl next to him, who stares at me like I am a mountain troll. I give up and return to my magazine. I am still incapable of reading, but at least I can look at the behind-the-scenes shots on the set of *Storms of Taffdor*.

It's not until we're boarding the plane that I get George's attention. He's already seated in one of the front economy rows when I inch down the aisle.

"Hey," I say.

He nods.

"Guess I'll see you on the other side."

He nods again.

So that's that. What great company. George is the one person I know who could make this trip unpleasant.

I check my ticket again. Judging from my row number and current position, I'm guessing I'm at the very back of the plane. My guess proves correct. The good news is the seat next to me is empty, so I get some extra legroom. The bad news is the flight attendant runs out of Biscoff cookies by the time she reaches me.

Kathryn Ormsbee

"This usually *never* happens," she says, and she gives me double the roasted peanuts instead, as though this makes up for it, and I'm left wondering why any airline still hands out peanuts when there are so many people out there with allergies. Which makes me think of Paul and his peanut butter kryptonite. Which makes me unspeakably sad. So I pull out my iPod and play St. Vincent so loudly I'm sure I'm doing long-term damage to my eardrums.

"Want to share a taxi?"

I've just hauled my suitcase off the baggage carousel when I find George hovering behind me like the freakin' Ghost of Christmas Past. So he's finally deigned to use words. That's an improvement, I suppose.

"There's a shuttle to the hotel, actually," I say. "It's a lot cheaper. I was just going to take that."

"Oh, really? Huh." George looks like I've suggested we ride bareback on mules down the highway.

"Sorry," I say, yanking out the handle of my suitcase and rolling it past him, toward the sign that reads BUSES & SHUTTLES.

"Hey, wait!" I hear. George hurries to catch up with me and says, "How often do they run?"

"Like, every thirty minutes. Why, you have somewhere you need to be fast? Adoring fangirls waiting for your autographs, Levin?"

George smirks. "They can wait, I guess."

It's not that bad a wait. The shuttle shows up in ten minutes and is well air-conditioned, a blessed relief after standing in the sticky ninety-degree heat. I make a mental note to not complain so much about Kentucky summers; Florida is way worse. When we get to the hotel, I grab my suitcase off the rack before the driver can, because I don't really need help, and I also don't know what tipping protocol is when it comes to stuff like that.

George and I stand in the hotel check-in line together. I am irrationally nervous that because my mom made the reservation, they won't let me check in and will call security on me. Like I'm some underage kid trying to buy a bottle of gin. But no one calls security. The problem, it turns out, isn't that I'm underage but that it's too early in the day, and there aren't any available rooms that have been serviced yet. The receptionist tells me to check back in a few hours, once housekeeping has made their rounds.

I roll my suitcase over to a couch in the corner of the massive lobby. Mozart is piping out of a nearby speaker, and the table in front of the couch is fashioned to look like a giant purple geode. It's gaudy, but overall pretty cool. I prop my feet on the table's edge and text my mom to let her know I've arrived safe and sound at the hotel. Then I text Thom.

Here, here, here! Still up for meeting at registration at noon?

That's the plan we made nearly a week ago. We're going to meet at the registration tables and then go to the convention's kick-off dinner together. Maybe, somewhere in between there, Thom will buy me cof-

Kathryn Ormsbee

fee from the little Starbucks kiosk in the lobby and tell me he's been secretly in love with me since he saw my first vlog.

Maybe.

Thom doesn't reply immediately, no matter how intently I stare at the screen. Then I hear someone clear his throat above me. For a wild moment, I think it's Thom, come early to surprise me.

It's George.

"Won't let you check in either?" he asks.

I shake my head.

He sits beside me with an irritated sigh. "Then what's the point of flying in early?"

I give him the stink eye. It's not intentional, just instinctual. I don't want to sit next to George, and I was seriously considering lying out on this couch and taking a power nap in public, dignity be damned.

"See anyone you recognize yet?" George asks, weirdly conversational.

"No," I say, "but I haven't really been looking."

"Greta Farrow is over there," he says, nodding to a corner diagonal to us. "You know, from *Greta Gabs*?"

"Oh." I note a petite girl with a hot-pink bob cut, who's wearing black denim overalls and chatting merrily with two guys a foot taller than her. "Yeah, she is kind of hard to miss."

"Isn't it wild to think any of them could be staying in a room right next to us?"

"I hadn't thought of that. But sure. I mean, they're normal people like us."

"Not exactly," says George. "Most of them are from L.A."

I cock my head at George. "Yeah, but being from L.A. doesn't make you less normal. Maybe more tan, more of an asshole. But they're just people, George."

"Yeah, I get that. You're . . . never mind. You're missing the point."

"I don't like star worship," I say. "Celebrities aren't worthy of a tenth the attention we give them. We just have this huge vacuum to fill because we don't believe in Hercules and Medusa anymore."

George snorts. "Production people always have inferiority complexes."

I glower at George. "Production people make movies *happen*. Actors wouldn't have a chance to get famous if it weren't for *production people*."

"Mmm-hmm, sure."

I narrow my eyes. "You have an acceptance speech prepared, don't you?"

He gives me a look. "That's your job. You're the showrunner."

"Yeah, but I bet you've still got a speech prepared."

George says nothing, but he's wearing a self-indulgent smirk. He gets up, lugging his backpack with him. "I'm going to explore some."

I nod, afraid that if I say anything else George will change his mind. I watch him go, then check my phone. Thom's texted back: *Hey, so sorry. Something came up, can't meet then. Call you later.*

Kathryn Ormsbee

I stare at the screen. *Call you later?* He's bailing on me last minute, with no explanation? Just *Call you later?*

I tell myself not to get pissed, not to overreact. Something urgent must have come up. A family emergency or a delayed flight or any other number of legitimate obstacles. Whatever it is, it's probably so urgent he doesn't have time to explain. When he calls me later—*soon,* I beg of the universe—he'll explain everything. Then we'll meet up, and everything will be great. It's probably better that way. If we met at registration, I would be so distracted with absorbing all the new information that I wouldn't be my most charming. So this is fine. It's all for the best.

If Thom isn't going to show up anytime soon, though, I might as well register for the convention and look around. I go back to the reception desk and ask if they can store my suitcase. They do, with a scary amount of courtesy, and afterward I stuff my claim number in my messenger bag and follow a glossy sign atop an easel that reads, GOLDEN TUBA REGISTRATION THIS WAY.

The hotel is even vaster than I expected. I turn past the reception area and find myself in a wide, high-ceilinged hallway filled with mingling people, most of them in their twenties and thirties, laughing raucously and sharing confidential whispers and telling stories with overlarge hand gestures. Everyone and everything around me is crackling with life and anticipation. Sets of double doors line the hallway, marked with hotel placards (BALLROOM A, CONFERENCE ROOM 2) and, above those, card stock signs with alternative room names (FRENCH HORN, SAXOPHONE).

Again, I think of Paul, and my heart twists. I refocus my attention on two long tables at the end of the hall. A gold-lettered banner hanging from the tables reads, REGISTRATION.

I get in line at the *P–Z* table, my eyes still wandering around the hallway. We're right outside the biggest set of double doors, marked BALLROOM C and TUBA. I'm guessing this is where the award ceremony will take place tomorrow night. From my obstructed vantage point, I see circular tables draped with white linen tablecloths, which makes me think they're holding the kick-off dinner there too.

"Name, please?"

It's my turn in line, and a cheery woman wearing bright pink lipstick and a *Doctor Who* T-shirt is looking up at me, expectant.

"Natasha Zelenka," I say.

She nods, flips to the last page of her stapled sheets, and runs her index finger down the row of names, chanting, "Zelenka, Zelenka, Zelen—there you are!" She drags a green highlighter over my name, then ducks under the table to retrieve a fat manila envelope. She hands it to me saying, "Everything you need is in there: schedule, ticket for tonight's dinner, name tag. Make sure you put that name tag on as soon as possible! You have to wear it to get into all our panels."

I nod dutifully, thank the woman, and slip out of line.

The hallway feels twice as crowded now as when I first set foot in here. There are so many conversations popping around my ears, so many running, shifting bodies. It's overwhelming, and I can't decide

Kathryn Ormsbee

if it's a kind of overwhelming I like. It is . . . *splendifying*. My eyes are strained and my whole body feels itchy and oily from the early morning travel. I really want to be alone in a hotel room, where I can splash cold water on my face and pass out for an hour-long nap.

Since that's not a possibility, and since my couch by the geode table has now been taken over by a family of four, I go to the Starbucks kiosk and order a tall iced coffee. Then I tuck myself away at a small table by the window and open my manila envelope. There are enough papers and brochures in here to keep me occupied for a while. I just hope Thom calls before I've gone through them all.

Hours later, Thom still hasn't called. I'm on my second iced coffee and reading the one carry-on book I brought with me—*The Death of Ivan Ilyich*, by my ever-so-talented boyfriend, Leo. At this point, I can't help but be well and truly pissed at Thom. It's after three o'clock, and he hasn't called, texted, *anything*. Not even a few words to let me know he's sorry and trying to get here as soon as possible. I mark my place in the book and attempt to look on the bright side: At least by now there has to be a room ready for me. I pack my things into my bag, drop my name tag necklace over my head (I've crossed out *Natasha* and written *Tash* over it in mechanical pencil), and head for the reception desk.

I receive a key for a room on the seventh floor, which I take to be a good omen, because why not. Then I retrieve my luggage and head upstairs with only one objective in mind: face-planting on my queen-size bed.

It is a well-earned, satisfying face-plant. I know I shouldn't nap, though, because it's too late in the afternoon, and I always turn into a mumbling Yeti-like creature if I nap after two o'clock. I decide it's best to power through, so I turn on the television before heading to the bathroom, peel off my sweaty travel clothes, and shower down my body. When I emerge from the bathroom, *The Fresh Prince of Bel-Air* is playing. The familiar voices of the Banks family put me in a happier mood as I remove my shower cap and untangle my wadded bun of hair. I decide to go ahead and put on my dress for tonight, considering the dinner is in under two hours. I'm applying mascara when my phone chimes. It's a text from Thom. Not a call.

I can be there in 30. Want to meet in the lobby?

Somewhere in the back of my mind I'm aware that I should be mad, but there's no way I'm going to spoil this newfound good mood. So I text back, *Works for me!* and spend the next twenty minutes choosing from the two pairs of earrings I packed and trying to beat down the feeling that I'm going to lose two cups of iced coffee all over this hotel room desk.

Then I head down to the lobby.

It's beyond weird, meeting like this. We both know what the other looks and sounds like from our vlogs, but we've never seen or heard each other in person. So we will recognize each other in the lobby, but not in the way most humans do. Only because of video cameras and the Internet. The marvels of the Modern Age.

Kathryn Ormsbee

I see him first. He's sitting, of all places, at the couch by the geode table. I take this to be a good omen, because I am taking *everything* as a good omen from here on out. He's wearing black skinny jeans, a white button-down shirt, and a thin, mustard-yellow tie. His hair is cut short but messy at the top, the same as it is in his vlogs. But he's *different* from the vlog version of himself too. His shoulders are narrower than I thought, and his profile is almost unrecognizable. It's like I've only known him as a flat, monochromatic stick drawing up until this moment. Now he is three-dimensional and pumped full of Technicolor. My intestines feel like they're crawling up my throat, but I'm here, and I've seen him first, which means I have to be the one to make this happen.

He doesn't catch sight of me until I'm close enough to tap his shoulder and say, "Hello, stranger."

He looks up, his face instantly breaking into a grin. "Oh my God," he says. "Look who it is."

He stands up, and I think we're about to embrace, but then he's wrapping an arm around my shoulder in a side hug instead. It's awkward, but how could it not be? This is us, Thom and Tash, Internet buddies, meeting in person for the first time.

I pull away and say, "Hello, Thom Causer" with mock formality, dipping into a little curtsy.

He returns the gesture with his own little bow and says, "Why, hello, Tash Zelenka."

He says my name wrong. He pronounces it like it rhymes with "ash." And my intestines are slipping back down my throat. It's such a small mistake, but it's a huge one too, and I wonder, how could he not know something like that? Something as simple as how to pronounce my *name*?

Because we've never spoken to each other before, that's how. It is a logical explanation that bears no blame on Thom. Still, I can't help but feel hurt—resentful, even.

Then he's talking, and I realize the moment is gone. I can't correct him now. It would be too bitchy to interrupt and say, "Hey, by the way, Tash is short for Na*tash*a."

So I clear my mind as best I can and focus on what he's saying.

". . . gets so chummy and boring, so I thought maybe we could go out for dinner. I know this great Italian place, Giuseppe's. I went there last year. It's not far from here."

I stare stupidly at Thom, still slow on the uptake. What is he suggesting?

"You want to ditch the kick-off dinner?" I hate the sound of my voice. It's high and thin, like a kettle whistle. "But it's a free meal. And aren't they going to make some important announcements there?"

Thom shrugs. "Nothing I can't fill you in on. It's been the same thing both years I've gone: mediocre food and condescending company. Plus, if we're stuck at a table with six other people, I won't be able to talk to you as much as I'd like."

I *do* like the sound of Thom's voice. It is low and crisp and rings around in my ears longer than all other noises.

"If you put it that way," I say, smiling.

Thom motions toward the hotel's front doors. "Come on. I've got an aunt and uncle here who are letting me borrow one of their cars."

It crosses my mind for a blip of a second that Thom could be a psycho killer about to drive me off to my doom. But this is *Thom*, a good-looking nerd who once posted a video defending me from Internet haters. It's Thom, and even if he doesn't know how to pronounce my name, he knows a ton of other things about me, like how I mentioned once that my favorite meal is fettuccine Alfredo. And now he's taking me to an Italian restaurant.

It looks like my reality is shaping up to be better than my dream. Dinner totally trumps a coffee date.

Twenty-Five

"So, no joke, I've been standing in line for two hours when, out of nowhere, this guy in a Chewbacca suit comes tearing across the lobby and bowls me over. My popcorn goes flying, and everything is *chaos*, and Matt is hovering over me like 'Oh my God, he's had a concussion. We need an ambulance, stat.' And the best part? Chewbacca *keeps running*. He runs out of the lobby and into the parking lot and God knows where after that."

There's a stitch in my side from laughing so hard. People at nearby tables are staring at us, but I don't care. It's Friday night, and I'm with Thom Causer in the flesh, eating the best fettuccine Alfredo of my life.

"Did you really have a concussion?" I ask, once my laughter is under control. I try to look concerned, but there are laugh tears dripping out the corners of my eyes.

"No, I was fine. Just a little bruised. And there was popcorn butter all over me."

"So you still saw the movie?"

"Tash, have you been listening? I stood in that line for more than *two hours*. It was the *midnight premiere*. Of course I still saw the movie."

I only wince a little this time when he mispronounces my name. There hasn't been an opportune time to correct him, but I'm beginning to not mind so much. I'm just so glad it's turned out this way, with me laughing, and our words overlapping, never a lull in conversation. I was scared things might be different in person, that there would be lots of awkward pauses and averted gazes and the whole night might crash and burn. But there's been none of that. This night is shaping up so much better than I hoped. I'm eating the most delicious Alfredo sauce I've ever placed in my mouth—apologies, Dad—and Thom is cracking me up with funny story after funny story. I never knew he had such a sidesplitting sense of humor; I guess texting doesn't really lend itself to the drawn-out anecdotes he's telling me now. Now that we've met. Now that he could reach across the table and hold my hand, if he wanted to.

And as we wait for our dessert, that's exactly what he does. His hand is warmer than mine, and a little damper, too. I curl my lips in on each other to prevent myself from smiling too big.

We share an order of tiramisu, and when the bill comes out, I insist we split it down the middle. Thom looks miffed, but he agrees. He lets go of my hand to fish out his wallet and says, "I didn't do anything wrong, did I?"

"Hmm?" I look up from my purse. "No. Why?"

"They say going Dutch is the sign of a date gone wrong."

The loony smile breaks free. "So this is a date, is it?"

Thom nods. "Absolutely."

"But splitting the bill isn't a bad sign. It's just modern."

I talk like I know a whole lot about the rules of dating. Like I'm a girl whose Friday nights are booked solid with classy adult dates at Italian restaurants. Right now, I *feel* like that kind of girl.

I leave an extra big tip for our waitress, who refilled our breadstick basket not once, not twice, but *three* times. As we leave the restaurant, my walk feels more like a waddle, and I'm convinced my body is composed of nothing but water and carbohydrates.

"Thom," I say as I buckle my seat belt. "My stomach is expanding at an alarming rate. I might blow up your car."

"You gonna go all Violet Beauregarde on me?"

I laugh and say, "I *love* that movie. And the book. Oh my God, my friend Jack is obsessed with that book. All the Roald Dahl books. Especially *The Witches*. She says her biggest regret in life is being born after Roald Dahl's death."

"So we can bet what *she* would do with a time machine."

For what feels like the hundredth time tonight, I laugh.

It's not until Thom is back on the road that I consider where we're going and what time it is. I check the clock. It's ten, but it feels much later. I could've sworn I aged a year inside that restaurant.

"Where are we heading?" I ask.

Thom glances at me. "Back to the hotel, I guess?"

Kathryn Ormsbee

"Oh." I'm not sure why I feel so suddenly deflated. "You want to hang out some more in the lobby?"

"Uh, yeah. Sure. Or, you know, your room. If you want."

I'm suddenly alert.

My *room*?

Is this what I think it is? What every teen movie out there suggests it is? Or does Thom want to go to my room and hang out, away from the noise and bustle of the Golden Tuba crowd? From nowhere, Jack's voice cracks into my head, shouting *Don't be so effing naive, Tash!*

Oh God.

So it's here.

That moment I kept pretending wouldn't arrive.

I should say something now, I know.

I should say something before Thom parks the car and we walk through the lobby and get into the elevator, before I punch the number 7 and we get off on my floor. I should, but everything has been going so perfectly until now. Everything has been good omens and laughs, and I don't want it to end yet.

But as I pull my room key from my back pocket, Jack's voice returns, full force. *Don't be unfair. He should know.*

First, I wonder since when did I allow my subconscious to assume the voice of my best friend and lecture me about my sexual identity?

Second, I wet my lips and get ready to speak.

But what the hell will I say? I haven't practiced this, haven't thought it through at all. How do I even begin? "By the way, Thom . . ."?

"By the way, Thom . . ."

It's too late. It's out there, and it can never be retrieved. So I press on, standing in the middle of the seventh-floor hallway, facing an increasingly uneasy-looking Thom. "Um. Just so we're clear, I don't want . . ."

I don't have to tell him everything right now, I think. *I could just say I don't want tonight leading to sex. That's a totally normal thing for a seventeen-year-old girl on her first date to say.*

But it's not the whole truth. It's an uncomfortable half-truth, and if whatever this is with Thom is going to keep existing, I'll have to tell the more uncomfortable half of it soon enough.

I've taken too long to sort out my words. Thom's face is creased in bad places as he says, "We don't . . . um, if you feel weird about going to your room, we don't have to."

I nod. Then I shake my head. "No, you should come in. But I have to talk to you about something."

I don't exactly want him to come in, but I can't carry on this conversation standing in the hallway, where anyone could peek out of their room or walk by. So I brush past him and pass a few more doors until we get to mine. I slide the electronic key into its slot, push open the door, and flick on every light switch within reach. My eyes fall immediately to the bed. We can't sit there. But there's only the bed and the desk chair, so I hurry ahead of Thom and take the chair. I know I'm giving off a nervous vibe. I'm already ruining this perfect night, and I haven't even told him yet.

Kathryn Ormsbee

I'm preparing to speak, threading together sentences that are by no means good but will have to do. Thom beats me to it.

"Tash," he says. *Tash like "ash."* "If you're worried I want to mess around . . . we don't have to do that. I just had a good time with you, and I thought we could be alone."

"Right," I say. "No, that's good. But I need to tell you something first. I think at this point it's important you know."

"Okay," Thom says slowly. "You're kind of scaring me."

"Sorry." My body floods with heat. "I'm an idiot, and I didn't think through how I'd explain this to you beforehand. So. So, the thing is . . . I don't like sex. At all. Like, I don't want to have it with guys. Or girls. I don't think of anyone that way. And I totally get that might be a deal breaker for you because, um, sex is pretty important to most people. I didn't bring it up when we were texting, because I didn't know where this was going. But now . . . Um. Well, now you know."

This moment cannot possibly belong to my life. I am a character in a made-for-television movie who's just read off lines from a terribly written script. I am a parody of myself.

Thom is looking at me as though I've slapped him across the jaw. I don't blame him. I know this has to be the last thing he was expecting. I feel like a sham, some fake version of Tash Zelenka. But how else could I do this? Even now, I don't see another way.

"Um, *what?*" Thom is still standing motionless in front of the bed. "Sorry, are you saying you don't like me?"

"*No.* No, that's not what I'm saying at all. I like you a lot. It's not personal, it's . . . I'm not attracted to anyone that way. Sexually, I mean. I'm, like, ninety-nine percent sure I'm asexual."

I say that last bit in a breezy, almost lighthearted way. I don't know how else to make this less monumentally awkward.

"You're not attracted to anyone?" Thom repeats. "But you, like, talk about your man crushes all the time on your vlog. Mr. Tilney, Mr. Darcy . . ."

I shake my head. "That's different. I *do* have crushes on them. On their personalities and on what they look like—like, *aesthetically.*"

"So just . . . objectively. Like works of art." Thom's voice has gone hard. He sounds incredulous.

"Well, not *exactly* like that. It's just, I don't fantasize about them or anything. Like, I don't want them ripping off my corset, or whatever."

I'm still trying to turn this into an upbeat conversation, trying to salvage all the goodness from earlier this evening. But I can read the look on Thom's face, and I know this is a losing battle. He doesn't understand.

"You're *asexual?*" he says. "You're, like, seventeen. No one knows they're asexual at seventeen. No offense, Tash, but don't you think maybe you're a little scared of sex? Or you don't want to try it yet? Because that's fine, but I find it hard to believe—"

"W-what does my age have to do with it?" I sputter. "I know what I want and what I don't want. I've never wanted sex. Never. I've never

Kathryn Ormsbee

understood why it has to be in every book and movie and television show ever made. I've never figured out why porn is such a huge thing. I'll be fine if no guy ever takes his shirt off for me. I'm not scared, I just *don't want it*."

Thom shakes his head. "So you're calling yourself asexual, because *why*? The Internet tells you so? Because no one out there was ever saying they were asexual before the Internet."

My body is hot all over. No more attempts at lightening the mood. No more timid explanations.

"What are you saying?" I demand. "That it's not a real thing? That I'm *lying* to you?"

"I don't know. I think maybe you're scared of where this is heading. Or maybe you're confused. But you can't like guys and say you're 'asexual.' That's not a thing. And you're not going to find any guy out there who will tell you it is. It's one or the other, you can't have both."

Now I am the incredulous one. "I don't need any guy out there to tell me what I'm feeling is real. The only reason I told *you* is because I was trying to be honest with you. Not because I want your opinion on whether I have legitimate emotions or not."

Thom groans. "Oh God, please don't turn this into a feminist rant. We were having a really good time. If I did something to freak you out, or if you changed your mind, you could've just told me straight."

"Why were you so late meeting me?"

I'm shocked by my own question. By the suddenness and the vehemence of it. It pierces the air between me and Thom, demanding an answer.

"What?"

This time, I ask it with cold resolution. "Why were you so late meeting me? You said we'd meet at noon. Then you didn't give any explanation for why you didn't show. So, what, was your flight delayed?"

Thom shakes his head slowly. "No, I had . . . something else come up. I ran into some guys I met here last year, and they wanted to have lunch. I tried to get away as quick as possible. But that's not really any of your business."

"So you wanted to network," I say flatly. "That was more important than keeping a promise."

"Wow, Tash. Melodramatic, much? That wasn't a promise. That was just some tenuous plan we had."

"Right," I say. "I'm just a tenuous plan you had."

"You know what? Fine. Yeah, I guess you were."

He's heading for the door, and I am incapable of following. I am stone, and so is this desk chair. We have melded into one unmovable statue.

He turns the handle. "I'll get out of here. Since that's obviously what you want."

I could chase after him. I could even kiss him. I could try to make this work the same way I tried with Justin Rahn. But I wouldn't be doing that for me, I'd be doing it for Thom, and when it comes down to it, I refuse to be that selfless.

Kathryn Ormsbee

Also, I am still cemented to the chair.

I stay stuck like that for a long, long time. Long after Thom closes the door. Long enough to develop a blood clot. Long enough, it seems, to decompose and waste away entirely. I only move when my throat begins to tickle with thirst. I break open one of the plastic-covered cups by the coffeemaker and fill it with water from the bathroom tap. I drink three cupfuls, but I still feel thirsty. I grab my wallet from my purse and leave the room. I remember seeing a vending machine in the ice-maker alcove, so I head that way. Maybe what my body really wants is sugar and carbonation.

I study the drink options before feeding the machine two dollar bills, and I leave with a bottle of Coke Zero and fifty cents in change. I'm at my door, fishing out my key, when I hear someone behind me say my name. I turn and find none other than George Connor standing in the hallway. He's two doors down and has his key card in hand.

"Hey," he says, pointing at the distance between our doors. "That's a coincidence."

I nod stiffly. "Um, yeah."

Why now, of all times, is George being conversational?

He frowns at me and comes a little closer. "Are you okay?"

I sniff loudly, rub together the two quarters in my hand. "Yeah, sure."

"You look like you've been crying."

Why now, of all times, is George being *concerned*?

"Yeah, I guess I've been crying."

"Well, uh, are you okay?"

Since I'm being so damn honest tonight, I say, "No."

George pockets his key and walks up to my door. He's squinting intently at me, as though I'm developing a genetic mutation before his eyes.

"What's wrong?"

I try thinking up an answer that is guaranteed to scare George off. I settle on "A boy was mean to me."

But George doesn't even flinch. Obligingly, he says, "Boys suck."

I break down into this ugly laugh-cry thing, and George says, "Why don't you sit down, you look unstable."

So I sit down right there in front of my door, and George sits beside me.

After a while, I speak. I say, "What do you think is more important: being honest, or being happy?"

"Honest," George answers, without hesitation. It's like he's been prepping for this existential query all his life.

"Why?"

"Well, that's my artistic philosophy: honesty first. Even if everyone else hates you for it, you have to be an honest performer. You have to be serious and dedicated and authentic. Happiness isn't really in the mix."

I feel as though I might laugh in George's face. "You're such an ass," I say, even though he's currently being the nicest he's ever been to me.

"I know," he says. "But that's the cost of being a good artist. Being

Kathryn Ormsbee

honest and dedicated inevitably means you're difficult to get along with. It means a lot of people won't like you."

I balk. "Says who?"

"Just look at the greats: Marlon Brando, Dustin Hoffman, James Dean."

"Kubrick," I add, thoughtful. "Coppola."

"I think most of the best artists were probably assholes."

"We should never meet our heroes," I say softly.

"So, you understand."

I try to ignore the fact that George basically called himself James Dean and say, "Yeah, I think I do."

"I can tell," says George. "In the way you direct."

"Wait. You think *I'm* an asshole?"

"No, I can just tell you're dedicated. But you care too much about people's feelings. *Unhappy Families* is great, but it would've been even better if you were a meaner person. You know, actually started filming on time instead of waiting for people to show up. Kept asking to reshoot a scene even though you could tell we were tired. You're too soft, Zelenka."

I give George a long, bemused look. "I can't tell if you're being nice or mean right now."

"I'm being honest."

"See, all this time I thought you were just a mindless prick, and it turns out you have this elaborate philosophy of prickiness."

"Think about it," says George. "You still kept me on, even though I was a prick and no one really got along with me."

"Yeah."

"Because I'm a good actor."

"Yeah."

"So my philosophy panned out okay."

I cannot argue with that. I twist open the cap of my Coke and take a long swig.

"So to answer your question," George continues, "it's better to be honest than happy. Because even if you're happy first, you'll eventually have to be honest with yourself."

"Does that mean honest people will eventually be happy?"

"I don't think it works that way."

"Boo."

After a beat, George says, "Where were you tonight, by the way? I thought you were coming to the dinner. I saved you a place at my table."

I jerk my head in surprise. "I thought you'd be busy hobnobbing."

"Well, yeah, but I also wanted to sit next to the woman who made my career what it is."

"Uh-huh. What happened to all that 'inferiority complex' crap?"

"I dunno, I'm feeling generous tonight. I got phone numbers from four different Kevin fans."

I look at George. I don't bother beating away the baffled appreciation on my face.

Kathryn Ormsbee

"You're all right, George," I say.

"I am fucking not," he replies, grabbing my Coke bottle and jumping to his feet.

I watch in disbelief as he chugs down the remaining soda in one go. He tosses the emptied bottle to me and says, "My fee for providing you with sage counsel."

"Night, George."

"Mmm-hmm. Till tomorrow. You going to that Taylor Mears meet and greet?"

I look him straight in the eye and say, "We should never meet our heroes."

Twenty-Six

While I'm still being honest, I guess I should tell you some things about my man Leo. Some not-so-impressive things. Because much as I like to pretend otherwise, he wasn't perfect. So here's the truth—the *whole* truth—about Tolstoy:

He had a tumultuous marriage. His wife, Sophia, was of the same social cut as him—a highbred Russian aristocrat. The stories say they were madly in love when they first met, despite the significant age difference (Leo was sixteen years older). Apparently, they were extremely passionate, couldn't keep their hands off each other. When they weren't busy with *that*, Sophia copied and proofread Leo's manuscripts and he listened to her input. But then they grew older. Sophia had thirteen—count them, *thirteen*—children. Leo developed his increasingly extreme ideas about money and social structures, and Sophia didn't agree with him. Their marriage was filled with jealousy, suspicion, and full-out hatred. It was a quintessential love-hate relationship, and it lasted for *fifty years*. They were an Unhappy Family like no other. Most people say

Leo was really unfair to Sophia, and in the end he abandoned her in an attempt to stay true to his new ideals. Not long after that, he died.

It's a much less rosy picture than I usually paint, I know, but it's an accurate one. The truth is, Leo would've made a horrible boyfriend. It would never work between us, and not just because of the chronological difficulties or my father's disapproval. If I ever met this particular hero of mine, I'd end up disenchanted for life. Kind of the way I feel now, after meeting Thom Causer.

I spend the night tugging the covers on and off, on and off again. My mind won't shut down. There are too many thoughts crowding the station, too many trains bound for too many destinations. I wish my brain's engineers would just go on strike already.

I keep asking myself if there was another way to do it, phrase it. Which is a particularly dangerous track to follow, because *of course* I could've done it differently, could've changed a dozen tiny things, from the prepositions I used to the length of the pauses between my words. The trouble is, I don't know if any of those differences would have made a difference.

For months, what I had with Thom was all raw potential, a steady uphill climb to the Great Unknown. Now the Unknown has revealed itself, and it's ugly and anticlimactic. All this for Thom to miss the point. To tell me I'm confused. I know it was a lot of information to throw at him, but I also know that even if we tried to talk this out, things couldn't go back to the way they were.

I finally drift off around five o'clock. My alarm wakes me at seven. Panels begin at eight. I debate whether I want to sleep an extra half hour or drag myself out of bed for continental breakfast. I choose food over sleep. On my way out, I stop to knock on George's door, but there's no answer. It's pathetic, but I'm a little terrified I will see Thom when I get to the lobby level, and I don't want to be alone if that happens, like every part of me is shouting, "Hey, I'm asexual *and* have no friends!"

But I don't see Thom at breakfast, or at any of my morning panels. During all the dead time yesterday, I made a handwritten schedule. It's a relentless lineup of discussions with titles like "Meta Media," "Comedy Vlogging," and "DIY Divas," with only ten-minute breaks in between. I give up trips to the bathroom for the sake of snagging a good seat, and by the time lunch break rolls around, my bladder is at the bursting point. I'm just coming out of the restroom when I catch sight of Thom's tousled hair, and I retreat immediately back into the swinging door, nearly taking out the girl behind me. I offer a meek apology, expecting an ugly look in return. Instead, I get "Oh. My. God. *Teatime with Tash*?"

I blink stupidly at the girl, who looks around my age and is wearing a giant polka-dot bow at the precise top of her head. Then I produce this dorky little laugh and say, "Um, yep. That's me."

"Oh my gosh, I *love* your vlog." The girl scoots out of the way of some other women departing the restroom, and I follow suit. "I was so

Kathryn Ormsbee

bummed when you went on hiatus. I mean, I love *Unhappy Families* as much as the next person, but your vlogs were adorable. And I agree: Wentworth is *totally* the hottest Austen boy."

I nod, mute with glee.

"You should think about doing some *Teatime with Tash* merch, because I would buy a coffee mug."

"Y-yeah, that's—that's a good idea."

The girl adjusts her boxy hipster glasses and nods enthusiastically. Her T-shirt reads, *Hufflepuffs Do It Best*.

"Well!" she chirps. "Just thought you should know. Oh, hey! Can I get a selfie with you?"

"W-what? Erm-hmm."

I'm barely coherent, but my lunatic smile seems enough confirmation for her. She whips out her camera, tapping it to selfie mode. Then she wrinkles her nose and says, "Maybe we could do it out in the hall? It definitely looks like we're in a bathroom here."

So we go outside and the girl positions us in front of one of the Golden Tuba posters.

"Perfect," she says after the third click. "Thanks so much."

"Thank *you*," I say, still a little dazed. "Really, thanks for telling me you liked it. That means a lot."

"Yeah, of course!" she sings, backing away with an enthusiastic wave. "Kevin forever!"

Which makes a pair of girls walking by do a double take. One of them very obviously checks my name tag, then yelps, "No way! *Unhappy Families?*"

I nod. I feel like an impostor, like I'm being mistaken for Meryl Streep and just going along with it. The girls both make an unintelligible screechy noise, and before I know it, I'm posing for another selfie.

"You know, Levin came too," I tell them. "He should be around here somewhere."

They go slack-jawed. One says, "WHERE."

"Um, I don't know. Sorry."

They set off at a run, as though speed will aid them in tracking down George Connor.

I've come down with a severe case of the jitters. *Fans.* Those were actual *fans*, and they treated me like I was famous. They wanted *selfies* with me. Granted, they'd probably much rather have a selfie with George, but still, I wasn't expecting this, and I don't know if that makes me humble or just stupid.

I realize something as I squeeze into the crowd swarming through the hallway: That first girl knew my name, and she said it *right*. Tash like "posh." Because I always introduce my vlogs by saying my name. So it's not that Thom didn't know how to say my name right; he just didn't care enough to get it right. And for some reason, this fact makes me more pissed off than anything else that happened last night.

I shake the anger out of my system. I'm not letting a boy warp my

Kathryn Ormsbee

Golden Tuba experience. I'm going to focus on those two glorious sel-fies. Sure, there's bound to be some *Unhappy Families* haters here too. Who knows? Silverspunnnx23 herself might be wandering these halls. But that doesn't matter. What matters is that there are definitely fans, and they are awesome fans, and that's way more than I could've said a year ago, when *Unhappy Families* was just an unrealized dream shared between me and Jack.

They're selling five-dollar sandwiches for lunch, but there's no vege-tarian option left, so I opt for a makeshift vending machine meal: granola bar, fruit snacks, barbecue chips, and an orange Fanta. I take my haul up to my bedroom and feast like a royal atop my queen-size bed. I'm aware that if I were a true professional, I would be downstairs "networking"—whatever that awful word means. But for once in my life, I don't feel like being a professional.

I check my phone. I don't know why I'm expecting texts from Jack and Paul. All lines of communication there are still down. I do have a text, but it's from George:

You want to go to the ceremony together, right? We could head down around 6:30.

I didn't think I'd ever find myself wanting to dress up and go any-where with George Connor, but his request actually warms my heart a little. I absolutely want to go to the ceremony together. Before today, I didn't consider how awkward it would be to attend alone.

Except, before today, I assumed I'd be going to the ceremony with Thom, knockoff clairvoyant that I am.

I write, *That'd be great, actually.*

I reconsider, delete the "actually," and replace the comma after "great" with a period.

George and I meet at the elevators.

On the way down, he eyes my sapphire-colored cocktail dress and says, "You look really nice."

I ignore the fact that he sounds surprised.

"You too, Konstantin Dmitrievich Levin," I say, aiming index finger guns at his black suit and tie.

We exit the elevator and, remembering my selfie session from earlier, I grab George by the sleeve and tug him over to a blank space of wall in the lobby.

"We need to document this before all the rabid fangirls drag you away," I say, holding my phone out.

I take a couple shots, then examine them with satisfaction. "Now I have photographic evidence I knew you when."

"Likewise," says George, without a hint of sarcasm.

Ballroom C/Tuba has transformed since I last peeked inside. The tables are gone, and the chairs have been arranged in long, deep rows before an elevated stage. The lights are dimmed, and pop music is thrumming from speakers overhead. An attendant at the door takes our

Kathryn Ormsbee

tickets and notes our name tags, then tells us to take a seat anywhere. We find two seats together on the far end of the fifth row.

Since we've still got time to spare, I slip out to use the bathroom. In the hallway, I catch sight of Thom. He's talking loudly to Chris Marano, a member of Taylor Mears's crew, and just as he seems to be reaching the crux of his speech, he catches sight of *me*. There's the briefest pause, during which I have the ridiculous fear he's going to bail on Chris and walk right over to me. To say he's sorry. Or to say something offensive, like "Look who doesn't have a date to the ceremony."

But he doesn't do either of those things, because this is life, not a movie. His eyes fix back on Chris and he keeps talking, with more enthusiasm than before. And I know then: That's the end of it. That's the end of months' worth of rambling e-mails and flirting texts and uncertainty and unrealistic expectations.

In the bathroom's fancy powder room, I pull out my phone and erase my entire text history with Thom Causer. I'm about to shut off the phone when I get a text from Mom.

First, just the words *Meet Baby:*

Then, a few seconds later, a picture pops into the conversation.

It's a photo of the ultrasound.

I can't make out anything. Seriously. There is nothing about the blob on my screen that resembles a human being. I need Mom and Dad here to tell me what is the head, the nose, the arms. One thing not even they can tell me: the sex. They've opted not to know that until the baby's born.

Another text: *Sorry it took so long! You know how bad I am with technology. Klaudie had to help. (:*

Then: *Hope tonight goes wonderfully! We're so proud of you.*

I'm writing a reply when yet another text arrives.

And I just heard the Harlows' news. I'm so sorry, darling.

I freeze.

The Harlows' news? What news?

Cancer, I think.

The word slices through the softest part of my mind, sending stinging chills through my body.

Mr. Harlow's cancer. That has to be it. But Jack and Paul never said anything.

Of course they didn't. Because we haven't been talking.

I sink down on the powder room couch, unsure if I have the strength to stand back up again. I call Mom.

"Tasha?" She answers on the second ring, her voice concerned. "Aren't you at the ceremony?"

"No. I mean, I am, but . . . Mom, what's going on with the Harlows?"

"Oh. I—I thought Jack would've told you. She didn't tell you?"

"No. No, Mom, *what's going on?*"

There's a long silence on Mom's end, during which tears gather in my eyes.

"He got some tests back from his oncologist," Mom finally says. "The cancer's back. It's spread. It's—it's bad, darling."

Kathryn Ormsbee

Tears fall fast down my face. I pretend not to notice the concerned looks I'm receiving from several women passing in and out of the room.

"Tasha?"

"I have to go, Mom," I whisper.

I hit end on the call. I close my eyes. Through the wall, I can hear the chorus of Katy Perry's "Firework," followed by a man's muffled voice on the loudspeakers. The Golden Tubas are starting. I wipe away one wave of tears, then another.

I have to get back to the ceremony. I will myself to move. I cross the hallway in an unfocused haze, flash my ticket to an attendant, and slip into a now dark ballroom. Onstage, a video is playing on a large screen. It's a montage of big moments from this year's web series, set to a peppy indie tune. Suddenly, George's and Eva's faces flash on the screen. It's their kiss from the Scrabble episode. Audience members have been cheering and *aww*-ing every clip, but the screams are especially loud for this one. It's so jarring that it takes me several seconds to realize that's our footage up there. *Our* footage—mine and Jack's.

Jack.

She should be here. She's as much a creator and storyteller as I am. She's as much responsible for *Unhappy Families*. And I'm struck now by how absurd it is that I'm here without her. How did I ever think that was okay?

If we're going to win Best New Series, the whole cast should be here. I would want Jack by my side. I would want Paul, even Klaudie, to be on that stage. If we win, and it's just me and George up there, it won't feel right. I will feel like a cheat.

The video ends, and the stage lights come up. Taylor Mears walks up to the microphone on center stage and launches into a speech, but I don't hear the words she's saying.

I can't be here.

The realization suffocates me as I back away from the audience and push through the ballroom doors. I need to be in Lexington, with Jack and Paul. I need to be there *now*.

I call Mom again when I'm in my hotel room, throwing my things into my suitcase, haphazardly stuffing and not bothering to put my still wet toothbrush into its toiletry bag.

"I'm coming home," I tell her. "I'm going to find the next flight back."

"Darling." Mom sounds extraordinarily calm given my own state of reckless insanity. "I know how upsetting this must be, but I'm sure Jack and Paul understand. Is one day going to make such a big difference?"

The memory of Jack sitting in my bedroom flashes through my mind, visceral and blindingly bright: *You take us for granted.*

"Yes," I say. "Yes. It is."

"You can't simply trade in your ticket for another one, Tasha. You'll have to pay for a new—"

"I know, Mom. I just . . . need to do this."

The silence gets thick as I stand still by the hotel room door, one hand on my suitcase handle, ready to leave.

Then Mom speaks. "Be safe. Call me as soon as you have something sorted out. I'll pick you up when you get here."

My throat stings. I puff out a sigh. "Thanks, Mom."

And I know my mom will probably have to do a lot of breathing meditations tonight until she's actually cool with this, but in this moment I couldn't be more grateful.

I check out, evading the concerned questions of the too helpful hotel clerk. I don't have time for the shuttle; I get a cab. On my way to the airport, I send a text to George: *I'm so, so sorry. There was an emergency. I'm sure your acceptance speech is way better than mine anyway.*

What I don't write is that his words from last night are plaguing me.

According to George, if you want to be a good artist, you have to sacrifice a lot—including the feelings of people around you. When George told me I was a good director, he focused on all the times I'd slipped up—the times I wasn't ruthless or honest enough. But now I'm horrified at the prospect of George Connor, prima donna extraordinaire, thinking I'm good at what I do. Because that means I'm *too* ruthless, too honest, too *selfish*.

Is that what's happening to me? Did I really get so caught up in all the fame and thrill of *Unhappy Families* that I didn't even consider how absurd it would be to go to Orlando without Jack?

My thoughts are a swirling, guilt-stricken mess when I arrive at the airport, but somehow I manage to devise a plan of action and book seats on the quickest route home—a Delta flight to Atlanta that leaves in less than an hour, and a late-night connecting flight to Lexington. I don't think about the fact that I've shelled out the remainder of my entire summer earnings from Old Navy. All I can think is, *Home, home, home.*

During my layover in Atlanta, I huddle up in a seat at my gate and check my phone. I've already let my mom know the situation. She's texted again to make sure I'm safe and not talking to any strangers in the terminal.

There's also a text from George: *Wow, okay. Doesn't matter, we didn't win.*

I don't even try to process the information. I think I've lost my right to process it.

I haven't texted Jack or Paul. I haven't called. Because it wouldn't be enough. They deserve more than a text or call. They deserve me there, in person, to prove I don't take them for granted.

Touchdown can't come soon enough.

Kathryn Ormsbee

Twenty-Seven

Mom is waiting for me outside baggage claim. It's past midnight, and the sky is moonless, which makes the Camry particularly dark. I tell Mom thank you at least five times, but it still doesn't feel like enough. I ask her for more details about Mr. Harlow, but she doesn't know any. She asks if *Unhappy Families* won, and I tell her we didn't, in a firm, dead tone that stops all further inquiry. Mom doesn't need me to tell her to drop me off at the house twelve down from ours, but I do anyway.

Both cars are in the Harlows' driveway. I go straight around to the back patio door. My fingers fumble on the handle before I realize it's locked, the basement dark. I'm about to make a run for the front porch, where I will knock on the door for however long is necessary. That's when I see that the entertainment room isn't entirely dark. There's a flash of blue and purple light coming from the television. When I peer closer, I make out Paul sitting on the floor, tilting a game controller side to side.

I knock on the glass, tentatively at first, because what right do I have to disturb Paul after the way I treated him the last time he and I were in this room? But soon enough my overwhelming desire to be there with him and Jack suffocates my shame. I pound on the door, effectively startling Paul. He tosses down the controller and hurries over to unlatch the door.

The moment he slides it open, I throw my arms around him. Forget what passed between us days ago, just for now. Forget all of it and put my arms around him, because it is instinct and it is the only thing I know to do that isn't wrong. His own arms are around my back instantly, and his head is pressed into my neck, and I hear him say in a muffled whisper against my hair, "*Fuck*, Tash."

That's when I notice something's off. I pat my hands over the width of his upper back, feeling around for the familiar soft cascade of his ponytail.

"Paul," I croak, pulling away. "What'd you do to your hair?"

"Chopped it off and donated it to Locks of Love. Because he's an idiot."

Over Paul's shoulder, I see Jack descending the basement staircase, arms crossed tight against her chest.

"What are you doing here?" she asks me.

"I got an early flight back," I say, not sure this is the answer she's looking for.

"I don't want a hug," she warns me, as I come closer.

Kathryn Ormsbee

So I stop my approach and instead move to the couch, where all three of us pile and stare vacantly at the paused *Call of Duty*. After a while, Paul clicks on the side table lamp and turns off the television. We sit in the yellow glow, silent. I keep stealing glances at Paul, unable to fully comprehend him with short hair.

"I don't know what to say," I finally whisper. "I'm just really, really, *really* sorry. And I'm here."

Paul scratches the back of his head, his fingers lingering just where the close-cropped cut ends on his neck. Apparently he, too, is unable to grasp what he's done.

"The best thing you could for me?" says Jack. "Make me think about something else. Like, I dunno, the Golden Tubas. I saw your photo with George. Am I going blind, or did you look genuinely happy to be one inch away from him?"

"It was all for publicity. You know how it is."

"Yeah, well, I was *expecting* to see a selfie with *Thom*."

"Yeah," says Paul. His voice is easy and interested. Too easy, too interested. Like he's trying to make up for past wrongs. "Yeah, how was that?"

I laugh. I drop my head in my hands. I laugh some more.

"I'm confused," says Jack. "Is that a rom com giggle, or a bloody horror giggle?"

"Horror," I say, in an appropriately raspy voice. "Definitely horror."

"Oh my God, I know what happened. He turned out to be

silverspunnnx23, didn't he? You totally got catfished. Some really convoluted version of catfished."

"Jack, that doesn't even make sense," says Paul. "He was the one who posted that video defending her, remember?"

"Defending her in a super patronizing way," Jack retorts. "Anyway, that just makes him more suspicious. He probably planned it out so that he wrote the post and recorded the video the same day. So he could pretend he was her savior or something."

"You guys," I say, lifting my head. "You guys, *no*. He was not silverspunnnx23. He was just . . . not very understanding."

Silence.

Jack says, "So, you told him, then?"

"He thought I was making it up. He basically told me the Internet invented how I feel and it's not a real thing. So. Worst possible reaction ever."

Jack's response is immediate and vehement: "Asshole."

Which she follows up with a half-dozen other variations on the theme of "ass."

Paul is conspicuously silent. Nothing he says right now won't sound vindictive or trite. Not after what's passed between us. We both know that.

"He didn't . . . try anything, did he?" asks Jack.

"What? No, nothing like that. He just peaced out. I don't know, maybe I was expecting it, because I don't feel all that shocked."

Kathryn Ormsbee

Jack mutters a few more choice words about what caliber of human Thom is, then surfaces from her plunge into profanity to say, "Damn, now *you* need to be distracted. Paul. Hey. What can we do to distract her?"

This is insensitive of Jack to say, and I think she realizes it soon after, because she beats Paul to an answer by saying, "I know. We need to start talking Kickstarter details. Goals, perks, how we're going to divvy the funds, which project we want to pick next. The Oscar Wilde one is the most fleshed out at this point, but I don't know if we want to go that—"

"Jack. Seriously?" I'm looking at her like she's confessed to being a deer hunter, and frankly, I think that's a very mild reaction on my part.

"Seriously what?"

"You just found out your dad's cancer is back. You haven't even told me the details of his condition, and you want to talk details for our *web channel*?"

"Um, what part of 'distraction' don't you understand? Have you been listening to me at all? Talking details for our web channel is *exactly* what I need to be doing. The show must go on. That's professionalism."

"Yeah, I think it's actually called emotional repression."

"Okay, look." Jack's voice turns jagged. "I am going to break down. At some point in the probably near future, I will ugly-cry and go on a drinking binge, and you will have to hold my hair back as I vomit. At some point, I will tell you all the details I know about my dad's fucking cancer. But I don't feel like doing that now, okay?"

"O-okay."

"Calm down, Jack," mutters Paul. "How is she supposed to know what you want?"

"She doesn't. That's the point: We're best friends, and none of us know what any one of us wants. It's all a big effing stew of repressed emotions, isn't it? So at least I'm doing Tash a service and telling her exactly how I feel."

Jack gets up, hurls the throw pillow she's been clutching at my gut, and storms out of the room and up the stairs. She has thrown the grenade and run for cover, and I can't decide if it was a brave or cowardly thing to do. I also can't decide if I should make a run for it too.

I'm suddenly so aware of Paul's presence next to me. The space he occupies, the rhythm of his breathing, his . . . lack of hair. It's bothering me so much.

"I should get going," I say, and I *know* that's the cowardly thing to do.

I'm halfway to the patio door when Paul says, "I felt like a bad person."

I stop, turn around. "What?"

He pulls his feet up on the couch and repositions himself so he's facing me straight on.

"I felt like a bad person, when I told you I thought my dad would get cancer again. Because I'm his family, so I'm supposed to be the optimistic one. And I wasn't. And I always felt guilty for telling you that. I felt

Kathryn Ormsbee

like somehow, because I'd said it out loud, that would make it happen. And now it has."

"Paul."

"So that's why I didn't tell you, when Dad first complained. That's why I told Jack not to let you know. Because I thought if we said it out loud, it'd definitely be true. It's not because I didn't trust you. I wasn't trying to hide anything, I just . . . felt like such a bad person."

"You're not a bad person, Paul."

He smiles grimly. God, how long will it take for his hair to grow back? *Years?*

I modify my previous statement: "You're the best person I know. Aside from my mom, maybe."

"No one beats your mom."

"Okay, yeah," I concede. "No one beats Mom. I spoke hastily."

Paul's smile turns pained. It looks like he's been forced to swallow kerosene. "I'm not ready to lose my dad yet. That's all I keep thinking, over and over: I don't want to be the guy without a dad. It's so selfish. It's worse than Jack not talking about it at all."

"It's not selfish." I step closer to the couch, where I can see Paul's face better in the lamplight. "You love your dad. You don't want him to die. And you don't want to be the guy without a dad. All of that is really natural."

"You'd be so disappointed in me. I'm thinking very un-Zen thoughts these days."

"Yeah, well, me too."

There is more to say here. There's more *I* should be saying. I should be apologizing. But to apologize is to bring up everything that happened before I left for Orlando, and now isn't the right time.

"I'm here if you need me," I say.

"Don't worry, we do. And you know Jack. She's just . . ."

I nod. I know.

But as I walk out into the night, I wonder if that's entirely true. I know that Jack shuts down and walks off when she's upset. I know she likes creepy stop-motion films. I know she doesn't like hugs. But I don't really know the *why* of it. It's not that she's a bitch or a sullen person or emotionally stunted. Those are all tidy explanations for Jack's behavior, but they're not the *why*. I don't know the why, and Jack is my best friend. So good God, what does that say about the human race at large?

People these days love to speculate on the apocalypse—whether our ultimate demise will be due to nuclear warfare or zombie epidemic or alien invasion. But I think it's more likely that our end will come on a normal day when we all stop trying to figure out the *why* of anyone around us and go live in separate houses and rot away, alone.

On the way back home, I notice an anthill forming in our next-door neighbor's yard, illuminated by a streetlight. It's begun in the grass and is now encroaching on the sidewalk. There's a steady line of ants filing in and out, so focused on their mission they don't notice the giant stooped over them, observing their work.

I wonder if ants *know* each other, or if they even try. Maybe they don't have to. Maybe they aren't hung up on a sense of self. Maybe they just *are* each other.

Once I'm in bed, fighting my way to sleep, I keep getting this crawling sensation on my arms. I don't know if it's chills or imaginary ants, but I've got a feeling it's not the last I'll hear from them.

Twenty-Eight

It's not like Jack and I have had an actual fight. Was it shitty for her to say what she did and then leave me alone with Paul? Absolutely. But her dad got re-diagnosed with cancer, the extent of which I don't even know, and I've no doubt if I were in Jack's worn-down Chuck Taylors, I would be just as shitty. Probably shittier.

I call her in the morning, and she answers. She tells me her dad is going in for his first round of chemo next week. According to the doctors, the cancer has made an aggressive return and spread to the liver, so the treatment will have to be even more intense than what Mr. Harlow endured the first time around. They're skipping the hormone treatment they used last time and are going straight to chemo. Jack tells me all this with a steady voice, no signs of emotional disturbance.

It's what I expect. Jack might break apart later, but right now this is how she's coping. That's why I don't launch into an elaborate apology over the phone, why I don't cry and tell Jack she was right, that I do take her and Paul for granted, and I'm going to be better. Jack doesn't do those kinds of apologies. Emotionally vomiting on her, all for the sake of obtaining her forgiveness, would be just another form of selfishness on my part. I already know Jack's forgiven me, and she knows I'm sorry, and we can leave it at that. And if, down the road, she needs me to beg for her pardon, I will do it. I know now, I would do anything to keep us okay. Even more than what I'd do for a good take of *Unhappy Families*.

Prostate cancer has to be *the* most awkward cancer ever. Especially when you are a girl, and you and your best girl friend are talking about it in relation to her dad. Back when Mr. Harlow was first diagnosed, I had no idea what "prostate" meant, and I kept mixing it up with the word "prostrate," including the time I looked the word up online, which led me to think for a full week that Mr. Harlow had a cancer that only affected him when he was lying down and therefore he would never again be able to sleep like a normal person.

It's an awkward, awful cancer, and its reappearance in our lives feels like an insidious inevitability. Cancer always seems to come back. It does, anyway, in all the sad cancer movies and books. It comes back like Mr. Harlow's—with a malignant vengeance. And in the books and movies, it's always the second wave that's fatal. I tell myself not to think these thoughts, but it's as good as telling myself not to think of the number 42. According to Jack, the doctors actually think Mr. Harlow has a good chance of pulling through. They've given him 60/40 odds. Glass more full than empty.

Mom is in all-out Angel of Mercy and Ministrations mode. Later in the afternoon, I hear her in the kitchen, marathon-calling friends and neighbors to set up a meal delivery schedule. Mrs. Harlow still has to travel for work and can't be home most of the week to cook. But with my mom's help, the Harlows will soon have more baked lasagna and chicken pot pies than they know what to do with. This is one social custom I can totally get behind. Flowers at funerals? Pointless. Everyone's too sad to notice. Cigars at a birth? Here's a brand-new life, let's celebrate by pumping our lungs with toxins! But food during illness—*that* I get. Food is always appropriate.

A week later, I'm walking up to the Harlows' when I notice a familiar black Jeep in the driveway. Jay Prasad is walking down the front steps, an empty wicker basket in hand.

He smiles and waves, quickening his steps to meet me in the middle of the yard.

"I misssss youuu," he sings in soft falsetto, bopping the tip of my nose. "How've you been?"

There's sympathy in his voice, which I know is partially due to the Golden Tuba disappointment.

I try to dispel it with an enthusiastic "Great!" before taking note that we are standing in the yard of a man who has cancer. "Um. Well, you know."

Jay says, "Cancer fucking sucks."

"Mmm-hmm." I feel like I'm going to cry. In an attempt to stave off a sob, I say, "How're you? How's Tony?"

Kathryn Ormsbee

Jay smiles in his cannot-be-repressed, heart-on-sleeve way. "Um. Good. Everything is very, *very* good."

I waggle my eyebrows.

"So," says Jay, "I dunno if you heard they're making this new web series in Louisville? I sent an audition tape and a link to that episode where Tony and I are ripping out each other's throats as Alex and Vronsky. And . . . I got a part."

"Jay, that's great! What's the series about?"

"Uuuh." Jay looks embarrassed. "It's, like, a slasher thing? Lots of fake blood."

"Oh. Wow. Diversifying your résumé."

"Yeah, I guess. Anyway, they called me up and said I didn't even have to come audition in person. They were all big fans of *Unhappy Families.*"

"O-oh. Wow."

"Basically, what I'm saying is you're famous and everyone loves you."

"Oh, Jay. You know how to make a gal feel real special."

He shrugs happily, and we fall into a hug. He's the kind of person I feel like I've never hugged enough.

"I'd better get going," he tells me. "Tony's started this new band, and I'm supposed to be fanboying all over him at rehearsal."

I store this away as information to share with Jack only when she's in an excellent mood. Then I wave as Jay pulls out of the driveway, and for some reason I'm sadder about seeing him go now than I was at the wrap party. Maybe because it's since become clear that we don't have any overlapping activities in the coming school year—nothing to keep us together. We do live in the Modern Age, though, so there are at least a few little things I can do. I can keep track of what shows he and Serena will be in this year. I'll go. I'll bring flowers. I'll text them every year on their birthdays, and they will be my Alex and Anna until the end of time.

On Saturday, we drive Klaudie to Vanderbilt. Our SUV is so packed that both Klaudie and I have to rest our feet atop Bankers Boxes crammed on the floorboard like Tetris pieces. There's a body pillow and a giant down comforter in the aisle between our seats, which makes for a nice sleep space, at least. We're not even to Bowling Green and I swear Dad has already made a dozen jokes about how much Klaudie has packed. She won't let it go, either. She keeps arguing back, with increasing irritation, "It's my entire *life*, Dad! I had to pack my *life* in this car!"

Somehow, Mom is able to sleep through the familial discord. Dad starts playing a Malcolm Gladwell audiobook, and Klaudie and I settle into silent scenery-gazing mode. When I attempt a by and large unsuccessful leg stretch, I notice Klaudie staring at me.

"Ugh," I say. "Creep, much?"

She doesn't reply, and she doesn't stop looking, which makes it even creepier.

"Ergh, stop it." I grab the edge of the body pillow and attempt to hide my face. When I peer back up she's still staring.

She says, "Is it my fault? I want you to tell me if it's my fault."

I abandon my body pillow barricade. "Is what your fault?"

"You not getting the Golden Tuba. Because I bailed for the last part of the show, and you had to change the script, and it made it less good of a show than it should've been."

It's so wholly unexpected, this line of conversation. I honestly haven't thought about Klaudie's departure from the show in weeks, let alone considered the role it might've played in Golden Tuba voting.

"Klaudie," I say, "I don't think that had anything to do with it. Like you said, you didn't leave until near the end, and some of those episodes haven't even posted yet."

Klaudie does not look at all convinced. There is guilt puddling in her deep brown eyes.

"I'm serious," I say, more forceful. "I'm sure it had nothing to do with us losing. The other series were really, really good. It was tough competition."

"I think maybe . . ." Klaudie looks out on the highway flashing past. "I don't know, maybe I made a mistake. I'm not even talking to Jenna now."

A couple months ago, I might have relished this moment. Now, not so much. Now, I'm just hung up on the fact that Klaudie won't be in this vehicle on our way home. I won't see her again until Thanksgiving.

"It's over now," I say. "It's over, it's fine."

I don't say it dismissively. I say it reassuringly. Like I mean it.

. . .

When we arrive on campus, I get a distinct summer camp vibe. Summer camp, but with a much better manicured landscape. Chipper students wearing goldenrod-colored T-shirts carry clipboards and tell us where to go. All four of us work up a sweat lugging Klaudie's things to her third-floor dorm room. Then, famished, we go to El Palenque, our favorite Mexican restaurant in town.

"You're going to know *all* the good places to eat once we come back," I tell Klaudie through a mouthful of refried beans.

"Don't count on it. I will subsist primarily on V8s. And dream of Dad's cooking."

She looks mournfully at Dad, and he looks mournfully back at her. Then, just as the whole table is reaching the point of utterly bleak, there's an eruption of claps and cheers from the other side of the room. The servers are singing a spirited "*Feliz Cumpleaños*" to a little girl with braces on her four front teeth. They place a bowl of fried ice cream before her and drop a hot-pink sombrero on her head. It hangs comically low, past her eyes, and her family busily snaps photos on their cameras. Seeing this little girl so happy makes our table cheerful again. Dad tosses a wadded-up straw wrapper into the striped pocket of Klaudie's T-shirt dress, and we cry out at the masterful precision of it all.

It's dark when we return Klaudie to her dorm. We pull into the only free visitor space and open the doors to an onslaught of humid air and cricket chirps.

Kathryn Ormsbee

Around this time last year, when we brought Klaudie to campus for a school visit, I thought I'd be moving here too. Now I'm not looking at the towering stone and brick buildings like they'll be my future home. They're just the place where my sister Klaudie lives. I'm not sure I'm entirely okay with that yet, but I think I will be. Eventually.

"I know they say you're not supposed to call the first week," says Mom, "but . . . *call*?"

We're all crying—Dad most of all.

"I'll call."

"And if your roomie turns out to be a psycho sorority girl," I say, "you can always come back home. Though I may have taken over your room by then."

Klaudie rolls her eyes and says, "I'll take my chances."

Her voice is shaking, though.

We form a sweaty group hug. Then Klaudie heads for the dormitory, waving off Dad's offer to walk her to the door, and she's gone.

The drive back is dark and quiet. Mom cries for the first half, and Dad keeps saying, "She seems so happy there," and Mom keeps saying, "I know, Jan, I know."

It gets me thinking that my parents will have this same conversation a year from now, and also *eighteen* years from now, about some Zelenka whose face I haven't even seen yet.

I still don't understand all the reasons behind why they're having this baby. I don't think I ever will. If I were their age and had already dealt with the early development of two girls, I would say no way in hell, give me early retirement. But I'm *not* them, and they're happy. I see it in the way they squeeze their hands over the gearshift, after Dad merges onto I-65. Like they're still head-over-heels-in-love teenagers out for a night drive.

I think about what Klaudie said on our own night drive—about how Zelenka Jr. is an addition to Mom and Dad's very small family. How that's true, accident or not. How it's a good thing. And that doesn't make leaving Klaudie in Nashville any easier, but it does make tomorrow look a little better.

In the morning, I walk to Holly Park. It's still early, just past dawn. I couldn't sleep again, and I decided that sitting in a creaky swing is better than sweating one minute longer under the covers of my bed.

I've only been swinging for a minute, listlessly pushing my heels into the gravel, swaying from side to side, when a pair of sneakers comes into view. I look up.

Paul is saying something, but I can't hear. I tug my earphones out and say, "What?"

He shakes his head, amused. "I called out when you passed by the house, but you didn't hear me."

"Oh. Sorry."

"Do you want to be alone?"

I seriously consider this. If I wanted to be alone, Paul would leave, no problem. He'd understand.

Kathryn Ormsbee

"No," I say at length. "I don't."

Paul takes a seat on the swing next to me. It judders under his weight.

"How's your dad?" I ask.

"Stuffed with pasta and cheese, so as happy as he can be under the circumstances. Some lady brought us a chocolate cake last night. With a caramel center. Who does that?"

My smile drops. "We didn't make you cake. Do you want more cake?"

Paul laughs. "God, no, Tash. You guys are doing more than enough."

"Are we? I don't really feel like we're doing anything. Anything that actually helps."

"You know," he says, "people always say if they could take their loved one's pain away, they would. But think about if you actually could. It'd be such a nightmare. You would take someone's pain, but then they would love *you*, so they'd just take it back, or someone else you love would take it from you, and someone they love would take it from *them*, and it would go on like that until the pain ended up with some person who loved but wasn't loved back. Some sad, unloved person. And they would get stuck with the pain."

"Damn, Paul. You go to dark places."

Paul pushes into a swing. The chains cough up rust and grumble in irritation. "All I mean is you're doing everything you can to help, and I'm kind of glad you can't do more."

The sky is pink. The sun is in my eyes. There's a congregation of birds chirruping in nearby trees. I squint at Paul and the haircut I'll never get used to.

This is when I should apologize. So I open my mouth and ruin the moment.

"I'm sorry. For how I treated you before Orlando. I—I don't even know what I was doing."

Paul stops the swing in a pullback. He looks dubious. "Don't you?"

"I . . . Well."

"Because it seemed to me like it was a striptease meant to convince me that loving you without sex would be torture and therefore impossible. Correct me if I'm wrong."

I don't correct him. Also, he said a form of the word "love," and I am having trouble breathing.

"Which was very ineffective, by the way, because I have seen you in less. You know, because we have been constantly around each other for more than fifteen years."

"Yeah, I know. Bad move on my part."

For so, so many reasons.

"Okay, I forgive you," says Paul. "The end."

He says it like he's finished telling a sleeping child a bedtime story—soft and final and relieved.

"God," I whisper. "I cannot take you seriously with that buzz cut. I just *cannot*."

Paul bursts into a laugh. I smile and drop my gaze back to the gravel.

Kathryn Ormsbee

"I really didn't know you felt like that," I say. "You've always treated me and Jack the exact same way."

"That's not true."

"For me, it's true. I never saw you treat us differently."

"I *felt* differently about you."

"Yeah, sorry, I can't see your feelings."

Paul sighs. "I said 'the end.' We don't have to draw it out."

I am burrowing a hole into the gravel with the tip of my sneaker. The earth grows darker and darker the deeper I dig.

"Paul," I say, "I like you a lot."

"Yes, well, word on the street is I'm the second-best person you know."

The canvas of my sneaker is stained and damp. "No, I *like* you. The way I like guys. I like you like that."

Nothing but the *creak-crick-moan-creak* of the swings.

"You know me," I say. "I don't have to explain things to you or impress you, because you know me, and you've seen me at my absolute shittiest. So it'd be really easy for me to say, 'Okay sure, date me.' But that'd be so selfish. Even if you don't think so now, you'll end up resenting me, and I can't let that happen."

"Don't you—"

"No, wait, I'm not finished. I've done a lot of research about this. About asexuals dating sexual people, and it's just . . . really hard. It takes a ton of communication and compromise, and you are a guy who wants to have sex, and that's totally fine, but why the hell you would want to date me is beyond the realms of logic."

Paul is staring hard at me. He says, "That was a really long sentence."

"Urmph," I reply.

"So you're saying I am an unhinged animal controlled by my libido."

"No. I'm being realistic."

"Actually, I think you're being kind of sexist, and *also*, you never asked my opinion on this subject."

"Paul—"

"Okay, this is going to sound crass, but here's the thing: I like you more than I like sex. I mean, I like sex. Like, a lot. But . . . call me crazy, but something about having a dad with prostate cancer makes you reconsider how important your dick is."

It's so unexpected, I have to laugh.

"Whyyy are we talking about your dad's penis?"

"I said nothing about my dad's penis. You did."

"Oh my God, Paul, uuugh." I'm embarrassed, but there's nowhere to hide, so I shut my eyes.

"I'm just being honest," says Paul.

Then, when I don't respond, he starts singing that line from Out-kast's "Hey Ya!": *"I'm—I'm—I'm just being honest."*

"Stop it." I kick at his swing, which results in a rusty cacophony of screeches.

Kathryn Ormsbee

When we settle down again I look at him, my cheek mushed against the chain of my swing. "Paul," I say.

I've been saying his name a lot, I realize. Just his name. Because it's so familiar, so comfortable. It's a better crutch than "uh" or "eh" or even "um."

"If you like me," he says, "why won't you let us try it out? It could be a flaming disaster, but we could try. You know, I've been doing a lot of research too, and I think we're pretty decent at communication and compromise. I've thought of how to deal. I think I can do it."

"You say that now . . ."

"Yeah, you know what? I *do* say that now. Now's all we've got. So maybe you should say 'yes.' Say 'yes' now, and you can always reevaluate in ten minutes, or ten hours, or ten months. Whatever. Maybe it will be too hard for me, or maybe it will be too hard for you, but at least we can try."

"You like the idea of it now, because it makes me different from other girls, but—"

Paul stamps his feet down hard into the gravel. He drops to his knees and grabs on to the right chain of my swing. There is so much light in his dark eyes.

"Tash. Listen. We have known each other for ages. I have kissed and dated and slept with other girls. You know that, because you were hanging around for all of it. Now, *listen*. I would. Rather. Hug you. Than be with. Anyone else. Just. Hug you. Do you. Want to. Hug me. Back."

He sounds like a robot who's recently developed the capacity for human emotion, and if this weren't the conversation it is, I would giggle. Instead, I want to cry. My voice is gone. Missing. I go on a hunt for it and find it curled up in the lowest part of my esophagus. I drag it back to its proper place. By the time I do, the light is fading in Paul's eyes.

I say, "Yes."

Paul says, "Tash."

I figure it out then. He feels about my name the same way I do about his: comfortable, at ease. It's on the tip of his tongue more than "um."

I slide off my swing and Paul scoots closer, and he fits his arms around me. We've hugged so many times before. I wonder the exact number. Is it in the hundreds? Thousands? Hundred thousands? We've hugged all those times, and this hug is exactly and nothing like all the ones before it. My cheek rests against his chest, and his blood pumps near my ear, and I feel warm and safe and known.

Because here is another thing I figure out, as we sit there in the gravel, hugging for minutes, chains creaking a chorus around us: Paul knows a little of my *why*. He's looked into some of the darkest parts of me, and he hasn't fled the scene. I would be an idiot to not try this out. At least for now, and however many nows that follow.

That night, Leo and I have a chat. I sit on the edge of my bed, and for once I scowl right back at him.

Kathryn Ormsbee

"Leo," I say. "Don't take this the wrong way, but sometimes you're a real disappointment."

Scowl, says twenty-year-old Leo Tolstoy.

"I'm breaking up with you," I say. "I think you've seen this coming for a while."

Scowl.

"But I'm very much enjoying *The Death of Ivan Ilyich,* and I hope you know I will always be a lifelong fan of your work."

Scowl.

Conversation over. At least I've done Leo the courtesy of telling him I'm leaving, which is more than he did for poor Sophia.

I take down the poster, gingerly roll it up, and stow it away on the top shelf in my closet. As this is not an acrimonious split, I leave his quotes on the wall. I even smile a little at my favorite one: "If you want to be happy, be."

There are two ways to take that quote, and if I were a scholar in Slavic languages, I guess I could translate the original Russian text and remove all doubt. But I kind of like that there are two possible interpretations in English. The first, more obvious one is such an oversimplification. You can't *make* yourself happy. Happiness isn't a matter of will but of feelings and biology and circumstances and a dozen other factors. So that's not how I read the quote at all.

This is my interpretation: If you want a *chance* at being happy, *exist.* Because yes, life can suck, but as long as you're alive, there's a chance you can be happy. And maybe that's a dismal way to look at life, but I think there's hope there. Like how the end of *Unhappy Families* leaves me feeling like a chunk of my chest has been carved out and will never again be filled. But then there's that hope for the next project, the newest venture. There's the hope of moving forward and making something even better.

Here's one thing I know has made me happier: honesty. Like George said, it's a decent policy to live by. Tonight, I'm being more honest with myself than I ever have before. And I like that feeling a lot—the feeling of being known by myself, and by someone else, too.

It's all that honesty that keeps me awake long after I've turned off the light. My mind wanders into a familiar but not recently visited land. There's a new project brewing here. I stay awake waiting for the lightning and thunder to show up.

Kathryn Ormsbee

Twenty-Nine

This year, for our combined birthday party, Paul and I are trying something new. Not another pool party. Nothing that requires paper plates or streamers or a store-bought buttercream cake. We decide this summer has seen enough pool parties. We decide that since we are turning eighteen and twenty, we should celebrate like adults. We're a little ironic about it, but we're a little serious, too.

So we plan a dinner. A joint family dinner to take place at my house. We plan it for the night of August 27—the date positioned evenly between our two birthdays. It's a Thursday night, nothing special, and no one else is allowed to help us prepare. Paul comes over to the house at four o'clock, right after his astronomy class at BCTC, and he and I cook the meal to a playlist that's an even mix of Travis songs for him and St. Vincent songs for me. Closer to six o'clock, I light candles, even though it's still sunny outside.

Mrs. Harlow is away on one of her business trips, but Mr. Harlow and Jack arrive and join my parents in the dining room. Paul and I come in and place the food on the table: a large salad of mixed greens tossed in vinaigrette, a basket of hot Sister Schubert's rolls, and the main event, fettuccine Alfredo. Because fettuccine Alfredo is Paul's favorite dish too.

"This is so wrong," Jack says, once we're all seated. "I can't believe you cooked your own birthday dinner."

"Not the cake, though," says Dad. "The cake was all me."

This is because Dad threatened to ground me if I made my own birthday dessert. Apparently, that is a line birthday girls do not cross.

"We're adults," I tell Jack. "Adults cook their own birthday dinners."

"Don't lecture me on what adults do," she says. "Adults go to fancy restaurants and get drunk on fine wines. *That* is what adults do."

"And where are you getting that information?" Mr. Harlow asks her, but Jack shrugs enigmatically and reaches for the salad tongs.

Mr. Harlow does not look good. He is thinner, though I don't know if he began to look like that before his chemotherapy and I am just now taking note. He doesn't look good, but he's wearing his usual unaffected smile. According to Jack and Paul, he's still gardening every day.

I offer him the platter of fettuccine first, ignoring an ugly look from Jack, who has already accused me once of treating her dad differently since the diagnosis. She says I was much cooler about the cancer thing as a kid than as a teenager, and I remind her that when I was a kid I was pretty self-absorbed and didn't know what "prostate" meant. Regardless of Jack's dirty looks, I think Mr. Harlow deserves the first serving of pasta.

Kathryn Ormsbee

It's been years since our two families have had a dinner like this. We used to do them a lot more often when Jack and Paul and I were little. Mr. and Mrs. Harlow and my parents would eat in the dining room, and we kids would scarf down our food at the kitchen table before running into the living room to watch Disney movies. Recently, I started to get nostalgic about those dinners. I told Paul we should reinstate them, and he agreed, and what better occasion for dinner than our joint birthday celebration?

Things won't be the way they were before, of course, because Klaudie is no longer here, and these days sneaking a glass of red wine sounds a lot more fun than repeated viewings of *The Little Mermaid*. But I like this new way. I think I like it even better than my memories.

Dad has made us a hot chocolate meringue cake, which is just as ridiculous as it sounds. He places a single candle in the center, and everyone sings "Happy Birthday" before Paul and I blow out the flame. Then Dad sloppily slices the cake—there's no way to do it but sloppily—and we dig into our crunchy slices with forks and knives.

Somehow, our parents get to talking politics, and that is when I throw down my napkin and say, "Is it all right if we head to the living room?"

"Tash, honey, what have I taught you?" says Dad. "Birthday girls do not *ask*, they *inform*."

"Okay. Dad. Mom. Mr. Harlow. We're going to adjourn to the living room."

This satisfies Dad, who flings his arm toward the living room in a gesture fitting a benevolent dictator.

So in a way, this night *is* turning out like all those memories. I'm actually about to suggest we pick out one of our old Disney DVDs, when Paul places a small, square package in my hand. It's wrapped in black-and-white-striped wrapping paper.

"What's this?" I ask. "My present?"

I already gave Paul his present on his real birthday, three days ago. It was a giant bag stuffed with packages of white chocolate macadamia nut cookies, Mr. Goodbar candy bars, and three 2-liters of Dr Pepper—all Paul's favorite snacks. At the bottom of the bag was some quirky book I found at Urban Outfitters called *College Students—Where Are They Now?* Subtitle: *Dead, Unfulfilled, or Having a Midlife Crisis.* Tucked in the front flap of the book is an unevenly cut slip of computer paper with a hand-written note that reads, *IOU one Ping-Pong table, once I have money.*

I wasn't expecting a gift in return until three days after today, on my actual birthday. This seems to be what's on Jack's mind too, because she says, "Paul, you effing asshat, how dare you."

Paul shrugs and taps the edge of the present, a pleased smile on his face.

"You want me to open it now?" I ask.

"Of course."

I take a seat on the couch, next to Jack, who is aiming lethal laser eye beams at Paul.

Kathryn Ormsbee

Paul pays no heed and instead sprawls out on the floor. His natural resting state.

I rip open the paper to reveal a wadded-up bunch of soft, jersey knit fabric. I lift it from my lap and it falls into its true shape. It's a light blue T-shirt in my size. On the front is the Seedling Productions logo Paul designed for us. The colors of the watermelon and sunburst are vibrant; they pop right off the tee. On the back, written in glittery black lettering, are the words *Team Zarlow*.

Jack cusses low and long. She rounds it off with a kick to Paul's shin and says, "Thanks a lot. Now I'm going to have to buy her a private island."

Paul props his neck on his folded arms and gives me a hopeful smile.

"Why are you looking at me like that?" I say. "You know it's perfect."

He settles his strained neck back down, smiling away.

Jack says, "Seedling Productions, you bastard brain child."

"Our blessing and our curse," I agree.

Moments like this I still have trouble believing *Unhappy Families* is all over and we're not just on some extra long hiatus. I'm not sure I'll ever fully believe it until I start filming something new.

Jack says, "So, I pulled a total you the other night, Tash, and made this list about what we can do to improve our game."

"Uh-huuuh?" I say cautiously.

"I think one of our goals should be to purposefully *not* pick up any more fans. I can't deal with the pressure."

I grin. "Me neither."

"In fact, maybe we should do something that will scare off some followers."

Paul lifts a hand and says, "Get me to act in your next production. Better yet, get me to sing."

"No," says Jack. "YouTube thrives on people making idiots of themselves. We'd go even more viral."

"I'm sure we'll think of something," I say. "Who knows? Maybe we'll get lucky and pick up a few more silverspunnnx23s and Horn-Rimmed Glasses Girls."

"We can only hope."

Isn't it funny how something can be serious for so long until one day it isn't? One day it becomes a joke. One day you can laugh about it, and the effort doesn't ache or rip out any sutures. It's painlessly amusing.

That's how I know Seedling Productions will start another project. It's how I know I am over the haters and disappointments and not-quite-professional moments of *Unhappy Families*. That's how I know I'm ready for a whole new wave of hate and disappointment and unprofessionalism.

A few weeks later, when I tell Jack and Paul about my new idea for a vlog, they both ask if I'm really okay with being that open. Because a vlog like this won't be a made-up story or tea-guzzling fangirling. And when critics come after me this time, the wounds might cut deeper.

Kathryn Ormsbee

I've thought about this, though. I've thought about it a lot. I've decided I can't be the only girl in the world whose mom got pregnant way later than usual. Whose best friends' dad is duking it out with cancer. Who loves Jane Austen *and* J. J. Abrams. Who has awesome, artsy friends. Who's nervous about college. Who misses her older sister. Who identifies as romantic asexual. Not a robot, not a freak, not *confused*. Just a girl.

Out of all Seedling Productions' current 84,203 subscribers, there has to be someone else who is, feels, experiences at least one of those things. So I've decided to talk about them, without tea and without Tolstoy. I might never live a life as impressive as Count Lev Nikolay-evich Tolstoy's. I might not be the next Francis Ford Coppola. But now that I understand a little better what it takes to be both those guys, I don't think I want it. I just want to be . . . honest. I'm going to say what's on my mind in a topical video every Monday morning. It may be a disaster. It may bring the trolls out from all the dark corridors of the Internet. It's a *splendifying* prospect—and at the moment, it's more terrifying than splendid. But it might be exactly what I need.

I turn on the camera. I settle in my seat. I look straight into the lens.

"Hi, guys! It's Tash here, officially back from hiatus. Today, I'm excited to announce a new project. . . ."

ACKNOWLEDGMENTS

It's my favorite time again! Here comes a bundle of thanks to the many people who made Tash Zelenka's story a possibility.

First, eternal gratitude to Super Agent Beth Phelan and the fantastic folks at the Bent Agency. Beth—thank you for your tireless work, for your general badassery, and for creating Tash fan art way before I even knew her story would make it on the shelves.

My magnificent editor, Zareen Jaffery—thank you for your invaluable insight and for giving me permission to add even more fun to Tash's story. Working with you makes me feel like one of the *lucky few*. (That joke will never get old, I swear.) A gigantic thank-you to everyone at Simon & Schuster BFYR: the inimitable Mekisha Telfer, top-notch publicist Aubrey Churchward, and the many others who helped make *Tash Hearts Tolstoy* a Thing That Happened. Thank you to my two-time copyeditor superstar Katharine Wiencke, and a very special thanks to Lucy Ruth Cummins for taking such care with *Tash*'s ah-maz-ing design.

Thank you, Kathryn Benson, for seeing me through another manuscript with your ever-incisive critique. You rock, name twin, and I still can't get over how you built an entire wall of bookshelves with your own two hands. Awe. Inspiring. Thank you, Kim Broomall, for taking a chance on me, a random Twitter DM. Your feedback, support, and general brilliance mean the world to me. Big thanks to wonderwoman Ashley Herring Blake, who read *Tash* way back in the day and gave me an encouragement boost just when I needed it most.

Marci Lyn Curtis, Jennifer Longo, and David Arnold—thank you, *thank you* for your wonderfully kind *Lucky Few* blurbs and general support. I am such a fangirl of each of you. Jen Gaska, Nicole Brinkley, Nita Tyndall, and Rachel Patrick—you've championed my books in special ways, and it's such a privilege to know each of you ridiculously creative and passionate women. Thank you also to Amanda Connor at Joseph-Beth for turning a childhood dream of mine into reality. My life and my books have been made better by countless other people in the kidlit community, both local and cyber. Thanks to you, and you, and all of you.

Friends, oh friends, you have seen me through a lot. Shelly Reed, my twinsie and ginger soul sister, I still freak out about how Fate threw us together all those years ago, across the pond. I never end a conversation with you not smiling. Hilary Rochow Callais, please never stop sending me #RockFacts. Kristen Comeaux, how is your hair always so great? Seoling Dee, we've earned our trip to Paris by now, *oui*? Badger, a.k.a. Nicole Williams, a.k.a. Honey Badger, a.k.a. Badge, a.k.a. Badge-Badge—thank you for traipsing around a freezing wood whilst carrying pounds of camera equipment, because that is TRUE FRIENDSHIP right there. Katie Carroll, my very best friend in all the world—thank you for not murdering me when I was making not one but two web series; you put up with so much, as only a best friend would. Also, remember that time your name was Samantha and you spoke in a British accent for a mafia movie? Hahaha, me too.

Very special thanks to everyone involved in the filming of *Shakes* and *Weird Sisters*. Hugs to Alec Beiswenger, Anna Stone, Beth Posey, Cathy Koch, Channing Estell, Cody Sparks, Ellis Oswalt, Garrett Bass, Matthew D. Whaley, Melanie White, Tim Childers, and Victoria Smith—talented actors I am so honored to know. Rebecca Campbell and Nicole Roberts, thank you for sacrificing space and time and general sanity to help out your friends. Clare "Cleh" Thomson, you are the best dramaturge and fake ghost around. Erin Wert—like, just wow. The Web Series Queen. Thanks for supporting me and Destiny in all we did. And, uhhh course, my pal and web series co-conspirator/creator, Destiny Soria. We did it. We made two web series, and we did not kill each other or cause a catastrophe (that we know of). Collaboration ftw.

A shout-out too to the many fantastic people behind some of my favorite web series—the folks at Pemberley Digital, the Candle Wasters, Kate Hackett Productions, and Shipwrecked Comedy. And, like, of course, Felicia Day. If the Golden Tubas were a thing, I would give my golden tubas to all of you. That is not meant to sound dirty.

Leo Tolstoy, thank you for writing some swell books. Tash hearts you, and so do I—but not as much as I heart Dostoyevsky, shh.

Mom and Dad—I love you. Thanks for always encouraging your weird offspring to go after what she wants. Thanks to Matt and Annie Snow for being my loudest cheerleaders and also just really cool siblings o' mine. Thanks to all the extended family for your love and support. KIDRON, oh hey, I put your name in a book.

Finally, a special shout-out to my ace readers. You are not alone. You are just right, and you are part of the *splendid* in this *splendifying* world. Keep being you.

<3
Kathryn